RICH MAN'S WAR

RICH MAN'S WAR

RICH MAN'S WAR

ELLIOTT KAY

SKYSCAPE

SKYSCAPE

Text copyright © 2015 Elliott Kay
Cover illustration © 2015 Lee Moyer
All rights reserved.

Published by Skyscape, New York

www.apub.com

Amazon, the Amazon logo, and Skyscape are trademarks of Amazon.com, Inc., or its affiliates.

ISBN-13: 9781477830840
ISBN-10: 1477830847

Cover design by Lee Moyer

Library of Congress Control Number: 2015930024

Printed in the United States of America

To my sister, Jennifer

"War is a racket. It always has been. It is possibly the oldest, easily the most profitable, surely the most vicious. It is the only one international in scope. It is the only one in which the profits are reckoned in dollars and the losses in lives."

—*War Is a Racket*, 1935
Major General Smedley D. Butler, USMC (ret.)
Two-time recipient of the Medal of Honor

PROLOGUE

Unfinished Business

"'Everyone loves a hero story, okay?' said Maria Pedroso, NorthStar's executive VP of Risk Management. 'But we shouldn't let Archangel's hype take us for a ride. That Malone kid was rescued, just like everyone else, by a Union fleet battleship—not by the Archangel Navy. And if Archangel had not unilaterally ended corporate security fleet coverage, the whole incident wouldn't have happened. Archangel doesn't have the ability to fully protect itself and its interests across the Union. They need us. It's only a question of how long it will be before Archangel realizes that and how much harm the system does to itself in the meantime.'"

—"Archangel Sticks to Her Tiny Guns,"
Solar Herald, March 2276

"Archangel has not seceded from the Union, nor will it. We have only withdrawn from some bad business relationships. It appears those businesses would have the Union believe this is no different from secession.

"We remain committed to the Union," President Aguirre continued, expecting neither applause nor murmurs of agreement from his audience. He knew how many delegates to the Union Assembly were bought and paid for—and how many others simply couldn't risk the confrontation that Archangel now faced. "We support the common causes of humanity, such as a unified diplomacy toward our alien neighbors and a common defense. We also support the rule of law. We believe in paying for services rendered. We also believe that when those services are not rendered, as has been the case with NorthStar, Lai Wa, and the CDC, that no payment is merited and further services should not be pursued. The current corporate educational regime has not served our young people well, and thus we have decided to provide for our own educational needs. Our security contracts have gone unfulfilled, as was made plain by incidents reaching back as far as the loss of the *Aphrodite* and the later loss of—"

Peanuts bounced against the flat image of President Aguirre as he spoke. "I'd pay good money not to hear about the fuckin' *Aphrodite* ever again," grumbled Ranjan at the bar.

"Shut up," snapped the pirate beside him. "I'm listening to this," Trevor said.

Ranjan glanced over his shoulder to take a look around the dimly lit dive. He saw little interest in the news broadcast on the large screen behind the bar. He also saw little in the way of customers other than his shipmates. "Yeah, you and all the other political junkies in here. Just download this shit to your holocom, and let's get the bartender to put on something interesting."

Baleful blue eyes looked up at Ranjan from behind Trevor's long blond hair. "I'm not payin' six creds to watch the news when it's on here for free."

"You don't have a subscription service?"

Trevor made a face. "Do you? What the hell do you put down in your subscriber info? You still have a bank account?"

Ranjan blinked. He glanced at his other shipmates at the bar, feeling awkward. "No," he lied. "Look, I'm just saying I'm sick of hearing about *Aphrodite*. We knocked over a fuckin' *planet*, but you don't hear him—"

"He just did, but you were talking."

"And shut up about that," hissed a shipmate opposite Trevor. Shahal leaned in with a scowl. "We're not on Paradise anymore!"

"Have you seen a single badge the entire time we've been on this rock?" Trevor asked, though he did lower his voice. "We didn't park the *Guillotine* at the spaceport because of the tight security service. We could land here with every gun turret exposed and nobody'd bat an eye. And I'd be happy if you'd both shut up."

"As anyone might expect, these changes have led to disagreements on all sides," continued Aguirre in a calm, reasoned tone. "We disagree on payment of primary debts and the terms of debts owed by individual citizens. We disagree on compensation for the state takeover of corporate property within Archangel territory, such as educational facilities. Careers and lives have been disrupted. We do not dispute that these changes are difficult matters.

"Yet when the corporations involved escalate to economic warfare—when they not only sever the ties of interstellar commerce and communication but indeed act to disrupt Archangel's efforts to provide such services for itself—then matters go beyond simple business relationships. At that point, the governments of the Union must ask, who really governs the Union?"

"He had to know they'd cut Archangel off from their packet ship services," Shahal noted.

"That's not the point," Trevor said, shaking his head. "Did you listen? It's not that they cut off service, it's that they're putting up barriers to Archangel taking care of itself. It's one thing not to deliver the mail, but it's another when you won't even let a guy pick it up himself."

"Why do you care so much?" asked Ranjan. "You aren't from there. None of us are."

"You don't think this will wind up affecting us?"

Ranjan frowned. "I don't see how." His eyes drifted to the door in the back room. Almost as if he'd given a cue, the door opened and Hannah Black walked out. The three pirates rose to meet their ship's elected captain. "How'd it go?"

"Well enough that I don't want to talk about it in here." Hannah grunted. Shahal returned her pistol as she passed, walking for the door with her long black coat billowing in her wake. The other crewmembers present, some of them closer to the exit, rose as soon as they saw her. By the time she'd stepped out into the night, her pistol tucked safely in its underarm holster, the crew had formed a pack around her.

The planet Edison had been settled early in the second wave of expansion from Earth. Though the world enjoyed rapid growth, later expansion developments and the whims of the markets had left its economy crippled, leading to its current status as an urbanized backwater. The spaceport city of Stilwell exemplified that demise, with miles of towers, bridges, and highways now showing far more decay and vandalism than its original ambitious beauty.

At this hour, not too many people roamed the streets. Even the homeless and the criminals had to sleep sometime. One could see scattered pedestrians and vehicles here and there—people did still live and work in this city, though few prospered—but Hannah and her crew walked unimpeded. "We've got a lead on a target," she said, "but I'm not sure everyone's going to like it."

"What's the trouble?" asked Ranjan.

He could see Hannah's frown and blue eyes looking at him from under her long black hair. "The info is an astronavigation protocol, not an actual flight plan. We'll have to park ourselves in one of three locations and hope we've picked the right one."

4

"One-in-three odds is still better than roaming around aimlessly." Shahal shrugged. "These are cargo ships, right? Should be a decent haul and not too much risk for the *Guillotine*."

"It's a matter of location. Like I said, not everyone's going to like it. And some people on the crew might like it too much." Hannah paused. "I don't think our seller was out to make a profit on stolen shipping data. This smells like someone pushing an agenda. He sold pretty cheap, given what he had to offer, and now that I know the location I understand why."

"Where?" asked Ranjan. Hannah didn't often go for ominous hints.

She held her hand up, nodding and looking forward as they entered a wide pedestrian tunnel under one of the city's major highways. A tall, young black man and a girl of Asian descent approached from the opposite direction, walking close together. Ranjan thought the girl was hot. Her tight pants and boots hinted at a great figure. The other pirates began their inevitable catcalls and whistles.

It hardly mattered if the girl turned away or walked in silence, or if she responded with a rude word or gesture, or if she politely asked to be left alone. The pirates would do whatever they felt like doing. That was the nature of pirates. Unfortunately, she made the worst of all possible choices: she smiled nervously and made eye contact as she passed.

Trevor reached for her ass as she came within reach. Other men let out further catcalls. The girl slapped Trevor's hand down but turned as she kept going in the same direction, walking backward to keep her eyes on the pirates. The tall black youth with her scowled, of course, but he didn't put up any sort of fight. Like his girlfriend, he just kept moving.

Ranjan quickly forgot the pair. "Hannah, what's the deal?"

Again, the captain shook her head and nodded forward. Yet another pedestrian approached on the bridge, this one a black woman wrapped up in a large gray overcoat. Ranjan paid her no mind. She'd inevitably step to the side. Anyone with sense would want to be on the outside of such a rough-looking group.

"Fuckin' random pedestrians, who cares?" Ranjan muttered. He glanced over his shoulder. The young couple was already at the end of the pack of pirates.

"I'm of a mind to be careful right now," Hannah replied quietly.

"Why?" he asked. "What's the deal?"

Fuming, Hannah looked to Ranjan and hissed, "Our contact had NorthStar Risk Management written all over him. Those coordinates are in Archangel space."

"What?" Ranjan blinked.

"They want us to do their dirty work for them. Now shut up. We'll talk about it on the ship."

Ranjan caught sight of the black woman again in his peripheral vision. She hadn't made a course correction. She walked between the pair of pirates in front of the group, directly into Ranjan's path.

He tried to say something, but the woman's elbow went right into his throat. Hard.

At the back of the group of pirates, Alicia Wong saw Janeka's first blow all but lift her target off the ground. The big overcoat fell from the gunnery sergeant's shoulders as she turned on her next opponent with a roundhouse kick, but Alicia had no time to watch. She and Ravenell had jobs to do—quickly and quietly.

A knife takedown from behind was easier for Ravenell, given his height. The last two pirates in the group never saw him coming, having discounted him as a wuss for not defending his girl and now distracted by Janeka. Ravenell's big hand wrapped around his target's mouth from the left, while his knife plunged into the side of the man's neck from the right, then punched straight out in a rough, ugly, and well-practiced motion.

Alicia didn't have Ravenell's stature to work with, but size rarely held her back. Given an unaware target, she had no reason not to commit her full power to her first move. Alicia drew the thermal dagger from her jacket sleeve, raised it to the base of her target's skull, and then yanked back on the man's hair to pull him onto the blade. Precision and six inches of strong, laser-hot metal made for an effective job. Alicia tugged to the right and then the left to jerk her sizzling weapon free. She had her sights on the blond bastard just a couple meters ahead before her first target hit the ground.

The blond pirate's first reaction when violence erupted in front of him was to go for his gun without looking behind. As with her first victim, Alicia tugged back fiercely on the man's conveniently long hair. Taken by surprise, he staggered backward as she'd planned. Alicia brought her blade around his chest and slashed upward, slicing his neck open in a vicious arc.

She didn't try for grace. These people were all mass murderers. Alicia had to break each man and move on to the next as quickly as possible, before anyone could fire off a gun or make some other attention-grabbing noise. The next pirate in line recognized the threat in time to meet her approach but not quickly enough to do much about it. The young woman didn't try to dodge his meaty fist. Alicia endured his awkward but heavy punch so she could step in close enough to stomp on his foot and throw him off balance. The pirate took a blade up under his ribcage and into his lung.

Bracing with both feet and twisting hard, Alicia flung her third victim to the ground. He had just enough fight left in him to break her grip on the dagger as he fell. With her targets down, her eyes quickly swept the field.

Ravenell's second target had reacted quickly enough to put up a fight, but Ravenell seemed to have the upper hand. The pirate leader—Hannah Black, according to the briefing—staggered back after a kick from Janeka while the gunny turned to deal with the last of the men standing nearest to her. Hannah reached inside her long coat, clearly going for a gun in a shoulder holster.

Alicia grabbed at Hannah's wrist and pulled. She slammed her free hand against the pistol. The push-and-pull motion took Hannah's arm one way and sent the gun in another, breaking her grip on the weapon at her thumb.

Hannah got one solid shot in across Alicia's cheek with her left hand. The pirate captain knew how to throw a punch, but Alicia had endured much worse. Tangled together in a standing grapple, both women struggled to apply the right footwork to throw the other off balance.

The contest was never in doubt, though Hannah couldn't have known it. They had a moment to lock eyes as they struggled. Alicia saw rage and a rising sense of panic. Hannah saw controlled ferocity. Then Hannah's whole world spun as Alicia got her leg around the back of Hannah's and shoved the pirate into the wall beside them. The back of Hannah's head hit hard against unyielding concrete. She blacked out even before Alicia's knee came up into her groin.

Alicia surveyed the field again. She saw Janeka's heel come down on a man's neck and saw Ravenell rise from the body of his defeated opponent. Alicia did a quick body count: the three she'd taken out, plus the captain, Ravenell's two, and the three men lying at Janeka's feet. They'd made a clean sweep of their enemy.

"You're both okay," observed the gunnery sergeant, receiving nods of confirmation in return.

"I got the captain," huffed Alicia.

"Is she dead?"

"Shouldn't be," replied the younger woman, kneeling down to check. "No, she's still good. Dunno if she'll be up for answering questions right away, though."

"Doesn't need to answer anything yet. We just need her warm and breathing in case we need her biometrics. And her holocom. See if you can find it."

The order wasn't necessary. Alicia had already turned to searching their captive. "Wow, I am never wearing my hair long again after this," she said, still rocky with adrenaline.

"Take a couple deep breaths," said Janeka. "Shake it off. Stay focused." As the gunnery sergeant spoke, she slid one finger over the holocom riding her wrist and then tapped it twice to signal the rest of their team.

"Ravenell, watch the tunnel entrance," Janeka instructed. "Stay calm, you got me? Breathe. Focus. Get over there, stop, and breathe again, then watch. Understand?"

"On it." Ravenell hustled off.

"Got a couple of data chips here," Alicia announced quietly, stuffing her pockets with items taken from her unconscious captive. She kept patting Hannah down until her fingers touched the pirate captain's earrings. One of them let out a beep. "Got it," she said and then worked to unclasp the large, pricy jewel that held Hannah's personal holocom. "Pretty sweet miniaturization here. These are expensive."

"Lotta money to be made in her trade, I guess," Janeka muttered. Her attention was focused on a black orb in her hands. It projected a small screen of orange light, into which the gunnery sergeant waved her fingers. The lights quickly went out with a beep.

"Anything else we should grab?"

"Just collect the guns. I've got the bag. We've gotta get gone." She knelt beside the dead man at her feet and placed the orb in his pocket. Inevitably, some random passerby would discover the bodies. That person would likely then try to call for help with a holocom, but the orb would jam signals going out of the tunnel. It would buy them at least another minute or two for their getaway.

"I'll take her," said Janeka, stepping up to Alicia and her captive. She grabbed the unconscious woman's wrists. "You're on point. Head out and let's get to the car."

Spaceport security and control varied dramatically from one planet to the next. Some worlds could afford tight restrictions and offered considerable equipment and infrastructure. Planets with sparse settlements sometimes had no control over interstellar traffic at all, and an incoming vessel could land practically wherever its crew pleased.

Edison fell somewhere in the middle. All of the heavy lifting to create the spaceport's infrastructure had been done long ago, but the planetary government couldn't afford to keep its systems up-to-date. Old scanners and chem sniffers were easily spoofed. Sparsely allocated guards and other personnel could be bought. Alicia found it all mind-boggling, especially in light of what their captive and their remaining targets had done on Qal'at Khalil little more than a year ago.

Targets, she thought, crouched in the shadows with the other plainclothes Archangel marines and their Intelligence Ministry "liaisons." That's what those people were now. They had to be. If she stopped to think of the bastards as people, she might hesitate. She couldn't have that.

Fuckers didn't hesitate to drop a fuel-cell bomb on a city, she reminded herself once again. Nor did these pirates, to be more specific, hesitate to hose down a spaceport with their ship's illegal weaponry.

Nor had anyone done anything about these particular pirates until now.

The spaceport berth was little more than a circular wall. Earlier reconnaissance revealed that the retractable roof was open and possibly inoperable. Inside the berth sat the *Guillotine* and her remaining crew, estimated to be around eighteen or so in total. After the fight in the tunnel, it didn't sound like such bad odds. Alicia wondered if perhaps the quick and dirty skirmish had made her cocky.

"Corporal Wong?" said Agent Willis, interrupting her thoughts. "Sorry, I mean lance corporal, right? Looks like we're partners for this one. You ready?"

Alicia blinked. The Intelligence Ministry agent hadn't spoken to her much during the mission, but he hadn't been standoffish, either. He worked mostly with the higher-ranked marines. "I thought you were with the gunny?"

Willis shook his head. "Doesn't fit with the layout. We need her in the middle guiding the operation with Lieutenant Crowder." He smiled a bit. "Don't worry, I've been through most of the same training you have."

Though she kept her thoughts to herself, Alicia's eyes flicked over to Ravenell and Janeka. For all the agent's training, she doubted he had run nearly as many mock boardings on as many different spacecraft as they had. Still, Alicia nodded, and when her holocom buzzed with a final check-in signal, she tapped it to confirm her readiness.

Sound-suppressed rifles coughed up above her on the wall of the spaceport berth. Knowing his cue, Ravenell activated the electromagnetic breaching pads on the nearby bay doors, forcing them open. "Go," ordered Janeka. Alicia and three others rushed through the entrance, weapons out and ready.

Though barely longer than a corvette, the *Guillotine* offered a broader profile to allow for extra space and comfort. She'd been built as a luxury yacht, but her original design hosted hidden weaponry and military-quality hull reinforcement, along with a power drive to match any corvette. Her crew, however, was not up to military-grade service, demonstrated by the way her entry ramp was still down and extended. The bodies of two sentries, shot by the snipers on the walls, lay to either side.

The *Guillotine* didn't take up the full space offered by the landing berth. That left the marine assault team with a few uncomfortable yards to cross before they came under her curved wings, but they'd been trained for actions like this. The team knew how to stack up, how to cover one another upon entry, and how to pick targets. They also knew not to squander the element of surprise, moving inside aggressively and gunning down the first handful of pirates they found with their pulse lasers.

Ravenell's team, leapfrogging Alicia's, broke off to head for engineering. Alicia followed Agent Willis through the passageways, eyes sweeping this way and that for targets as shouts and gunshots rang out. A tattooed, scraggly haired man at the bottom of the steps leading up to the next deck had his weapon out as Willis and Alicia appeared. His panicked shots hit neither of them before they put him down with quiet blasts of blue light that burned through his torso.

Willis ran for the ladder well. Alicia followed, then felt her heart stop when he yelled, "Grenade!"

She saw the little orb clatter down onto the base of the ladder in front of them. Willis jumped to the side. Alicia grabbed the body of the man they'd just killed and heaved it over the grenade before jumping back and away to curl up in a ball on the deck.

Despite the body smothering the grenade, the explosion still shook the passageway. Alicia felt bits of debris and gore strike her body. Something burned her leg, but she knew right away that it wasn't serious. When she raised her head, she found that Willis had recovered a heartbeat faster than she had, and was hurling his own grenade up the ladder. Unlike the pirates, Willis knew how to time his before throwing, thereby leaving the enemy above less of a chance to react.

They heard screams amid the boom of the grenade. A bloody, smoldering woman fell dead through the ladder well. Willis covered the opening with his pulse laser while Alicia got to her feet and followed up with a second grenade, this one built to stun with flashing light and booming sound. As soon as it was out of her hand, Willis followed after it. Alicia stuck close to him.

As expected, they found the bridge locked up tight. Alicia set up her breaching kit while Willis shouted, "Surrender now and you'll live through this!" By the time they were ready, other marines had caught up to them. Perhaps two minutes had passed since the first sniper shots had taken down the sentries outside.

The team stacked up at the hatch. Alicia got behind Willis, passed the breaching activator to the marine behind her, and held her weapon ready. As soon as the breaching unit opened the hatch, Willis and Alicia opened up with their guns. The team did everything right, yet that didn't make anyone invincible. Willis caught a gunshot in the face. He went down in front of Alicia, who in turn cut down one of the three remaining pirates on the bridge.

Lasers and bullets flashed by her in both directions. Alicia looked for targets and fired. Another gun went off beside her, almost right next to her head, thankfully firing lasers rather than solid shells that would have deafened her despite the miniature baffles plugged in her ears. Someone else on her side screamed. She stepped into the bridge compartment, took cover behind a console, and forced herself to aim before shooting, lest she wreck vital controls.

Again, the laser rifle beside her flashed distractingly close to her head. It cut down the last of the pirates, ending the fight. "Clear," Gunny Janeka announced, placing her hand on Alicia's shoulder.

The younger marine swallowed hard. "Clear," she replied, then looked back at the others. She didn't know when Janeka had gotten there. Of the three men who'd breached the bridge with her, only one still stood. Willis lay dead in the entryway. Another marine slumped against the wall, clutching a wound on his arm that wouldn't likely be fatal.

"Breathe," said Janeka once more, looking each of her marines in the eye. "Stop and breathe."

The quick pause made all the difference. "Wong, take the helm. Fire it up. Lieutenant Crowder, do you copy?" Janeka asked over her holocom link. She glanced at the wounded marine, who winced but nodded. Then she grabbed the hatch to the bridge and pulled it shut again, setting the magnetic locks to reboot.

"Lieutenant Crowder took a pretty bad hit, gunny," reported another voice. "We're working on him, but I don't know if he's gonna make it."

"Engineering is secure," added Ravenell. "Not much damage. Primary systems were kept warm. Life support looks good. We put down a bunch of targets in the galley, too."

"Exterior remains secure," reported one of the snipers.

"Then I'm assuming command," said Janeka. "Everyone get on the ship and secure for liftoff. We are extracting immediately."

She sat down beside Alicia, who dutifully had her station powered up, but Alicia's eyes were turned toward the closed hatch. Willis lay dead on the other side. He wasn't alone.

"Wong. Listen to me. Breathe."

"I'm breathing," Alicia said, nodding and turning back to her work. She checked the skies and traffic above them and started up the systems diagnostic. "Are you breathing?"

"Breathing is for lesser mortals," said Janeka, her hands moving over the controls.

Alicia froze. She blinked and turned to Janeka. "Okay, now I know I'm too ramped up, because you made a joke and I'm not laughing."

"You did good," Janeka told her. "Real good, like I knew you would. You fought like a marine and now you're gonna run the helm like a navy crewman, just like you were taught. We're gonna make our rendezvous and FTL it straight home to Archangel. We'll be back on the *Los Angeles* in a week."

Alicia nodded. She turned back to her controls and watched the condition tracks run up toward full readiness. "Gunny, thanks.

For picking me for this, I mean. Not 'cause I enjoyed the fight, but . . ."

"I knew you had what it took. That's why I picked you."

Again, Alicia nodded. She glanced once at the gunny, then away, and then something jerked her attention back to the older woman. "Did you just smile?"

"I did not smile, marine. *I do not smile.*"

"Right. Understood," said Alicia, turning her face dutifully back to the controls.

"You're bleeding from your leg," Janeka observed without looking. "Tend to it when we get clear. I've gotta look after Hernandez over there."

Alicia looked down at her thigh. Sure enough, she had taken a bit of shrapnel from something—probably the grenade on the lower deck—and hadn't noticed.

Janeka rose from her station to see to the other wounded marine. As she passed, she laid a hand on Alicia's shoulder and gave a single warm squeeze.

It occurred to Alicia that it was just as well that this whole op was covert and classified. No one would ever believe Janeka would show such affection, anyway.

• • •

"Tight-beam transmission from *Guillotine*," announced the comms tech. He read from a screen at his station, not turning around toward the ship's captain or first officer. A navigational display near the tech showed the former yacht passing by. Both ships were just outside the two light-minute safe navigation zone around Edison.

"How'd it go?" asked the gravelly voice of the captain. He stood from his chair to walk over to the comms station. His first officer, Aaron Hawkins, stuck close to his side.

"*Guillotine*'s captain is in custody, all other hostiles KIA. Three friendly casualties, including the agent in charge. Marine team leader also seriously wounded." He paused and then looked over his shoulder. "The acting mission leader is asking to speak to the captain."

Hawkins opened his mouth to speak but found himself cut off. "The captain is unavailable," said the captain. "Acknowledge their report and tell them to hold to the original plan. They jump to FTL as soon as they're outside Edison's gravity well."

"Aye, aye, sir."

Hawkins eyed the ship's captain. Though officially the first officer, Hawkins had much more of a background in intelligence and covert operations than ship handling. Few first officers had to keep their captains completely restricted to the ship as part of their duties. "Looks like all the intel on where we'd find the *Guillotine* and her crew was right on the money," said Hawkins.

"Yeah, what a shock," came the somewhat annoyed reply. Casey looked his personal watchdog in the eye before passing him on the way back to his captain's chair. "Can't imagine who gave them all that great info."

• • •

"Yup. Request denied, hold to the original plan." Alicia looked over to the gunny. She'd known Janeka long enough to learn the nuances within Janeka's repertoire of expressions of displeasure. "Is that dodgy?"

Janeka glared at the large ship on the holographic display. "Only because the captain never met with Lieutenant Crowder, either." She frowned. "Or Willis."

"That's weird?" asked Alicia. Their course was locked in. Janeka and the computer had done most of the work. Alicia gave the ship on the screen another look. Her recruit company had received more than a little training in ship recognition from Janeka and Chief Everett, but the vessel on the display didn't look familiar to her at all. It might have been a stock passenger liner once upon a time, but it had clearly been through considerable modification.

"At your rank, it wouldn't be weird for you not to meet with a ship's captain, no," explained Janeka. "At my level, one would at least expect a handshake. But this ship brings us into a sovereign system for a covert op, and the captain doesn't want to meet anyone in charge? That's dodgy."

Considering it further, Alicia suggested, "Maybe it's for the sake of deniability?"

Janeka shook her head. "No. A ship's captain doesn't get to play dumb. He has to know everything that happens on his ship. Doesn't matter if he's military or civilian. They hung around to monitor, too, not just drop us off and go on their way."

"FTL jump in sixty seconds," Alicia noted. They wouldn't be outside Edison's legal FTL line for it, but that paled in comparison to the other laws they'd just broken. Alicia dutifully announced the countdown as *Guillotine* passed out of the gravity wells of Edison and its moons. Laws against FTL jumps within a system existed for good reason, but at this distance from large bodies, the risks of a gravitic disaster were reasonably low.

Janeka input the commands to execute. Everyone on the ship felt the lurch as the ship transitioned from well below light speed to something far beyond it, but the lurch was much less pronounced than on most other vessels. It was a reminder of *Guillotine*'s original purpose; once upon a time, she'd been a luxury yacht built for a smooth and pleasant ride.

That thought pushed Janeka out of her seat once she was satisfied with immediate responsibilities. "Keep everything under control here," she said. "I'm gonna make the rounds."

"Aye, aye, captain." Alicia grinned. She dared a wink when Janeka looked back at her.

The gunnery sergeant checked in on the wounded. She surveyed engineering and made sure someone was already dealing with the dead pirates strewn about the ship. She gave instructions to collect all the small arms on board. These were all necessary steps, but she had one other duty to fulfill. For that, she retrieved the big gray overcoat that she had ditched just inside the ship's entryway upon boarding.

She found Hannah Black in a chair in the ship's galley. The pirate captain had her hands and feet tied to the chair, which was itself securely bolted to the floor. Awake and aware of her surroundings, Hannah watched but said nothing until Janeka stepped up to her.

"You're military," said Hannah. "Whose?"

"You'll figure it out before too long."

Hannah scowled and spit on the deck. She noted the look in Janeka's eyes. "Have we met?"

"Not personally, no," said Janeka. "I've wanted to meet you for a long time, though."

Hannah didn't respond. She just watched and waited.

Janeka reached into her coat. She drew out a soft, stained bit of comfort and warmth and put it on the table in front of Hannah. Then she walked away, leaving Hannah under the lifeless stare of an old, battered, bloody teddy bear.

ONE

Pieces on the Board

"*Primary debt is a specific subset of sovereign debt. It's the long-term debt owed by an extraterrestrial colony for all those massive start-up costs of getting out into the stars in the first place. The Big Three of Lai Wa, NorthStar, and CDC own almost all of that debt. Ironically, the government of Archangel is in the position to break from corporate dependency precisely because its primary debt is among the lowest in the Union, thanks to the financial support of the Catholic Church during the Expansion Era.*

"*Archangel's economy is the strongest of any state based around a single star and the ninth strongest in the Union overall. Yet the system's anticorporate stance and cessation of primary debt payments have sent Archangel's credit plummeting to the bottom of the Union's ranks. Given the enormous cost of the services Archangel must now provide for itself, it's anyone's guess as to how badly the system's economy will tank.*"

—Matt Gao, "Can Anyone Go It Alone?"
Union Business Review, April 2276

"We're looking at open warfare breaking out on Scheherazade within the month, sir," explained David Kiribati, head of Archangel's Intelligence Ministry. He leaned in close beside President Aguirre as he moved his fingers through the holographic projection in front of them, starting with a projection of the multiple stars that made up the Kingdom of Hashem and then zooming in on a single system, enlarging the fourth planet out from its star. "This system is nominally under Prince Kaseem's oversight while remaining loyal to the king, but in reality the security forces, the government, and most of the big domestic businesses are split between Prince Kaseem and Prince Murtada. We know Murtada is covertly stockpiling weapons and troops on the planet. The king knows it. NorthStar and Lai Wa know it. And given all that, it's hard to believe Kaseem doesn't know it."

"What makes us think NorthStar and Lai Wa know?" asked President Aguirre. Numerous advisers and aides filled the president's comfortable office, some seated and some standing. Only a handful would do the talking unless called upon.

"We have reason to believe that NorthStar has decided to back Murtada, sir."

Aguirre looked up with surprise. "I thought they wanted to tamp down on this whole feud before it gets worse. We expected them to back the king."

"Murtada's political and religious platform makes him more attractive than the status quo, sir," explained Theresa Cotton, Aguirre's foreign minister. "For one thing, Murtada takes a much stricter line over the hajj. He was deeply inspired by his own journey years ago, and—"

"I don't need the theological underpinnings," Aguirre cut her off. "What's it all mean strategically?"

Theresa managed to control her frown. "It means a significant long-term uptick in travel if Murtada comes out on top, which puts easy money in NorthStar's pocket. This also puts a theological twist on what was initially a straightforward fight for succession that will draw religious conservatives to fight for Murtada."

"People will shoot each other over how low they set the economic bar for going to Mecca?"

"Mr. President," spoke up Admiral Yeoh, cutting through the room with her soft tone, "we still have communities in this system that denounce you as a false pope, when you've never claimed any religious authority. We humans seem bent on finding ways to separate ourselves from one another."

Aguirre blinked at that, as did several others, mostly because Yeoh rarely offered existential commentary. She usually concerned herself with empirical matters—as did the president. "So what do we expect?" he asked, turning his attention back to Kiribati. "If they start up a fight over Scheherazade, doesn't the whole kingdom wind up in a civil war?"

"It seems likely, sir," said Kiribati. "That may not happen right away, but in the meantime a ground war will break out on Scheherazade. Most of the serious combat spacecraft are on the other side of the kingdom facing off over the shipyards. When this gets rolling, we'll see an initial rush to secure strategic assets on the ground. Government installations, the ground-side spaceports, infrastructure.

"And it'll be ugly," he added. "Part of the reason we know about this movement is that we were able to identify particular officers in Murtada's forces. A lot of them were involved in the initial massacres on Qal'at Khalil after the pirate attack there. Murtada has a thing for strong-arm tactics."

"What are the other parties doing about this?"

"Union Assembly diplomats are making the usual overtures, but they're toothless. Lai Wa seems content to let NorthStar take the lead in Hashem; we think there's probably a quid pro quo arrangement there in exchange for concessions elsewhere in the Union. NorthStar has offered up intelligence and planning aid.

They may even provide some of the heavy lifting to transport Murtada's troops. It's also possible they plan on providing manpower later to help stabilize the situation under a peacekeeping contract. We've got reports that they've increased training and simulations for occupation ops."

"And what are we doing?"

Kiribati glanced at Yeoh before answering. "We're moving in assets for evacuation. We have an Archangel Navy corvette in the system, and a covert vessel under an Independent Shipping Guild registry should be there the day after tomorrow."

"Is that enough to evacuate our people? We've got a full consulate staff there, right? Some civilian business operations?"

"Yes, sir." Kiribati nodded. "The covert vessel should be able to handle the load."

Admiral Yeoh spoke up. "It wouldn't hurt to have more in the way of military assets present, sir. Right now Prince Kaseem accepts his father's instructions to allow foreign naval traffic, probably because it complicates Murtada's plans. If and when Prince Murtada attacks, he'll order all foreign vessels out of the system. That will naturally leave foreigners in the middle of a war zone until Murtada decides to let them go, and no one can say how long that might take. We need to be able to get in and get our people out as soon as the shooting starts—if not sooner," she suggested pointedly.

"It's complicated either way," Theresa said with a shake of her head. "If we wait too long, we put our people in jeopardy. However, if we pull out based on these suspicions, we could damage our relationships and maybe be blamed for creating a crisis atmosphere—especially if the king or Prince Khalil has some sort of diplomatic work going on to settle things down."

"More importantly, we risk tipping our hand if we move in too soon." Kiribati frowned. "Keeping one or two ships in the area seems like a reasonable precaution. If we evacuate preemptively, we'll give the impression that we know too much, which will jeopardize our sources."

"I understand," Aguirre said, holding up his hand. "Admiral, we can't pull out now. I know it's tough, but we have to wait and see how this unfolds."

"Then, as I said, sir, more overt military assets would help in the event of violence," Yeoh replied.

Aguirre glanced toward Kiribati, who nodded. "We can't send in a large force," Kiribati warned, "but even adding one more navy ship to the mix is a definite improvement."

"I don't see a drawback, either, sir," Theresa concurred. "We have every legal right to extract our citizens if fighting breaks out."

"All right, fair enough." Aguirre nodded. "Admiral, go ahead and move some more people in, but don't send anything big. We want to get *un*involved, not sucked deeper into our neighbors' mess." He stared at the holographic star system and snorted. "NorthStar is planning to put people on the ground to stabilize all this?"

"I think so, sir," Kiribati replied. "And frankly, the more deeply they're involved in someone else's civil war, the better off we are. It'll take their attention off us."

"I'm afraid I must disagree, sir," said Admiral Yeoh. Again, eyes turned toward her.

"You heard what David said about them training for an occupation?" asked the president.

"Yes, sir. I've seen the reports."

"You don't think they're doing that to get ready for this?"

"No, sir," maintained the admiral calmly. "I don't believe that it's the Kingdom of Hashem they plan to occupy, sir."

She didn't say the rest. It would have sounded alarmist. Her warning carried more weight if it went unsaid.

"That sounds like a topic for another meeting," noted Victor Hickman, the president's chief of staff. He looked at the time on his holocom.

Aguirre took the hint. "Right. We're late for the next one. I've got a line of CEOs outside the office waiting to see me. It's one thing to alienate the Big Three, but I don't want to leave our home-grown companies feeling snubbed, too. Was there any other urgent business?"

"No, sir," answered Kiribati, Yeoh, and the other officials simultaneously.

"Thank you, ladies and gentlemen," said the president. Everyone else stood as he rose. The meeting promptly broke up.

Yeoh ducked out of the conference room before Kiribati and his people. She dismissed her aides outside the office and then waited. Standing with her hands clasped behind her back just outside the door, Yeoh caught Kiribati's eye as he walked out with a couple of aides in tow. "David. A word?"

He nodded to his companions to send them on their way, then moved a few steps down the hallway with her. "What's on your mind, admiral?"

She noticed the change in his tone. He knew he was free to use her first name. Aguirre tried to maintain a collegial atmosphere among his top advisers, but Kiribati's walls were up. She knew then that she would get nowhere, but she might as well ask and watch his reaction. "I had some questions about the operation on Edison. A few points were not covered in the briefing documents."

"Such as?"

"The initial insertion," Yeoh said, looking at him directly. The poker face Kiribati presented fit her expectations. "You listed a vessel under a 'covert private registry' out of New Corsica, but no other details. I'm aware that it was a large ship, perhaps a converted passenger liner?"

"More or less."

"Is it an Archangel asset or some external resource?"

"It's one of ours. I wouldn't outsource something like this. What are you getting at, admiral?"

Yeoh didn't blink, but the man's attitude raised her concerns. "The Intelligence Ministry has always had vessels of its own, but something of that size surprises me. Mr. Kiribati, who is the captain of that ship?"

"As I said, it's one of ours. I'm afraid the details are on a need-to-know basis."

"You don't believe I have a need to know about a combat-ready ship of that size operating in tandem with our military?"

"Admiral, all I can tell you is that the president has been fully briefed, and you do not have a need to know. I'll thank you for leaving the matter alone." With that, he turned and left.

Yeoh watched him walk away with thoughtful, narrowed eyes. She'd expected polite lies, not stonewalling. She'd smelled something fishy when Kiribati had first proposed the operation—lacking pertinent details then just as now. Given the value of the mission, she'd agreed to provide a strike team, but her concerns remained. She was unable to relay her suspicions to those marines and still expect the operation to go smoothly. She had, however, made sure to fill the team with smart, observant people who'd think for themselves. They reported back to her that the insertion vessel was most certainly not just an ordinary passenger liner.

Unfortunately, none of them got the full tour during their brief time on board. They didn't get to meet the captain, either, which increased Yeoh's concerns. Archangel held only so many people qualified to run a ship of that size and complexity who could also be trusted for dangerous and covert ops. Yeoh could account for all of them—those on active duty, the retirees, and those in the private sector. As Kiribati had said, it wasn't like him to outsource such a matter, so he wouldn't have hired someone from beyond Archangel . . . would he?

Given the impending problems on the planet Scheherazade, it seemed likely that the ship would be in play again soon. Once the shooting started, the ships' captains on scene would have to take charge and make decisions on behalf of all Archangel . . . and Yeoh had no sense at all of who commanded the largest ship.

Yeoh headed out toward the elevators. The admiral quickly dismissed the idea of approaching President Aguirre directly on the matter. Kiribati's bonds with the president ran deeper than those of a career military officer who'd been in place well before Aguirre was elected.

She couldn't let this go, but she couldn't make noise about it, either. Military intelligence would likely be too unreliable here; the bonds between that division and Kiribati's Intelligence Ministry were too widespread. Someone, perhaps even a well-meaning subordinate, would inevitably tip her hand.

Her current approach had gotten her this far. Yeoh could probably get further with simple passive research. Still, her ploy on this last operation had borne some fruit. She'd put good people in the field and trusted in their abilities, and they had delivered. Her mind began considering other personnel who might be good to put into play. It wasn't long before she decided which ship she would send, based largely on its captain. Concerns about her staff also came to mind.

Stepping out of the elevator, Yeoh walked into the upper lobby overlooking the grand entrance to Ascension Hall. Below, tourists filed past the original oversize paper copies of Archangel's colonial charters. Two marines in full dress regalia stood guard beside them.

The sight triggered an idle thought. She walked to a navy crewman posted at the top of the stairs, also in dress uniform. His posture stiffened just a bit and he saluted sharply for the head of Archangel's military. "Crewman Jones," she said, reading his name tag as she returned his salute, "I'm looking for another member of the honor guard. Do you have today's duty roster on your holocom?"

"Yes, ma'am," he said. Technically, he did not break the stance of attention—he looked straight ahead, remained stiff, and didn't turn his chin, but something in his expression lightened as if to affect a grin. "But I imagine I can tell you where to find who you're looking for off the top of my head."

• • •

Nothing surprised him more than the frequency of one question: "Hey, would you mind if I took a picture with you?"

He'd gotten it from celebrities, ambassadors, wealthy political donors to the president, and politicians in offices high and low. Six months ago, the most sought-after personalized souvenir of any visit to Ascension Hall was a picture of oneself standing alongside the president. While everyone still wanted that picture, they now also wanted their picture taken with Tanner Malone.

His fifteen minutes of fame seemed mostly over. He didn't hear his name on the news anymore, nor were there requests for interviews. Talk of film adaptations of his experiences had died off. He'd expected to fade back into obscurity. Yet there was still this.

At times, he was flattered, even excited. At other times, less so. He didn't agree with the politics or practices of everyone who came through the palace doors. Yet as a member of the honor guard, he had a responsibility to be respectful, politically neutral—politically mute, to be more accurate—and exceedingly, unfailingly polite.

As such, he didn't feel he had much of an option to decline.

Tanner answered the request before him as he always did: he smiled, stepped around from the desk to stand with the petitioner, and said, "My only condition is that I get a copy, sir." He shook the man's extended hand. Tanner wore his dress uniform, with medals and badges and well-polished sidearm just as regulation required for duty at Ascension Hall. The man who stood beside him with a well-practiced smile and perfectly groomed goatee wore a business suit that cost at least three months of Tanner's base salary.

"I'm Jonathan Hartmann," said the gentleman, "though I guess you might've already heard that," he added, gesturing toward the civilian receptionist.

"Yes, sir," Tanner replied with a friendly nod. "Briarwood Capital is the largest independent investment firm in the system."

Hartmann seemed gratified by that. "It's always nice to be recognized, isn't it?"

Tanner kept his mouth shut. He made a habit of looking up every individual scheduled on the guest book upon arriving at his post. People who entered Ascension Hall through this checkpoint tended not to be ordinary, anonymous citizens. They also enjoyed being recognized.

The man's aide pulled her holocom from its earring mount, activated it, and took a few steps around the pair to get a solid frontal-arc image. Few people went for the full three-sixty recording. Soon, Tanner instructed his wrist-mounted holocom to receive a tap transfer and touched it against her slick, state-of-the-art device.

"That's a nice piece," Tanner said idly as the holocoms executed the file transfer.

"Thanks." She smiled at him and then tilted her head curiously. "Hey, you're wearing an earring. I thought servicemen weren't allowed to wear those?"

"Old naval tradition, ma'am," Tanner explained. He hadn't meant to draw any attention to the humble gold bead in his left earlobe. "Sailors who survived a wrecked or sunken ship were entitled to wear one." He gave a little wink. "I'm pretty sure it's more myth than tradition, but if it lets me get away with pushing the uniform boundaries, I'll take it."

"I had a couple of friends on the *Pride of Polaris*," said Hartmann, his glowing and genetically perfect smile still on display. "I heard the whole story from their perspective, so I've wanted to shake your hand ever since."

"Thank you, sir," Tanner replied. "Pleasure to meet you."

"Mr. Hartmann," spoke up one of the civilian staffers, "I'll show you in. Right this way."

Tanner walked back around the desk. Predictably, with Hartmann out of earshot, the needling from the woman who ran the reception desk began. "Sooner or later, one of these people will just come straight out and ask if they can adopt you."

"They're not that interested in me, Beth."

"Oh please. 'Oooh, you're Tanner Malone! Can I have your picture? Will you sign my briefcase? Are you doing anything later?'" she mimicked.

Tanner rolled his eyes. "I have never once been asked out while on duty—"

"That you actually noticed"—Beth smirked—"but you are a little dense."

"—and who actually uses briefcases anymore?"

"I've seen a few. Besides, it's either that or sign a napkin. Or someone's breast, but you'd probably get in trouble for doing that here." She paused. "You've never been asked out while on the job? Some people might presume you and Andrea Bennett are still seeing each other, but it's not like that ever stopped anyone in this town."

He bit down on his first response. Beth was just teasing him, and he knew it. He also knew her last comment was a marginally subtle probe. He didn't feel like opening that line of discussion. "They're not actually interested in me. They just want the picture."

"You don't think people want their picture next to you because they're interested in you?"

"I think they want the picture so they can show it off to create a certain impression." Tanner jerked his thumb in the direction

Hartmann had taken. "It lets big, important people like him show that he associates with ordinary, everyday people like me."

Beth frowned at him. "You aren't ordinary people, Tanner."

"Yes, I am. There are hours and hours of media stories to tell you so."

"You don't think that proves my point?"

"I think it proves that not everyone understands the concept of irony," he quipped.

Rather than let him get away with that by laughing, Beth smacked him on the shoulder. Tanner accepted it without complaint. "Still. That's a pretty cynical view of things, isn't it?"

"How long have you worked in Ascension Hall?" Tanner asked. "You haven't gotten cynical yet?"

"Oh, I'm plenty cynical"—she shrugged—"but you've only been here a few months. I figured it'd take at least a year or two for a kid like you to get that way." Beth looked at him thoughtfully. "You've never been asked out?"

"Not the way you're suggesting, no. Have I been asked out? Sure. Have women dropped hints? Sure. But nobody just walks up to me while I'm here in my shiny dress uniform and—"

Tanner always kept his eyes on the hallways. His job mostly involved simple crowd control, courtesy greetings, and a certain amount of pageantry. Dress uniforms were part of the spectacle of the palace. But neither he nor his sidearm were purely for show; he was also a part of the building's security force, and as such he kept his eyes and ears open at all times.

He saw the admiral coming well before she was within conversational range, but he popped to attention the instant she appeared. Unperturbed, Beth merely turned her eyes back to her computer displays.

"Crewman Malone," said Admiral Yeoh, "how are you?"

"Fine, ma'am. Thank you for asking, ma'am."

The corners of Yeoh's mouth cracked in just the slightest show of amusement. "I wondered if you might join me for some coffee."

"Yes, ma'am. Soon as I can get relief here, ma'am." He wasn't due to have a break for another hour, but this was Admiral Yeoh. Every officer in the guard would tell him that his break would happen whenever the admiral damn well pleased.

"Excellent. I'll see you in the south dining room."

"Yes, ma'am."

With that, Admiral Yeoh turned and headed back down the hall. Tanner relaxed his posture. He glanced at Beth and then grimaced at her amused expression. "Don't," he warned in vain.

"Don't what? I was just gonna say she's still rather pretty, especially given her age. You like that, don't you, Tanner? Pretty, powerful, and much, much older than you?"

Tanner let out a loud, grumbling sigh. He tapped his holocom to call his watch commander.

Beth didn't bother to restrain her teasing. "So, I want to know: Is it the feeling of conquest that draws you to women like that? Or are you only interested in women who can conquer you?"

"That's exactly it," Tanner replied. "That's why I have erotic dreams every night about Gunnery Sergeant Janeka from basic training."

"Wait, you have dreams about *what*?" asked the voice of the watch commander on his holocom.

• • •

"So, what are your thoughts on choosing a rating?" Yeoh's eyes stayed on him as she sipped her cup of coffee. A handful of the other tables also hosted people in dress uniform—all of them officers, except Tanner—but by a wide majority, occupants of the south wing dining room wore civilian business wear.

"I'm sorry, ma'am?" Tanner had yet to touch the drink on the table in front of him. He sat up straight with his hands on his lap.

"Tanner, it's one thing to observe military etiquette, but you don't have to call me ma'am with every sentence." She smiled. "This isn't the first time we've met. Or even the third. Relax."

His lips tensed for a second as he processed his reactions, but he nodded. "Yes, ma'am," he exhaled, and then grinned a bit at himself. "Meeting with you still isn't something I would expect to happen on a random Tuesday."

"No, but you interact with plenty of other VIPs and dignitaries here on a daily basis. You are not so tongue-tied with them. I've seen you be perfectly friendly and laugh in such company. Some people come to that sort of grace naturally. Others have to learn it. I think you're more of the latter, but you're quick. I only adapted gradually as I climbed through the ranks. What's your secret?"

"I've learned not to put people up on pedestals."

Yeoh gave the slightest of nods. "Andrea?" She waited for an answer, but heard none and couldn't blame him. "This is the point at which a lowly crewman can tell the head of the military that something is none of her damn business, Tanner. But I suspect you don't have many people you feel comfortable talking to about it. For what it's worth, I'm not judging."

"Yeah, that'd make you about the only person in this town. Ma'am," he added gratefully.

"Politics makes for a rough game. Andrea is very good at it, but even she takes hits. You might consider that she thought you're worth taking a few."

"It's not just about politics," Tanner replied, shaking his head. "At least, not that kind. I appreciate your offer, but I'm not sure this is a good time and place to get into it. But thank you."

"Then back to my question: You must have given thought to choosing a rating. You're twenty-two months in. By now you could be in a rating school . . . but you aren't."

"I wanted to do a tour here at Ascension Hall, ma'am."

"And after what you went through and what you accomplished, you had your choice of billets." Yeoh nodded. "You could have named your duty station. You chose to stay here and open doors for people coming to meet the president."

"People work pretty hard to get this post, ma'am," Tanner pointed out.

"Most of them aren't trying to hide in plain sight," she countered gently.

Tanner blinked. The heavy, unsettling sensation he'd felt in his stomach from the moment Admiral Yeoh asked if he wanted to grab a coffee break with her intensified. "Ma'am?"

"I don't actually know what ratings might appeal to you, but if I made some educated guesses, they would all require a full year of time in a starship billet. You have nine months." She paused, watching his reactions. "That sort of detail wouldn't slip by you. At first, I thought you requested this duty to be close to Andrea. But after I gave it some serious thought—the kind of thought you would give it—I believe you knew the odds of that relationship going the distance. From the start, I'd imagine. And yet you still requested duty with the capital honor guard.

"As I said, any duty in the service would've been open. No one was going to break any rules for you. It wouldn't have looked good. But if you'd needed to fulfill some prerequisite or qualification, plenty of people would've made that happen. I think you knew that when you requested this assignment over all the other options.

"You're hiding out, Tanner. You're hoping to go unnoticed."

"I like this assignment, ma'am."

"Oh? Tell me why."

The answers came to him with agonizing sluggishness. "I've got a regular schedule here, ma'am. The capital's a great city. I can take—I have taken classes here. I get weekends off. I get along with my roommates in the barracks. And I've learned a lot just by being here, about how the government actually works, about things most people only read about in news articles, and . . ."

His voice faltered under her skeptical gaze. She ran her finger across her holocom to activate its display, projected a small file, and turned it toward him. Tanner saw a record of his military passcard use. Every visit to a military or affiliated facility spread out before him. "Two visits a week to the tactical shooting range at Fort Bentley," Yeoh noted. "Twelve hours every week at the gym at the Joint Capital Security Services complex, including their hand-to-hand classes and their urban obstacle course. You completed the two-week wilderness survival course at Camp Horizon and a refresher course in advanced first aid. The only remotely academic course you've taken is introductory Arabic."

". . . You've been checking up on me that closely?"

"I'm the head of the military, Tanner. Your training records are only under the lowest privacy classifications. I looked them up while waiting for you to join me." She tilted her head. "And while the honor guard looks pretty and performs ceremonies, I know the training this post involves. You aren't here just for show. But to add all of that extracurricular activity on top of the day job? That's an awful lot of active training for someone who's happy to spend the rest of his enlistment on a safe and stable ground-side billet."

Tanner wasn't sure what to say. He felt himself being backed into a corner. This conversation felt more and more like a chess match that he was bound to lose. "I had a long talk with my psychiatrist about whether or not this was paranoid behavior, ma'am."

"And what did your psychiatrist say?"

"He said it was fine if it left me feeling more empowered and less vulnerable. And as long as I was ready to question myself on it, I shouldn't worry too much." Tanner paused. "I'm not sure he's such a good psychiatrist, to be honest."

"Is that why you're going to all this effort?" she asked, indicating the training record. "Paranoid behavior? Empowerment?"

"No, ma'am."

"Then why?"

He couldn't meet her eyes at first. Tanner looked around at the people in fine, formal business wear in the ornate but comfortable dining room. The setting felt peaceful. Everyone seemed to be at ease, or at least perfectly accustomed to a high-pace, high-stress lifestyle. Tanner could name more than a few of them off the top of his head and identify what made them important enough to be at Ascension Hall.

He read the guest book every day. He knew who was here, and he could easily guess why.

"They're coming for us, aren't they, ma'am?"

"Who?"

"NorthStar. Lai Wa. CDC. Maybe with friends." His eyes came back to hers. "We're not trying for any reconciliation. I've seen the president's speeches. He's not dialing anything back. The navy is at its maximum fleet size—beyond it, depending on how you count—but we're still recruiting like it's going out of style. The incentives keep getting better.

"We're moving further and further away from the corporations while they're preoccupied with the mess in Hashem, but when that's over, they're gonna come after us. It's not going to stop at punitive trade sanctions and a lot of passive-aggressive rhetoric . . . is it, admiral?"

Yeoh looked at him soberly. Her voice had never risen during the conversation, but she lowered it a notch as she said, "If it weren't for the mess in Hashem, they'd probably be using the Hashemites as proxies against us already."

Tanner nodded toward the screen showing his passcard record. "That's your answer, ma'am."

Her holocom beeped. She checked the holographic display and quickly closed it up again. Unlike many people Tanner had seen at the capital, Yeoh knew how to focus on her living, breathing company rather than her communications gadgets. Had it not been some sort of priority message, she probably wouldn't have checked it at all.

"I need smart, capable people in the field, Tanner. I need people who are good in a crisis. You may think you don't belong in the military, but we both know your record says otherwise. No one who didn't belong in the navy could've pulled off the things you've done."

"I'm really important enough for all this, ma'am?" Tanner asked. "I'm worth the head of the Archangel Navy coming down to talk to me personally?"

"Unlike a lot of officers, I know which people actually make things happen in the military. I keep tabs on quite a number of enlisted people. You may be a lowly crewman . . . but you're also Tanner Malone. Not too many people are walking around wearing the Archangel Star. And nobody else ever managed to win one in what is allegedly a time of peace. So, yes, you are worth a two-minute records check and a cup of coffee when I happen to be in the same building."

Tanner winced. He knew that was coming before he'd spoken. Tanner scratched at his left ear, his fingertips bumping the small gold bead in his earlobe. He'd won that in peacetime, too, on exactly the same day. "Allegedly?"

"Yes," she said, idly turning her wrist to indicate her holocom. "If that weren't the case, it might be lunch instead of just coffee. But I've got to get back to the office. Thank you for your time, Tanner. It's always a pleasure."

• • •

Her office was well out of his way back to his post. The public affairs department wasn't high-security territory; anyone who could access the "business" portions of Ascension Hall had all the clearance they needed to enter. Tanner didn't make a habit of visiting—to the contrary, he generally stayed away—but no one gave him a second glance when he passed through. His friendship with the press secretary was public knowledge.

Speculation as to whether or not he might be more than just a friend only occurred in discreet conversations.

Tanner knew how busy Andrea could get at the drop of a hat. No matter how organized or skilled the presidential press secretary might be, the job could go into crisis mode without warning and stay that way for days. Even without a crisis, Tanner expected to find her door shut or to see staffers or journalists meeting with her, but he made the trip, anyway.

As it happened that morning, he found nothing of the sort. Tanner caught the eye of Andrea's assistant at her desk in the office next door. She threw him a quick nod and waved him on through. With that, Tanner took a deep breath and knocked on Andrea's door with his free hand.

She looked up from the holo screens spread out in front of her desk and offered a soft smile. "Hey," she said. "How're you?"

"Little thrown off my routine today," he admitted. "I had some unexpected time in the south dining room and figured I'd bring you something." Tanner came inside and placed the tall mug on her desk, careful not to reach through any of the holo screens, lest he accidentally input a command.

"Couldn't ever say you aren't thoughtful." Andrea knew without looking that the mug of coffee would be exactly the way she liked it. "How did you know I wasn't busy?"

He shrugged. "I thought I'd just come check. I'd make some observation about how things look on this end of the building, but I don't want to jinx you."

"Thank you for that."

He didn't sit down. In truth, the dress uniform seemed designed to keep a man standing, anyway.

Andrea rose from her desk, stepping around it to walk to her door and close it by hand. Tanner looked her up and down as she moved, appreciating her slender figure and the way her curly black hair was pinned up to leave the nape of her neck exposed. Andrea never dressed provocatively at the office, but she always looked good. It was part of her public image.

He'd been lucky enough to see the rest of her. Tanner had developed his crush on the press secretary when she'd only been a far-off media personality. Up-close exposure turned that crush into something he couldn't properly label. Not a serious relationship. Not a romance. She liked having someone on her arm at state dinners and social functions, and liked taking him home for the rest of the weekend too much for him to think that he was just a photo op and a convenient date for appearance's sake.

Yet there was always a distance there, too. Always a sense of trepidation. Things conspicuously left unsaid.

"It's been a few days," she observed. Andrea stood close enough to reach out and touch, but she didn't step closer. Neither did Tanner. "I wondered if you were mad."

"I figured leaving you alone for at least a few days was what you wanted. I didn't know whether or not to make it more. I'm frustrated," he admitted, "but not mad."

Andrea nodded. "That's fair. Fairer than I've been to you. It's not like I told you a time frame."

"I didn't think 'We need to back off' would have a schedule. It's fine."

Silence hung between them, each unsure how much to say. He decided to go for it. "Is there something I did wrong?" he asked evenly. "I tried to follow your lead. I know you have more concerns than I do."

"No. You didn't do anything wrong." He heard affection in her voice. "Hell, you did more things right than I could've ever reasonably expected. Thirty years ago, I couldn't have said that without blushing," she added. "It's not anything you did or didn't do, Tanner. It's the thirty years. We could ignore the other ten and it'd be fine, but the rest . . . Tanner, I had a Senate seat before you were in school. This isn't something that'll go away."

She didn't look even ten years older than Tanner. Physically, she looked to have only a handful of years on him. "I never felt like we ran away from that."

"We didn't," she conceded, "but I kept telling myself it was all just for fun, and all 'just this once more,' but it kept on going. And if all I had to think about was you, me, and my inevitably disapproving family, we might get by. Like I said, you never did anything wrong, I just . . . I'm already taken, Tanner. I'm married to my career."

"I figured that out the moment I met you. Well, okay. The second time, anyway. I didn't have much of a chance to think the first time."

Andrea laughed in spite of herself. It was a good memory. Still, her mirth quickly faded. "Tanner, I've been selfish all along. The first weekend together was selfish, but I told myself it'd do you some good, too."

"It did. You don't even know."

"I think I do, Tanner . . . which was why I convinced myself it was okay to go beyond that. And then to the next weekend, and the next. And I didn't care about the gossip stories because they seemed harmless enough, and you sure as hell didn't care, but I'm starting to get subtle hints from my bosses. The ones who have to care what everyone says, you know? And frankly, it's my job to care what people say. It's one thing for private citizens to throw convention out the window and not care about age differences and all that shit, but I've got to get this president reelected. I put my own political career on hold to make all this happen. We need conservative votes. Every little thing his staff does matters. This matters."

She'd thought all of this through before saying it, of course. She hadn't expected Tanner to grin in the middle of her letdown talk. "What?"

"You don't normally swear."

Again, Andrea laughed. "Great. I can't imagine where I picked that up." She gave him a long, thoughtful look. "You're trying to make this easy on me. And I don't know why I should be surprised."

"We were a long shot to begin with. If you've thought of all this to say, I can't imagine I'm going to debate you into changing your mind." He paused. "But it hurts."

"Yeah." She nodded, looking down at the floor. "Yes, it does. Probably more for you than me. I saw this coming all along. That's what I'm saying. Look, Tanner, I don't want you to just go away. It's not like I've been faking anything. I just . . . I *can't*, you know?"

"Well, I might be going away, anyway. I've had some pretty blatant hints dropped on me," he explained as Andrea's expression grew quizzical. "People above my level don't want to see my career stagnate. I think I'm gonna be transferred out."

"I'm sorry to hear that. I know how you've felt. Ship duty?"

"Probably. I don't know. It's still just hints. But I figured I should talk to you now rather than waiting too long. Next thing I know there might be some crisis in here and I'd have to send you a letter."

"I can understand that." Her hand reached up to his chest. "I'm sorry, Tanner. About the transfer, too, but . . . well. Everything."

"Don't be. I'm sad, sure, but I'm also grateful." His holocom beeped. "I've gotta get back to my post."

"Yeah. I've got work to do, too." The soft kiss she placed on his lips lingered, but she didn't risk any real passion. It wouldn't have helped. Andrea turned from him then, returning to her seat. She heard the door open and looked up to watch him leave.

He paused at her door and offered a small grin. "You have any plans for what to do with your life when this guy isn't president anymore?"

"Tanner, don't." She shook her head. "It's not fair to either of us."

He let it drop, nodded, and walked away.

Andrea's assistant poked her head through the doorway. "That went okay, then?"

"Yeah." Andrea sighed. "Yeah, he knew the score. Just . . . two adults having some laughs," she muttered. "Took it like a man." Her eyes fell to her desk. "I need something to do other than reading. What have we got?"

・ ・ ・

Tanner held his neutral expression until he was out of the public relations department. He found a bathroom, slipped inside, and locked the door.

He only needed a moment. The tears didn't stain his uniform. The redness in his eyes quickly faded. Other men might not have even needed that much, but this was new territory for him. The short time he'd had with Andrea left him with a long way to fall. Nor was it any easier to face after his coffee break.

He couldn't expect anything to last while he was in the military. He couldn't put down roots. People would come and go. His life would be like this for the next few years. He had to accept that and push on. Someday, when his enlistment was up, he'd be able to choose his own directions. For now, all he could decide for himself was how to face whatever turns came.

Tanner checked himself in the mirror, took the sort of long, deep breaths he'd been taught in basic to settle his nerves, and walked back out into the world.

TWO

All Things Change

"'We can absolutely afford a state-funded twelve-year educational system,' said presidential spokeswoman Andrea Bennett. 'Marketing aside, the Big Three derive the illusion of indispensability from their size and scope, not their uniqueness. There's nothing they do that smaller organizations—including other corporations—can't do themselves.'"
—"War of Words Escalates," *Solar Herald*, April 2276

"All hands, secure from takeoff," said the voice over the PA. The message went through everyone's helmets via the shipboard comm network, too, creating an odd sort of echo. "Repeat, secure from takeoff. All hands to the cargo bay for briefing."

The announcement required little of Tanner, though it did allow him and his fellow deckhands to pull off their helmets. They were already straightening up *Joan of Arc*'s cargo bay as the corvette took off. He'd arrived late that night and found the crew both tired and busy. Yet despite some signs of stress and a full workload, everyone he encountered welcomed him aboard with handshakes, smiles, and some friendly banter—the exact opposite of his first arrival on *St. Jude*.

The rapid pace of arrival and takeoff didn't surprise him, given the urgency of his orders to report aboard at Fort Stalwart. Beyond that, though, Tanner found one sign after another that this would be a decidedly different experience from *St. Jude*.

"See?" said one of the other deckhands. "Told you we'd get a rundown of what's going on soon as we got underway."

Tanner looked around at the clean cargo bay and its neatly stowed supplies and shook his head. "It's not that I didn't believe you. It's just not what I'm used to. Is this gonna be an organized thing? Formation by department and all that?"

"Nah, man. Just everyone standing around while the captain or the XO explains what's going on." Crewman Apprentice Sanjay Bhatia was good-looking and fit, a little taller than Tanner, and about the same age. He'd only been on the ship for five months, not yet long enough to qualify for the rank step up to crewman. It appeared the crew respected him well enough. No one seemed to treat Sanjay as "the boot." "Why would that be formal?"

Tanner shook his head. "*St. Jude*'s captain used to call us all to attention at chow and lead everyone in a prayer."

"You're shitting me. Everyone went along with that?"

Tanner realized he didn't want to say too much on the subject. He always felt the weight of the dead whenever it came up. That said, some of his old ship's idiosyncrasies weren't exactly a secret. "Didn't seem like something a non-rate was supposed to bring up, y'know?"

"Shit, I'd have said something. I might've said a lot. Anyway, no, nobody calls 'attention on deck' when the captain walks in. You only need to salute her and the XO the first time you see 'em on a given day. Nobody plays reveille on the speakers in the morning. The captain wants people to handle actual procedures like watchstanding by the book, but all the extra etiquette stuff just gets in the way."

"Something's wrong if Sanjay's giving lessons on etiquette," said the ship's XO. Junior Lieutenant Darrell Booker strode into the cargo bay in the company of several other men and a couple of women in gray navy vac suits. Though Booker, like Sanjay, appeared to be a relatively new member of the crew, Tanner appreciated the lieutenant's confidence. "We figured the only reason they'd loan us someone from the honor guard was to teach Sanjay some table manners."

Sanjay threw Tanner an annoyed look and shook his head. "You bite a guy one fuckin' time . . ." he grumbled.

The rest of the crew filed in, most of them similarly in good cheer. Tanner kept quiet and observed, but he had to wonder how different his life would be if he'd been sent to a ship like this one out of basic rather than *St. Jude*.

Eleven men and women in total took up spots to stand or sit in the cargo bay along with Tanner, comprising the full crew of *Joan of Arc* minus her current watchstanders and her commanding officer. Lieutenant Kelly arrived last, stepping into the cargo bay with a pair of active screens from her holocom floating beside her. Tanner remembered her from Oscar Company's first trip into space. Her striking green eyes and bright, short red hair would let her stand out in most crowds.

"First off, everyone, thanks for a fast and smooth departure," she said. "I wish I could've told you more than I did when this trip came up, but our orders were classified. Hopefully I dropped enough hints that those of you with families got everyone at home prepared for a long deployment." She threw a wink toward a couple of the engineers off to one side, who nodded in understanding.

"We are heading into Hashemite space, specifically toward the planet Scheherazade. We're going as fast as we can, so we should be in the system in a few days. Our orders are to establish comms with our consulate on the ground and with *St. Patrick*, which has been in the area for about a week with a civilian-registered Archangel passenger liner. Command advises that the situation in Hashem may be about to go to hell again and it may start on Scheherazade. We're to hang around in the area and observe. If shit hits the fan, we evacuate our people in the consulate and any other Archangel citizens. Most of them will go out on the liner, but we'll be there to lend a hand.

"Obviously, this mission has 'hurry up and wait' clearly written on the label. Command admits that. We may drop out of FTL in the middle of a crisis or we may wind up sitting on our hands for weeks and then come home. In the interim, we'll run drills and we'll answer any distress calls per Union laws, but our priority will be to evacuate our people from Scheherazade at the first sign of trouble.

"I've been given a basic rundown that I'll share on everyone's holocoms. We'll meet with *St. Patrick* and refine our plans from there. Inevitably, a situation like this will be fluid and chaotic. We'll work out some contingency plans and try to adhere to the basic objectives, but all the planning may go out the window in the first two minutes. I'll be relying on you all to adapt quickly."

Tanner glanced around at the other assembled crewmembers. As if to answer his prayers, one of the midranking engineers asked, "Ma'am, do we have any sense of how many people we'd be taking on?"

Oh my God, Tanner thought. *Is she taking questions?*

"We've got fifty cots, Erin." Kelly glanced at one of the bo'suns for confirmation. "That's about as many as we can squeeze in between the cargo bay and the other available spaces, but ultimately we'll take on however many we need to. If people have to sleep in shifts and spend most of the trip home sitting against a bulkhead, I imagine they'll prefer that to hanging around in a war zone." Her tone remained even and matter-of-fact. She seemed to think it a reasonable question.

"Has there been any preliminary evacuation?" another crewman asked. "Nonessential personnel and families?"

Kelly shook her head. "Given the transit time for news, I don't know any more about what might've happened over there in the last few days than you do, but I doubt it. Some of this comes down to politics. Nobody wants to create a self-fulfilling prophecy by pulling their people out." Her frown deepened. "Obviously that's the sort of thinking that makes sense to politicians *before* a crisis, and if things explode they'll all start blaming each other for not acting sooner. But it's not our call.

"I want to emphasize that we may be going into a genuine shooting war," Kelly warned, her gaze sweeping the group once more. "We don't want to get involved and we're not there to pick sides. We will make every effort to hold fire, but we will defend ourselves and our people. I'll have more for you once I've had a chance to confer with the other ships on scene. Like I said, we'll have to make sure we stay adaptable.

"On that note," she added, looking at Tanner, "we've got an extra pair of hands to help us out for at least the next couple months. Crewman Malone, welcome aboard. We're glad to have you."

"Thank you, ma'am," Tanner said with a nod.

Kelly grinned. "You look eager to get moving."

"Ma'am? No, sorry, it's just . . ." His voice trailed off as he realized what he was about to say. From the first days after the disaster on *St. Jude*, he'd resolved not to speak ill of the dead. Six months later, he still wasn't sure how much he should share, but . . . "I'm not used to crew briefings, ma'am. This is all new to me."

Chuckles and snorts followed. The captain just smiled. "We'll try to get you acclimated quickly. But unless anyone has something urgent to share, I know it's pretty late and a lot of you would just as soon hit the rack. Any other questions? No? All right. Good work, people. Dismissed."

As the meeting broke up, Booker lingered. "Tanner, have you met Grzeskiewicz yet?"

The thin man beside the XO wore third class ops specialist's markings. He rolled his eyes as he put out his hand. "Call me Stan," he said. "XO here just likes to show off the fact that he can pronounce my last name."

"Good to meet you," Tanner replied, shaking hands.

"Stan's the old man in the forward berth," Booker explained, "so he'll make sure you're all set up. There's seven of you now with only six racks, but I'll let you all sort that out."

"I've got it, XO," Stan assured him.

"Hey," Sanjay spoke up, "I could always just share a rack with Ord—ow!"

She had to reach up to hit him on the back of the head as she passed, but the gunner's mate seemed to have practiced that. Her short black hair bounced along as she moved. "Ordoñez, hi." She smiled by way of introduction to Tanner. The young woman never broke her easy stride, raising her middle finger up over her shoulder in Sanjay's direction before she left the compartment.

Tanner glanced around, wondering if he'd finally found a source of tension between the crew, but no one seemed the least bit bothered by the exchange. "Anyway, that's it," said Booker. "Tanner, we're still working you into the stations bill for damage control and all that. We'll probably have it by morning. If anything happens before then, just stick with Stan or Sanjay, okay?"

"Yes, sir."

With that, the XO moved out. Tanner followed Stan and Sanjay out as well, turning with them to head for the forward crew berth. This, too, was unlike Tanner's experience on *St. Jude. Joan of Arc* had the exact same narrow compartment holding three stacked-up bunks embedded on either bulkhead, with the same small lockers and the same tiny head opposite the entry hatch, but the space looked and smelled considerably better than Tanner's old living space. They found Ordoñez already in one of the top bunks, reading something from her holocom. The others were mostly empty, though one of them held Tanner's few bags.

"I've already been told we can't just grab one of the cots from the cargo bay and put it on the deck for you," Stan explained. "I hate to say it, but you're gonna have to hot-rack with someone. Which is going to require some extra shuffling, too, since you won't be in the same watch rotation as everyone else until you qualify for helmsman."

"What do you mean by hot-rack?" asked Sanjay.

"It means he has to use someone else's rack while they're not in it," said Ordoñez, looking over from her reading. "Stan, they're seriously sticking him in here with us? Don't they have an extra space back in the NCO berth?"

Stan shrugged. "He's not an NCO."

"Sorry about this," Tanner offered. "I know it's gonna be a pain."

Ordoñez shook her head. "I don't care if you use my rack when I'm not in it, long as you don't do anything gross. We're all sleeping in vac suits, anyway, it's not like the mattresses ever get sweaty. Just make sure you swap out pillows and it's fine. I just half-expected they'd put you in the chiefs' stateroom or something."

"Why would they do that?"

"Don't you get extra privileges with an Archangel Star? Officers having to salute you first and stuff?"

Blushing fiercely, Tanner said, "That's only if I'm actually wearing the medal. Or the ribbon. It's never supposed to be a privilege thing. Honestly, the whole saluting deal just gets confusing, too. I get officers staring at me wondering why in the hell I don't salute. Anyway, it's fine, I'll take whichever rack is open. There's locker space for me at least, right?"

"Yeah," said Sanjay, "right over here."

Ordoñez seemed to frown a little as she rolled onto her back again, calling up a new article on her holocom. The others set to sorting themselves out, mostly crawling into their own racks as Tanner stuffed his bags away. "Which rack is open now?" Tanner asked, gesturing to the empty spaces.

"Mike's on watch and Teddy tends to stay up late," Stan explained, "so you should probably take Mike's." He pointed to the rack underneath Ordoñez's. "I'll send him a note so he doesn't crawl in with you when he comes off watch. We'll just shuffle around until morning and then figure it out."

"No worries."

"I just think they ought to treat you better after everything you did," grumbled Ordoñez.

Tanner hesitated, unsure of how to address this. "I feel a lot better being treated like everyone else, to be honest. I don't expect to get out of cleanup details or mess duty. I'm still a non-rate."

"It's not about you personally," said Stan with a knowing grin. "Ordoñez is 'new guard,' like you. She's still kinda bitter about all the initial teasing you guys got when you first showed up." Stan flinched but laughed when Ordoñez pelted him with a piece of candy.

"When did you go through basic?" Tanner asked her.

"I went to Fort Melendez in the summer of '74," Ordoñez answered. "We started with the old-school program but then they heard about the Fort Stalwart program and decided they wanted to shift over before we were done with the second week of training."

"I did the six month deal, too," groaned Sanjay, "*and* weapons and tactics afterward."

Tanner was still stuck on the time line. Ordoñez must have enlisted only a month or two after Tanner, and yet she was already through her rating school and promoted to third class. The schools for ratings classes came open at irregular intervals based on the needs of the service, which was one reason why Tanner couldn't get into the ratings he most wanted. Before this conversation, he'd felt indifferent about the wait. If he finished out his enlistment as a non-rate because his school never came up, that didn't seem too bad. He didn't want to make a career out of this life, anyway.

Yet now he wondered how many of Oscar Company's navy recruits were probably on their way to ratings schools already. *Joan of Arc* had been the destination of one Oscar graduate—a guy named Garrison—who left for school months ago. Tanner remembered watching older friends go off to universities while he sat in the wreckage of his own future plans. He wondered if he wasn't setting himself up for the same experience all over again by sticking to his earlier priorities of slow-moving science or health ratings.

"So other than the saluting thing," Ordoñez said, "what else is there with the Archangel Star?"

Again, Tanner blushed. He felt like putting the pillow over his head rather than under it. "Ordoñez, leave it alone," said Stan.

"I'm just curious," she said. "If it bothers you, I'll shut up."

"No, it's fine," Tanner replied with a sigh. "I'm supposed to get an invitation to the Annual Address every year. I get some of the retirement benefits after I get out, too, even if I only do this one enlistment. But mostly it's just another medal, so like with some of the others it bumps me up a bit on transfer wish lists and promotion rolls, but I still have to jump through all the same—"

"Holy shit!" Ordoñez blurted out. Suddenly, Tanner found her head and arms hanging down over the side of her rack above his. Her short, dark hair dangled freely. Tanner had no idea how she was holding herself up. The holographic article came down with her, too, and she pointed at it. "You get an extra five hundred creds a month *for life*?"

"Jesus Christ!" gasped Stan.

"Uh . . . y-yeah," Tanner admitted, "but it's all going to educational debt."

"Five hundred? That's it?" asked Sanjay.

"What do you mean, 'That's it?' He's making more money than I am!"

"Yeah, but you gotta pay taxes on it, right?" Sanjay asked. "Just seems like a crap benefit when the Hashemites would've paid ten million credits for that pirate captain Tanner caught."

"I heard they offered to pay him, anyway, but the government said no, we're not mercenaries," said Ordoñez.

"Wait, what?" Tanner blinked. "Where did you guys hear that stuff?"

Ordoñez shrugged. "I read it someplace."

"Look, all that money is going to educational debt," Tanner repeated. He couldn't blame anyone for making a big deal out of the money. Anyone could use that sort of bonus.

"Hey, we've got educational debt, too," said Sanjay. "Wanna help me with mine? I'll let you have my desserts at chow."

Rolling his eyes, Tanner reached up to jerk his privacy curtain shut.

A hand from above peeled the curtain back. Ordoñez's grinning face still hung over the side of her rack. "Okay, we'll leave you alone, but you're taking us all out drinking next time we're in port at least, right?"

• • •

Sarah Kessler seldom attended meetings of NorthStar's executive committee in person. She often viewed the video or read the transcripts of them afterward, or at least portions that related to her department. She'd been to enough such meetings, though, that she hardly found them exciting or intimidating when she did attend. Her position required intelligence, a sharp memory, excellent social skills, mental stamina, and unflappable nerves.

None of that put her in a seat at the table with some of the most powerful human beings in the known galaxy—not that she wanted such a seat. It had, however, gotten her into the seats that formed a ring around that table. Sarah Kessler, executive assistant to NorthStar's director of education, sat behind her boss with her holo screens open and her eyes and ears attuned to any chance that he might need anything.

It was all routine enough that being present didn't make her nervous. Behind her masterful poker face, though, Sarah had good reason to feel rattled to the core by this particular meeting.

"With Union certification all wrapped up, we are ready to implement the Test this year for all graduating secondary students as planned," explained her boss, Edwin Garber. He stood at his seat at the conference table, gesturing to a large holographic display floating above the table's center. Lights in the wide room remained dim to allow for clear visuals. "We expect our profit margins in many systems might increase. Simply put, kids across the Union may figure that if Archangel is ditching the current educational regime, the educational system's days are numbered and they have less reason to take the Test seriously. That misperception will lead to better returns for us. That point also brings us to the elephant in the room."

Garber gestured through his holographic control display to shift the larger image that served the whole audience. NorthStar's director of education looked sharp as always in his finely tailored suit and tight, well-groomed beard. It seemed a far cry from how he'd looked just a few months ago, when he'd been forced to backpedal on one unfulfilled projection after another regarding Archangel's unexpected "reforms"—which, to NorthStar's view, involved state theft of company property and massive poaching of employees.

Sarah knew neither she nor her boss had quite gotten over the stress of those days. They'd been forced to make projections based on a situation with no modern precedent. The executive committee demanded to know what to expect even if it was based on wild conjecture. Garber noted the impossibility of that task, directed his people to comply with those impossible demands, and then naturally had to make one retraction after another. Before long, Sarah wondered if he'd be asked for his resignation.

Fortunately, the situation steadied out into something predictable as time went on. Garber and his department did their research and gathered their data. Sarah played a major role in crafting the report.

Or, as the private message that came across her holocom asked, "You put together all these graphs and charts yourself, didn't you?"

She stepped on her nerves, forcing herself not to gasp or shudder when the real-time message window appeared. Passing messages was nothing new for the assistants on hand. Sarah glanced up across the table toward Greg, another executive assistant seated behind his boss just as Sarah was, and saw him wink knowingly.

In this case, Sarah felt grateful that Greg had been the one to initiate contact between their personal holocoms. He'd never have suspected anything had she been the one to open the point of contact, but, just the same, she took this as a chance to get on with her real task.

Sarah's fingers traced over a small icon in one corner of her holo display, input a confirmation code that no observer would think strange, and then did her best to look natural as the icon disappeared. In her head, she prayed she would remain unnoticed.

Her boss went on speaking. "We can reliably project how much revenue would have come from the current graduating class in Archangel if they took the Test. In the grand scheme of NorthStar's educational arm and our corporate profits as a whole, the losses naturally aren't crippling, but it's still a significant number. Those losses are put into better context when one considers the division's low operating costs." Garber didn't need to rub it in; of all of NorthStar's major divisions, from consumer goods to finance, education had always demonstrated one of the largest profit margins. Every young person in the Union had to go to school, after all, and NorthStar held great sway with the people who set the standards for success—which translated into the financial profits from a given student's failure. Other corporations such as Lai Wa offered competition, but ultimately they relied on the same business model and reached for the same outcomes. The system had always seemed secure until the events of the last year.

"After a good deal of lobbying and consultations, I can report that a full fifty-five percent of public universities across the Union have decided not to accept diplomas and transfer credits from students graduating from Archangel this year. The report also includes a cost-benefit breakdown of—"

"Fifty-five percent?" broke in an already fuming Jon Weir. The chief administrative officer sat several places up the table from Garber. "That means forty-five percent of them *are* accepting students from Archangel? That's almost half!"

Sarah quietly sent Greg a private note: "Does your boss ever actually read the reports before these meetings?"

"Again, we're only talking about *public* universities," Garber explained. "They aren't afraid of us pulling our financial support, and while admittedly they make up a large share of the most prestigious universities, they're still a distinct minority overall. They feel like Archangel's schools are doing much the same job as they did under our management. The rest—"

"Of course those schools are doing the same job," snorted Weir. "It's all still the same staff teaching in the same schools that *we built*. What was the last figure you cited? Ninety-one percent of our people stayed on the job through the takeover?"

Greg's response arrived before Weir finished speaking: "He has people for that, obviously."

"As I said back in November and December, Jon," Garber continued patiently, "the only way to hang on to most of those people would have been to offer new positions elsewhere along with relocation assistance."

Weir waved off that argument, as he had months ago. "Gimme a break. If they'd wanted that kind of special treatment, they wouldn't have gone to work as glorified babysitters." He glanced around the table, looking for nods of agreement, and found more than a few. "I'd just expect a little bit of corporate loyalty given all we'd already done for them."

"We must not show resentment," counseled the steely voice of Anton Brekhov. The CEO of NorthStar sat at the head of the table, his chair tilted somewhat to the side to present a relaxed, calm image. His salt-and-pepper hair and minimal signs of age belied his exceptional lifespan, courtesy of the best longevity treatments that untold wealth could buy. "This is a struggle for public opinion. Right now, it is merely a single-system government making a shortsighted gamble at the expense of its people."

Like everyone else in the room, Sarah looked up at Brekhov's face. No one missed the cold resolve in his eyes or in his voice. He expected his subordinates to hold to the company line as he stated it. "NorthStar and our friendly competitors are the glue that holds humanity together. The Union needs us. The people of Archangel need us. Regardless of what their leaders allege, we are looking out for them. It's unfortunate that the people of Archangel are suffering the natural economic consequences of their leadership's gamble, but that can't be helped—until they come back into the fold.

"When this is all over," Brekhov continued, sweeping the room with an even gaze and a measured, firm tone that didn't match the warmth of his chosen words, "we'll need to help Archangel recover. We will implement programs to help them rebuild their economy, to *pay their debts*, and to become good citizens of the Union once more. Until then, we will take the high road in every venue, in every interview, and through every public statement. We will keep our hand open and outstretched.

"And we will *not* allow this matter to set a precedent for other systems. We will not allow this to spread further. This is *not* a revolution—and we will not be cast as oppressors."

Sarah had seen Brekhov's talent for warmth and positive oratory. She'd seen him hold babies and cut the ribbons at new hospitals with a broad smile on his face. At every Christmas party, Brekhov asked about her family with a perfect memory for names. But after working for so many years at this level of the corporation, Sarah also knew the other side of Anton Brekhov. She knew how bad life could get for anyone who did not heed the implicit threats in his tone. So did the rest of the room, as the chill silence settling over the conference table demonstrated.

"Now, Edwin," said Brekhov, his gaze shifting and his demeanor softening somewhat, "did you have more to share? We are all listening."

To his credit, Garber took the interruption in stride. "The rest of the data I have to share is in my report, and I know the committee has more pressing business."

"Nothing is more important than the situation with Archangel, Edwin, and you are at the fore of one of our key points of concern. But in terms of timeliness, yes, we have other matters to attend to." Brekhov's eyes flicked over to a couple of other executives—one of them Commodore Eldridge, the uniformed head of NorthStar Security Forces. "We'll pick up with those matters after lunch."

Scattered conversations began as Brekhov and a couple of other executives left. Other attendees, Sarah included, began gathering their things. Many would not be back after lunch. As exclusive and tightly managed as attendance was for this meeting, the list of individuals involved in the security meeting would be smaller. Neither Sarah nor her boss had any business at that table.

Greg would be there, though, as would the quiet, unobtrusive program Sarah had loaded onto his holocom during their chat.

She wondered how anyone who did this sort of thing for a career could live in such a state of constant paranoia. It surely wasn't what she'd have wanted to do with her life. By comparison, being one of NorthStar's executives seemed like a relaxing job.

• • •

Six hours later, Sarah rode the elevator sixty-three floors to the suites at the top of the Fairhaven Hotel. She felt certain that everyone in a two-mile radius could hear her hands vibrate and was simply too polite to say anything about it.

No one batted an eye at her in the lobby. No one rode the elevator with her. It was always like this. Perfectly calm, perfectly casual, and perfectly nerve-wracking.

In the movies, meetings like this always happened in public, right under everyone's nose. They happened in parks. In restaurants. On waterfronts. Something about the scenery seemed to say, "No one would dare shoot us out here." In reality, she found, this sort of thing generally occurred in private.

Finding the correct room, Sarah glanced up one end of the hall and down the other—she couldn't help herself—and then pressed the door chime. A moment later, the door opened. She walked inside.

It was a pleasant suite. Clean, comfortable, quiet. Nice artwork and furnishings. Probably a nice view, but for the closed blinds on the windows. Sarah could afford this on her own. Her boss would've considered these accommodations rough living.

"It's good to see you, Sarah," said the sole occupant of the suite. Vanessa extended her hand, smiling warmly. Her clothing was a touch more business casual than Sarah's suit, but she wouldn't look out of place at Sarah's side. The outfit complimented Vanessa's light-brown skin and took advantage of her athletic build. Sarah wondered where Vanessa could be hiding her gun. Movies suggested that a spy like Vanessa could have a weapon hidden in the back of her collar, tucked under her long black hair. Then again, Sarah's experience with Vanessa made her abandon everything she'd ever heard before about spies.

Vanessa snapped her thoughts back toward conversation. "Any trouble getting here?"

"No. Not at all." Sarah shook Vanessa's hand, then took a seat at the small table.

"Are you nervous?"

Sarah blinked. "Do I look nervous?"

"No," Vanessa said, still with a calm smile. "You cover it well."

"I am, a little, actually, yes."

"Tell anyone where you were going?"

"Nobody asked, so no."

"Good. Then I wouldn't worry too much about it." She then fell silent. Sarah, too, fell silent, and the silence quickly became awkward. The door chime rang again. "That should be Raoul," Vanessa said, rising to get the door.

"Raoul?" Sarah blinked again. "Who's Raoul?"

"He's your cover." Vanessa grinned a bit mischievously. "Just let me handle this part." Crossing the room, Vanessa checked the screen at the control panel and then opened the door to greet a tall, unarguably handsome young man in a suit.

"Hi," he said. "I'm Raoul."

"Yes, you are," Vanessa agreed with a decidedly flirtatious tone. "Raoul, could you wait in the other room, please?"

Raoul glanced at Sarah, then back to Vanessa, and nodded. "Of course," he said as if there was nothing at all odd about this. He walked to the bedroom and shut the door behind him.

"What's that about?" Sarah asked.

"I thought you might have been nervous at your meeting. You came to an upscale hotel instead of going home. I wanted to provide some plausible explanation in case anyone is watching you."

Sarah's head turned toward the closed bedroom door, then back toward Vanessa. "That man's a prostitute."

"Mm-hm." Vanessa nodded. "Licensed, certified, and worth every bit of his fee, or so I'm reliably told. I haven't tried him out myself."

"You want people to think I'm having a fling with a prostitute."

"I want people to think you aren't doing anything odd at all," Vanessa corrected. "But if they do think you're acting suspiciously, I'd prefer it be over something harmless. No one who'd keep tabs on you would think a fling with a prostitute is something to cover up—but *you* would, and those people would know that about you."

Sarah wanted to be mad. As she considered her retort, though, she realized that Vanessa was absolutely right. She'd have laughed it off if she had discovered any of her friends or coworkers had hired a prostitute. She wouldn't have thought it virtuous behavior, but as personal scandals went, it was pretty mild. Sarah didn't exactly have anyone to cheat on.

"That guy looks young enough to be my son."

"Maybe he is. It's just embarrassing enough to keep secret, but not a security concern."

Sarah looked toward the door again. "So he's just going to sit in there?"

"If that's what's asked of him, yes. He'll stay until we're finished, and then I'll leave. And then he'll wait around until after you've left. You should let him know when you go, of course. But if you just want him to sit in there, he'll do exactly that. It happens. He won't tell a soul about sitting in that room alone for an hour . . . or about whatever else you might ask of him. He's a professional, and he'll be paid regardless.

"Like I said," Vanessa continued, "I wanted to provide a plausible explanation for your nerves and your whereabouts. That's why he's here. What you do with him when I'm gone is entirely up to you. I won't judge."

Sarah put a hand on her face and laughed. "This is beyond surreal."

"Should we get down to it, then?"

At that, Sarah took a deep breath. "Yes. We should. There's a lot to tell you."

"Did you try the ghost program?"

"Yes. I loaded it onto the holocom of the executive personal assistant to Jon Weir, chief administrative officer. I opened up another exchange with him to extract everything after the security meeting broke up. I only tried it the once, like you said."

"That's outstanding, Sarah," said Vanessa, not bothering to hide her interest or her appreciation. "One target is all we need. Trying for more would only lead to more chances of exposure. I felt torn about asking you to try this at all. Taking risks is supposed to be my job, not yours. At any rate, you're here, and you pulled it off. Let's do the transfer." She produced a small device from one pocket. It looked more like a fat pen or a marker than a piece of jewelry or any more elegant style of holocom, but Sarah knew it had considerably more functions than the average personal computer. "How did the meeting go? They discussed the primary debt payment issue?"

"Oh yes. They discussed that." Sarah pulled off her earring holocom and placed it on the table. She activated it with a swipe of her finger, then brushed her hands over the holographic screen to key in her security codes. "Debt collection, PR campaigning, education plans, and more. Even the usual stuff that gets covered in these meetings like stock performance and new product rollouts were oriented toward the Archangel issue. They talked a bit about

Hashem, too, but every time it came up they tabled it until later in the day, so I didn't hear much about that."

Vanessa set up her holocom for the file transfer and put it next to Sarah's. "Just call up the files and let them play through. This will run optic scans so there won't be any record of a file transfer or duplication. Run it on fast-forward. I'll still catch everything."

Sarah did as directed, watching images and spreadsheets fly across her screen. She didn't have a visual recording, but she had crystal-clear audio along with copies of each file shared at the meeting. In the morning, she would compile a condensed version for Garber's easy reference. Before that, she would erase everything taken from Greg's unwitting file transfer.

"You don't seem nervous anymore," Vanessa observed, though her eyes watched the file icons flash by. On a second screen, the automated transcript of the meeting as recorded by Greg's holocom scrolled along.

"I don't? How do I seem?"

"Angry."

Sarah didn't think she seemed angry at all. Vanessa was good. "It's in the files I grabbed on my own. It's about the Test this year, and things Edwin has said that I've had to look up. The whole thing is rigged, Vanessa. The Test has a subroutine that measures how students perform and adjusts the questions as it plays through to double up wherever a student is weak. It's not disclosed in any of the public documents or the contracts."

"Huh." Vanessa's eyes didn't come off of the flashing screens.

"You don't seem surprised."

"We've suspected that for a long time. A lot of people have."

"Well, now you have proof."

Again, Vanessa just nodded. "That's a major coup, Sarah," she said, still not meeting her eyes. "I'm listening to you. This is a big deal. I'm just looking for something that may be time sensitive. But I hear you."

"Tell me that doesn't make you mad," Sarah dared her quietly.

"It does," conceded Vanessa.

The spy didn't seem mad. She didn't seem anything. Yet Sarah was sure she detected sympathy. "They think they're so much smarter than everyone else," Sarah said.

"How long have you worked at this level?" Vanessa asked with a wry grin.

"Twenty-two years, after forty years working my way up. I used to consider myself lucky, you know. School debts covered. University paid off. Longevity treatments. Healthy, happy kids. NorthStar provided all of that . . . and then I read the files and find things like this. I wish to God I could just leave."

Vanessa glanced up at her. "Why don't you?"

"They'd never let me go. You know that. They'd ruin me in a heartbeat."

The spy slowly shook her head. "The minute you want to go, say so. You've done more than anyone could've asked for already. If you want to disappear, you just let us know and we'll get you out. Your kids, too. I guarantee you we can place you with a good employer and your kids in good universities. We may not find a match for your salary, but you'd be comfortable and safe. You've done more than enough for that."

Sarah snorted. "Are you going to be one of my references? You could tell people all about how faithfully I served my previous employer."

Vanessa paused the transfer. "Sarah, do you know what they look for when they recruit people like me?" She let the question hang for a moment. "They want someone healthy and smart and quick on her feet. All that. But what they really look for is integrity. *Honesty*. They train us up to lie, cheat, steal, and worse, and so the first thing they look for is trustworthiness.

"In eighteen years, Sarah, how many times has someone like me tried to recruit you?"

"Seven."

"Seven. You turned down every one of them. But not me. Why?"

"Because you didn't offer me money or sex or any other bullshit."

Vanessa slowly nodded. "I offered you a chance to do the right thing. And you've done it. Over and over."

Her eyes turned back to the holocoms, where she resumed the file reproduction. "As soon as this is done," Vanessa murmured, "we scour your holocom of everything you recorded. There'll be even less to trace on it than there is on your friend's."

". . . I'm not sure I can call him my friend after all this."

At that, Vanessa merely offered a sympathetic glance. She had nothing comforting to say. Her attention turned back to the flashing files, and finally her sense of urgency got the better of her. She touched the holographic display of her own holocom and said, "Search for words in proximity: Hashem and Archangel or Hashemite and Archangel."

The display shifted through the transcript to highlight the specified words. Sarah couldn't read it from where she stood, as the text was all backward to her, but she watched Vanessa's eyes move. "Expand to related document displays," Vanessa instructed. More screens appeared in thin air, showing lists, a star chart with travel times, pictures of people, and a couple of well-annotated city maps.

"Oh my God," Vanessa breathed. "Scheherazade." She expanded the star chart and traced out a couple of routes, looking at the time frames to each and growing visibly concerned.

"What is it?" asked Sarah.

Vanessa's eyes flicked back up to hers. She waved a hand through the displays to close them all up. "I have to go off-planet. Immediately. Sarah, I hate to do this, but I have to hand you off to one of the other operatives here on Fairhaven. We need to extract you. I think we've got time for you to resign and leave gracefully or come up with some other cover story, but I'll let you work that out with him."

"I—extraction? You're sure? What's going on?"

"Sarah, I can't explain, but I have to get this information off-planet right away, and I can't make any sure predictions of what will happen when I deliver it. I'll be in transit for a while, but pretty soon after that, NorthStar may realize there's a leak and start investigating. It may come to nothing, and it may be fine, but things could get very ugly. I don't want you exposed.

"This is the end of the line. You've done more than anyone could've asked of you already."

"Do you think," Sarah asked, choosing her words carefully, "there's more for me to do?"

"I don't make policy. You have to understand that. I can't tell you what will be done with this information. I swear to God I won't leave you hanging and I don't believe for a second anyone above me would, either, but screwups happen. All I know for sure is that I have to jump on a situation before it unfolds, which means I don't have time to consult with the higher-ups. It happens in my job. Part of operating light-years away from the office." She shrugged. "Since I don't know how this will turn out, it might be better to just tell you everything will be fine, but I can't do that. It wouldn't be right."

Sarah looked her in the eye. "That's the other reason I never turned you in," she said quietly. "You're the only one who played straight with me."

• • •

"Three contacts within our bubble: one Hashemite freighter, one Hashemite liner, one Lai Wa destroyer. Courses for the liner and destroyer are holding as listed, freighter has parked for repairs, and all have returned salutations. We had an inbound private yacht blow through here kinda fast just a bit ago, but that's about the only interesting thing that's happened. Comms traffic with the consulate on Scheherazade and our friendly ships in the area have been quiet. EM1 Cervantes has just assumed the watch in engineering. Any questions?"

"Nope." Tanner took in the three-dimensional projection representing two light-minutes of space around *Joan of Arc*. Other contacts and points of navigation beyond the two-minute bubble floated at the edge of the projection in alternate colors to make them easier to differentiate from closer contacts. Traffic in and out of Scheherazade stayed light to Tanner's thinking, but then, he'd never traveled outside of Archangel before now. He knew his basis for comparison was therefore a bit thin. "Looks like it's all under control."

Sanjay slid the logbook across the astrogation table to Tanner. "All yours," Sanjay said, looking down with dark eyes while Tanner signed in as the helmsman of the watch.

"You are relieved," said Tanner.

Sanjay nodded. "Aye, aye."

"Deck officer, I have the helm," said Tanner.

"Deck officer," said Sanjay, "I stand relieved."

"Crewman Malone has the helm," answered Chief Romita from the port-side chair. The ops specialist leaned around to look back and ask, "Tanner, did you see the XO down there? He coming up?"

"Captain asked to see him before he went on watch. Said he'd only be a couple minutes."

"Hope so," Romita yawned, covering his whole face with his hands. "I am wiped out."

"Better tank up on the caffeine, buddy," Sanjay counseled, slapping his hands on the ops specialist's shoulders. "Gonna be drill, drill, drill again today as soon as we're done with breakfast!"

"I'm so tired I can hardly smell your sarcasm," groaned the older man.

"What? Sarcasm? Me?" Sanjay stepped back to make exaggerated gestures of shock and innocence. "Why would you think I'm being sarcastic? I love drills! What's better than spending all day pretending the fuckin' ship's about to explode? Am I right Tann—oh." Embarrassment brought his rant to a sudden halt. Sanjay made an apologetic face, scratching the black stubble of his scalp. "Uh. Wow. You know I didn't mean anything, right?"

"I'll back him up on that," said a woman's voice from the rear of the bridge. All eyes turned that way as the captain entered. "Sanjay can go pretty low, but the only way he'd sink that low is if he tripped . . . over his foot while it was on its way into his mouth."

The two crewmen came to attention and saluted as Romita stood to do the same. Kelly returned the motion quickly, murmured, "As you were," and kept a mildly disapproving yet amused look fixed on Sanjay.

"Well, okay"—Tanner frowned at Sanjay—"but if I wake up screaming in the middle of the night, you'd better hug me and tell me everything's okay. You're morally obligated now."

Kelly and Romita chuckled. Sanjay needed a moment to realize that Tanner couldn't be serious, and then snorted. "Shit, I'm not *that* sorry. I'd just smother you with a pillow."

"That might be more practical," conceded Tanner.

"Time for drills, ma'am?" Romita asked the captain.

"Nah. No drills planned for today. People need a chance to get caught up on regular work. I came to take over the XO's shift so he could handle some admin stuff."

"Really, ma'am?" Sanjay blinked. Kelly allowed a reasonable amount of downtime, but she knew it was important to keep everyone sharp. Since arriving, the ship had run drills every day, be they battle stations or some other emergency scenario.

The captain offered a mild smile. "I'm not saying everyone gets the day off, but I figure we can scale back the drills just a bit at this point. Who's my helmsman, anyway? Even I'm losing track of the new watch rotation with an extra body in the mix."

"Uh, actually, I just got here, ma'am," said Tanner. "Sanjay's on his way out."

"Oh, right. See you later, Sanjay." The crewman merely nodded and left. Kelly turned to Romita and added, "I figure getting six-month performance reviews from the XO is much more fun than running drills, right?"

It was then Romita's turn to wince. "Yes, ma'am."

Tanner waited until the changeover finished and the captain sat down before he claimed his seat on the starboard side of the small bridge compartment. Qualifying to stand watch on *St. Jude* had taken several months—something Tanner only now began to accept was hardly his fault—and along the way, he'd become somewhat accustomed to standing through his whole shift. Having the chance to sit during his watch still felt like an odd privilege.

Working alongside the captain was something else that he'd never done on *St. Jude*. In fact, he'd never heard of the captain taking up any slack in the watch rotation.

Given the vast distances of space, much of the work performed by the helmsman and the officer of the deck was actually done by automated sensors and computer processes. *Joan of Arc* sat well outside the two light-minute line from Scheherazade's moon. The ship had little more to do than monitor communications and nearby traffic. Tanner and the rest of the crew soon found that standing watch on the bridge often amounted to a lot of time for idle chatter.

He expected this watch might be a bit awkward, given the customary social distance officers put between themselves and enlisted personnel—particularly those at the lowest ranks. Tanner opened up a few screens on the control panel and looked for something productive to do to fill the expected silence.

"I'm glad to see you can joke about it all," said Kelly. Tanner looked over at her and blinked. "*St. Jude* and everything that happened with you. I'd guess that's a good sign, right? Obviously everybody's been deliberately avoiding the subject."

He slowly nodded. "Yes, ma'am."

She eyed him suspiciously. "They *have* avoided the subject, right?"

Tanner couldn't entirely hold back the small grin. She didn't need to know about the first night's chatter in the crew berth. "Pretty much, ma'am. I figured on the first day it was just a way of showing I wouldn't be treated differently from anyone else. After that, I kind of caught on that it must be a conscious effort."

"It is," Kelly confirmed. "I had the XO warn everyone about it. Like you said, we don't want to give the impression that you'll be treated differently. But it's also just a matter of respect. All the media wanted us to see was how you're a big hero. But you went through hell. I can't imagine that's been easy to get over."

"No," Tanner replied. "No, it hasn't." His eyes drifted to the transparent canopy. *Joan of Arc* sat too far away from any planet or moon to see much but stars. Yet here, Tanner still had all the reassuring surroundings of a ship. He knew what it was like to be surrounded by nothing but distant points of light in an otherwise complete void.

"You know we'll leave it alone, right?" The captain sat back in her chair in a relaxed posture. "Sanjay wasn't trying to goad you. He just said something dumb."

"No, it's okay. I'm fine, ma'am. I stopped having trouble sleeping through the night a couple months ago. No more appointments with the therapist. I'm okay with talking about it. Usually."

Kelly's green eyes occasionally drifted to the controls or to the astrogation table behind them, but she seemed mostly focused on the conversation. "There was plenty of talk when we got word you were coming aboard. Cervantes wondered if it was a sign that we'd be sent into some crisis."

"Do you think we are?" Tanner asked. The question came just a little too quickly.

The captain shrugged. "I dunno. I don't hold back much from my crew. Any captain has to be ready to make snap decisions on behalf of Archangel—the captain of any ship, large or small, represents the whole system. That responsibility goes all the way down from me to you and the other non-rates. I figure it's best if we're all as well informed as possible."

"Pretty heavy stuff."

"It can be. It gets easier once you put yourself in the right frame of mind. Accept it, put the needs of the system first, and do your best in good faith, and then someday you might get used to it."

"I don't think I'd want your job, ma'am," Tanner deferred with a grin.

Kelly smiled back at him. "Not shooting for a commission? I imagine you'd have a leg up on competition for an academy spot."

"No, ma'am. I want to do my time, get out, and get on with my life. No offense to you or any other career types."

"Oh, I'm not necessarily a career type."

That surprised him. "I didn't think many people would go into the officers' ranks if they didn't want this as a career." Tanner looked at her thoughtfully. He wondered if she'd had longevity treatments yet. Officers signed up for terms in five-year increments, and nobody made it to the rank of lieutenant—let alone command of even a small ship—in a single term.

Physically, Kelly seemed only a few years older than him, but then, so did Andrea. Her green eyes and short red hair stood out against her smooth skin. *Is it the feeling of conquest that draws you to women like that?* Beth's voice asked in his head. *Or are you only interested in women who can conquer you?*

Kelly smiled, finding something funny in his response. "That might be the case for the ones in the capital. How many officers do you know who aren't already at commander or above?"

"Good point. Just yourself, the XO, and the officers on *St. Jude*. I've only met others in passing. But you can't be on your first term, either."

"No. I thought about only doing the one term, but I wanted command experience." Then she paused and seemed to want to look over her shoulder before saying more. "Started my second term in the spring of '74." Tanner all but dropped his jaw, which she seemed to expect. "I'm twenty-six. And yes, a lot of older officers wanted this chair."

"How . . . ?"

"Hey, according to regs, there's nothing odd about this at all." Kelly tried to hold back a slightly smug, slightly amused grin. "I did the requisite time at each rank. Granted, those regs were all written back when longevity treatments were a new thing. Nowadays officers can't make more than one rank step per five-year hitch . . . unless you shine brightly enough. Hell, the XO's only on the last year of his first term, too."

Tanner shook his head. "I had no idea. Guess I haven't met the right sort of officers at all."

"I knew Lieutenant Stevens from my first duty station," she ventured. She watched Tanner for a reaction. He merely nodded, so she came out a bit further: "He was kind of an asshole."

Tanner snorted. Then he looked away and down at the controls. He wondered if he might turn red. "That's not something I'm sure I should comment on, ma'am."

"Why's that?" Kelly asked. "You afraid I'll reprimand you for agreeing with me?"

"Ma'am, Lieutenant Stevens—that whole crew—they left behind eight widows, a fiancée, and eleven kids. All of them had other family and friends. I'm the guy who's left alive. I'm the face of all that. I'm old news now, but the moment there's something embarrassing or salacious to report, it'll be headline stuff all over again. Only this time it'll open up new wounds for people who don't deserve the ones they've already got."

"That what the public affairs people told you?" Kelly prodded gently.

"No. I learned a few things about media and politics from all the attention I got after St. Jude, and then from being on the honor guard. Learned a lot, really. No one ever told me explicitly what to say or not to say, but you hang around someone like the president's press secretary long enough and talk about her job, you start to pick up on things. It's not that I don't want to talk about it, but . . . I'm the only voice. They can't defend themselves anymore."

"That's understandable. Commendable, even." Kelly glanced around the bridge compartment. "Still, I don't see any of the recorders active. I promise I won't tell. Scout's honor."

"Do you have these sorts of talks with all of your crew, ma'am?"

"When I think they could use it. When I think it'd be good for them and for the ship. I'll let the department heads or the XO handle it if I think that'll do the job, but when it comes down to it? Sure. I'll always listen. I've only got fifteen people under my command, Tanner—sixteen with you on board. That's not too many people to get to know personally.

"And you *are* Tanner Malone," she added, looking him in the eye. "Some of my people have had it pretty rough, but I don't think anyone's got fresh scars like yours."

Tanner glanced at the control panel. Nothing new seemed to be happening. No signs of an emergency in sight or anything else to interrupt this.

"He was an asshole, ma'am. Not just 'kind of.' Stevens was a monumental asshole, and so was just about everyone else on that ship. It was miserable. I think I can count on one hand the number of times Stevens spoke to me, and here I am now talking to you, and . . ." Tanner wasn't sure how much to say. "All I've wanted was to serve my time and get out. I felt like I had a brick sitting in my stomach when I got orders to come on board this ship. I figured this would be more of the same. *St. Jude* was bad."

"How bad?"

Cry-yourself-to-sleep bad, Tanner thought. "Well, like I told the XO, it took forever to qualify for helmsman on *St. Jude*. I'd never done a damage control or battle stations drill until the last month or so on that ship. I mostly avoided casual conversations because I couldn't handle all the venom. Whenever we were underway, I spent as much time as I could in my rack, which I'm told is a sign of depression. Didn't know it then, but it fits.

"The thing I don't tell anyone is that I finally snapped about a minute before we lost the ship. The BM2 and I were about to go at it. One of us was gonna wind up with a broken neck. Then I saw the laser flash and there's the BM2 floating out into space right in front of me and everyone else was just gone. That doesn't come up in the interviews."

Kelly slowly nodded. "Sounds pretty bad."

"Yes, ma'am."

"Stevens really fucked up."

"It wasn't just Stevens, ma'am," said Tanner quietly. "It was all of us. Myself included."

"Shit rolls downhill, Tanner," Kelly replied, shaking her head. "Like I said, these corvettes have only so many people on board. If Stevens was that out of touch, it's no wonder things went badly. Every other problem got that much worse because the captain didn't do his job. Why do you blame yourself?"

"I should've thought of some way to address it." Tanner shrugged. "I'm not gonna shift all the blame onto other people. I still don't know what I could've done, but throwing up my hands and saying it wasn't me isn't good enough, either."

"Maybe punching out the BM2 would've been a start. We could talk about what you might have done, but I can't say if it would've done any good. There's not a doubt in my mind that the problems came from well above your level. Not from what you're describing. And after a ship like that, I don't blame you if you weren't excited about coming on board this one."

"I wasn't, but this ship isn't the same at all, ma'am. This is like night and day from what I'm used to."

"Oh? Enough to give the service a second chance?"

"Not a chance in hell, ma'am," he said with a weary smile. "I am very grateful that there are so many people who are willing to deal with all this, but it's not for me. I don't want this to be my life. When my time's up, I'm gone."

Kelly laughed. "You're preaching to the choir, actually. But that's not for a few more years. In the meantime, there's a lot of good a body can do in the military . . . for yourself, and for other people. And I know you care about that at least, right? You're here for the duration, so you might as well get what you can out of it."

"Yeah, I know." Tanner sighed. "I've had a couple conversations about picking a rating, but I'm not sure any of my options come close to what I want to do with my life."

"This doesn't have to be your life. You said before you want to do planetary surveys, right? You have to go to college to do that, anyway. If I were in your shoes, I'd want to learn things they don't teach you at a university."

"I hadn't thought about it like that," Tanner admitted.

"It's half the reason I signed up," said the captain. "How much longer have you got? Three and a half years? Hell of a waste to spend it running out the clock."

He chewed on that thought. Eventually, he found himself looking at the captain once more. "Ma'am . . . your first name doesn't begin with an *A*, does it?"

• • •

Final adjustments to the plans continued even now, less than an hour before showtime. While primary overall plans were cemented weeks earlier, before the freighter landed on Scheherazade, the nature of a beast like this included constant tweaking and accounting for targets of opportunity. The world outside the freighter was busy and vibrant, with a large population. People came and went. Local forces moved around according to their training schedules. Nothing remained static for long.

Harris strode through the freighter's massive, crowded cargo bay toward the line of tanks parked on one end. Green paint, scarves, and other bits of randomizing did much to make Harris's top-of-the-line NorthStar defensive gear indistinguishable from the not-quite-uniform fatigues of the Hashemites around him. His natural complexion was a bit paler than theirs, and the thick stubble of his scalp used to be blond rather than black. An experienced eye would see much more significant differences between Harris, his comrades, and their Hashemite hosts. Harris and his men had considerably more training and medical conditioning, not to mention greater experience.

He saw squad leaders and officers—some of whom, at least, deserved such titles—readying their men for combat. Directions changed. Time for preparations evaporated, heightening stress and anxiety. A handful of the Hashemite troops looked nervous or grim. Harris had no problem with them.

The guys who looked overly eager, though, concerned him greatly. He found far too many of them for comfort. If they'd been rookies, he would have blown off their eagerness as nervous bravado, but many of these guys had seen combat . . . or, at least, they'd seen violence. Much like the sketchy worth of the ranks and titles claimed by the leadership around here, Harris wasn't sure he'd call their prior experience "combat." He wouldn't call this a unit, either. Some were soldiers. The rest amounted to a mob of thugs in military gear.

At first, Harris had been impressed that so much in the way of men and materiel could be smuggled onto Scheherazade. This freighter and other ships in the advance landing force received covert assistance from the local boarding teams and inspection crews, meaning people with expert inside knowledge had done a lot of good planning and bribing. Such logistical feats were encouraging, but as zero hour approached, he decided not to equate strong logistics with solid troop discipline.

Harris found his quarry standing beside one of the looming tanks. Holo screens spread out around Major Basara and a couple of his subordinates. The major wasn't difficult to find—not with the gaudy epaulets on his combat jacket and the scimitar on his belt. Beside them stood Mr. Abnett, another NorthStar employee like Harris himself—only rather than a member of the corporation's uniformed security services, Abnett came from Risk Management. He wore the same slightly disguised gear as Harris and the other NorthStar rangers, and he knew his way around a gun, but Abnett's real work wouldn't come until the shooting stopped. In the meantime, Abnett represented another minor wrinkle in the chain of command, which was something Harris never liked.

"We have eyes on the objective now," said Basara, pointing to one of the maps. A large, square building in the middle of a cityscape stood out thanks to computerized highlighting. "They could send us live video, but the consulate may well have good monitoring gear. No sense giving them something to pick up until it is time to jam their communications."

Abnett nodded. "Excellent."

"What sort of eyes?" asked Harris, looking over Abnett's shoulder.

"Snipers, Mr. Harris," Basara assured him. "Experienced men loyal to Prince Murtada. They will provide assistance for our assault."

"By 'snipers,' do you mean two-man teams or lone-wolf jack-offs?"

Abnett's eyes went wide as he turned to face Harris. "What?" Harris asked. "It's an honest question."

"Mr. Harris," fumed Basara, "these are all brave men who have seen combat. They brought order to Qal'at Khalil after the pirates left."

"Uh-huh. Listen, major, ops like this depend on the right people *not* gettin' killed. You sure that went all the way down the chain to the grunts and the privates?"

"You have reason to believe it hasn't?" Basara folded his arms across his chest.

"Your men are talkin' about cutting people up and looting," explained Harris. "Some of these guys carry trophies, the kind that grew on another human being. They need to throw that shit away. It brings a whole lot more trouble than it's worth."

Basara's eyes flared. "I shall make these decisions, not you, Mr. Harris. These are fighting men. I am surprised that some-one of your experience cannot recognize this. Do you come to lecture me on how to lead men? Do you think I do not under-stand why we undertake this errand instead of pursuing more vital strategic objectives? If you are not pleased with the forces at hand, I will gladly cancel this mission and fold these forces back into Prince Murtada's army of liberation while you and your 'advisers' sit here in—"

"Major, if you'll allow me," Abnett broke in, gesturing for Harris to follow him away. He didn't know whether Harris would actually take the hint but felt a bit of a relief as the old soldier turned from

Basara and started walking with him. "You think now's the time for this?" hissed Abnett.

"No, the time for it was when we first got here and found out who we'd be workin' with," grunted Harris, "and the guy for the job is *you*. But I didn't see you takin' it up with anybody, so I figured I'd better give it a shot."

Hashemite fighters moved all around them as they walked, carrying weapons and ammo. Everyone slowly picked up their pace as a voice over the public-address system began to relay announcements in Arabic.

"Harris, I don't get this," said Abnett, shaking his head. "You know what we're about to do. Hell, you came up with half the planning. But you're lodging moral objections on the conduct of our host forces? Now? This isn't a peacekeeping mission, Harris, it's the exact opposite."

"Behavior like this is a bad sign, Abnett. You let soldiers run around picking up random loot and trophies, they start worrying more about their collections than they do about securing a perimeter or watchin' out for their buddies. The major back there has the same problem. It's 2276 and he's carrying around a *sword*, for fuck's sake. My problem isn't about morality, it's about professionalism.

"And another thing: conduct like this doesn't make it any easier to work with the locals. You can scare a civilian out of your way, but it's a long way from there to getting any active support. This ain't a peacekeeping op yet, but it's gonna be. We're gonna have to come in here with a real army and clean up the mess this jackass prince and his cousin the major make on their way to the top."

"All above our pay grade, Harris," said Abnett. His voice dropped and he leaned in as he jerked his thumb back toward Basara's tank. "Besides, the fact that these guys are a bunch of savages just makes our cover story more plausible. We're not gonna change anything now. Let's just do our job and get out."

Harris headed back to the NorthStar team along with Abnett, falling a step behind. "We're gonna be back here in six months fighting an insurgency," he grumbled. "Not that you'll be on board for it."

THREE

All Necessary Measures

"*The Kingdom of Hashem suffers from one of the classic pitfalls of monarchy: three capable heirs, two of whom have no lack of ambition. Though all seven systems of the kingdom remain nominally under the king's control, no one expects the peace to last. Earlier flare-ups between the king's sons in the wake of the pirate raid on Qal'at Khalil seem to have been the prelude to greater conflicts. Peace overtures on the part of the king, the Union Assembly, the Lai Wa Corporation, and Prince Khalil himself have all failed to achieve any sort of reconciliation.*"

—"Medieval Problems in a Modern State,"
Union Relations Monthly, April 2276

A large, bright holographic screen winked to life in front of Kelly's chair with an unmistakable beep of urgency. Other screens disappeared in keeping with the protocol she'd set up for it. Kelly sat up in her chair, immediately dropping her conversation with Tanner as she read quickly. "Oh shit," she breathed. While still reading,

Kelly waved a hand at Tanner. "Sound battle stations and haul ass for Scheherazade. Go!"

Though the sudden appearance of the message took Tanner by surprise, he didn't blink at the captain's instructions. With the course to Scheherazade preset, all he had to do was press two buttons. Alarms on the bridge sat next to each chair on old-fashioned metal toggle switches. Tanner threw the red one for battle stations and then called up the helm controls. He also hit the intercom. "Engineering, we are maximum acceleration for Scheherazade," he warned while alarms blared throughout the ship.

He fought the urge to throw on his helmet the instant he heard the sound. The captain gave him instructions and her tone made plain that every second counted. He'd get his chance to don his helmet as soon as his hands weren't busy with other things.

"Understood," came the response. "We're not at a cold start, but it's gonna take us a minute to get up to full speed."

Tanner double-checked all of the contacts within the two-minute bubble. Nothing seemed to have changed. Tanner saw no inbound invasion or other cause for alarm. The Archangel Independent Shipping Guild's liner lay closer to Scheherazade than *Joan of Arc*, but only by a matter of light-seconds. The corvette would soon overtake her.

"ETA to Scheherazade approximately sixteen minutes," Tanner announced. He looked to his side. Kelly already had her fingers flying over the controls at her station.

"Adjust course to bring us closer to *Argent* on the way," she instructed without looking at him. "She'll be moving in the same direction if she isn't already. Let's shave a couple seconds off the comms lag between us."

"Aye, aye, ma'am," Tanner acknowledged, keying in the proper commands. He felt a brief hum run through the ship as the engines climbed toward maximum sublight power. His eyes flicked up to the astrogation feed once more to watch Kelly's prediction hold true. *Argent* turned directly toward Scheherazade and got moving.

Tanner bit back all of his questions. Training took over. The captain called for battle stations and gave a course; at a time like that, one simply shut up and followed orders. He knew enough about *Joan of Arc*'s mission and conditions in the Kingdom of Hashem to put together some ugly expectations.

Less than twenty seconds after sounding battle stations, Tanner snatched up his helmet from the hook on the side of his chair. He glanced over to the captain and realized she hadn't picked up hers yet, either. He thought about saying something.

Stop it, he told himself. *Nobody's in range to shoot at us yet. She knows what she's doing.*

Not for the first time, his eyes glanced down to her leg. No blood stripes had appeared on her suit in the three weeks since setting out from Archangel, nor on anyone else's. Concerns for rank and age and greater experience evaporated as he considered one unwelcome thought: *Nobody here has ever seen combat except me.*

Tanner saw the battle stations readouts on the control panel light up as the crew arrived at their posts. Kelly activated the electrostatic reinforcement of the hull, strengthening the ship's armor at a molecular level. Stevens, by contrast, had utterly failed to activate the ES system before *St. Jude*'s demise. Armored plating slid up over the bridge canopy, completely blocking the view though high-resolution projections inside the compartment created a near-perfect illusion of transparency. Chaff missiles stood at the ready. Missiles and guns came online. Kelly wasn't flying into anything blindly.

The captain is solid. So is the crew. We'll get through this.

"ASG *Argent*, this is ANS *Joan of Arc*," Kelly said, her fingers on the transmit key. "We are inbound for Scheherazade at emergency speed and see you doing the same. Please confirm."

The hatch at the rear of the bridge opened up as the XO and both ops specialists stepped inside with their helmets already on. Stan turned to the astrogation table. Chief Romita came up to stand beside Tanner's chair, while Booker moved to join Kelly.

"We're on a course for—" Tanner began to explain to his relief, but the chief ops specialist held his hand up to silence him as the captain began speaking, both to them and to the rest of the crew through their helmet comm network.

"People, we just got an urgent message from the consulate planet-side," she explained. "They say solid intel has the planet getting hit any minute now, and our consulate is a direct target for ground forces. We are in full emergency evac, and—" She cut herself off when a light on her control panel winked on.

"ANS *Joan of Arc*, this is ASG *Argent*. We confirm emergency course for Scheherazade. Message from planet-side received. Please advise."

Kelly keyed up her response. "*Argent*, *Joan of Arc*. We're closing to within live comms range. Please put your captain on." Then she called up one of the overhead maps of the consulate and its vicinity. Several possible landing sites had been highlighted in blue during earlier planning sessions. Given the densely urbanized nature of the area, none of those landing sites were closer to the consulate than two kilometers. Even the broadest streets were too cluttered with concrete dividers and such to accommodate the corvette.

"We'll do a flyover, try to figure out which route is safest for our people and land accordingly. If the consulate is under fire when we get there, we'll strafe and engage, but if we wind up making a target out of the ship, it's gonna put *Argent* and *St. Patrick* in a bad spot, too."

"Why the hell would they hit the consulate?" Romita wondered.

Kelly shook her head. "Message doesn't say."

"Have we heard from *St. Patrick*?" asked Booker, glancing to Tanner. "Are they still on the other side of the planet from us?"

"Far as we know, sir." Tanner gestured to a tactical display. Information at that distance was at least three minutes old.

"We've all been sitting as close as we're allowed." Chief Romita shrugged. "We all knew something was fishy when they wouldn't let two little ships like ours stay close together for more than a couple hours at a time. Probably so somebody could arrange this exact problem."

"Yeah, and we may only be minutes ahead of their timetable," added Kelly. "We'll have to hope *St. Patrick* can make her pickups on the other side of the planet as planned."

"How solid is this intel?" Booker asked.

Kelly pointed to the priority message screen still visible at her station. She turned to another matter. "Are they getting back to me this week?" she muttered, looking at her comms channel with *Argent*.

"Multiple course changes in our light bubble, ma'am," announced Tanner, still in the middle of handing his duties off to the chief. "Several ships now inbound for Scheherazade. Outbound ships are picking up speed."

"Did we send out any warnings?" asked Booker. "Or did the consulate? Any comms from those other ships to us?"

Tanner shook his head. "No, sir."

Stan took in the changes displayed on the astrogation table and quickly figured things out. "They probably saw us tearing toward the planet and put two and two together."

"Should we talk to them?" Booker considered.

"We're here to look after our own, and the intel didn't say anything about anyone else's consulates being hit," said Kelly. "If I had more, I might've shared, but as it stands we're giving away enough by moving like we are. Goddammit, we're almost in live comms range with *Argent* now. Where's—there," she grumbled, keying up the comms panel again.

"*Joan of Arc*, this is First Officer Hawkins on *Argent*," said the helmeted man appearing on a new screen. Unlike Archangel Navy helmets with their metal faceplates and separate eye lenses, Hawkins wore a model with a fully transparent facial visor. "I imagine you got the same message we got?"

"Seems likely," said Kelly. "Where's your captain? We need to confer."

Seconds passed before Hawkins could answer because of the time lag. "Captain's busy, lieutenant. I'll relay. Right now we're planning to set down at the spaceport to pick up the bulk of our people per the original plan. If the consulate is a target, I don't think we can land anywhere close enough to be of assistance, anyway."

Tanner watched Kelly's face as she looked away and consulted her map. No one would've missed the tension in her voice, but he suspected she was still the calmest person on the bridge.

"Good call," said Kelly, "that's what I would advise, too. Stick with the original priorities. You worry about the bulk of our civilians; we'll focus on the consulate. Until and unless you receive contrary orders from the consul or from *St. Patrick*, our initial protocols hold. That includes rules of engagement. Send out a scream signal the instant you come under fire."

Hawkins nodded. "We've got it under control, *Joan of Arc*. Comms will remain open on this channel. *Argent* out." The screen shifted to the soft-green static of standby mode.

Kelly looked over her shoulder at the senior ops specialist. "You catch that, chief?"

The older man merely nodded. "I'm sticking with my first guess, ma'am. That guy's gotta be Archangel Intelligence. Maybe he was navy once upon a time, but not anymore."

Tanner watched the exchange curiously. Two weeks ago, after *Joan of Arc* met up with *Argent* and *St. Patrick* for a command conference, Kelly, Booker, and Romita returned with some concern they would not voice in front of the crew. Circumstances now sent that sense of discretion out the airlock. With Romita fully in control at the helm, Tanner called up the file on *Argent* at his station and took another look at the ship.

He couldn't shake the feeling that he'd seen the liner before, or one like it.

"Nothing we can do about that now," grumbled Kelly. "I can't imagine they'd put an inexperienced captain on a ship like that. We'll have to have faith that he isn't an idiot. Pretty sure our original plans will fall apart as soon as we hit the planet."

"That's the way of these things, ma'am." The chief nodded. "All we can do is improvise."

• • •

Status reports and other announcements flew across *Argent's* bridge. Internal sensors displayed full readiness throughout the ship, with defensive systems online and all compartments sealed. The general quarters alarm cut out once the captain was satisfied . . . with the condition of the ship, at least.

Everyone on the crew had served on other vessels, though those experiences varied wildly. Several were veterans of the Archangel Navy, or the Union fleet, or civilian vessels. Almost half the crew came from outside the system, signing on for a two-year cruise under strict, isolated conditions for the promise of citizenship and a clean slate. A few of the Archangel natives had signed on in search of amnesty for past crimes. They were screened and hired by the Intelligence Ministry: a band of has-beens, second chancers, and refugees with vital skills.

The ship's doctor had lost his medical license ten years ago over ethical matters. *Argent's* chief engineer, who had once held the same position on the Union fleet battleship *Fletcher*, was two years past mandatory retirement age, divorced, childless, and desperate for the only job he'd ever loved. The head astrogator was an alcoholic. Adultery scandals had derailed the Union fleet career of the duty helmsman. And Casey had no idea how many of his crew were undercover agents of the Intelligence Ministry.

Casey could work with all of that. His feelings toward his first officer were another matter entirely.

"You realize we're at least ten minutes away from any actual trouble, right?" the captain asked in a low, quiet voice. His baleful eyes lifted from the holo screens at his station to regard the first officer with contempt. Casey's helmet remained on its hook on his chair.

Hawkins blinked. "Yes. What—"

"You look like an idiot." The captain gestured to the rest of the bridge crew, who had also donned their helmets, gloves, and other emergency gear. "You're supposed to set an example, but you're also supposed to be a reassuring presence for the crew. They all got themselves squared away as soon as the alarm went out. You rushing to get wrapped up in your security blanket sends the message that we're all about to get our asses blown out of the sky. Take a breath."

The first officer opened his mouth, but promptly closed it. "Anything else . . . *sir*?"

"Yeah. We're not gonna have any more time for this 'playing telephone' crap. You're gonna have to let me talk directly to the other captains."

"No can do," said the other man, shaking his head.

"Why not? You afraid one of them is gonna recognize me?"

Hawkins stiffened. For all the need to maintain proper decorum and deference to the man who was in almost all appreciable ways the sovereign captain of the ship, the channels of authority on *Argent* were not entirely so traditional. This captain had a few specific limitations. "You know it's not part of the deal."

"I also know shit's about to hit the fan and every second counts, Hawkins," Casey seethed. "We can go back to normal when we're on our way out of the system, but this moment right here is why I'm the one in the chair and not someone else. So you've got two choices, spy guy. Either you get the fuck out of my way and let me do the job, or I go back to my cabin and drink until I pass out and leave you to handle this mess on your own. At least I won't die sober."

Silence fell between the two, punctuated only by further call-outs from various bridge stations. Hawkins took a long breath and put his hands on his hips—though that left one hand pointedly leaning on his sidearm in a silent reminder. "I'll release your comms switch," he said, "but don't use it unless you absolutely have to. Anything else?"

"No," sneered the captain. "You might wanna go look busy or check on another station before the kids think Mommy and Daddy are fighting again."

• • •

"Contact! Ship dropping out of light—multiple new contacts around Scheherazade's outer orbitals!"

The "naked eye" projections against the armor plating of the bridge canopy showed the planet as a distant orb, too small for anyone to make out details without adjusting the optics. Smaller features around the planet like satellites and spacecraft remained absent. That would change in seconds, though, given *Joan of Arc's* speed. More than one of the men on the bridge wondered when Kelly would give the order to slow down. No spacecraft could stop on a dime at this speed.

"I see them, Stan," said Kelly. The captain leaned in at her station, taking in data from her view screens. She didn't look back at her junior ops specialist as she added, "No need for position callouts."

The newcomers arrived with considerable space between them—at least in relation to the planet. Fleets in simultaneous FTL transit usually kept themselves spaced farther apart than this, but the scene unfolding over Scheherazade saw ships appearing more or less evenly spread out in an arc covering half the planet.

"Jesus, they cut inside the moon's orbit," observed Chief Romita. "Lucky they all survived the drop out of FTL that close to—oh man, maybe not," he corrected himself. He pointed to a contact on one display that continued on toward the planet while the others altered courses to burn off excess momentum. A second contact soon demonstrated the same behavior.

Tanner watched the canopy projection and found he could now make out the streak of bright light across the planet's atmosphere made by a torn-up and out-of-control ship. A flash erupted from the wreckage, almost certainly from the ship's engine room exploding. He glanced at Kelly's display and saw the computer's evaluation of the second disaster. While the first ship mostly held together until its explosion, the other came apart completely under the stress of dropping out of FTL so deeply within Scheherazade's gravity well.

Lessons from physics classes about the strange behavior of mass during shifts into and out of FTL rattled around in the back of his head. This sort of thing was one of the big risks of a surprise planetary assault; attackers wanted to come in as close as possible to achieve the greatest degree of surprise, but coming in too close risked a loss of control or even the complete destruction of a ship simply from gravitic stress. Tanner figured the fleet up ahead was lucky to only lose two ships out of the three dozen or so present.

Kelly's voice pulled Tanner from thoughts of FTL physics. Tactical concerns took priority here. "Give me a rundown," she said.

"Holy shit, they've got two assault carriers," Stan announced. "We're looking at . . . four cruisers and the rest are all smaller. How old have those carriers got to be?"

"They're not old," explained Romita, looking over much the same information. "They're new. Think those are NorthStar carriers painted up to match the fleet. Standard operating procedure for providing a Union state with military assistance."

"What?" Tanner blinked. "So that's the king's fleet? Or are you saying NorthStar decided Murtada's the legal king? How's that work?"

Romita shrugged. "Money and influence. They'll beg forgiveness of the Union Assembly later rather than ask for permission up front. It's been done before, just not like this."

"Are those NorthStar troops on those carriers?"

"I doubt it. The crews, yeah, but you're probably looking at fifteen thousand or more of Murtada's guys on each of those ships. And look, see how they're holding back from the rest? I'll bet NorthStar only signed up to do the lifting and logistics here. Carriers like that have serious armor, but they'll let Murtada's real fleet fight their way through Kaseem's ships and his planetary defense guns before dropping troops. His other ships will have their own landing craft, too." Romita shook his head. "This shit keeps getting uglier."

Tanner understood history well enough to know that no one occupied whole planets anymore—at least, not planets as developed as Scheherazade. The numbers didn't add up. However, the assault carriers brought enough troops to take key cities. Since the days of the Expansion Wars, planetary conquest involved only select occupation on the ground, along with a constant threat of orbital bombardment.

"They'll prioritize the comms satellites," Kelly predicted as she shifted her view screen to another display. "First priority is to make sure nobody planet-side can yell for help."

Fulfilling her prophecy almost as soon as she said it, beam weapons and missiles shot from the newly arrived ships in numerous directions, creating a brief web of light all around the planet. Each line ended with a burst as various communications satellites exploded. Some of those satellites served to unite communications across the planet. Others contained FTL-capable drones, each of which carried millions of private messages and public news to other systems at regular intervals—and when given emergency orders. Until and unless someone found a way to make transmissions travel faster than light on their own, the Union relied upon such drones and upon manned ships for communications.

It was a vulnerability that any sensible enemy would always exploit. The opening seconds of the assault on Scheherazade saw the planet cut off from the rest of the Kingdom of Hashem.

"Ma'am, I've got several other ships nearby altering course and heading for the planet," warned Stan at the astrogation table. "A couple look military, probably local militia."

"Then hopefully they'll make a fight of this rather than running away or rolling over." Kelly grimaced. She opened up a closer tactical display of Scheherazade, drew out a course, and sent it to her ops chief's station. "Put us down right through here, chief."

Romita's eyebrow rose. "Um. We gonna slow down, ma'am?"

"Soon as we're past that net of ships."

"Some of those ships are just outside the atmosphere," noted Booker.

"Yeah, we might wind up scuffing the paint a little," Kelly muttered.

"*Joan of Arc*, this is *Argent*," came a voice over the live comms channel unaccompanied by a visual. The liner continued on in a path behind the corvette, unable to keep up at the same speed but still moving impressively fast for a liner. "Obvious problems up ahead. Please advise of your plans."

Kelly frowned absently. The voice on the comms channel sounded a little distorted, but she saw no other evidence of comms jamming in the vicinity. She wondered if *Argent* had a problem on her end. As Scheherazade loomed ever larger in the canopy, Kelly hit the transmit key and said, "*Argent, Joan of Arc* here. Continue on as planned. We'll handle the new arrivals."

"They're not gonna just let us through," warned the other voice.

"They'd fucking well better. Stand by." Kelly keyed up another channel, leaving the audio with *Argent* active as she said, "Attacking fleet, this is Archangel corvette *Joan of Arc*. We are escorting the civilian liner *Argent* behind us to Scheherazade to evacuate Archangel citizens. We have no hostile intent. Please acknowledge."

Heartbeats passed. Kelly continued working the controls and tactical displays and gave her bridge crew silent instructions with hand motions and nods. Scheherazade grew ever larger up ahead. The light show around it intensified as the invading ships exchanged fire with ground-based defense guns. Spacecraft already in orbit around the planet either tried to escape or, in a few cases, engaged with the invaders. Though the attacking force clearly held fire superiority, the situation grew chaotic.

Serving mostly as an extra pair of hands and eyes on the bridge, Tanner did more watching than working. He felt a sense of dread build in his gut. Scheherazade's skies looked nothing like Raphael's, or Michael's, or any other planet in Archangel. The worlds of his home system had solid defenses. Its militia was professional, unified, and growing.

Yet even Tanner, an untrained observer when it came to planetary invasions, could tell which way this battle would go. The scene before him didn't leave him feeling terribly confident about his home's ability to defend itself.

A face appeared on the comms screen, revealing a Hashemite naval officer with his helmet visor up. "*Joan of Arc*, this is cruiser *Ambar*. Alter your course immediately and await instructions."

"Negative, *Ambar*," Kelly said calmly, "we are here to pick up our people and be on our way."

"*Joan of Arc*, *Ambar*. I repeat, alter your course. You will not be permitted to land on the planet."

"*Ambar*, *Joan of Arc*. Understood. Per your statements, Prince Murtada has declared war on Archangel. I will alter my course to an attack vector while the liner behind me carries word back to my fleet. Please confirm."

"I—what? That's not what I said!" stammered the flustered officer on her screen.

"Sure sounds like you're threatening me, *Ambar*," Kelly pressed. "We can skip straight through the formalities and get down to business or you can let me through. Just depends on how many fights you want to pick today. Your call. Might want to decide fast."

"Ah—I—what?" the officer sputtered. He looked away from his screen, calling out something in Arabic. *Joan of Arc*'s comms computers offered a translation in text, but Kelly ignored it.

"ETA to atmosphere?" she asked.

"Fifty seconds," said Chief Romita.

Booker reached over to mute their transmission. "If they're attacking the consulate, aren't they already declaring war?"

Kelly shook her head. "I'm betting these assholes don't know about that part of the plan," she said. "Hitting a consulate of a neutral state without provocation? That's gotta be a black op. The main fleet probably doesn't have a clue."

Another face appeared on the comms screen. This officer looked a bit older than the first, and the insignia on his collar, shoulders, and helmet surely denoted a higher rank. He spoke entirely in Arabic, unlike the first officer, but the computer translated his words almost instantly: "*Joan of Arc*, this is *Ambar*. We are not at war with Archangel unless you take hostile action. This operation is a Hashemite matter. Stay clear for your own safety.

You will be allowed to retrieve your citizens when the situation is settled."

"Acknowledged," said Kelly, her tone flat and firm. "Glad to hear you won't fire on us. We will continue on our way and we will stay out of yours."

The new officer seemed only slightly less taken aback by her words than the first. "Are you mad? Do you not see the active guns down there? They will shoot you, too!"

"You look like you'll clear a path for us quickly," Kelly replied. "We'll take our chances. Stay out of our way and we'll keep out of yours. *Joan of Arc* out." With that, she cut the channel with *Ambar*. Her communications with *Argent* remained live. "*Argent, Joan of Arc*. We are continuing on our mission. Transmit peaceful intent on all channels while you land. Hopefully the guys on the ground will get the message, but there should be a clearer path by the time you hit the atmosphere. Good luck."

With that, she turned to her ops chief. "Okay, now we should probably slow down a bit. I'm gonna take over the helm from you, chief."

• • •

Casey flicked the mute button on his chair controls and turned his eyes toward his first officer. Hawkins looked on in shock as *Joan of Arc* screamed into the outer atmosphere of the planet, darting past a frigate and its ongoing exchange of fire with a pair of ground-based laser cannons.

"Christ," Casey grunted, "I might actually like that bitch."

• • •

Artificial gravity generators offered a great deal of stability and protection within a vehicle, canceling out the internal effects of a vehicle's momentum. Even within an atmosphere, *Joan of Arc* could jink, wheel, and roll while her crew stood upright and steady. Sudden shocks could cause the interior to shake and rumble— though the computers controlling the internal environment adjusted with amazing speed, nothing was truly instantaneous. Still, as long as the grav systems held, everyone could remain on their feet with a little effort.

None of that prevented *Joan of Arc* from shaking violently as she entered Scheherazade's atmosphere. On the bridge's canopy projection, the eternal night of outer space shifted into the light-purple shades of the planet's sky. Multicolored streaks of lasers, plasma blasts, and missile contrails shot back and forth all around the rattling ship as her hull grew hot and smoke began trailing in her wake.

Alarms blared on the bridge. "We're being targeted!" warned Stan. "Chaff and ECM deploying!"

Kelly watched and waited, holding the ship on a steady course with only minor corrections. The corvette's defensive measures worked well, distracting missiles and energy blasts, but not every single shot was led astray. She waited until a particularly close explosion gave the ship a good jolt and then wrenched the manual controls low and to starboard. Kelly put *Joan of Arc* through a long, loose roll, orienting her course more directly toward the ground. "Cut the ECM!" she ordered. "No more chaff! Let it go!"

Joan of Arc's systems complained in a variety of ways, mostly through audible alarms and buzzing warnings, but Kelly held firm. Soon, much of the blaring stopped. "And that," she huffed, "is how we make the antiair guns think we're falling debris until we're too low for them to target us."

Her eyes flicked up to her stunned bridge crew. She threw her ops chief a wink. "You said something about improvising, right? Anyway, check the planetary chart," she instructed. "Make sure we aren't on the wrong hemisphere right now, or I'm gonna feel like a complete idiot."

• • •

"Jamming is pretty bad around here. If they're sending anything out, we can't pick it up."

"I thought it would be more chaotic," mused Stan. His table now offered a downward view of the city below the ship. *Joan* flew only a hundred meters over the tallest of the towers and stylized minarets. "People running around in the streets and shooting at each other and stuff, y'know?"

Standing nearby, Tanner shook his head. "Most people are already hiding in basements and shelters. Anyone old enough to have grandkids lived through the last war on this planet. They know what to do."

The ops specialist blinked. "How do you—"

"I read a lot," Tanner answered. He didn't need to look up to know the question was coming. "We've been waiting for this for three weeks now. Figured I should probably read up on the local history and stuff."

"Jesus, is that a blood trail on the roof there?" The XO brought up a mobile holo of the overhead view of the simple, rectangular consulate building, moving it to where the captain could see it from her seat.

Tanner brought up a similar picture from *Joan of Arc*'s optics at the astrogation table. Several metal boxes on the flat rooftop sat smoldering in the sun. A wide trail of blood led from a spot near those boxes to a rooftop access hatch nearby. "Those boxes look like comms gear, ma'am," he suggested. "You can see permanent fasteners there. Looks like they were slagged. Either someone was right next to them when they blew, or whoever went out to fix them got hurt. Or maybe shot. Look at the blood splatter."

The neighborhood offered many buildings that rose taller than the consulate's few stories. The lack of traffic made it impossible to determine who, if anyone, controlled the area. Nobody saw people in the open inside the consulate's small walled perimeter. Yet apart from the rooftop, the building seemed undamaged.

"That would explain why they can't power through any jamming," Kelly mused. "Chief, take the helm back. Go in low and swing around in a wide angle. We'll see if anyone waves to us from a window or something."

"Aye, aye, ma'am, I have the helm on manual," said the chief, taking her place at her chair as she stood and went to the astrogation table. The usual bubble had been replaced by a partial view of the skies above, showing the Hashemite warships up in orbital distance along with various debris that would eventually fall back to ground. At the bottom of the table, the ship's systems worked up a three-dimensional map of the neighborhood around the consulate.

"Aw shit," said Tanner, his eyes still glued to *Joan of Arc*'s tactical displays. "Ma'am, there's a group of tanks and other vehicles approaching the neighborhood from the northeast." He thought quickly as he spoke, checking the map on his other screen. "That's almost a direct line from the spaceport. I can't make out any flags or symbols, so I'd guess they aren't local."

"And that implies they aren't friendly. Dammit, we could hover over the rooftop with the gangway down and let people run up," Kelly muttered, "but if we wind up taking serious ground fire it could get ugly. Tanner, can you give me an ETA on those tanks?"

He already had the computer working it out. "Ten minutes at the earliest, ma'am. There's some traffic and obstructions in their path. Hard to say for sure."

"A tank like that could actually do some damage to us," concurred Booker, "particularly if it's loaded with antiair missiles. And I don't know why it wouldn't be."

"We can't get away with shooting first," Kelly grunted.

"They're waving, captain!" called out Stan. "I saw someone in a window. Looked like a marine uniform."

Anticipating Kelly's next command, Romita reversed course and swung the corvette back the way she came. Given the ship's antigrav capabilities, he didn't need to reorient the ship. *Joan of Arc* could move sideways at these speeds with no trouble.

"There. I see him," Kelly said, spotting the figure in the window. "He's not staying visible long, though."

"Even if they lost the gear on the roof, they should have portables capable of cutting through the jamming," Booker thought aloud. "Shouldn't they?"

"You suggesting we toss them a radio, sir?" asked Chief Romita.

Booker turned his attention to the captain and said, "No. I'm suggesting we go one better."

Tanner kept his eyes on his screens throughout the conversation, but he followed their thinking just fine. He didn't need the XO to spell out his offer any more than the captain did. A familiar feeling of dread suddenly announced its presence in Tanner's gut. He'd had no time to think about himself since the call for help reached the bridge, but the sensation couldn't be ignored any more than Booker's unspoken suggestion.

"XO," Kelly began, "this is already getting away from us—"

"If I had another option, I'd suggest it," said Booker. "They can jam all the signals they want, but they can't jam face-to-face communication."

"Yeah," she exhaled, "I just wish I could go instead."

"It's my job, captain."

"Okay. Go."

Tanner winced as Booker took off. He cursed inwardly, already knowing where this would go. *At least I won't be jumping into a void*, he told himself. *Or jumping alone.* "Send me with him, ma'am," Tanner spoke up. "I'm a spare hand on this ship, anyway. Less shuffling on the stations bill if I go."

Kelly hesitated for only an instant before she agreed with his assessment. "Okay. And Tanner!" she added as he moved out, catching his attention before he made it off the bridge. "Bring my people back alive." With that, she activated the ship-wide comm net and announced, "I need two volunteers to go ashore . . ."

He didn't listen to the rest. Tanner followed the XO, hustling through the passageway and down the nearby ladder to the lower decks. They encountered no one in their brief rush through the ship. With a crew of only sixteen—seventeen with Tanner on board—everyone had a specific place to be at a time like this. Tanner was, indeed, somewhat superfluous.

So instead you're about to jump out of the ship into a war zone, he thought. *Good job, Malone. Way to run out the clock.*

Coming out into the cargo bay, the two men found Ordoñez pulling gear from the weapons locker and tossing it onto a nearby countertop against the bulkhead. Once again, Tanner felt a flash of gratitude for whomever decided his experiences justified the expense of buying combat jackets for the navy. Not every crewman got one—the cost was prohibitively high, even with domestic manufacturers and Archangel's military expansion programs—but *Joan of Arc* carried enough to outfit a boarding team.

"You coming with us, Ordoñez?" Tanner asked as he threw on his jacket and pulled the seam tabs to adjust the fit.

"No. I'm here to get you set up, then I gotta run back to the main gun." She quickly laid a pulse rifle and one of the riot guns on the table, then disappeared back into the locker. "I offered, but the captain wants me here."

"It's always the thought that counts," Tanner grunted.

Ordoñez appeared again, setting down bandoleers with pouches of ammunition for each weapon. She glanced over at Tanner. "Everyone volunteered."

The comment made him stop and blink. "This ship really is different."

Two more men arrived in the cargo bay then, each of them promptly joining Tanner and the XO in collecting gear. He glanced up and took stock of the team. Cervantes hadn't spoken with Tanner much, but the ship's electrician's mate seemed solid enough, and having a tech along was wise. The final member of the team also made sense: Sanjay had been through the same sort of extended basic training program as Tanner.

Ordoñez appeared from within the weapons locker once more, this time holding up a black backpack with padding shaped around its boxy metallic contents. "Who gets the comms pack?"

"I've got it," said Cervantes, stepping up to take the pack from her.

"Anything else?" asked the gunner's mate.

"Tanner, Sanjay, grab medic packs," instructed Booker. "We don't know if anyone's hurt down there. Ordoñez, I think we've got it from here. Head back to your station."

"Aye, aye, sir. Good luck, guys," Ordoñez added, punching Sanjay in the arm on her way out.

"Hey, all I get is a pulse rifle?" Sanjay called after her.

"They won't let me stock anything bigger!" she complained before closing the hatch to the cargo bay.

"Guys, the ship's moving in over the consulate now," explained the XO. "We step off the ramp and get inside as fast as we can. Whatever happens, remember that we are here only to take our own people home. This is an evacuation, not an intervention. *Do not* fire on anyone unless you have a target who is threatening us or Archangel citizens. And don't spread out too far. As soon as we step off the ship, we're probably gonna lose holocom signals. Got it?" With that, Booker turned toward the cargo bay ramp and hit his holocom. "Captain, we're ready when you are."

Mild tremors rippled through the cargo bay as the engines shifted and the antigrav generators did their work. "Acknowledged," came the captain's voice over the holocom net. "Moving into position now. Ramp is coming down. Get to cover and try to establish comms as soon as you can. Remember the evac plan, gentlemen. If we can't stay overhead and we have to set down, we'll stick to our original landing site priorities."

As she spoke, daylight and the roar of the engines broke through the first cracks between the hull and the cargo bay ramp. Tanner stepped forward with Cervantes, unlocking the safety catch on the pulse rifle in his hands. Up ahead he saw the urban skyline of the capital city. Thus far, the city all around them seemed to hold steady. None of the towers showed smashed windows or other damage, though plumes of smoke rose in every direction farther out.

He glanced left and right, checking on his teammates. Booker gave Tanner a wave as soon as the ramp lay parallel to the deck. Tanner moved forward, finding the rooftop of the consulate less than two meters below. Assured the fall wouldn't likely injure him, Tanner jumped. The others followed.

Something small, loud, and shockingly fast streaked over Tanner's head and straight into the cargo bay. He fell forward as he heard the explosion, flinging himself to the rooftop and then rolling to his side to look around. All three of his shipmates made it out before the small missile hit. *Joan of Arc* lurched up and away.

"Motherfucker!" blurted Sanjay.

"Stay down!" ordered Booker. "Anyone hurt?"

"I think I'm fine, sir," said Cervantes.

Another missile flew overhead, striking the underside of *Joan of Arc* with a loud boom that forced all four men to cringe.

"I think they figured out how to jam face-to-face communication, sir," warned Tanner. He scrambled for the nearest cover, though that only amounted to the damaged electronics gearboxes. A bullet ricocheted across the rooftop just a foot away, causing him to reconsider his placement.

Sanjay and Cervantes took advantage of the small parapet that rose at the edge of the roof. It offered less than a meter of coverage, but it was better than nothing. Sanjay lay alongside the parapet and raised his pulse rifle over its edge, firing back along the line drawn by the contrails of the first missile to an apartment window several blocks away. Blue bursts of energy struck against the windowsill and the wall around it, but more than a few made it inside.

"Sanjay," Booker shouted, "do you have a target?"

The crewman paused. "No, sir," he admitted angrily.

Tanner stayed behind his cover for only a moment before moving away. Another shot struck the damaged boxes. It couldn't have come from the same direction as either of the rockets. "Snipers!" he yelled out. "Don't stay in one place! They're on more than one side!"

Cervantes rolled away from his spot in time to avoid a bullet that struck the parapet. He pushed himself up and dove for another spot while two more rounds hit the roof near him. "The fuck do we do?" he demanded.

Tanner glanced up to the sky. *Joan of Arc* swung around in a semicircle beside the consulate, trailing smoke but putting herself between the building and the side facing the missile fire. Whatever damage the first missile had done to the cargo bay didn't seem to impede the ship's maneuverability. Tanner suspected that the missiles were portable infantry weapons rather than anything heavier. The corvette could only provide cover in one direction, though, leaving the men vulnerable at several other arcs.

More shots rang out all around them, close enough that Tanner could hear the weapons—but not the impact. He realized that someone below the roof was shooting outward to offer the team some further protection. Looking to his team again, Tanner found the XO hustling to the rooftop access hatch. It flew open before the XO got there. "Get inside!" someone yelled from within.

"Cervantes! Sanjay! Let's go!" Booker waved. The electrician's mate came first, swinging his legs over the side and all but dropping down below. Sanjay hustled toward the hatch but fell to his left with a sudden jerk and an angry cry.

Tanner instantly understood the implications of Sanjay's fall and came up with a way to deal with it while rushing to his shipmate's side. He aimed his pulse rifle at the parapet as he ran, firing off several bursts that kicked up a cloud of masonry dust and debris. If the snipers targeted with motion sensors, bounced signals, or ordinary optics, the debris would offer at least a momentary disruption.

"Sir, jump down!" Tanner yelled. "I've got Sanjay!"

"I've got myself, goddammit," Sanjay growled, pushing himself up before Tanner reached him. "I'm moving, just go!"

Another boom split the air around them as a third small missile hit *Joan of Arc*'s side. Though a few infantry weapons offered enough firepower to damage a corvette, they would need to land an exceptionally well-placed shot to inflict critical harm. *Joan of Arc* shook but held her position until Tanner jumped down the rooftop hatch after Sanjay and Booker. Then the corvette rapidly rose in the sky, turning and shifting to evade further targeting.

Tanner took the landing as he'd been taught in basic, crouching down with one arm out and rolling forward to redirect the energy. He found himself on his back in a darkened hallway among his three shipmates and a pair of armed Archangel marines in service uniforms. One of them wore lieutenant's bars.

"Everyone okay?" asked the lieutenant.

"I'm good," grunted Tanner over a similar response from Sanjay. He found Cervantes already on his feet, clearly unharmed by his fall. The XO seemed to have fared just as well. Tanner got up and moved to Sanjay's side, finding a bleeding hole in the tall crewman's shoulder. "Jesus, Sanjay, sit down. You took a hit."

Sanjay pushed the faceplate of his helmet up with one hand before he shook his head. "Can't be too bad if I'm still moving okay."

"I'm Lieutenant Adams," said the marine officer, "head of the garrison here. Glad to see you." He reached out to the XO as much to help him up as to shake his hand. "If you're all well enough to move, we should regroup in the security office downstairs."

"Good enough." The XO accepted the tug back to his feet. "Lieutenant Booker, *Joan of Arc*. What's the situation here?"

"Not good. Snipers took out our rooftop comms gear about the same time that fleet showed up overhead. We had reports of fighting here and there about a minute or three before that, but we didn't know we had threats in the vicinity until I sent a couple guys up to check on the gear. A sniper killed one of them. The other's in bad shape, but we've got him stable."

The group walked quickly through the halls as Adams spoke. All of the doors were closed. Drapes covered most hallway windows, though Tanner spotted desks propped up on their sides to block a couple of others. They found another marine standing by the stairwell door, holding a laser rifle and still wearing her dress uniform.

"I've got fifty-three civilians here and my 'garrison' is about a squad and a half of marines. That and a couple of armed Intelligence Ministry agents is all we've got," Adams continued. He led the group down the stairs. "That's not enough to send out teams to hunt down snipers and guard the building at the same time. Worst thing anyone ever planned to deal with was a protest riot or the like."

"Yeah," said Booker as they exited the stairwell, "we were hoping to move everyone to a landing spot nearby or hover over the roof with the cargo ramp extended at worst. But with those snipers out there, I'm thinking those aren't such good ideas anymore."

"Right. Hell, when we first saw that invasion fleet appear over us, we figured you wouldn't make it through," Adams confessed.

"I wasn't sure we'd make it, either," Booker agreed. "We moved as soon as we got word."

"Yeah, that's another story there," muttered Adams, but soon he came to an armed marine standing guard outside a secure room. The lieutenant exchanged brief words with the sentry before the door opened, and then he ushered the navy team past.

Inside they found a large security and communications room. Hard screens and computers lined the walls, though more than a few of them displayed static or standby graphics. Only a couple of the people inside wore marine uniforms. The others dressed in civilian clothes.

Tanner looked over to Sanjay again as the officers moved off to meet with the consul and a pair of his staffers. "Sanjay, take a seat," he said, gesturing to the table. "Let me look at that wound."

"Yeah, okay." The other crewman winced. He sat down as instructed.

"Is it getting worse?"

"Well, now I've had a couple minutes to feel it." Sanjay shook his head. "Still moving okay, though."

Tanner unslung his medical pack as Cervantes helped Sanjay pull off his combat jacket and helmet. He glanced around the room, wondering if there might be a dedicated medic on hand, but seeing no one step forward, Tanner pulled off his helmet and then saw to Sanjay's shoulder.

"Doesn't look too bad," observed Cervantes. "Pretty nasty gash, but it doesn't look deep."

"Yeah." Tanner drew the fabric shears from his kit and cut away the sleeve of Sanjay's vac suit at the shoulder, then gingerly peeled it back to get a better look. "The plating in the combat jacket must've forced the bullet to turn a bit. You don't have a hole here, you've got a tear."

"I've got a tattoo to get fixed, is what I've got," Sanjay corrected.

Tanner pulled a chemical-laden sponge from his kit and held it to Sanjay's shoulder. "Yeah, you do," agreed Tanner. The sponge worked quickly, creating a foam that drew little bits of inorganic matter from the wound while cleansing it with antibacterial agents. Sanjay endured the pain without complaint. With that finished, Tanner held a second sponge to the wound to fill the affected area with a mild numbing agent and clotting boosters to aid in natural healing. Then he set to stitching the skin together with a pen-size auto-suture.

"Congrats, Crewman Sanjay," said Tanner. "You just earned your first Purple Heart."

"For that? I could get hurt worse from slipping on a banana peel."

"You got shot. Bananas don't actively try to kill you."

"XO?" Cervantes called, looking up from his holocom and walking away from the two crewmen. "We were right about the comms gear. I've got the ship on the portable." His voice drifted off as he joined the officers and consulate staff.

Sanjay nodded toward one of the monitors against the wall. "Good thing, too," he noted. "Looks like the ship's pulling way off."

Tanner followed Sanjay's gaze and saw what he meant. Though the consulate had been rendered deaf and mute, it wasn't yet blind. Cameras and scanners mounted outside the building still worked. *Joan of Arc* flew up and over the buildings surrounding the consulate. It appeared her attackers decided to hold fire after the shore party had made it inside.

"What do you think?" Sanjay asked.

Glancing around the room once again, Tanner shrugged. "Somebody's gonna have to clear a path to one of the landing sites. Those snipers won't go away until somebody makes them."

"That marine just said he didn't have enough people to do that."

Tanner's grim frown held in place. "He's got four more people here now, and we're all wearing better protection than anyone else. And somebody's gonna have to do it before those tanks get here."

"Tanks?" Sanjay blinked. "What tanks?"

"Oh, I guess nobody had time to tell you. They might not come here. Maybe they've got other shit to do."

"You don't sound like you believe that."

"I'm hoping," Tanner replied sincerely. "We've dealt with enough bullshit already today."

"Hey, excuse me," spoke up one of the other marines in the room. The two crewmen glanced up at the man, who stood with two of his comrades. "I just . . . wow. I was right. You're Tanner Malone."

"Um. Yeah?"

The first marine smiled broadly, stepping back and punching one of his fellows in the arm. "I told you we'd get out of this mess."

Tanner's mouth fell open. He tried to formulate some sort of response, but nothing came to mind.

"You don't get that often?" asked a woman standing nearby. Her long black hair hung limply to her shoulders while her lips curved into a smirk. Her clothes seemed closer to civilian attire than military wear, but the gun belt, black long coat, and rugged boots marked her as something quite different from a consulate staffer. Tanner realized she'd come over from the conversation between the officers and the civilian bigwigs.

"Tanner Malone, poster boy for the Archangel Navy, and this surprises you?" she pressed mildly, gesturing to the three marines.

". . . Yes," he finally answered, getting his brain back on track once again. "It's weird. I'm still not used to people telling me who I am." He glanced at the marines once more, meaning to say something friendly or at least to add, "No offense," but they had already returned to other matters. That didn't stop them from looking over their shoulders toward him—or toward the woman beside him.

"Who are you?" Sanjay asked.

She hesitated, glancing between the two crewmen, but offered her hand. "Vanessa Rios. Archangel Intelligence Ministry."

Both young men blinked. Tanner shook her hand mostly out of reflex but recovered from the slight surprise quick enough. A consulate seemed like a reasonable place for an intelligence agent to be. "This is Crewman Sanjay," he said, gesturing to his companion.

"Crewman." Vanessa shook his hand. She turned her attention back to Tanner. "I thought you were on the capital honor guard now?"

"Temporary duty on *Joan of Arc*," he answered, his brow furrowing. "Does the Intelligence Ministry keep track of me or something?"

"It's not my job, but I'm sure somebody does. I've just had a personal interest since your story broke. We have a few things in common."

"Like?"

"Wish I could tell you." She smiled ruefully. "My job doesn't work that way."

He paused for a second, trying to catch up. "Then should you be bringing it up?" he wondered.

She shrugged. "Far as you know."

". . . Wait, what?"

"Sanjay, Tanner, you two good to go?" asked Lieutenant Booker as he returned. An older man in a suit accompanied him. Tanner figured he must be the consular. "That shoulder okay?"

"Fine, sir." Sanjay pulled his combat jacket back on. "What's the plan?"

"The security systems here tracked the trajectories of some of those missiles down to a few specific buildings while we were getting shot at. If we can take those snipers out, we'll have a clear path for a rooftop extraction. But they'll obviously stay mobile, so we'll have to go room to room to find them." As he spoke he brought up a flat projection from his holocom to show an overhead map of the neighborhood. He highlighted a particular apartment building, tracing out a route to it from the consulate that took advantage of several points of cover.

"Normally that's marine work," the XO explained, "but they're a little short-handed for a job like this, and we're wearing better protection than they've got, so we're gonna help them out. The marines will take one building and we'll take another. Cervantes will stay here to run comms for the consulate."

"We're going for the apartments there?" asked Sanjay. "That building looks like a nice enough place to have decent security. Sliding doors and computer locks like they've got here. No old fashioned hinges and doorknobs."

"Got that covered already. The marines are loaning us a bumper unit. Not exactly subtle, but we don't have time for subtlety. Borrowed a couple chaff grenades, too."

"What about the ship, sir?" asked Tanner.

"She swung around to make sure *Argent* has a safe landing and starts collecting people without any problems. Don't worry, she'll be back when we call for her."

"Gentlemen," spoke up the suited man, "I cannot stress enough to you the importance of engaging in absolutely minimal violence." Tanner caught the slight wince in Booker's eyes, but if the other man noticed, he ignored it. "Archangel cannot afford to become embroiled in a civil war *or* a conflict with whomever comes out on top in this mess. The one thing we must not do is escalate this situation further."

"Wait"—Sanjay scowled—"aren't they *shooting* at us?"

"We can't prove who 'they' are, crewman," Vanessa answered before the suited man could reply. "Those snipers probably aren't wearing uniforms or identification. The bad guys here want some level of deniability until the last second, so they can wash their hands of this in case it all goes wrong. As long as they have to do that, they're limited in how much force they can use. If that goes out the window, they can use whatever the hell amount of force they want."

"And then Archangel is obligated to respond," added Tanner. "Or at least there'll be a huge political fight back home over whether or not we do anything about this."

Vanessa pursed her lips at Tanner's suggestion, but whether she was impressed or amused, he couldn't tell.

Sanjay cared little for such concerns. "Motherfuckers shoot at me, I'll shoot back. It's that simple."

"I understand how you feel, er, crewman," said the suited man, "but you have to understand that if we handle this poorly—"

"Mr. Regan," interrupted Vanessa, "I think they understand the situation. Why don't we let the military types handle this?" She took his arm and began leading him away, tossing the XO a quick glance as she moved.

With a quick gesture, Booker got both of his crewmen on their feet and gathering up their gear. "Did she say anything to you?" Booker asked quietly, looking over his shoulder again.

"What, the spy lady?" Sanjay chuckled. "Didn't say much. I think she wanted Tanner's autograph."

"Not the impression I got." Tanner slipped his arms through the straps of his medic pack, tightening it down and then scooping up his rifle and helmet before walking out of the room with the two men. "I'm not sure what she wanted. Is she part of the consulate here, sir?"

"I'm probably not supposed to say anything," replied Booker. "Just thought I should ask."

They followed a marine guide down to the bottom floor and through a service hallway toward the back of the building. A handful of frightened and concerned people crossed their path along the way, all of them mindfully staying clear of the windows. Tanner guessed that most of them were consulate staff, but a few looked like they might be dependents, or perhaps tourists or expats who were closer to the consulate than the spaceport when the warning to evacuate went out. He saw a few small suitcases and other belongings, and even one or two children in the mix. Some people were clearly more ready than others.

He also saw more than a few faces look up with recognition in their eyes as he passed. Some turned to their friends and whispered. A couple pointed.

Eventually, Tanner put his helmet on and slammed the faceplate down.

At the rear entrance, they found a couple more marine sentries armed with rifles. Like several of the others, they still wore dress uniforms under their protective gear. Booker talked his crewmen through a simple weapons check, then opened up his holo screen once more, reminding everyone of their planned route. Then he looked to the pair of marine sentries. "We'll clear that wall faster if someone's there to give us a boost. You two up for it?"

"Yes, sir," the two answered without hesitation. "That wall's built to hold up against a truck, sir," one of them added. "He won't be able to shoot through it, at least, and we'll put a chaff grenade over the wall after you. Might give you a couple more seconds of cover."

"Good. I'll take the lead. We're first," Booker said, gesturing to Tanner and himself, "then help Sanjay here and then get back inside. Any questions?"

Tanner glanced briefly at Sanjay before he spoke. "Sir," he said, "don't take this the wrong way, but, um . . . have you had infantry training?"

For a second, Booker plainly didn't know what to say. Then he let out a breath. "Not a whole lot, no," he admitted. "Boarding team school and a couple of orientation classes at the academy. That's about it. But I can't let you go out there alone, and the marines are used to working with their own."

"Sir, I'm not saying you should stay." Tanner felt relieved that the XO didn't explode at his question. Many officers certainly would have in the same situation. "I'm just . . . those snipers are probably watching the exits, and they've had time to study the layout here. The chaff grenade might scramble any fancy electronic targeting, but not an optic scope, and the smoke will spread only so far. They know where to watch when we run for cover."

Booker glanced to Sanjay, who merely nodded in agreement. "Suggestions?"

"Just that we should know to expect it. Don't stay under one bit of cover for long. One, two seconds at the most, and don't run in straight lines or at a constant pace. You don't want to give him a chance to predict your movements or focus in on a spot where you're hiding." He thought for more to say, then shrugged. "That's what they taught us in weapons and tactics school, anyway. I'm not pretending I've done this for real before, either."

"No, it's better than nothing," said the XO. "Good advice, Tanner. Thanks."

"Tanner?" piped up one of the marine sentries. "Holy shit, are you Tanner Malone?"

The faceplate on his helmet prevented anyone but the XO from seeing Tanner wince. "No time for it now, gentlemen," Booker said. "We're out of here at the count of three. Ready?" he asked, giving everyone a chance to get set to the sides of the door. "One . . . two . . . three!"

The metal door to the rear of the consulate slid up in a flash. The group rushed out in the next instant. A small patio area lay between the door and the rear wall of the consulate property. Tables and chairs for small receptions and the like sat arranged in an elegant fashion.

Tanner slipped up with the wall to his left. A marine held his hands low with fingers knit together for him and grunted, "Good luck, buddy," as Tanner put his left foot in the man's hands and lunged upward. The burly marine gave him a bigger boost than he'd expected; Tanner had meant to grab the wall with his left hand and swing his right limbs over, but found himself turning and moving all too fast. In a single second, he went from executing a well-planned move to flailing over the side of the wall. "Shit!" he blurted out before the concrete sidewalk rushed up and clobbered him from head to toe.

He heard the chaff grenade go off with a boom as he rolled away from his spot of impact, wanting to stay mobile rather than give the sniper a chance to zero in on him. The fall left him feeling a bit shaken, but adrenaline and his protective gear blunted the pain. *Just wouldn't be combat if I managed to do anything gracefully,* he thought as he rushed for the nearest parked vehicle.

Pieces of concrete burst from the street beside him as he got under cover. His gaze swept in an arc to find his shipmates. Both men had already made it farther along their path. Tanner also noticed the small depression in the consulate's outer wall caused by the sniper's bullet at about the point where he had fallen.

Not far away, the chaff grenade continued to send smoke, burning bits of phosphorous with loud pops in every direction. Much like the disruptive effects of chaff missiles on ships, the device served to throw off the high-tech aids offered by modern sniper rifles. Bouncing signals and thermal trackers couldn't work through such a mess, though the distraction would be short-lived.

Tanner put his own advice to use. He dove out from behind the vehicle and then rushed forward and slightly to his right, breaking into a full run as soon as he was behind the cover of a tree, rather than pausing to let the sniper keep up with him. Once more, small chunks of concrete exploded behind him as a bullet ricocheted against the street.

The urban landscape left Tanner feeling like a gunman lurked in every window. Escaping the snipers felt more like an outcome of random chance than a payoff for his tactics or speed. He spotted

Sanjay and Booker at the edge of the alleyway up ahead. They'd both made it. He swallowed his rising fear and shifted over to his left again as he ran and deliberately slowed his pace for a second rather than breaking into a dead run like his gut demanded.

Another bullet cracked against a wall beside him just as he reached the edge of the street, vindicating his choice to rely on training rather than letting his flight instincts get the better of him. Two more such shots ricocheted around him as the sniper made a last desperate attempt to hit Tanner before he was out of sight, but then the young crewman was in the shadows and behind cover.

"Jesus Christ," he huffed, painting himself into the nearest doorway in the alley. He glanced down the alleyway to the tower of glass and steel looming above them across the street, and then spotted a pair of marines at the tower's base, running for the entrance. Tanner hoped the snipers were so focused on him and his comrades that they'd failed to spot the marines entirely.

"You okay?" asked Booker.

"Yeah. You?"

"We're good." Though their run had taken them barely forty meters, adrenaline and fear had all three men breathing heavily. "Okay, through this building and on to the next. Ready? Tanner, you take the lead."

Booker reached for a button near the door and found it unsecured. The door slid up without any trouble. Tanner moved in, bringing his rifle up and at the ready and sweeping it from left to right to take in his surroundings. He saw only boxes and refrigeration units, quickly remembering from the map that this was some sort of coffee shop or restaurant. Tanner pushed on with his shipmates following, hoping neither he nor they would accidentally blow away some terrified civilian hiding inside.

The optic systems in his helmet worked perfectly, though jamming signals still blocked communications. He could not see the status lights of his teammates on his heads-up display, but the onboard computer still overlaid every bit of Arabic text in sight with a soft-green English translation. Though the system offered potential distractions, it also eased movement through a foreign environment. In truth, Tanner hadn't gotten far in his first classes in Arabic. The translation program made it easier to identify exits, storage closets, and bathrooms.

They found no one within the main room or the hallways. Empty chairs and tables still held food and drinks. As Tanner initially suspected, people here knew to go to ground when the shooting started. He moved with his rifle at the ready, just as he had been taught. The reflective part of his mind found the empty dining room eerie and sad, but he couldn't dwell on it. This was only one of three buildings he had to pass through on the way to their target.

The next building did not open so easily, as its security systems remained online, but the apartments were built only to keep out casual trespassers and not determined soldiers. A pair of shots from Sanjay's rifle brought down one of the transparent plastic panels that made up the exterior wall, and though this resulted in an internal alarm and flashing lights, nothing further barred them from entry. The three men rushed through the hallways and the lobby of the apartment building.

Crossing the courtyard between the side exit and the next tower, though, they exercised greater care. All three of them made sure to look before they leapt, pointedly casting their eyes skyward, lest a grenade or some other danger drop down on them from above. This apartment building, fancier and more modern than the last, was their destination.

Tanner stayed on point. The clear glass doors slid open as soon as he stepped forward. He snapped up his rifle and almost shot the lobby greeting hologram when the image of a man behind a desk appeared and started speaking to him pleasantly in Arabic. Once more, his helmet optics quickly translated the signs and labels within the lobby.

He waved the other two men forward. "I figured some sort of alarm would go off when we came in here with guns," he said. "This seems like a pretty modern building."

"Well, there's already a sniper here," Booker considered, "so he may have already taken care of the security systems."

"True enough." Sanjay shrugged. "Okay. We're here. How do we do this? Any idea which floor we should start on?"

"He has to have at least good enough elevation to see across the roof of the consulate," Tanner thought aloud, "so that means, what? Fifth floor at least?"

"Seems like. Plenty of floors above that, though. And we'd be idiots to use the lifts. Looks like the stairwells are that way. Welcome to the infantry, I guess," muttered Booker.

. . .

Complications arose with the first few apartments the team checked. Though they found no civilians in their sweep—something Tanner considered a priceless blessing—most of the apartments were locked. The bumper unit coaxed most computerized locks open, but in a few instances they had to resort to naked force. Furniture, differing configurations of apartment rooms, and the occasionally still-active holographic appliance offered a great many advantages for anyone trying to hide. In most of the apartments, home environmental control programs activated as soon as they entered, turning on lights and sometimes offering a greeting in Arabic, which only served to keep their nerves on edge.

Tanner never liked playing hide-and-seek, nor did he particularly enjoy being "it." The expectation that this particular game would end with gunfire made it worse.

They came to a corner apartment, sliding up along the walls and looking down the hallways for any signs of movement. Booker took one side of the door. Sanjay took the other, with Tanner right beside him. The one hopeful sign Tanner took from their search was that Booker quickly caught on to the tactics that the two crewmen had learned in basic. Before they'd finished with the fifth floor, it seemed Booker had the techniques down. By the time they'd cleared the sixth, the disparity in training felt all but erased, and the XO was solidly in charge again.

Sanjay tried the door controls and found them locked. He grabbed the small, shoebox-size bumper unit hanging from his belt and held it against the panel. The bumper unit promptly overloaded the door controls with so many garbage data signals in a single high-powered pulse that it essentially forced the security system to reverse its default lockdown condition.

Tanner swung around Sanjay with his rifle up and ready, covering the left of the entryway while Booker covered the arc to the right. Inside, they found a spacious, clean living room nicer than the others they'd seen. The lights didn't activate as they moved in. A spiral staircase at the far end of the living room led up to the second floor, making this the first two-level residence they'd found. Beyond the living room, tall, clear windows offered a corner view overlooking the consulate building.

They moved in cautiously, identifying and clearing corners and furniture large enough for a body to hide behind. As with the other apartments, they found no one on this level. Tanner cleared the small dining area and kitchen, rounding it and coming back to the living room to focus his attention on the stairs. He made it to the bottom step, but soon realized that he didn't have anyone ready to follow him.

Moving to the other side of the living room, Sanjay looked out toward the consulate. "Aw shit!" he hissed. "XO! You'd better look!"

Booker moved to join Sanjay and let out a stressful groan. "Oh, son of a bitch."

Tanner kept his weapon and his eyes trained up the stairs toward the second floor. He thought he saw a steady, smooth shift in the shadows on the ceiling above, perhaps from the ripple of a curtain. Wanting to see it again with his vision unaffected by the lenses of his helmet, Tanner raised his faceplate and watched.

"*Joan of Arc*," said the XO, trying to keep his voice low, "this is Booker. We have tanks moving into place around the consulate with troops in support. Do you copy?"

"Ssshhh," Tanner warned, waving one hand, but if the others listened, he couldn't tell. He dared not look away. The ripple of shadow against the second-floor ceiling happened again, but that didn't bother him nearly as much as the strong, unpleasant smell he detected now that his faceplate was up.

"Dammit, I think the jamming signals are still active," he heard Booker grumble, but his voice drifted farther away. Tanner's feet began slowly carrying him up the stairs, keeping him close to the edges, lest some creaky board give him away.

His head and the barrel of his weapon crested the opening to the second floor, where he found a hallway leading to rooms in each direction. Slowly, he turned in place, getting a full circular view of the hallway . . . and feeling the breeze on his face as he looked back toward what must be the master bedroom.

The door lay open. Natural sunlight illuminated the room. Shadows moved along the ceiling. He'd found the room with the open window and the source of the smell.

The woman lay on the bedroom floor with her eyes staring lifelessly at him. Beyond her, he saw a shattered mirror over a dresser and personal items in obvious disarray: an overturned glass, a hairbrush on the floor, a broken statuette. She must have put up a struggle.

Tanner heard Booker's voice again from downstairs and in the earpiece inside his helmet, but it seemed overlaid with another. He realized the second voice came from the bedroom. He couldn't make out what the other voice said, but like Booker's it seemed a bit hushed. He took another slow, careful step up the stairs, and then another. He had the elevation then to see the blood pooled around the dead woman, staining the carpet. A third step gave him the chance to see the bloody holes in the back of her dress left by gunshots.

He crept up out of the stairs. She wore her hair in a braid secured at the back of her head. Perhaps the fabric dangling from her dresser was her hijab, if she wore one. Perhaps she didn't. Even if it were a common practice for her, she didn't need to wear it in her own home. She lay with one arm stretched out to another doorway beyond, perhaps the bathroom. He couldn't see yet.

Tanner rounded the bannister and slowly advanced on the door. He heard more of the voice inside the bedroom and less of Booker or Sanjay. He worried that his shipmates would notice his absence and call out, giving him away to whomever occupied the bedroom.

From his vantage point, Tanner guessed the bedroom was big. This woman either made a very good living or was part of a wealthy family, or maybe both. She couldn't be from a world of guns and bombs. Tanner steadily put one foot in front of the other.

At the edge of the door, he saw another pool of blood on the floor of the bathroom. He saw a small shoe attached to a small, bloodstained leg. The rest of the child's body lay inside the bathroom. He didn't look further.

"*Joan of Arc*, this is Booker," repeated the voice in his earpiece. It snapped him out of his focus on the room and the bodies. "We have tanks and troops right outside the consulate, do you copy?"

Tanner silenced his holocom and swallowed hard. He heard the man inside—he knew for sure it was a man's voice now—say something in Arabic, though he could only make out a couple of the words. The man didn't sound upset or distraught. He sounded controlled. Calm. Steady.

Steadier than Tanner. The body on the floor stared at his feet now, rather than at his eyes, which he closed to gather himself. The man had to be talking on a comm system, given the way no second voice responded. Someone knew he was up here. If he were speaking to the tanks and the soldiers below, they'd know he was here but not necessarily that he wasn't alone. Nothing in his voice spoke of a concern for intruders.

His eyes opened again. The dead woman stared at his feet. The plea in her eyes seemed obvious. He was too late to answer it . . . which only made him angrier.

At the doorway, Tanner glanced around for reflective surfaces to get a sense of the room before stepping in. He found a man with a rifle sitting on an open windowsill, partly covered by one curtain. The other curtain billowed in the wind behind him. A small backpack and a jacket with an urban camouflage pattern sat on the bed. His missile launcher sat there, too, but Tanner saw no ammunition for it. Apparently he'd run out.

No one else in the room still drew breath, let alone spoke. Tanner didn't see any holo screens or a hand unit. The sniper had to be talking over an earpiece.

Tanner paused for one last moment to think. He needed to make sure he got the conjugation right.

His mind set, Tanner slipped into the room and cut a path around the large bed toward the man in the window. He cared less for stealth than speed now. He couldn't afford hesitation. Just as he came within arm's reach, the man sensed his presence and turned.

Tanner mercilessly slammed the butt of his rifle into the man's throat. Then he dropped his rifle and seized the sniper. Tanner yelled out a single phrase in a high-pitched, almost panicked voice: *"Alanzaliq! An alanzaliq!"*

The man tried to cry out through his spasming throat. He managed it just after Tanner shoved him out of the window.

"Oh shit!" Sanjay fairly shrieked from downstairs when the sniper tumbled right past the living room window.

Shifting to a spot behind the curtains, Tanner risked a peek down at the street below. It allowed his first look at the infantrymen arranging themselves behind various bits of cover outside the consulate. He saw a single large tank taking up much of the street leading to the gate. Other tanks moved into position at each of the nearby perpendicular streets.

He lingered for only a second, two at the most, verifying that several of the troops rushed to check on the dead sniper now lying on the sidewalk below. Then he turned from the window and nearly jumped when he found someone standing in the bedroom doorway. His mind processed the sight while he dove behind the bed for cover. Vanessa Rios had her pistol pointed up to the ceiling rather than at him.

"Sorry about the surprise," she said. "I came up behind you and didn't want to spoil your approach."

"Tanner?" called out Booker. He and Sanjay quickly rushed up the stairs. Vanessa held her hands up in a gesture of peace, watching to make sure they didn't mistake her for a threat.

"How'd you get here?" Tanner asked as he stood back up.

"Your exit made for a good distraction. I figured you might need the help." She caught the obvious doubt on Tanner's face and added, "It was either that or hide in the consulate. This seemed more important. I don't have any responsibilities there."

Booker looked from her to Tanner. "You should've gotten us before coming up here," he said, moving into the room past Vanessa.

"Sorry, sir," Tanner replied. "You were distracted with whatever's going on downstairs. I saw movement and kinda got tunnel vision." He took Booker's lack of response as acceptance; the XO seemed more focused on checking the sniper's gear than dwelling on Tanner's decisions.

Vanessa tilted her head curiously as she gestured toward the window. "I slipped?" she translated. "Is that what you shouted?"

"That was you?" asked Sanjay.

"I . . . yeah." Tanner swallowed. "If those guys down there know someone took him out, they might send people up to investigate. If they think he had an accident, maybe they won't bother."

Both Sanjay and Vanessa blinked, though the young man's surprise was a bit more pronounced than hers. "Wow, man," Sanjay huffed with obvious approval. "You play dirty."

"Not what I'd have expected," murmured Vanessa, "but I'm not throwing stones."

"Here. He had a jamming unit," said Booker. He pulled the large electronic device from the pack, revealing its active lights and status readouts. "This thing looks pretty sharp. Might be the only one they needed to drown out every signal for a few blocks."

"Don't turn it off, lieutenant," warned Vanessa. "Not yet. Tanner's right, we can't let them know we're up here." She moved to look out the window, taking advantage of the curtains to conceal herself. Tanner slipped up alongside her.

The consulate sat at the end of a T intersection, surrounded by its walls and neighbored by a pair of smaller buildings. A single tank rolled up along all three roads. Tanner suspected a fourth sat somewhere on the far side of the consulate. They heard someone's voice over a loudspeaker. "I can't make out what they're saying from here," he muttered.

"It's pretty obvious, isn't it?" asked Sanjay. "Gotta be demanding everyone come out with their hands up before they level the place."

"The building does them no good," Vanessa explained. "By now every bit of sensitive tech or recorded data has been slagged. That's half the reason the marines are there. They'd know that. They don't want the building; they want live prisoners. Listen closer. They're offering 'protection' so they can grab everyone without a fight."

"Is this what the intel said?" asked Tanner, still watching the tanks and the men below. "The info that warned the consulate was in danger? Did it specify tanks?"

"It didn't have a full layout of forces involved." Vanessa shook her head. "Just a list of certain people who'd be involved in the operation and plans for what to do with prisoners."

"So why don't we shut off the jammer, call in the ship, and have it blow the shit out of these assholes from the sky?" pressed Sanjay.

"At least one of those ships up in orbit is bound to have eyes trained on this situation," Vanessa answered. "They don't necessarily know what's going on with this op, but if they see your ship fire on the ground, they'll open up on her. They can't complain about us evacuating our people or even taking out a couple of crazy random snipers in a war zone to do it, but an Archangel ship firing on Hashemite tanks complicates everything. Archangel can't afford to get involved in this war—and the people who sent those tanks know it."

"Hey, XO?" said Tanner, still looming at the window.

"What is it?" Booker responded. "Anything changed?"

"No, sir, but . . . they're arranged in a really thin line. And they've got a couple of huge weak points."

Booker's already grim expression turned doubtful. "What are you suggesting?"

Tanner glanced over to the camouflage jacket on the bed and shrugged glumly. "Nothing I haven't done before."

FOUR

Absolutely Minimal Violence

"NorthStar is committed to peace and stability. I look to the turmoil within Hashem, to the growing distance between Archangel and the Union and the economic struggles of so many honest, hardworking people all across our sister worlds, and I see so much work to do. But we will do that work. In the words of Abraham Lincoln, 'We are not enemies, but friends. We must not be enemies. Though passion may have strained, it must not break our bonds of affection.'"

—NorthStar CEO Anton Brekhov,
Letter to Shareholders, April 2276

"Get back inside the goddamn tank, you stupid asshole."

"Excuse me?" asked the Hashemite tank driver. He turned to Harris, who leaned in beside him at his station within the tank. "Are you—oh. You are talking to your friend, not me."

The frown on Harris's face shifted slightly as he nodded. "Yeah, yeah, sorry," he grumbled, pointing to the solid view screen in front of them. The tank's control compartment offered enough room for half a dozen crew and one or two extras, as long as the crew all remained in their seats. There certainly wasn't need for anyone to stick his head out of the turret in his tank, or in the tank at the bottom of the *T* intersection shown on the screen. At most, the tank's commander had an excuse, since that allowed for a human face to be seen delivering the offer of "protection" to the people inside the consulate.

Sadly, no one in the tank seemed to have pointed that out to Abnett. He stood in one of the open hatches in the top of the turret, right next to Major Basara. Both of them had their heads and torsos fully exposed. *All that armor and antitargeting tech*, Harris thought, *and you decide all you need is your helmet. Without even pulling the visor down past your eyes.*

Harris turned his attention briefly from the scene unfolding at the intersection to the status feeds at the crew stations around him. As he'd warned Abnett, things did not go according to plan. The slight delay in transit from the freighter to the consulate was predictable enough. Civilians rushed home from work. Mommies and Daddies risked their lives to retrieve their kids from school or day care or wherever they might be. All things that one might expect people to do the second their whole world goes to hell. Though the tanks could smash their way through most obstructions with their weight and powerful treads, and though they had antigrav capability to float over trouble they could not drive through, chaotic streets could slow anything down.

Yet what concerned Harris—and surprised Abnett—was the arrival of those Archangel ships almost in tandem with the invasion fleet. Their presence in the system was no surprise, but they shouldn't have been able to get through the fleet's cordon around the planet, let alone show up so quickly. The fact that the corvette managed to drop some people onto the roof and get them in past the snipers offered further concerns—could they have comms gear that would defeat the jamming? Had they known this was coming in advance? What if they dropped antitank weapons along with those guys?—but Abnett seemed focused only on the most obvious complications.

"Harris," came Abnett's voice over the comm net, "do we have a location on that corvette?"

If you were inside the tank looking at a status screen, you'd know, dipshit, Harris thought bitterly. "Still over the civilian spaceport, Abnett. She could take to the air and fly high enough that we can't touch her, and we'd still be at point-blank range for her turrets."

"It's only a corvette crew," Abnett countered. "That thing can't have anyone higher than a lieutenant in command. You think anyone that low in rank is gonna have the balls to risk an all-out war?"

"If that ship fires on us, our vessels in orbit will destroy her instantly," added Major Basara. "But unless she threatens us, the fleet cannot take action against a ship of a sovereign state."

"Ain't sayin' they should, major," replied Harris. "My point is, just having her in the atmosphere is a serious problem. Everyone at this card game has a shitty hand."

"These people know they have more to lose than we do," Abnett assured him. "They'll fold."

"Yeah. If they don't flip the goddamn table."

• • •

They only risked taking the elevator down to the second level before shifting to the stairs. Thankfully, they found the lobby unoccupied, without a single soldier in the street directly outside the apartment tower. As Tanner had noted, the force surrounding the consulate did so with a thin line.

Hiding behind the couches, chairs, and plants near the exit, they watched the troops down the street settle into positions. They counted no more than a couple dozen soldiers, though the number of others covering other directions outside their view had to add up to a much greater force.

"Tanner, I don't think I can let you do this." Lieutenant Booker frowned. "It's too crazy."

"Sir, I don't *want* to do it, but we need to resolve this fast," Tanner maintained, speaking as calmly as he could. In truth, he already felt his heart pounding. "Waiting for the ship only gives the bad guys time to get a better grip on the situation. She can't fire on them. We have to step up and do something."

"Yeah, I understand"—Booker nodded—"but we are seriously outnumbered and outgunned."

"We don't have to destroy the enemy, sir," he countered. "We just have to wreck their plans." Vanessa let out a grunt. Tanner found an amused grin on her face. "What?"

"Sun Tzu? That's your secret weapon?"

He let it go without a response. Booker still looked skeptical. "Sir, I'm not looking for any more medals. I just wanna go home alive with everyone else. But we have to get this ball rolling or nobody will make it out of here."

"XO, what about those other marines?" asked Sanjay. "The ones who went after the other snipers?"

Booker gave it a moment's consideration, but shook his head. "They must've seen this mess by now. They'll have to move when they see the opportunity." With that, he turned to Tanner and gave his nod of assent. "Okay. If you're sure you're up to this?"

"You have to stay back and coordinate, sir. Rios and Sanjay would both stand out too much." Tanner took a last look out at the scene. "Helmet's probably gonna be a dead giveaway, too," he muttered, handing that, his jacket, and his rifle off to Vanessa.

In return, she held out the sniper's coat. Grenades still dangled from attachments on the chest. "All warfare is based on deception," she quoted with feigned gravity.

Tanner blinked at her. "Are you enjoying this?"

"Maybe a little. You could, too, if you'd let yourself." Vanessa winked.

126

No witty retort came to mind. Tanner donned the sniper's long coat before he moved toward the exit. Sanjay followed, but split off from him once they were out in the street to take cover behind a large concrete planter. He glanced back into the apartment lobby to see Vanessa and Booker ready themselves. Booker had the jamming unit out on the couch in front of him, ready to deactivate it at the right moment. He hissed instructions to the others, coordinating their selection of targets.

Down the street waited a monstrous engine of destruction and at least a platoon of soldiers. With the deep tan common on Michael, the dark stubble of his hair, and the collar of his coat popped up, Tanner could at least pass as one of the locals at a distant glance. The sniper's coat disguised him from his shoulders down past his hips, but offered nothing like the protection of his combat jacket. The vac suit pants complete with Archangel blood stripes remained a dead giveaway, though. His only real defense lay in the likelihood—on which he bet his life—that all those soldiers had their eyes on their target rather than on one another.

He stepped out of cover and into the street, walking down a sunny lane devoid of life but for the tank and scattered troops up ahead. He glanced this way and that, seeing nothing but empty storefronts and apartment lobbies. Just off to his left was a NorthStar Education testing facility.

"Do what I'm doing. Join the military," Tanner muttered. "You don't have to go infantry or marines. There are more noncombat roles than you can count." His hand fell to the grenades hanging from the jacket. He wished he could spare one of them to throw into that stupid testing facility.

Tanner shifted into a jog, but not a run. Moving too fast or too slow would draw attention. He needed to look enough like a part of the operation that no one would look at him twice.

"God, I wish I could just go to college," he grumbled.

His jog took him past one set of buildings, then the next. He marked the halfway point, and then half of that distance, soon having much the same thoughts that he had about running through a sniper's field of fire. The hull of the tank rose a little more than two meters in front of him, resting fully on its tractor treads rather than floating in the air via its antigrav engine. Tanner reached the tank without obstruction, pointedly not looking left or right, lest he jinx himself and draw the attention of the foot soldiers crouched behind trees and parked vehicles.

He jumped up to get his arms over the hull, throwing both arms over the side. His right hand still held the sniper rifle; his left grabbed hold of a sturdy cleat, allowing him to hoist himself up. The pair of men standing in the tank's open turret hatches didn't seem to notice him until he'd heaved a foot up over the edge. Tanner ducked his head but waved one hand, calling out in Arabic, "*Ustaaz! Ustaaz,*" hoping the Hashemite dialect didn't have some other more accepted way of saying "sir."

The turret was little taller than a single meter. The pair of men in the hatches stood within arm's reach of one another. Tanner got to both feet, glanced up at the two men just as the officer in the hatch on the right did a surprised double take, and then launched himself onto the turret.

The butt of his rifle came into the right-side officer's cheek hard, crushing bone and leaving the man stunned with pain. Tanner immediately shifted left, meaning to slam the middle of his rifle into the head of the other officer, but the Hashemite reacted too quickly and grabbed hold of the rifle with both hands. The struggle lasted only a heartbeat. The officer with the epaulets on his shoulder was no slouch, twisting the rifle hard and wrenching it from Tanner's hands, though he, too, lost control of it as it flew away.

Tanner planted the back of his left fist into the officer's face, knowing he couldn't let up. Once more, though, the major managed to get the better of his young opponent, catching hold of Tanner's ankle with both hands and yanking him off balance.

Tanner landed on his shoulder on top of the turret but kicked back hard while trying to get control of himself. He heard shouting all around him at that point and knew he couldn't let this struggle continue. While he kicked again, slamming his foot into the major's shoulder, Tanner yanked one grenade off his jacket. He twisted the activator, rose to his knees, and hurled it down the major's hatch right between his legs.

The major let out a cry of alarm and pushed himself up out of the hatch, shoving Tanner out of the way as he moved. That sent Tanner rolling right off the turret, flailing for anything he could grab. Thankfully, he managed to wrap his arms around the tank's cannon before he fell off entirely.

On top of the turret, the major could only scream out a useless warning before the grenade went off. Tanner saw smoke and a little flame burst from both open hatches on top of the turret. The man in the other hatch, apparently still reeling from the blow to his cheek, screamed out in agony before falling down inside the hatch. The major shot Tanner an enraged glare and drew the scimitar from his belt.

For a brief instant, Tanner considered abandoning the tank. Then he noticed the trio of soldiers in the street nearby who now had a clear shot at the idiot hanging in front of them.

Okay, Tanner decided. *My plan sucks.*

• • •

Discipline hadn't come naturally to Sanjay. Had he been better about doing what he had to do, when he had to do it, he'd probably have been a better student and a better son. He might've had better things to do with himself after school than fuck around with dumber kids than him, stealing shit and getting into fights and generally making bad choices.

To his credit, Sanjay never chalked those decisions up to the circumstances of his upbringing or the influence of his peers. He'd been smart enough to know right from wrong. Stealing might have helped put food in his stomach, or covered the rent when his mother came up short, or made the difference between clearing the family's monthly debt payments or slipping further down the economic ladder. Yet all of those outcomes came after the crime; Sanjay might have done good things with the money, but he didn't steal to make that happen. He stole because he was frustrated and bored, and in the few times when some adult tried to set him straight, they told him so. He'd known they were right.

That hadn't stopped him from hating them for it. Or from stealing. Or from hating himself.

He only learned discipline during basic training, where he first found people who would neither lower their standards nor buckle for his anger. Unlike school, the military wouldn't put him through their system only to kick him out with a massive bill. He either met their expectations or he kept trying until he did. He didn't like his drill instructors, but he liked the things they taught him.

He liked the man he'd become.

He liked his crew, too. No attitude. No pretension. Half of the crew came from backgrounds as poor as his. The officers never talked down to him, never came up with unnecessary busywork... and never let him slack on the things that actually needed doing. They listened to him when he had something to contribute, as the XO did when Sanjay and Tanner coached him through tactical entry. He had to respect that and had to do his part.

As much as Sanjay wanted to watch what happened as Tanner jogged down the street and then got up on that tank—and as much as he felt like he should go down that street with him—he instead did what he needed to do without complaint. He stayed down behind the concrete planter, kept his rifle up, and looked down its sights at the rifleman hiding behind the parked hovercar near the tank, just like the XO said.

He watched as the men reacted to the activity on the top of the tank. He saw them shift their rifles over, saw his target grab the barrel of another man's gun, and lower it, lest he shoot a friendly target. And then he saw his target change his attitude and raise his weapon.

"Fire," ordered Booker.

Sanjay pulled the trigger, releasing three pulses of lethally hot energy. He watched his target jerk forward, smoke, and crumple to the ground. Agent Rios fired off her rifle in the same instant, bringing down another man. A third soldier threw himself to the ground as his comrades died, but Sanjay didn't watch, let alone train his rifle on the guy. He shifted his attention to a second pair of targets who took cover behind a large tree as Booker had predicted.

Something blew up near the tank. Maybe it was on top of the tank. Maybe it was Tanner, but Sanjay hoped not. He couldn't spare the moment to look. That was Booker's job. Sanjay had to trust him to do that, just like Booker trusted Sanjay to stay focused on his shooting.

Another target went down. More scrambled for cover. From the way they acted, one would think they were being attacked by a whole platoon.

• • •

Everything seemed to be going okay until Harris heard a crunch and a moan from Abnett over the comm net. He had his eyes on the tactical feed from the ships overhead showing the spaceport many kilometers away. "What's that, Abnett?" he asked. "You okay? Abnett?"

Harris turned his attention away from the tactical feed to scan the other view screens, but by then he heard the grenade go off. Abnett screamed over the comm net. Harris saw Basara stand up on top of the turret with smoke billowing from both hatches behind him, raising his sword over his head as if he was about to execute someone hanging from the cannon, while pulse lasers flew all around them.

"Get in there!" Harris demanded over the comm net. He turned to the status screen and jabbed at the icon for the infantry platoon leader. "The command tank! Get that guy on the command tank, now!"

. . .

Tanner had to let go of the cannon with his left arm to swing himself away from the scimitar coming at his head, but that left him with a new problem: hanging on at all. Despite the officer trying to cut him in half from above, there was enough gunfire all around Tanner that the tank was the safest place he could possibly be. He couldn't hang on with one hand. He wanted to wrap his legs around the cannon, but that would only offer easier targets for his enemy. The glove of his vac suit offered a decent grip but not the sort of traction he could get with his bare skin.

Then it all came together in his head.

"Suit clamps!" he yelled out as the major steadied himself for another blow. Tanner grabbed the tank cannon with his free left hand, let go with his right, and repeated, "Suit clamps!"

The magnetizing relays in his vac suit activated all at once. Tanner's grip went from fair to ironclad. He put one knee against the underside of the cannon, all but locking himself to it. He wrenched himself upward through a single punch, using almost every muscle in his body to swing up and plant his fist into the side of the major's knee.

The major fell from the tank with a yelp, brushing against Tanner's shoulder but doing no harm on the way. Tanner scrambled up on top of the cannon and then the turret in mere seconds, turning off his suit clamps as soon as he had decent footing once again. He pulled the pistol from his hip holster and heaved himself through one of the open hatches. The padding of his suit did little to protect his right knee from his painful landing on the cramped, tiny command platform inside the tank.

Unfamiliar with his surroundings, Tanner found himself surprised at how intact the interior was after the grenade blast. Most of the smoke had already cleared, but an uncomfortably warm haze still filled the air. The other officer from up above seemed to have survived, though he now hung halfway out of his hatch platform in a bloody and whimpering mess. Wherever the grenade had landed, it seemed his platform had offered partial protection, but that still left him to suffer countless shrapnel wounds. The other men in the tank, it seemed, suffered worse.

Tanner focused on the hardware rather than the carnage. A seat toward the front and right within the hull offered a bow tie–shaped steering mechanism and an intact view screen. The man in the seat gave no signs of life. Climbing out of the hatch platform as quickly as he could, Tanner picked his way over to the seat and unfastened the man's seat belt.

The driver groaned. Tanner flinched. The driver's chair and helmet had protected him from much of the blast, but as with the officer in the hatch, he had still caught a good deal of ricocheting shrapnel, not to mention the grenade's concussive force. Tanner froze. Some frightened, guilt-ridden reaction leapt up within him as if trying to seize control of his body.

The man hardly had a left arm anymore. Blood flowed from a major gash in his cheek. His eyes were open but didn't track anything.

No time, urged a voice inside of him. *No time for this.* His hesitation only lasted a heartbeat or two, but it felt like much longer. Pushing past his feelings, Tanner unclasped the man's seat belt. With one hand still filled with his pistol, Tanner awkwardly grabbed the driver's shoulders and pulled. If the driver felt anything, he gave little more reaction than a low groan. Then a forceful impact slammed Tanner against the side of the compartment as someone tackled him from behind.

He heard an enraged, frightening voice yell out a command he couldn't understand. Hands struck at his side and his chest. Anguished demands in Arabic rang in Tanner's ears as he struggled to turn and face his attacker. Tanner bashed and kicked back, trying to find leverage against a plainly much larger opponent.

The break came when Tanner's elbow came against the drive controls. He braced himself against them and pushed back on his opponent, trying to get room to use the gun in his other hand, and felt the tank lurch forward. His assailant lost his balance with the vehicle's sudden motion, stepping back far enough to give Tanner the opening he needed.

A blind man could have made the shot, but he wouldn't have seen the tank crewman's young face. In a single instant, Tanner's laser pistol cut a vertical line down through his opponent's chest. Tanner saw his eyes go wide and his mouth open in a silent scream. He fell backward, almost sitting down on the deck before he collapsed.

He looked to be Tanner's age. Maybe a little younger. Bigger, more muscular, but clearly trying to grow in a beard that wouldn't come fast enough. His last words and actions had been in defense of a comrade, maybe a friend. Tanner registered all of it as the youth fell over, but once again, he had no time to process such thoughts. He turned back to the driver's seat.

Tanner pushed forward on the bow tie–shaped controls. Again, the tank lurched forward. "Good enough," he grunted, shoved the pistol back into his holster, and then pulled back hard on the controls. He bent at the knees in time to keep himself up as the tank revved into reverse. On the view screen before him, he saw vindication of his actions as the consulate fell farther and farther away.

Then he saw the consequences of those actions as the tank off to the left of the *T* intersection rose in the air through its antigrav engines and swung around in pursuit.

Tanner's eyes flashed from one view screen to the next. He tried to hold the controls steady, but in truth, he knew he didn't have to drive the tank far, or well. He half expected that he'd have to abandon the tank where it sat once he'd neutralized the crew, which he'd predicted to Booker in the first place. The goal was chaos and disruption, not a stand-up fight. Still, moving the tank away from the consulate obviously constituted a positive outcome.

Escape from pursuit clearly wouldn't happen. His few options flashed quickly through his mind: back, left, or right. He never considered stopping or charging forward. Tanner looked at the view screens again and spotted the NorthStar Education building off to his left.

"Fuck it," Tanner growled, knowing a once-in-a-lifetime opportunity when he saw one. He turned the tank hard and watched as the office rapidly grew larger on his rear view screen. The impact shook the whole tank as it demolished everything in its path, rolling backward through the office with the cacophony of shattering concrete, glass, and steel against the armor filling the compartment until Tanner lost his footing. His hand slipped from the controls as he tried to steady himself, bringing the vehicle to a halt.

The view screen showed that the tank was fully embedded within the building. Tanner's eyes made one last sweep of the compartment for unrecognized dangers. To his left, at a station similar to the driver's, sat another dead man. On the station's targeting screen, Tanner saw the pursuing tank pull up directly outside, still facing down the street but with its turret now turning toward Tanner's tank.

He rushed to the control station. He didn't understand even half of the labels, but the enemy tank sat right in front of his cannon. For all the complexity of modern military technology, everyone knew what a big red trigger on a control stick did.

• • •

Sanjay's tunnel vision held out only so long. He couldn't ignore a tank backing up at high speed in his direction. Much like the soldiers down at the end of the street, Sanjay instinctively held fire as the vehicle got rolling. "Shit, what's happening?" Sanjay yelled out.

Then the other tank, hovering rather than rolling, whipped around from the corner up to the left and gave pursuit. The fleeing tank only held its course for a couple dozen meters before making a hard left as it continued backward, crashing into the NorthStar Education building up across the street from Sanjay's position.

"Tanner must be at the wheel!" Vanessa called back. She shifted her rifle into full automatic fire, sending rapid blasts down the street to suppress the remaining infantry.

"How do you know?"

"Because he can't drive for shit! Booker, I'd say the enemy is pretty distracted!"

Though he'd taken part in the shooting, the XO focused more on suppressive fire and spotting for his comrades rather than aiming for specific individuals. Heeding Vanessa's advice, Booker turned from the firefight to the jammer pack sitting behind the planter that served as his cover. He deactivated the device and immediately sent out a signal over his holocom. "*Joan of Arc*, this is—"

A loud hum split the air as the tank half-buried in the demolished office fired its main gun. The wide red particle beam struck the other tank across its rear flank with a sustained blast that burned through both armor and engine. The explosion shattered windows up and down the block.

• • •

"Fucking Christ!" exclaimed Harris. His own tank had barely advanced into the intersection when the explosion occurred, blanketing the area with smoke and debris. His tank's scanners worked to compensate for the mess, but then the destroyed vehicle's chaff systems began to spontaneously ignite and cause further problems.

"Why are we stopping?" he demanded of the tank's Hashemite commander. "Get in there! We've got to get after them!"

"You see what just happened?" the commander retorted, his accent thick but still understandable. "I am not rushing in blind!"

"So go in from the flank!" Harris countered. "You're a tank driver, do you not know how to do this shit?" He knew the answer before he finished asking: of course the other guy had thought of that already.

"I *am* the commander, yes, and *you* are the guest here. What of our mission?"

"*Fuck* the consulate. We can't keep that place surrounded now. The whole mission's fucked. And—dammit, that ship is moving," Harris said, pointing to the overhead tactical map. "We've lost the consulate. We can at least get those fuckers there!"

• • •

Time to quit while I'm ahead. Tanner left the weapons station to climb into the turret. He found the hatch impossible to open, and then cursed himself for an idiot. He'd all but buried the tank in the collapsing floors above. The hatch could have a half ton of debris sitting on top of it. He needed another way out.

Tanner crouched down on the platform so he could read the internal view screens again. The front of the hull looked clear, he realized, and he might find an overhead hatch or two there. He slipped one foot off the platform, then the other, and heard someone groan, "Oh God, help me."

He froze. *That's English.*

The man lay right in front of him, having fallen from the other turret hatch platform onto the deck in a wounded sprawl. He sounded nothing like a Hashemite with that accent. The wounded man fought to pull off his helmet.

One could surely find blond men and English speakers in Hashem. Tanner took such diversity for a given. Yet the incongruity of this man in this tank remained. Further, Tanner realized, he wore no unit patch nor rank insignia.

Tanner pulled off the fallen man's left glove and found a sturdy, high-quality holocom on his wrist. "Wait," the man tried to protest, but his words fell on deaf ears. Tanner tore the device from the man's arm, then rushed for the escape hatch at the front of the vehicle.

Behind him, Abnett coughed once and slumped back onto the deck. "Aw shit."

• • •

Dust and debris fell from the hatch as it popped open. Tanner climbed out as fast as he could. If the soldiers at the end of the street regrouped and made a quick advance, or if the other tank followed the first, he knew he'd never make it out of the wrecked building.

To his relief, he found his comrades hurriedly picking their way through the wreckage. "Tanner, let's go!" Sanjay shouted. "We gotta move!"

Tanner rolled off the tank's hull, falling and jabbing himself with more debris for his trouble, but he pushed past the pain and rose to his feet. "Where are we going?"

"Out the back," Vanessa said, gesturing to the hallway that still stood—more or less—behind him. "You got the front door open, seems like a waste not to take advantage. What are you holding?"

"Holocom from an officer in the tank. He didn't look like a Hashemite. I figured it might be important . . . ?"

Vanessa came to a halt, allowing Booker and Sanjay to overtake and pass them. She snatched the holocom from Tanner and looked at it with wide eyes. Then she shoved it down a pocket of her long coat and grabbed his arm. "Come on," she urged. "We're on our own."

"The ship . . . ?" Tanner asked as he followed.

"Still needs a distraction!" called Booker. "Those assholes are pursuing, and that's what we need them to do! Let's go, Malone!"

He needed no further encouragement. Tanner followed Vanessa through the wreckage to the hallway. The glass exit doors were shattered, either from the impact the tank made on the whole building or from Sanjay or Booker blasting their way out. Regardless, he saw Vanessa take a hard left turn as she made it onto the street outside. He picked up the pace in order to keep up, made it outside, and pivoted on his right foot to follow.

His knee bent but seemed intent on going forward rather than turning. He felt something pop inside his leg as he collapsed on the sidewalk. Tanner tried to ignore the pain and pick himself up while leaning on his left leg, but taking the weight off his injured knee didn't help him rise.

A soldier wheeled around the corner into the doorway, his rifle up and ready to fire. Another soldier rounded the corner while staying low, holding a kneeling position. It all seemed to happen in slow motion. Less than ten meters separated Tanner from their guns.

He pushed up from the concrete with his hands, wanting to roll away, but someone's foot shoved him back down to the ground again. He heard the coughing sound of a pulse rifle on rapid fire over his head and saw the soldiers fall under the barrage of energy blasts.

Vanessa roughly rolled Tanner onto his back, snatched the last grenade off his jacket, and hurled it down the hallway. He heard someone shout as it landed. The boom of the grenade and its flash of fire and smoke left screams in its wake.

"Are you hit?" she barked.

"It's my knee," he said, trying to rise once more. He found himself capable of at least sitting upright. "I'm not hit, but I fucked up my knee."

She didn't listen for further details. Vanessa simply shoved the rifle into one of his hands, then grabbed his arms at the wrists and pulled. Before Tanner knew it, she had him over her shoulder in a fireman's carry.

Down the street he saw Booker and Sanjay pause in their flight. Given Vanessa's quick movements and his awkward position, he couldn't track much; as soon as she turned, he lost sight of his shipmates. Vanessa let out a determined growl as she launched herself into a run, naturally moving slower than before but surprising Tanner with her pace just the same.

The rifle in his hands bumped once against the concrete before he shifted his grip to keep it up. He looked back the way they came and saw movement, but by then more pulse rifle blasts flew down the street as Booker provided covering fire.

"Get him down here!" Booker called as Vanessa caught up. "I'll carry him."

"No, I've got this," Vanessa said. "Stick to the plan. Sanjay needs to get us a vehicle, and you've gotta lead. I'm okay. He's not heavy."

"Christ, you gotta be kidding me," Tanner grumbled, feeling useless.

"What?" Vanessa huffed. "Got a problem being rescued by a girl?"

"Yeah," Tanner shot back, "of all the shit that's gone wrong today, *that's* what I'm upset about!"

"Is he being sarcastic?" she asked one of his shipmates. He couldn't tell which. His head still hung entirely in the wrong direction to follow the conversation.

"Most of the time, seems like," answered Sanjay.

"Stow it! Sanjay, move!" ordered Booker.

Tanner tried to keep up with what was going on, but Vanessa turned and jostled too much. His upside-down view alternated between Sanjay hauling ass down the street, Booker calling out turns and working to keep the group together while he ran, random views of seemingly empty buildings and parked vehicles, and the tank that appeared at the far end of the street behind them.

Though he'd never given it serious thought, Tanner always assumed a tank's turret wouldn't turn so fast. "Tank!" he called out. "Tank behind us—"

The vehicle's weapons drowned out the rest of his words. Its main cannon let loose with a blinding red beam that demolished a parked hovertruck nearby. Vanessa wobbled as she ran but never ceased in her flight. Tanner heard the ricochets of many bullets against all manner of unintended targets as the antipersonnel guns on top of the turret chased them out of the street and into a small alley.

"Sanjay, double back!" called Booker. Vanessa came to a halt. Tanner watched as his fellow crewman reversed his course through the alley, but Booker continued through. "We'll fake them out," Tanner heard Booker explain as he ran to the far end of the alley.

Sanjay rushed past Vanessa and Tanner. Booker made it to the opposite end of the alley, tore a grenade from his jacket, and hurled it into the street. Tanner heard the loud shriek and magnesium pops of the chaff grenade while Booker ran back up.

"How are you doing, Malone?" Vanessa asked.

"Holding it together. Is this gonna work?"

Something exploded in the next street over as if in answer. Tanner heard more roaring gunfire and ricochets, this time followed up by a second and third blast of the tank's particle beam cannon. He saw the monstrous vehicle rush down the street, knocking aside debris as it shot past the alleyway. With the chaff grenade inhibiting sensors, the tank commander clearly preferred hot pursuit over standing off and waiting for his view to clear.

"Negative, captain, you've *gotta* make the consulate pickup," Tanner heard Booker say nearby. He craned his head around to find the breathless officer leaning against a wall. A holo screen floated beside Booker, but the lieutenant had his eyes on activity in the street—presumably Sanjay. Tanner couldn't hear Kelly's response, but he saw Booker argue emphatically, "Captain, the situation overhead is still the same! If they see you open up on that tank, you'll be a target for the ships in orbit! We're drawing them off, let us worry about evasion."

"Has he been on with the ship this whole time?" Tanner asked.

"Yes. Officers gotta multitask," said Vanessa. "C'mon, Malone, keep up."

"Still glad you followed us into that building?"

"Sure." Vanessa grinned, her breath heavy but still holding up. "I'm a spy, Malone. All I have to do is drop you and find someplace to hide for a day or two and then pretend I'm a native. You're the ones in trouble here, not me."

"Good to know," Tanner said to the concrete as he dangled from her shoulders.

"Move!" Booker called out. "That silver rover there, go!"

Vanessa took off, jostling Tanner over her shoulders until she got out onto the street again and came to the parked vehicle. She crouched and helped Tanner off her back. He managed to get into the backseat of the rover all on his own, growling at the pain in his right knee while hauling himself inside. He let his bad leg lay along the bench-style backseat. Tanner saw neither blood nor an obvious misalignment at his knee, but the pain told of a serious problem.

He pushed himself back along the seat, saving Vanessa from having to crawl on top of him as she followed inside. The door swung down behind her. Tanner glanced over to find Booker in the shotgun seat. Sanjay threw the vehicle into motion before the doors sealed shut.

"Mark VI," Vanessa observed. "Good call. You've got fast hands."

"Anyone want a vehicle security system?" Sanjay asked as he dropped a dislodged hunk of electronics hardware over his shoulder.

"Always appreciated your versatility, Sanjay," grunted Booker. He pointed out toward one corner, directing Sanjay away from the last known position of the pursuing tank. "*Joan of Arc*, this is Booker," he said into his holocom. "We have transportation and are moving away from the consulate."

"Let me look at your knee," said Vanessa. She produced a knife from one pocket and quickly sliced a long line up the leg of Tanner's vac suit with sure hands. The expression on her face didn't change as she examined his injury. "I don't think it's broken. Not a lot of swelling yet, but it's only been a couple minutes," she noted. "I think I can fix this here. You've got a corrective bandage in your pack. You'll be sore but mobile."

• • •

"Damn, they're gone," Harris fumed. His eyes swept the internal displays for any sign of his quarry but found nothing. Though he held out little hope, he activated the sound analyzer. A quick nod to his driver brought the vehicle to a halt while the computer listened.

The sullen Hashemite officer who technically commanded the tank sat at his station with his arms folded across his chest. He shot Harris another glare as the foreigner continued to give orders but didn't raise serious objections. The tank crew knew they'd been loaned to NorthStar for this. They had to play along until the operation was over . . . not that it seemed it'd be going on much longer.

"We have a vehicle moving one street over," announced one of the tank crew.

"Get on it," Harris replied.

"Mr. Harris," said the tank commander, "your friend is alive." He held out his holocom toward Harris and swiped one finger across the display in order to share the transmission. The computers took care of the rest.

"Abnett, you okay?" Harris asked.

"He's got my holocom," came the weak, coughing reply. "Fucking bastard tore off my holocom when he bailed out."

"Aw, son of a bitch." Harris didn't need Abnett to explain the rest—the moron probably had any number of sensitive files on his personal holocom, and while it had to be encrypted, no such security was foolproof. Harris looked up once more at the tactical screens and scanner feeds. The computer identified the fleeing vehicle as a rover through its sound profile. It was the only moving vehicle within a kilometer. "Go!" Harris shouted. "Get that rover now!"

. . .

Tanner let out a loud growl as the rover hit a bump, but he bit down on his urge to make more noise than that. Still sitting sideways on the bench seat, Tanner watched the thick green corrective bandage around his knee ripple and constrict. A small strip of circuits down one side of the bandage directed the application of various drugs, electrical shocks, and pressure to cause a rapid realignment under the skin. Though the drugs included a couple of painkillers, Tanner still found the process exceptionally unpleasant.

"Will he be able to run?" Booker asked from the front seat.

"More or less," Vanessa answered, watching the little holographic display projected by the bandage's circuits. "Probably have a limp until he sees a doctor."

Gritting his teeth, Tanner huffed, "Hooray for modern medicine."

"Where are we going?" asked Sanjay from the front seat. He drove like a madman through streets lined mostly with houses and lower buildings than the neighborhood they'd just escaped.

"Away from here," said Booker.

"Yeah, but—"

"We're going the right way. The spaceport is only a few dozen kilometers out. If we're lucky, we can get there before *Argent* lifts off and hitch a ride."

"Won't there be bad guys around the spaceport?" Sanjay pointed out.

"Captain said there's fighting underway, yeah, but I don't know where we might find another ride home. We'll see when we get there. Might have to shoot our way through."

"This your plan all along, lieutenant?" asked Vanessa.

"Pretty much. I'm open to suggestions, if you have a better idea."

"No, it's good," she replied. She focused most of her attention on her patient.

"What?" Tanner scowled.

"I'm sorry?" she asked.

"Why are you looking at me like that?"

Vanessa hesitated but then seemed to disregard her concerns. She tilted her head toward his injured knee. "I guess it's nice to see you're a mere mortal like the rest of us after all."

Tanner opened his mouth for an exasperated reply but never got it out. A sudden explosion outside the rover interrupted him. It lifted the rover several inches off the ground on one corner, peppering the windows and hull with debris.

"Aw fuck, that tank is back!" shouted Sanjay. He put the rover through a hard right turn and pushed the accelerator to the floor, then wrenched the vehicle to the left again as soon as he rounded the corner. "Shit!" he yelled out, weaving left and right to avoid the fleeing civilians he found in his path.

Tanner sat up and watched as the locals scattered. His eyes swept the truck for his rifle, but Vanessa had already grabbed it. All he found within reach was the hunk of vehicle security circuitry that Sanjay had slagged and his combat jacket. Tanner snatched the jacket and sat up to throw it over his shoulders. The jammer that Booker had confiscated from the sniper and a few other bits of gear fell from within one pocket to clatter to the floor by his seat.

Vanessa leaned over Tanner and fired his rifle, blasting through the rear window at something behind them.

"What good will that do?" he asked. "You won't make a dent."

"Depends on how experienced the tankers are," Vanessa explained as the vehicle swerved hard, breaking her line of fire. "Most people flinch when someone shoots at them. And it makes me feel better."

Tanner couldn't fault her for that. *I'd rather shoot back than just sit here, too.*

Sanjay drove on, then suddenly put the rover through a hard turn punctuated by another particle beam blast. "Shit, there's the other one!" he yelled. Tanner caught a glimpse of it as they rolled past the new pursuer emerging from another side street.

"They could probably overtake us if they wanted," noted Vanessa. "Why haven't they?"

As if in answer to her question, one of the hovering tanks shot forward in a sudden burst of speed. It tilted forward to allow the main gun to dip low enough for a decent shot, but all that the effort produced was a short, smoking trench dug through the middle of the street. Recognizing the move as an attempt to ram more than a try for a point-blank shot, Sanjay braked and spun hard. Though the tank's antigrav systems and computer-assisted controls made for excellent handling, its driver was not quite up to the task; the hovering tank turned but couldn't slow down quickly enough to avoid crashing into a two-story house nearby.

The lost momentum left the rover open for a shot from the other tank. Once more, Sanjay acted just in time, slamming down on the accelerator, racing past the tank, and swerving to evade the blast from the twin antipersonnel guns atop its turret. Before the tank could follow, Sanjay rolled between a pair of houses and through their backyards. Environmental control pylons and lawn furniture flew everywhere as the rover battered away any small object in its path. Soon, Sanjay had the vehicle back out onto a clear street but knew their pursuers would catch up fast.

"XO, how many more chaff grenades have you got?" Sanjay asked.

"I'm fresh out."

"Shit. Hold on," Sanjay warned, putting the rover through further sharp weaving just before another particle beam shot past them. Again, he made a hard turn at the nearest corner. "Y'know, if they use the missiles on those things, we're fucked."

"I can't believe they haven't tagged us already," said Vanessa.

"Me neither," confessed Sanjay. "Must be on manual targeting."

"Sanjay, just pretend like you're running from the police," suggested Tanner.

"Got a lot of experience with that, Malone?"

"I will after I get my hands on the guy who decided not to let us evacuate this rock early."

"You and me both. XO, am I going the right way anymore?"

"I don't know, I'm trying to track too many things. Tanner! You up to handling comms for us? I've got to navigate."

"Sure," Tanner grunted. He fired up the communications interface on the holocom on his wrist. With a few swipes of his fingers, he joined a channel with their ship. "*Joan of Arc*, this is Malone, do you read?"

"We've got you, Malone," came Stan's voice. "We're coming in over the consulate for a rooftop pickup now. No hostiles in sight. Marines all back inside. Stand by."

Tanner glanced up as Vanessa fired his rifle out the back again. *Nope. No hostiles where you are. All the hostility is focused on us.*

• • •

"That invasion force is about to become the least of your problems, kid," Casey snarled. Despite being fully preoccupied by the stresses of their own tasks, several of the bridge crew visibly cringed. The captain had a singularly intimidating voice. Though only a few specific officers on the ship knew the truth about him, no one who'd met the man doubted that he was fully capable of murder.

The young Hashemite officer on Casey's screen quickly came to much the same conclusion, but he at least didn't have to share space on a ship with him. "Captain," said the spaceport officer in flawless English, "we have several battles within the spaceport right now! Surely you can see this! The enemy had at least one of their ships already here, maybe more. If I open the checkpoints between your ship and your assembled passengers, they will be exposed to great danger. If you will only wait for us to secure the spaceport, we can—"

"You and I both know you can't hold this port," interrupted Casey. "You think the enemy would attack here without enough people to take the place? Look at your map, for fuck's sake! You have too much territory to hold and not enough troops to do it."

His assessment wasn't wrong. An overhead map of the space-port floated near Casey with markers for known firefights and security threats. As with most similar facilities on developed worlds, the spaceport sprawled across several square kilometers. Though much of the layout allowed for wide-open spaces for ships the size of *Argent* and larger vessels, it also made for numerous internal choke points.

Only two such points concerned Casey. They lay between the landing zone occupied by *Argent* and the designated assembly area for the majority of Archangel's civilians. Things at that site had gone swimmingly up until now. The consulate had had foreign service people on-site around the clock for the last few weeks to make sure someone would be there to oversee collection and take care of head counts and other such crowd control, and apparently they'd done a damn good job. Now the only problem lay in getting those refugees from point A to point B.

Casey bristled at the thought of putting his life on the line for the sake of a couple thousand tourists, expats, and other worthless fucks from Archangel. The thought of not even pulling off the job had him ready to strangle someone.

"I have armed security teams of my own," Casey growled. "Get your guys out of their way and let them retrieve the civilians them-selves, and we won't have any problems. Maybe my guys will take out a few of those attacking assholes along the way. But, buddy, if you don't get this shit moving, I will open fire on this space-port myself. This boat might not be a military ship, but I goddamn guarantee you I have more than enough firepower to waste that fucking control tower you're sitting in."

"You're insane," the officer protested. "You would never make it off-world!"

"Who's gonna stop me? All those balls of fire raining from the sky are the remains of your local defense forces, kid! And it won't make any difference to *you* if I make it off-world or not when your ashes are floating around the spaceport!"

The officer swallowed hard. He looked away from his screen, probably hoping to get someone senior to him to take over this issue, but found no such help available. "Captain, you will be sending your people through the shooting! Many will be hurt!"

"That's my problem, not yours," Casey pressed. "You let me decide on acceptable losses. Just unlock those checkpoints and get your people out of my way."

"I cannot—"

"Goddammit, have it your way. Tactical!" he called out. "Target the control tower!"

"Sir?" stammered the man at the fire control station across from Casey's command chair. "We can't fire on a civilian—"

"Mother*fucker!*" Casey roared. He rose from his seat to storm over to the tactical station a few meters away. The crewman at the station stood as he saw the captain approach, clearly unsure what he would do about his predicament. Casey had not a shred of doubt, which anyone could recognize in his voice. "You will follow orders, or I will pitch you off this bridge with my bare hands!"

"But, sir, that's a civilian—"

"You're relieved!"

"But I—"

Casey's fist rammed straight up into the man's gut, leaving him crumpled on the floor in a winded, helpless heap. He then shoved the fallen man out of his way and keyed in the commands to assume full weapons control. His eyes swept the bridge.

Every officer stared back at him. Some had the visors of their helmets down, but others did not. Casey saw nothing but silent surprise. No one stepped up to challenge him, let alone drew a weapon or tried to defend their fallen shipmate. Not the ops officer, nor the comms officer, nor the pair of armed security specialists at the bridge entry hatch. No one.

He took for granted that many of these people had military experience. At the very least, they'd all been vetted by Archangel Intelligence for service on the ship. A couple of them probably had training and experience in combat. But none of them stopped him. He didn't see loyalty, to be sure, but he saw an understanding of the situation.

He was the captain of a ship in the middle of a crisis. He had to be obeyed.

With a few commands on his holocom, Casey routed the spaceport control comms screen to the weapons station. "Okay, asshole, I'm done discussing this." His hands turned to the weapons controls. "That little buzz you're probably hearing is the sound of your tower sensors realizing they've been targeted."

"Stop!" blurted out the control officer. In the background, several people began to cry out in alarm as they heard precisely the warning buzz Casey described. "All right! We will open the checkpoints! Have your security team open a communications relay on this channel," he instructed hurriedly, sending along computer commands. "Just cancel your targeting solution!"

Casey's eyes narrowed. Clearly the port officer was worried about keeping his people at their stations. Between all the security feeds and their bird's-eye view of the spaceport, they probably already knew everything was going to hell. Casey revoked his targeting commands, turning *Argent*'s small turrets away from the tower. In truth, he could have targeted and destroyed the tower without using active signals to aim his weapons, but the technique served as a meaningful shot across the bow.

"Thank you." His gravelly voice dropped a few notches. "You'll hear from my team. *Argent* out." Then his eyes swept the bridge again. "Anyone else gonna have a problem following orders? No? Then someone get this dick off my bridge. I'll handle tactical myself."

One of the security guards came over to haul the fallen officer off his knees and off the bridge, but Casey paid it no mind. He patched himself into the tactical comms net and signaled Hawkins. "Landing team, bridge," he said. "We're dropping the gangway now. Control and I have come to an understanding. I'm sending you a comms channel for their security teams. Be advised, you might have to shoot a few fuckers to get this job done. I recommend extreme prejudice."

"Acknowledged," came the response. "We're on our way."

Casey glanced up at the gangway camera as men and women in combat jackets and helmets rushed out with Hawkins in charge.

He turned his attention to other matters. The tactical station involved more than weapons control. He tied in to numerous comms channels and looked over the display showing the presence of ships overhead. Casey set to immersing himself in the data.

Then he heard the voice.

"*Argent*, this is *Joan of Arc*'s landing party!" said the voice over the local ground comms net. "We are inbound to your location with tanks in pursuit! We can't get back to our ship, so we need to extract with you! Do you copy?"

"We read you, landing party," responded a woman not four meters away from Casey on *Argent*'s bridge. "What's your location?"

Casey's eyes widened as he heard the voice relay a frantic, shaking answer. He heard something explode in the background. He saw the comms officer turn to him with a questioning look. Casey merely nodded to her.

He would recognize that voice for the rest of his life.

Coming to this ship, he thought with a mix of awe and fury. *He's coming to my goddamn ship again.*

His eyes flicked around the compartment, seeing only a bridge crew of mostly strangers. *No. Not my ship. Not yet, anyway. Maybe never. I don't have their loyalty. Might never have it.* Regardless of the lack of objection to the way he'd ejected his tactical officer, he couldn't expect these people to help him deal with this . . . and the moment Hawkins knew that fucking kid was on the ship, he'd lock the "captain" in his own quarters for the duration of the trip.

But Hawkins didn't know about this yet. He had too much to deal with. And it wasn't like the kid identified himself to the ship's comms officer.

Trembling from shoulder to fist, Casey looked over the tactical station and weighed his options. *Argent* had launched several overhead monitor drones upon landing in the spaceport to maintain a bird's-eye view of the area. He watched as the drones used info from the comms officer to locate the landing party and their pursuers.

For the first time in his life, Casey found his survival instincts outweighed by an even greater need.

· · ·

"Take a breath or three if you need it, Ordoñez," counseled Lieutenant Kelly. On the canopy screens, she saw a beautiful skyline contrasted with the rain of debris from the violence in Scheherazade's inner orbit. Her personal display screens, however, showed *Joan of Arc*'s position as she hovered at a level just above the consulate's rooftop. Another of the holographic displays floating in front of her relayed the feed from the corvette's main cannon as the gunner's mate programmed in a short, sustained blast on a tight plane.

"I've got this, ma'am," Ordoñez replied over the ship's comms net. "Just a couple more seconds to confirm."

"If you have any doubts, say so. Don't feel like you have to go along with this just because I suggested it. This isn't a 'whatever the captain wants' kind of thing."

"No, no, no, ma'am, it's fine. I can do it. This is a great plan." She paused. "I've always wanted to do something like this."

"You're sharing too much again, Ordoñez."

"Can't talk now, ma'am. Aiming a big gun." Again she paused. "Hey, if I fuck this up, they're gonna court martial *both* of us, right? I mean, it's not just gonna be me?"

Kelly groaned but didn't answer. Her eyes flicked over toward the two men who shared the bridge with her. Though he'd relinquished much of his manual control to the ship's computers for this, Chief Romita still had plenty to do in keeping *Joan of Arc* steady. With the astrogation table now converted to display tactical info, Stan had his back to the captain. "Stan? How are we doing?" she asked.

"No trouble in sight for us. I'm worried about our guys on the ground. I keep hearing the blasts over the net," he explained, tapping his helmet at his ear.

"We'll get 'em," Kelly assured him. "First things first."

"Captain," spoke up Ordoñez on the comm net, "I'm ready to go."

"Fire at will, guns."

The bright-red blast from *Joan of Arc*'s chin-mounted main cannon lasted only two seconds as it swept from left to right across the roof of the consulate, disintegrating concrete, steel, and everything else it touched. With most of the material reduced to dust, there was little debris, and that which fell inside the building landed in small bits of rubble. Simple civilian buildings were rarely built to hold up to the sort of punishment dished out by starship weaponry. The consulate now stood with a gap of several meters cut through the center of its roof.

"Consulate, we have our rooftop opening," Kelly announced over the external comms net. She gave Romita a single nod. The chief spun *Joan of Arc* 180 degrees around. "We're pulling clear. Your turn."

"Acknowledged, *Joan of Arc*," answered Lieutenant Adams. "Just a second."

Kelly watched the rearview video feed. Within seconds, a small explosion inside the consulate blasted a hole through the exterior wall in line with the gap in its roof. Large blocks of masonry crashed down to the street below. *Joan of Arc*'s cameras filtered out the dust to reveal a pair of marines, who quickly kicked and shoved some remaining debris out of the way to clear the path.

"Looks good, lieutenant. Get everyone up to the stairwells. We're backing in with the ramp now." Again, she gave Romita only a slight gesture to get the process going.

Kelly thought at first that her crew or the consulate staff would object to her plan. Given the situation in the immediate area, though, a ground-level pickup was too risky. Taking everyone out through the roof meant bringing people up one by one through the rooftop access hatch, a slow process that would still leave people exposed in at least 180 degrees. Yet by blasting off the roof and creating a single hole, *Joan of Arc* could hover in backward with her ramp extended, granting a much wider and flatter pathway for her passengers while offering protection from—

"Sniper!" cried out one of the marines.

Kelly saw both men jerk away from the hole to hide behind the consulate's remaining walls. She couldn't tell if one of them was hurt or not, but she saw the small burst of concrete dust as the sniper's second bullet hit.

Then, just as she opened her mouth, she saw and heard the wide red beam of *Joan of Arc*'s main cannon as it blasted through the corner of a nearby apartment building, leaving a smoldering black hole three meters tall. "Guns?" Kelly blinked.

"Sorry, ma'am!" Ordoñez replied. "Um. Reflex, ma'am! Think I got him, though!"

The captain bit back her immediate reply. She looked over to the tactical table, expecting to discover missiles or targeting signals raining down on her from above, but saw nothing other than Stan's shocked expression. Kelly took a quick breath, swallowed hard, and nodded. "Next time, wait for my command, guns," she said in a deliberately calm voice.

"Yes, ma'am. Aye, aye, ma'am."

Kelly looked to the canopy display again at the destruction wrought by her main gun. Ordoñez likely blasted away someone's whole apartment with that one shot—and cut straight through the next building in line with it across the street, and probably well into whatever lay beyond. The captain sighed. "Carry on."

"You know what they say." Chief Romita chuckled without taking his eyes or hands off the controls. "If you can pass the psych eval, you're not qualified to be a gunner's mate."

• • •

If nothing else, the chase through the city's streets distracted Tanner from the pain in his leg.

"Sanjay, *Argent* says we're heading straight into a neighborhood firefight," he warned. "We've gotta veer left or right at the next corner to avoid it."

Another building façade exploded as the rover hit the corner, sending debris flying out at the vehicle and directly into its path. Rather than slow down or swerve, Sanjay plowed straight through the cloud of dust and smoke, ignoring the heavy thumps of broken masonry and other rubble against the rover. Within a second, he had full visibility again, minus the cracked windows and thin coating of dust now clinging to the windshield.

"Straight ahead?" asked Sanjay. He pointed at the oncoming intersection, where everyone could clearly see the flashes of laser fire that darted between a pair of buildings. Black smoke wafted up from several windows, along with the fires from burning vehicles that lined the street. "Up there?"

"Yes!"

"Good!" Sanjay pressed down harder on the accelerator. Another particle beam flashed by, cutting through a parked car to leave it a charred wreck.

"Aw Christ," grunted Vanessa. Like Booker, she promptly ducked as low as she could and covered her head while the rover blew straight through the exchange of gunfire. Lasers and bullets alike struck from both sides, several of them shattering windows as they passed straight through, and a few others piercing the rover's hull and tearing through upholstery.

Like the rush through the cloud of debris, the moment lasted only a few rapid heartbeats. Tanner heard Vanessa yelp and thought he heard much the same from Booker. He, too, rode out the barrage with his arms reflexively thrown up around his head, but despite his fear Tanner managed to recognize the end to the small arms fire against the rover. He propped his head up and looked out the back.

Though the rover's approach had been a complete surprise, the pursuing tanks didn't enjoy the same advantage. Reacting mostly out of reflex, belligerents on both sides of the street turned their guns on the tanks. Tanner saw what had made such a mess of the parked vehicles and the buildings; from one end of the street, a heavy pulse laser opened up on the tank with rapid-fire bursts. Someone on the opposite side fired off a small missile. Small-arms fire hit the tank from both directions.

Tanner let out a shout of approval as the tank tilted heavily forward, its nose scraping deep into the concrete of the street. The resultant mess of dust and debris blocked the rest of his view. Such damage might not destroy the tank, but any disruption or delay of its pursuit was a good thing.

He turned his attention to Vanessa, who groaned as she shifted and sat up in the leg space between the front and back seats. "You okay?"

"Fine. Just cut myself on some piece of the window." She looked at the blood dripping from her hand. "I'm fine."

"XO? You okay?"

"Yeah," gasped Booker. "Combat jacket stopped it."

"You sure?" Tanner asked. He turned Vanessa's wrist to check her wound but found nothing particularly life-threatening. Given two or three minutes, he could easily clean it out and apply sealing gel or at least a bandage. His eyes glanced back up to the front seats.

"I'm good," said Booker. Tanner couldn't see his face, but when the XO turned his head he could see the black scoring left by the laser deflected by his helmet. The young crewman swallowed hard and tried not to think too much about it. Had that blast hit at a different angle, it likely would have gone straight through metal, bone, and brain.

"Well, that bought us a little bit more space," said Tanner.

"Won't last long," grunted Booker. "Good job, though, Sanjay." He paused. "Don't do that again."

"No, sir," agreed Sanjay. "No argument."

"Landing party, this is *Argent*," said the voice on Tanner's holo-com. "We have firefights all along the perimeter of the spaceport and within the interior. We're loading up passengers as we speak, but we'll hold the door for you. I've laid out a path for you to follow into the spaceport. Sending now."

Tanner saw the small navigational icon appear on the screen projected by his holocom. He passed a finger through it to route it to the team's holocom net, then specified it to open for Sanjay. At the front of the rover, a new holographic screen winked into existence to provide Sanjay with an overhead map and a three-dimensional image to show him what to expect from his own ground-side perspective. "Acknowledged, *Argent*," Tanner said. "Directions received."

"Either one of those gates could be a live-fire zone or they could be secured by one side or another by the time you get here," added *Argent*'s comms officer. "No guarantees. Overwatch drone says you still have tanks in pursuit. You need to open up some space between you."

"Didn't think they'd give up," Tanner muttered.

"Landing party, this is *Joan of Arc*," spoke up another voice on the comms net. "We're almost done loading. Be overhead in a flash. Hang tight and stay alive and maybe we can give you some cover."

Tanner watched as the navigational screens showed the rover draw closer and closer to its destination. The entry gates to the spaceport were just around the next corner. He thought for the briefest of moments that they might not need air support from the corvette.

Then another particle beam shot through a nearby house, igniting it instantly and announcing the return of their pursuers. "Fire support would be good right now, yeah!"

• • •

Hawkins would have greatly preferred a more orderly evacuation, but he couldn't blame these people for running for their lives. Sustained gunfire could be heard in almost any direction. Locals ran or hid with panicked cries that proved contagious among his civilian charges. Several bits of debris from satellites and destroyed ships left foreboding trails of black smoke across an otherwise blue sky. At least the orbital bombardments seemed to have stopped, but that only meant troop landings would start any minute now.

Hangars, tall storage bays, and administrative buildings created canyons of concrete and metal. Some stood open, allowing Hawkins to bring the crowd inside and keep them from being exposed. Other buildings remained shut, forcing him and his security team to make quick decisions. He'd rather have brought people through in small groups and handled the load in stages, but the situation didn't allow for such delays.

Standing in a cavernous hangar, Hawkins looked back over his shoulder at the stream of men, women, and children entering through open garage doors at the back end. Security troopers from *Argent* in combat jackets and helmets worked with a couple of consulate staffers to guide everyone inside. He had to hand it to the consulate workers—regardless of the sudden chaos of the invasion, their preplanning and diligence had paid off. Initial assembly of the evacuees went as well as anyone could have hoped. Running them through the spaceport had resulted in some sprained ankles, stumbles, falls, and many out-of-breath and frightened people, but that part couldn't be helped.

Managing Casey already ranked as one of the toughest assignments Hawkins had ever had. Shepherding a crowd of nearly a thousand frightened civilians through a war-torn spaceport complex surely ranked as a close second. This was not the sort of thing he'd envisioned when he entered the Intelligence Ministry.

The garage doors at the rear of the hangar came down with the arrival of the last two security personnel. One of them carried a small, crying boy over his shoulder. The other signaled Hawkins with a broad wave of her arm. Hawkins turned his attention to the hangar entrance, where the doors remained partially closed and two of his men stood with weapons ready. He ran to the entrance to look outside at the broad and mostly empty flight line beyond. To his left, perhaps a football field away, loomed *Argent* with her broad cargo ramp extended under her bulk. To his right, Hawkins saw yet another pair of his security people crouched behind a load lifter. Far beyond them, much farther away, stood one of the spaceport's perimeter gates. He could see flashes of laser fire all around the gate.

Hawkins rushed from his position to join his people at the load lifter. "How's it look?"

"Not good," grunted the woman on his right. The lowered visor on her helmet offered her much better vision than the naked eye. "Only a few stray blasts have come this way, but even so, it'll be risky."

"So is staying here," noted her partner. "We can't tell who's winning out there."

"Point," she conceded.

"*Argent*, this is Hawkins. We're grouped at a hangar a hundred meters south of the aft section of the ship," he explained over the holocom net. "I don't think we can get to closer cover. We may have to make a run—"

"Hawkins, stay down!" barked Casey in reply. "Keep everyone bottled up. There's trouble inbound at the gate and—Marquez, tell them to get a better lead or they're fucked!"

Contrary to instructions, Hawkins naturally peered up over the edge of the load lifter again. Though the fight continued to rage at the gate, little enough of it seemed oriented in his direction. "What's he on about?" Hawkins muttered.

The loud crash at the southern gate answered his question, along with the red particle beam that continued on past him along the flight line.

• • •

"We'll never make it through those barriers!" warned Booker. He clutched at the dashboard with one hand, watching the oncoming obstructions with wide-eyed alarm.

"I know, I know!" shouted Sanjay. His eyes darted back and forth from the road ahead to the rearview displays. He'd have preferred the ancient but reliable technological wonder of rearview mirrors, but those had already been shot away. "Might wanna throw on seat belts back there!"

"Shit," Tanner grunted. He hauled his legs up and sat up straight, enduring less pain than before but still wincing as he bent his knee. Vanessa took up the spot beside him, buckling in just as he did. "*Argent*, we are almost at the gate with tanks still—woah!" He slumped over into Vanessa's shoulder as Sanjay jinked hard to the right, timing his maneuver just before a pursuing tank's particle beam fired.

Tanner saw the destruction wrought by the tank's gun up ahead. Part of the tall wall near the gate crumbled and fell in a smoking wreck. Warring factions fled. Their path, though bumpy, lay clear. Beyond the gate lay salvation. *Argent*'s engines rose many stories above the flight line.

Rockets shot from a battery on top of the ship's hull and arced toward the gate, the rover, and its pursuers.

Tanner swept away his seat belt and lunged for the jamming unit still lying on the floor.

• • •

Joan of Arc swept overhead mere heartbeats too late. The barrage of rockets crashed into the ground, detonating in a series of fiery blasts over a wide area. Though clearly fired from *Argent*'s antimissile defenses, resulting in more chaff than explosive power, each was still lethal to ground vehicles and exposed individuals.

"*Argent*, cease fire!" shouted Kelly. She watched as the rover and the pursuing tanks disappeared within the bursts of flame, smoke, and debris. "Those are our people! Cease fire!"

The corvette banked left and flew back around over the liner. Kelly's eyes swept the field below. She saw a mob of people rushing out of a hangar toward the ship now that the gunfire toward the gate had ceased, but at the gate structure itself she saw only rubble and smoking ruin. Sensors were still too disrupted by all the chaff to make out anything more than simple optical images. A lone, flaming tire rolled away from the mess.

Nothing and no one moved.

"Captain! Vessels overhead have altered course and orientation!" warned Stan. Each of the targets had been given arbitrary designations. "Destroyer *Tango* and frigate *Charlie* have—targeting signals!"

"Chaff! Fire!" Kelly ordered. She had no time for her anguish; all she could do was shove her feelings aside before more people died. In fact, she didn't have time to give Romita orders as her helmsman. She reached for the computer—knowing human hands couldn't react as quickly as necessary here—and set *Joan of Arc* into "screening" mode for *Argent*. The corvette spat out chaff missiles and lasers to disrupt and intercept incoming missiles while *Joan* flew straight over the liner and held steady in the air.

Only three missiles streaked in from the sky toward the spaceport, but they were more than enough to do the job against a less prepared defense. A starship firing from outer orbit at a target on the ground was more or less shooting at short range. *Joan of Arc* barely managed to deflect all three, shooting down one missile with its laser turrets and sending the other two flying off in the wrong directions.

The beam weapons that cut through the sky above to strike at the corvette were not something the ship could evade. *Joan of Arc*'s reflective hull blunted much of each blast, withstanding all but the most direct hits. Every corvette captain knew what a destroyer's main guns could do to their ship after the demise of *St. Jude*, but that ship had been caught unawares and without her ES reinforcement generators working. *Joan of Arc*'s damage-control systems warned of malfunctions and threats, but the ship stayed aloft.

Kelly looked to her ground-side displays again. She couldn't make out anything but smoke, rubble, and debris where her shipmates had been. Holocom signals from Booker, Sanjay, and Malone no longer registered. It amounted to the last thought she could spare for them. She saw no further movement on the ground around *Argent* and took that to mean the last of the passengers had made it on board, or at least under the protection of her hull. The liner's ES generators wouldn't work until she was fully buttoned-up, but even a tough ship like *Joan of Arc* could withstand only so much punishment. Kelly had to get her out of the line of fire.

"Helm, lay in an attack vector on frigate *Charlie* and execute," she shouted, speaking simultaneously to Romita and the corvette's computer. "Gunners, fire at will."

Still drawing fire away from *Argent*, *Joan of Arc* banked left once more, tilted up toward the sky, and blasted away from the urban landscape at a speed suited to space combat. Blue skies turned black. *Joan of Arc* rushed headlong toward the orbiting frigate, her small size and sudden acceleration doing far more to protect her than her hull ever could.

As Kelly expected, she saw the angry red beams of *Joan of Arc*'s main cannon fire off ahead of her well before she could make out the frigate with her naked eye. Smaller beams from her turrets joined in. Missiles streaked out from the corvette's wings as if to chase after the lasers. The stars spun as Romita added evasive patterns to the course of the ship, but *Joan of Arc* continued to charge in against a larger opponent with guns blazing.

Kelly's chest rose and fell rapidly. She wanted a trigger to pull, something she could actually do other than shout commands, but that wasn't her place. *Joan of Arc* had a great crew; Kelly had trained them hard to make them greater. She'd already seen that training pay off in getting them this far.

"Hits on the frigate!" Stan announced as the tactical computer relayed the results. Kelly saw little damage from the main gun on her own screens but understood instantly what her gunner's mate had done. The broad cannon blast had swept away a good amount of the frigate's own defensive missiles and chaff, leaving it momentarily open for the missiles that followed in. Ordoñez let loose with another shot from the main gun as soon as its cooling system allowed, this time hammering the frigate with a much deadlier blow.

"*Argent* is lifting off now, captain," Stan added. "She's firing her own chaff systems. I think she'll make it off the ground okay if we keep this up."

As he spoke, *Joan of Arc* sailed past the stunned frigate. Though still too far away to register as anything but a speck of light in a field of so many others, the frigate showed up just fine on *Joan of Arc*'s optics and active scanners. "Helm," said Kelly, "alter course to engage the destroyer at range. The frigate's knocked for a loop right now. We've gotta keep the heat off *Argent*."

"Aye, aye, ma'am," answered Romita.

Kelly shifted the priorities on her tactical screen, watching the numbers shift as *Joan of Arc* moved in. She saw beam weapons strike the destroyer from planet-side almost as soon as she had the ship on her screen. "*Argent*'s firing!" Stan shouted.

"I see it," she interrupted, watching the destroyer turn and accelerate. A second flash of red light missed the destroyer, but it confirmed what she'd already seen: for a liner, *Argent* packed some serious weaponry.

• • •

Casey worked the tactical station in a frenzy, directing *Argent*'s weapons and countermeasures with swift and sure hands. The ship's automated guns responded instantly; the gunnery crews followed his instructions without a hitch. "Helm, that corvette made a hole for us," he said without looking away.

"Aye, aye, sir," came the response. "Course laid in."

"Get us the fuck out of here! Turrets, when we're out of the atmosphere, fire at will," Casey directed. "Focus on that frigate. Keep it off balance. Hold back on the cannons and missiles; let's not show all our cards unless we gotta. Damage control, how we doing?"

"Minor damage so far, captain," answered the voice on his comm. "Critical systems all still holding up. We've got some injuries among the passengers."

"Yeah, well, better injured than dead or held hostage." One corner of his mouth spread out into a half grin as *Argent*'s weapons landed another hit on the destroyer. He saw missiles streak in from *Joan of Arc* as well, keeping the destroyer preoccupied while *Argent* made her violent escape. True to his assessment, the frigate had been bloodied badly enough that her guns went silent. She didn't want any more attention from either of her opponents.

Hawkins made it onto the bridge then, breathing heavily within his helmet. He noticed immediately that Casey stood at the tactical station. He also noticed that the captain's helmet was still back in his otherwise empty chair. "What's our status?" he asked as he strode over to join Casey.

"See for yourself. We're doing fine. None of the other ships will move in to intercept in time to catch us. They're all busy, anyway. Helm, you got a course ready to get us out of the system?"

"Yes, sir!"

"Outstanding," said Casey. He didn't bother to look up at Hawkins. "See what I mean?"

"Where's Peterson?" Hawkins asked.

"Who? Oh, was that his name? I threw him off the bridge. Didn't follow orders. Can't have that on a ship. Bad for discipline. You're the XO, so you get to deal with it. Lemme know how that turns out." He knew Hawkins would be opening his mouth to say something, but he promptly cut the other man off. "I have this under control. Why don't you go back to managing all our passengers?" Casey didn't look at him, choosing instead to work the tactical boards.

It wasn't the sort of job Hawkins could do better than Casey. Both men knew it.

"Understood," Hawkins grunted before he stalked off.

Casey and his gunnery crews continued firing as they put the destroyer and frigate behind them, as did the corvette, but the contest was already won. Neither of Archangel's ships would have trouble getting away now. A triumphant grin spread across the captain's face.

Casey's gaze swept the bridge once again. The other men and women in the compartment felt it, too. They'd shared their first danger together and come through under his command. His leadership had carried them through. For all his harsh measures and surly demeanor, they'd survived. The crew wouldn't forget it.

Nothing won a crew's loyalty like a victory.

With danger drifting further away, Casey opened up a holo screen and replayed the video of *Argent's* last few seconds on the ground. He scrolled through camera options to find something focused on the spaceport gate, then watched as his chaff rockets fell all around the rover and detonated. He saw nothing but smoke and rubble. Certainly nobody had moved to check for survivors, and there was no way the corvette would be able to return to the planet now. She had passengers of her own to protect.

Hawkins hadn't asked about that yet. Perhaps all he'd seen was the blast of particle-beam fire that offered Casey his excuse. He'd find out sooner or later, but by then Casey could review every recording and ensure that he'd covered his tracks. It wasn't as if he didn't have any justification.

Fucking kid might not be dead, but this day keeps getting better and better.

FIVE

The Last Flight Out

"NorthStar Security personnel are instructed to adopt emergency protocols to protect corporate property and personnel. All other NorthStar employees and their families are advised to shelter in place. NorthStar and its employees are expressly not targets of either hostile party. Please stay safe until further notice."

—Emergency Communiqué to Employees
on Scheherazade, April 2276

The whole world was made up of frightfully intense light, deafening whistles, and heat. Tanner hunched over in his seat as the blaze seemed to engulf the rover, arms wrapped around his head. Time seemed to slow down until he became aware of the particularly searing heat on his shoulder. Understanding dawned on him—a piece of chaff had embedded itself in his seat and partially broken off onto his coat.

Tanner opened the door and threw himself out, tumbling into the smoking rubble around the rover. His fumbling, panicked fingers tore the fabric off before the chaff ate through the material and did him real harm.

Outside the rover, the world felt louder. A burst of force shook the air, knocking him to the ground once more. He was dimly aware of Vanessa, who followed him out of the vehicle, but the thunder in the sky drew his attention.

He looked up in time to see *Argent* lift off. Her chaff rockets and laser turrets fired upward while missiles streaked down out of the sky at the liner only to be intercepted or lured away by false readings. The air and ground shook from both missile impacts and the rumble of *Argent*'s engines. The liner remained horizontal for several long seconds, offering Tanner a good look before she tilted her bow skyward and her aft thrusters roared to life.

No one shot at him amid the charred rubble of the gate, the security wall, and the rover. If anyone had tried in those first seconds, he probably wouldn't have noticed. His ears still rang at a shrill pitch. Several shrill pitches, and maybe a scream or two.

No. That's a real scream.

Vanessa lay on the ground beside him, coughing but alive and uninjured. His eyes turned up toward the rover, and then he saw the rapid flashes in the driver's seat.

Oh God. Sanjay. Tanner forced himself to his feet and got to the driver's side door. Sanjay's left arm burned with an intense bright light, and he howled in pain as he tried to fight his way free of his seat belt and jacket. Not a single window in the rover had survived, allowing Tanner to reach in and open the door from the inside rather than fighting with the exterior lock. He felt the heat of the pieces of chaff in Sanjay's arm and smelled his shipmate's burning flesh.

"Get him out!" shouted Booker from Sanjay's other side. He was clearly doing all he could from his seat, but it amounted to little more than unclasping Sanjay's seat belt. Tanner threw his head and shoulders under Sanjay's burning arm to get ahold of the panicked crewman's torso and haul him out. They landed roughly on the concrete, but Tanner at least managed to do it without getting seriously burned.

Sanjay could do little more than thrash and scream. Tanner had to fight him to keep the arm isolated and look at it, but by then Vanessa was there to help keep Sanjay down. The chaff continued to burn as designed in Sanjay's arm, just as it would even if submerged in water or in the vacuum of space. It would burn until it had exhausted its own chemical fuel, or any fuel it might be able to draw from—in this case, Sanjay's flesh. With Sanjay pinned to the ground now, Tanner realized that he'd already lost fingers and a good deal of flesh at several points. Smoke streamed out of little holes all along the ruined arm from elbow to shoulder. The disgustingly sweet stench left Tanner gagging.

He'd never dig it all out in time. Not before it burned right up to the joint and perhaps into the veins. Tanner jerked his survival knife from its sheath on his leg and activated its heating element. He shifted on his knees to keep Sanjay pinned to the ground and caught Vanessa's eye.

"Do it," she urged.

Sanjay screamed. The faceplate of his helmet did nothing to muffle the sound. Tanner swallowed his own horror and despair and shoved his hot knife through his friend's shoulder. He made himself watch as he held the blade against the severed joint, making sure the wound was cauterized before he pulled the knife away. It only took a couple of seconds.

Tanner then dropped the knife and turned away, shutting his eyes tightly while he tried to breathe and Sanjay's cries turned to an awful sob of pain. He afforded himself only a breath, perhaps two, wanting for all the world to vomit or run away or both, but he couldn't. He instead turned back to his friend and pulled open the small first aid kit on his belt.

"Booker, are you all right?" Vanessa yelled.

"I'm okay," came the grunting reply, "just tough to get out of here. Help Sanjay."

Booker tumbled out of the rover. His helmet and jacket were both gone, suggesting that he'd suffered the same sort of problems with chaff as his subordinates but had managed to escape it before it got into his skin. Without a word, Booker joined Tanner and dug into his own first aid supplies. Together they quickly applied painkillers and antishock injections, clotting gels and bandages. Vanessa released Sanjay and turned to keep watch over their surroundings.

"You're doing good, Sanjay," said Booker. "You're gonna get through this."

"Did you have to cut it off?" Sanjay asked, his voice wavering. Booker worked Sanjay's helmet off, revealing an anguished face covered in sweat and tears.

"A hospital can grow it back for you," answered Tanner. "I'm sorry. I'm so sorry. You're gonna be fine."

Sanjay swallowed hard. His breathing eased quickly as the painkillers kicked in. "You don't sound like I'm fine," he managed.

"Hey, I'm a little freaked out right now, too," Tanner replied, trying to flash a reassuring grin.

"Oh God, was I crying?" shuddered the other crewman.

"I cry when people call me names. Listen, I gave you stuff for the pain and shock, okay? You're gonna be pretty loopy."

"*Argent's* long gone," reported Vanessa as she returned. Only then did Tanner realize the explosions and roar of engines had ceased moments ago. "Looks like everyone thought the whole spaceport was being bombarded and went to ground."

"Even the frigates carry ship-to-ship missiles that'd wipe out the whole spaceport with a single hit." Booker frowned, looking skyward. "They were being careful. Won't take long for ground forces to realize that."

"That ship looked familiar," Tanner noted, still focused mostly on his first aid work.

"It should," said Vanessa. "You docked with it about a million times."

Tanner looked up at her. "Huh?"

He saw Vanessa all but bite her lip. "Sorry. Rough day for me, too." She cast her attention further afield again, though whether it was to keep watch or to avoid Tanner's gaze, the young man couldn't tell. "How'd you know the jammer would throw those rockets off?"

"I didn't." Tanner shrugged. "I just wanted something to do. Made me feel better."

Again, he saw Vanessa's eyes glance at his over her shoulder. This time, he caught sight of her grin.

With Sanjay somewhat stable, Tanner took in their surroundings. The gate area had been completely demolished around the rover. He saw destroyed tanks off in one direction and a mostly empty flight line in another. Buildings out beyond the gate had been damaged in the explosion of chaff rockets but still stood. A few others inside the spaceport had clearly suffered the brunt of missed laser cannon blasts and deflected missiles from space. Fighting continued to rage here and there out beyond their immediate area, but the fight for the gate had been thoroughly resolved by *Argent*'s chaff missiles.

"Wait, the jammer?" asked Booker. With a look of sudden realization, he jumped back toward the rover and stuck his head in the passenger door. Booker reached inside, found the jammer unit, and turned it off, and then checked his holocom again. "Dammit," he sighed. "*Joan of Arc* and *Argent* are off the net. They probably think we're dead. Couldn't come back for us regardless, not in the middle of all this and with civilians on board."

Tanner winced. "Did I screw up?"

"Not if you saved our lives." Booker tossed the unit over his shoulder. "Those chaff rockets swerved at the last second. Now I know why. But either way, our rides just took off."

Though weakened and disoriented, Sanjay managed to follow the conversation. "Then what do we do?"

"Guess we'll have to find another ride"—Tanner frowned—"but God only knows where to start. This place is fucked."

Again, Vanessa grinned at him. "You must learn, grasshopper, to scope out the parking lot before you walk into the party."

• • •

The wreckage inside the tank forced him into awkward angles, but with some effort Harris pulled his leg free from the collapsed console. It hurt like hell, but he gritted his teeth, sucked up the pain, and crawled toward the hatch over the front driver's seat. With the turret blown half to hell, he couldn't get out any other way.

Thankfully, the hatch flew open upon the pull of its release lever. Harris saw blue sky above. Favoring his bad leg, he climbed halfway out to look around. He found the spaceport largely still standing despite the destruction in his immediate surroundings. The other tank clearly got hit worse than his. The rover lay a couple dozen meters up ahead in a smoking ruin.

Its former occupants shuffled across open terrain.

Harris's hand went to his sidearm. Four people, one of them limping and one of them outright carrying another. No cover, moving in a nice and predictable line. Obvious injuries. He could take at least two down before they turned and reacted, maybe another before they returned fire. His hand was a bit shaky, given all he'd been through, but he could manage this. His pistol offered computer assistance even on rapid fire.

He had it halfway up before he considered how many times those four had surprised him already.

They'd chewed through a couple tanks and the better part of an infantry platoon before hitting the spaceport. They'd survived this much, and Harris wasn't in the best shape right now. He had a pistol. He saw at least two rifles among them. And he was alone.

He could take down maybe two of them, three at the most, before he suffered any return fire. But he *would* take that return fire, and he might not inflict much damage in his opening shots. His leg hurt like hell. So did his back, come to think of it.

Abnett might suffer some heat for losing his stupid holocom if Harris recovered it, but that would be the end of the matter. It wasn't as if Harris would get a commendation or a bonus or a "pat on the back" letter in his file for all his efforts. Just as likely, fucking Abnett would cover up the whole issue so he wouldn't get in trouble for having lost it in the first place.

NorthStar Security recognized Harris as an elite but still a grunt. He led squads and platoons of similarly elite grunts, but nothing beyond that. His last promotion had been over a decade ago. The ceiling above him now could only be broken by the sort of networking and connections that a guy like him never got the opportunity to make.

Somewhere along the way, Harris's career had become a job.

His leg hurt, his back hurt, and he knew it'd be a good long while before he could rest again. Better to dig out the medical kit and take care of his injuries than to knock himself out trying to clean up some other guy's mistakes. Hell, at this point, all he had to do was say he wasn't sure if they'd lived through the explosion. Abnett would be perfectly happy to keep his mouth shut and hope nothing further came of the matter.

Harris holstered his weapon and turned his attention from the fleeing enemy. It didn't exactly cost him a chance at a bonus in his paycheck.

• • •

"I can't believe we're just floating on out of here after all that," said Booker from the copilot's chair.

"Malone, hit him," said Vanessa. She sat in the pilot's chair of the boxy packet ship. After Vanessa led the others right to the ship's hangar and defeated the building's security within seconds, none of the men were of a mind to object when she took the seat. She was the only one who could read Arabic without the aid of translation software, anyway.

"Why would I hit him?" asked Tanner. He stood behind the two, looking out at the void and hoping it would remain so nicely empty.

"He just jinxed us."

"No, I think he's right." A holographic display of the packet ship's sensor bubble floated over the controls. "Looks like all the nearest ships are engaged. Any one of them could hit us pretty easily at this distance if they wanted to. I guess we don't rate the attention."

"What'd I say about jinxing us?"

Booker adjusted the display. "If they haven't done it yet, I don't think they're going to . . . and I think I've figured out why. Look." He called up the computer's analysis of the nearest contacts. One read as a destroyer, positioned tens of thousands of kilometers out and limping away. Another, nearer and perhaps once directly over the spaceport, drifted helplessly. "That's a frigate."

"Wow," said Tanner. "You think *Joan of Arc* did that, XO?"

"*Joan* or *Argent* or a combination of the two. I don't read anything that looks like either of them floating around out here, so that's a good sign."

"I wasn't sure a corvette could take down a frigate."

"It's possible, but you have to get pretty lucky. Pretty lucky and pretty good."

"The big question is still open, lieutenant," said Vanessa. She turned to look at him expectantly.

Booker took a long breath. "We hit the lunar orbital line in another minute. We can keep going for a while before we jump to FTL, but we're almost clear of the red zone. Obviously, I don't think we can wait until we get all the way out to the legal FTL line, so . . . thoughts?"

"It's your call, sir," replied Tanner.

"I wouldn't ask if I didn't want input," Booker assured him. "You saw what happened to some of the ships that dropped out of FTL close to the planet. We could end up like that. We're farther out than they were, but you know the risks," he reminded, looking from Tanner to Vanessa.

"I've done some time as an astrogator," she told him. "I understand. Do it."

Booker glanced up at Tanner, who in turn looked back toward the small living compartment aft of the cockpit. His fellow crewman lay on one of the two bunks. "You want me to try to get a vote out of Sanjay, sir?"

"I'd bet my entire salary I know how he'd vote," said Booker.

Tanner took another look at the sensor bubble display. The invading ships held their positions. Most of the other contacts were identified as wrecked or destroyed spacecraft. The spacer's ethics drilled into Tanner by Chief Everett in basic training demanded that they at least try to make some sort of search-and-rescue sweep, but that was plainly suicide. "I say let's get out of here, sir."

With that, Booker turned back to his controls and laid in a course perpendicular to Scheherazade's orbit around its star. "Giving it about a minute-long run to get us clear," he explained, "then we'll work up our best course back to Archangel."

He waited with his hands over the controls as the packet ship floated steadily away from home and the numbers on his screens shifted. A dot representing the ship moved closer and closer to the line that denoted the orbital path of Scheherazade's moon, which offered a relatively reliable benchmark for minimum safety—at least by civilian emergency standards. Military operations could cut things closer, but no one on the packet ship thought their vessel capable of such feats.

The ship crossed the line without incident. Booker counted down from ten to give them a little more distance, then executed the FTL jump. The packet ship rumbled and lurched much as they expected, with the stars growing fuzzy and blurred as the ship's speed exceeded that of the light around them.

Everything in the ship held together. No alarms blared. The rumble faded as quickly as it began.

"That's that." Booker sighed. He sank back in his chair, as did Vanessa. Tanner relaxed slightly as well, knowing the worst of the danger had passed. Now all they had to face was a long stretch of boredom and the common perils of space flight, but that was a far cry from being shot at.

"You should probably get off that leg for a little while, Tanner," Booker suggested.

Tanner spoke mostly in a mumble. "Aye, aye, sir. I'll go check on Sanjay."

He limped back through the very short passageway into the "berthing" cabin between the cockpit and the similarly small and cramped storage and engineering space. Embedded in one bulkhead were bunk beds and small storage cabinets. The other bulkhead offered several humble appliances for cooking and cleaning. Sanitation facilities, which amounted to a small closet, were equally limited. A packet ship such as this sometimes had cargo modules attached, but, unfortunately, this one had no such extra frills. Even an empty container module would have at least offered a little more in the way of living space.

Tanner slumped down into one of the two chairs at the compartment's small table. On the table lay a pile of foil-wrapped packets of food Tanner had appropriated from a vending machine near the packet ship's hangar berth before launch. He'd grabbed other emergency supply bags and even raided a break room refrigerator before they left as well. The results of his hurried scavenging littered the deck of the small living space.

It would be a long trip—considerably longer than the voyage would take *Joan of Arc* or *Argent*. The packet ship's short-range practicalities meant that it would have to travel at a slow clip in order to stretch out its fuel supply.

Tanner frowned, trying to make sense of his thoughts. He felt the ship lurch as it dropped back out of FTL, but that was expected. Rather than return to the cockpit, Tanner gathered the foil packets of food, sorting and counting them out. Before long, the ship shuddered as it jumped to FTL once again.

"Hey," croaked Sanjay. "Guess we made it out, huh?"

"Yeah," Tanner said, forcing a little bit of a smile. "We're out of the shooting, at least."

"That's good. Getting shot sucks." The injured crewman sighed. With his shoulder now sealed in a gel pack, the biggest concern was blood loss. Still, Sanjay had made it this far and remained stable.

"You're awake?" asked Booker as he and Vanessa stepped out of the cockpit.

"Doesn't feel like it," Sanjay mumbled.

"I think he's gonna be okay, sir," said Tanner. "If we keep him warm and off his feet and make sure he drinks plenty, he should recover from the blood loss."

"They teach you a lot of emergency medicine in basic these days?" asked Vanessa.

"Yeah," Sanjay managed, "and he's got a half-dozen medical textbooks on that holocom of his."

"It's true," Tanner confessed.

"Nobody's complaining," said Booker. "Well, the FTL drives on this thing aren't bad at all. We're looking at eight days before we're back in our own territory—probably get there a couple days behind *Joan* and *Argent*. I'd take us to the nearest safe port if that were practical, but there's nothing closer than other Hashemite territory. Given the shifting politics out here, I'd say it isn't worth the risk. So we're looking at a long and boring ride home."

"Air and water look like they'll hold up fine," said Tanner. "This thing's old, but they kept up on all the maintenance. Ship's food stores were only set up to support two people for one week, though. It's all emergency survival stuff." He paused, glancing at Vanessa. "Agent Rios picked us a good one."

"It pays to plan ahead," she replied.

"And the extras you picked up?" asked Booker, gesturing to his pile of foil packages on the table.

"Meals might be skimpy and a lot of this is snacks rather than substantial food, but doing the math in my head, I think we'll be okay."

"You know, I admit I thought you were going a bit overboard"— Booker grinned at the assortment of boxes and bags on the deck— "but I guess it comes from experience, huh?"

"'Abandon ship' kind of leaves an impression once you've done it for real, sir."

"We did good out there today," said Booker, looking to each of the three people in the cabin with him. "I don't think we could've pulled this off if any one of you hadn't been there. Agent Rios, I'm glad you decided to join us. Thank you."

"My pleasure, lieutenant."

"XO," spoke up Tanner, "you did good, too, sir. You held us together, kept us on the right track. Hell, if *Argent* hadn't panicked and opened up on us along with those tanks . . ." The thought threw him off, making Tanner lose track of whatever he'd meant to say. Eventually, he shrugged. "I'm glad you were all there, too."

• • •

Tanner awoke in the dark living space of the packet ship, forced to consciousness by the buzz of his holocom's preset alarm against his wrist. He rubbed his face, stretched his arms out, and yawned, reflecting that he must have slept more deeply than he'd expected. Climbing out of the top bunk, he found that his knee hurt somewhat less than before, that Sanjay's medical monitors all gave steady readings, and that Booker, lying on a makeshift bed of emergency blankets on the deck, snored louder than any officer should.

He needed only a moment in the ship's tiny head to freshen up. Careful not to wake his shipmates, Tanner stepped back out of the head and then into the cockpit, closing the door behind him. He found the internal lights relatively dim. Light from the stars quickly streaked past the canopy, blinking in and out as the ship moved faster than any photon could naturally travel.

Tanner found Vanessa in the pilot's seat with her feet up on the control panel. A pair of holo screens floated in front of her. He noticed sharp differences in style and format between the two screens, although both showed mostly alphanumeric code and little in the way of user-friendly icons.

"Have a seat." Vanessa tilted her head to the copilot's chair. "Hope you don't mind if I hang around up here for a while longer."

"Not a problem." Tanner settled into the chair and gave the control panel a quick look. Nothing was out of the ordinary. FTL travel continued on, as it would for days to come. As long as the ship held steady, there would be little to do. Military piloting standards mandated that a constant watch be kept regardless—and it gave a very bored crew at least a little bit of structure and activity. "What are you up to?"

Vanessa's eyes slid over to meet his. Tanner frowned, nodded, then held up one hand. "Never mind. I know the joke. Don't tell me so you won't have to kill me."

"That joke is ancient." Vanessa held up the holocom that sat in her lap, causing the two screens to ripple as the devices compensated for movement. "Trying to crack the holocom you swiped from inside that tank."

"Getting anywhere?"

She let out a sigh. "No, and I don't expect to. It would be a miracle if my little piece was enough to beat the encryption on this thing. Cryptology isn't one of my stronger skills, but I have nothing better to do. How'd you sleep?"

"Fine." He noted the change of subject and decided not to press the issue. Someone like Vanessa probably had to exercise great care in casual conversations like this. "I imagine the longer we're stuck on this ship, the harder it'll be to sleep. Not much physical activity."

"I imagine there wasn't much physical activity working in Ascension Hall, either. That why you signed up for more shipboard duty?"

"You seem to know an awful lot about me," he said, hoping to sound playful rather than sour.

"Hard not to. Your girlfriend made a point of everyone knowing."

"She's not my girlfriend."

Vanessa chuckled. "I'm shocked."

Tanner gave up trying to mask his irritation. "You've been taking shots since we met. What's your problem with me?"

Vanessa bit back her immediate response. She stared at her holo screens for a moment longer, then swept the screens aside to float beside her, away from the conversation. "Envy," she admitted with another sigh. "It's envy and a lot of self-criticism and doubt, and it's a problem with me, not you. But you're right here and it's hard not to kick. Sorry."

"What have I got to envy?" Vanessa huffed in response, half laughing, and he added, "If you wanted to be famous, I imagine you wouldn't be a spy."

"It's not the fame. It's the success."

"How so?"

"You did what I couldn't do. Or what I thought I couldn't do, but then I saw you pull it off."

Tanner fell silent, watching her and waiting. Vanessa frowned. "How high is your security rating?"

"Only Delta. They do the background check at the palace to clear you all the way to Epsilon, but they don't actually give the rating. It's just in case you see or hear something by accident."

"Right. I didn't know if they'd gone further with you because you're . . . well, you."

Tanner shook his head. "Nobody made any special exceptions for me." Vanessa snorted. It only got him irritated again. "I'm here because—" He stopped, looked away, and sighed. "Okay, that's stupid. I'm here because Admiral Yeoh decided she wanted me here."

"Uh-huh. Listen, I'm a top intelligence agent, and I don't have anyone like Admiral Yeoh calling me out by name."

"She stuck me on *Joan of Arc* because my qualification time underway didn't add up to a year yet," he grumbled. "That's what I mean. So, yeah, people know who I am. But nobody's bending any rules for me. Lots of ratings require a full year of time on an underway billet as a non-rate, so here I am. I got onto the honor guard, yeah, but so do a lot of other non-rates, okay? I have Delta clearance. Seems pretty high to me as it is."

Vanessa shook her head. "Okay. Sorry. Still kicking, I guess. But I suppose you must know how to keep your mouth shut. All that time in the limelight and you didn't say or do anything stupid, so that's gotta count for something . . ." Her voice trailed off. Tanner waited.

"You've seen *Argent* before, only she used to be called *Aphrodite*. We recovered her a little less than a year after Casey's crew grabbed her."

Tanner sat up in his seat, staring at her. "She's—*we've* got the *Aphrodite*? I thought she disappeared from that haven Casey's guys used! Why's the government keeping that a secret?"

"Hey, I'm an operator, not a policy maker. Couldn't tell you why for sure. Still, if we admitted we recovered her, we'd have to admit to how and where. The pressure would be on to follow up, but the navy wasn't ready to go after the pirate haven. As to why we didn't say something to the Union fleet or anyone who did have the muscle? Hell if I know. Maybe the info did get shared, and you and I don't know it. But the other reason is that Archangel wanted to keep that ship. If we admitted we had our hands on it, we'd have to give it back to NorthStar."

"She's that important to keep? Why?"

"Because she can fight her way out of a planetary invasion, like she just did. She looks pretty on the outside—maybe not as pretty as she was when she was called *Aphrodite*, but she's still got the look—but on the inside, she's built like a destroyer, Tanner. A lot of the liners are. NorthStar builds them like that to dodge the Union's armament limits. If there's a war, they can put their liners and some of their other ships in for a refit and within a couple months they'll have three times as many warships. Lai Wa does it, too."

Tanner's gaze seemed to dart around the cabin as his mind processed the implications. "Aren't there inspectors and approvals and . . . How can they get away with that?"

"Holding the big boys accountable would be inconvenient for everyone. The stocks would all take hits, which would cost a lot of people money beyond NorthStar and Lai Wa themselves. The Union and system governments would have to take actions to correct it all, and that would cost money and probably embarrass important people. I have to assume Archangel isn't the only system that knows what's going on, but it's like I said about how we covered up having *Aphrodite* in the first place." She gave a shrug, not of indifference but weariness. "It turns out if everyone thinks you're indispensable, you can get away with all kinds of things. If everyone pretends nothing is wrong, then nobody has to do anything about it."

"That's insane!"

"You've never seen anyone turn a blind eye to a bully?"

"But they . . ." Tanner searched for the words but closed his mouth. Vanessa hardly needed to offer up other examples. If anything, he wondered if she knew how well she'd made her point. "So Archangel just added *Aphrodite* to the navy without putting her on the books?"

"Not the regular navy, no. Probably under the Intelligence Ministry. I don't know how much of a refit she's been through, but like I said, she's a lot tougher than she looks. A plain old knife might not be the best weapon you can carry, but it can make a pretty big difference if nobody knows you have it. And with arms limits the way they are, every single warship can make a difference."

She watched Tanner as the wheels spun in his head. "Obviously that's a little higher than Delta clearance," she noted. "I could get into serious trouble for sharing all that, but . . . well, like I said. You seem to know how to keep your mouth shut."

"Yeah, but why tell me? We were talking about . . . ?" The answer came to him. "What does that ship have to do with you and me?"

"You asked how NorthStar gets away with fitting out ships like that. Part of the reason is that it's not easy to get hard evidence." She hesitated, staring off through the canopy. "And you asked why I would envy you. It's not you. It's what you did, and what I didn't do in the same situation.

"I was on *Aphrodite* when she got hit. I was undercover as part of her bridge crew. There wasn't a chance for me to get away when the pirates took the ship, but when they separated us out so Casey could give his recruitment speech, I thought . . . I thought I couldn't do any good for the passengers. Not on my own. But I figured I could follow the pirates and find out how they operated, so I took the offer and joined up." She paused again. Tanner saw no tears on her face, nor did her voice crack. Her emotions showed just the same.

"I've been an operative for twenty years. I'm one of the best agents I know. I've lost count of all the gunfights and tough scrapes and . . ." She swallowed. "You were a non-rate navy crewman floating in space with a crowbar and a roll of tape, and you saved *everyone*. I held to my cover and let them die."

Tanner kept his mouth shut. He watched and listened, waiting for her to speak again.

"I let those bastards space *Aphrodite*'s passengers and told myself I couldn't do anything about it, promising myself I'd make them pay later. And I did. I made them pay. I hurt them as much as I could, and I moved on." Her jaw set firmly as she looked back at him. "That worked fine until I saw you on the news."

Unsure of what else he could say, Tanner said, "I'm sorry."

"Sorry for what?"

"I'm sorry you went through that."

"Huh. Yeah. Me, too. But mostly I'm sorry I didn't have it in me to do what you did. I'm better trained. I have more experience. I should've . . ." The words failed her. She shook her head. "I *could've* done what you did. I could've at least *tried*."

"Are you sure about that?" Tanner asked, and then held up his hands when he saw her glare. "Look, I'm not questioning your ability, I just . . . do you think you had the opportunity? You said you were with the crew. I was on my own. They didn't know I was there."

"I could've slipped away."

"You just said you couldn't."

"Yeah, but I could've tried harder and found a way—"

"You could've died with no one to know any better, too," interrupted Tanner. "And you're only second-guessing yourself now because you're on the other side of it. Vanessa, I thought I was committing *suicide*. You know that, right? No. You don't," he said as he noted her expression. "They edit that part out of the interviews because it's not inspiring. Look, I figured it was better to go down fighting rather than hang around on what was left of *St. Jude* until my air ran out. I got lucky. I got insanely lucky along the way. In your shoes, I'd probably have done the same exact damn thing you did. If I'd been that smart in the first place. The last person in the world who's ever gonna second-guess you for what you did is me."

Her frustration didn't go away, but Tanner saw his words sink in. "I think you made your own luck," she muttered.

"And you didn't? Obviously, you got away. You said you made them pay, too. What happened?"

"I'm the one who stole *Aphrodite* from them as soon as they got it back to their little hidey-planet," she answered. "Me and one other gal I got to help me. Couple of the other pirates, too, but they weren't exactly reliable travel buddies. Didn't make the whole trip." She looked him in the eye again. His amazed expression seemed to make her feel a bit better, so she added to it. "You actually saw *Aphrodite* when we first got her into Archangel space—which took almost a year. *St. Jude* landed on her a bunch of times because somebody was working on some sort of obnoxious training qualifications. I presume that was you, knowing what I've read. And your stupid gunner's mate tried to hit on me during the boarding."

Tanner blinked. "Wow. What are the odds?"

"I asked myself the same question when you walked into the consulate on Scheherazade. The galaxy can be a small place sometimes."

"I'm glad you were there," said Tanner. "You saved my life. You saved all our lives. Like the XO said, we wouldn't have made it without you."

Vanessa looked down at her holo screens. She didn't speak right away. "You might not have been there in the first place without me," she said, and then called up another screen. "Told you things I shouldn't have already," she then muttered to herself, "not like this will make it any worse."

"What do you mean?"

"My last assignment was . . . I had a source inside NorthStar. A very good source. I caught wind of this whole invasion with just enough time to drop everything I was doing and haul ass for Scheherazade to warn the consulate before the invading force got there."

"So you're why we got that warning?"

"Yep. Made it to the consulate with all of about five minutes to spare, from the sound of things."

"That sounds about right," Tanner mused.

"I didn't think I'd make it at all."

"So you knew about the invasion?" he asked. "You knew they contracted with NorthStar for those assault carriers and stuff?"

"I knew more than that." She held up the holocom Tanner had grabbed during the battle. "This is the sort of model that NorthStar's covert security and espionage teams use. It's not an actual NorthStar model because they wouldn't want it traced back to them, but it fits all their standards." She dropped it in her lap again.

Tanner's brow furrowed. "So those were NorthStar guys. Murtada wanted them to hit the consulate? Why? That never made any sense to begin with."

"It doesn't. Turn your question around the other way. Murtada doesn't have anything to gain by kidnapping a whole consulate staff. NorthStar does, though, as long as someone else does it for them.

"It wasn't about the consulate staff themselves," explained Vanessa. "They'd be more pawns in the game, but it's just another drop in the bucket. One more bit of harassment from NorthStar when the order of the day for them is to screw with us at every turn. One more problem on our hands. They're doing whatever they can to make our lives difficult all over the Union. A hostage crisis would be one more example to the rest of the Union of how nobody can take care of themselves without corporate help."

"Harassment?"

"Yeah."

"Bullshit."

"Watch these guys as long as I have," Vanessa suggested. "Ask anyone who's watched them as long as I have. They'll believe it, too."

"Doesn't that make it too easy?" Tanner asked.

Vanessa turned to look at him. Her face slowly betrayed a grin. "Wow, you are bright, aren't you?"

He frowned. "Okay?"

Vanessa considered it and let out a breath. "I think they wanted to see if we'd find out." She turned from her holo screen to look at him. "I had a good source inside the company. An amazing source. I think they floated this op just to see if Archangel would find out and react. It got to me kind of late in the process . . . I don't think they had any idea they were compromised so high up. I didn't have a lot of time to think much. It came down to either jumping on the information immediately or just sending the info up the chain, which would've taken weeks. And if I didn't jump on my own, the op would've happened. People probably would've died."

"Like on *Aphrodite*."

"Yeah. So I pulled my source, sent copies of everything I had to Archangel with another agent, and hauled ass for Scheherazade. I'm not gonna let another *Aphrodite* happen to me ever again."

Tanner shrugged. "Can't blame you there. But why now? Why would they do this now?"

"To make sure their house is in order. I think they plan on making a bigger play somewhere down the line. Something big and something soon. And they wanted to make sure they're moving from a secure base first. But don't ask me what the next move is, 'cause I don't know."

That sounded reasonable enough. "Is this gonna cause trouble, though? Pulling your source and all?"

Vanessa grinned a little bit. "Yes. For them." Then she tossed him a wink. "Sorry. Think I've shared enough sensitive info for one confessional. You'll have to wait for the rest to go public."

"Fair enough. I'm surprised you shared so much already."

"Listen, Tanner, that 'aw shucks' act you put on for the interviews is a winner for the media and the crowds, and maybe you actually believe it yourself, but don't try it with me." Vanessa smirked. "I saw you out there in front of that consulate. I was right there with you the whole time. And I know who you tangled with on *Vengeance*, and now you ask me all this?" She shook her head. "You're a player, Tanner, whether you want to admit it yourself or not."

He scowled. "I'm just another crewman."

"The people who run for office aren't the ones who make the world go 'round. Voters like to see a clean suit. People who make things happen have to get dirty. You make things happen."

Tanner stared off into space, chewing on all the thoughts she had sparked. "Vanessa . . . who's her captain?"

"Whose captain?"

"*Aphrodite. Argent.* Whichever."

"Couldn't tell you. Either it's above my pay grade, or I don't have a need to know. Why?"

"Because Captain Kelly didn't know, either. And *Argent* took a shot at us."

"Tanner, we had a pack of tanks right on our ass and *Argent* had civilians to protect. I wouldn't take it personally. Listen, I can connect a lot of dots on my own, but there was more going on with that mess than either of us know."

"Your *pirate* killed three of our people, including a goddamned state hero."

"Four people, Mr. President. Far as I can tell, I lost one of mine, too. He also saved hundreds of civilians. Scheherazade's a sideshow now, anyway, what with—"

"Oh, don't give me that shit, David!" Aguirre's skin flushed red as he glared at the man standing before his desk. Like any good spy, David Kiribati knew how to maintain a neutral expression. As much as Aguirre found that aggravating, he figured any other tack Kiribati might take would only annoy him even more right now. "That's not the point and you know it."

"That is the point, sir," maintained Kiribati. "We sent him in there to rescue civilians, and when they were put in the line of fire, he acted to save as many people as he could."

"And you think it's a coincidence that he killed Tanner Malone in the process? Of all the goddamn people to have run into each other in the middle of all that?"

"He had no more idea that Malone was in the system than I did. I reviewed all the logs myself. Casey wasn't on the comms channel and Malone never identified himself, nor offered a visual, and when I talked to Casey he didn't know about—"

"No chance he's putting one over on you, huh?" Aguirre interrupted with a dry scowl.

"I like to think I haven't been out of the field so long that I can't read a guy like Casey, sir," Kiribati replied with an icy but controlled tone. "He won't shed any tears once he finds out what happened. Hell, I'm sure he'll drink himself into a celebratory stupor. That doesn't mean he knew Malone was there."

"We should never have let that bastard out of his cell."

"Due respect, sir, that bastard is half the reason we've come so far."

Aguirre shot his longtime partner an irritated glare. "You don't think he's outlived his usefulness?"

"No, sir, I don't, and I'd point to the operation on Scheherazade as the reason why. We got all of our civilians and consulate staff out of that mess while only losing a handful of military people, and I'd say that's a bargain. Casey is a big part of that. He did everything right."

Fuming, Aguirre sank back into his chair. "There's nobody else we could put in charge of that ship?"

"Yeoh has at least a dozen people. You want to hand the whole thing off to her?" He waited for that to sink in. Aguirre understood the implications of what could happen if Yeoh got her own people on board *Argent*. Even a completely blanked-out log history would raise too many more questions. "Sir, Casey got a lot done for us in the three years leading up to his capture—"

"Not out of loyalty," Aguirre snorted.

"—and this is the fourth mission he's taken since we put him on that ship, and every mission was a success. Yes, there were losses. Yes, the fact that Malone was there is a giant PR headache, and it'll have people asking questions."

"It's already got people asking questions!" Aguirre snapped. He pointed across his office, empty except for the two of them, to the closed door on the other side of the room. "We've got a security briefing to start. The navy already knows that their people died from friendly fire. We can't keep it from the media much longer, and we have to notify the families. They're all gonna want to know who was in charge of that ship! We can't just tell them it's classified. The media won't shut up and nod and accept that like good soldiers."

"We don't have to keep it from the media, sir. I have a cover story for this. I have a captain to give to the media. He's a retired agent. We're prepping him now so he'll know what to say. Yeoh will probably see through that, but she also knows that *Argent* is an Intelligence Ministry asset. She'll toe the line."

One of Aguirre's eyebrows rose in a doubtful arch. "She lost three of her people over this. She's not going to let this go."

"As far as I can tell, I lost one of my best operatives, too, sir." Kiribati frowned. "Yeoh will have to let it go and she'll have to move on, just like me. Besides, we've got much bigger matters to deal with. Like I said, Scheherazade was a sideshow. Everyone will know that once we're ready to go with the intelligence we've gotten."

"We can't go public with that for months," Aguirre said, waving his hand dismissively. "In the meantime, this is all the public is going to care about."

"This is a dangerous business, sir. It will get much uglier before we're done. And we'll need Casey and people like him."

"We needed someone we could rely on, not some freelance criminal."

"Gabe, we never had the time to build a better asset up from scratch. You know that. You knew it at the time. We needed the genuine article, and we found him, and he delivered. 'The enemy of my enemy' is always a dicey proposition, but it paid off here. You also know how many ships we acquired completely off the books because of him—before and after he got caught—to say nothing of the cover he provided for the public face of the buildup.

"Malone's death is a PR headache. I get that," Kiribati continued, taking on a reassuring tone. "We don't have to cover up the friendly fire angle. It's the kind of tragedy that happens in combat. Look, forget about all the hype. He was just another enlisted kid. He didn't want to go back into the field. Tell Andrea before the news breaks, give her a little time to get her head back in the game, and then I'm sure she'll pour her heart into some sort of martyr spin. That'll probably be worth more than we'd have gotten out of him if he'd lived. You ask me, we're getting a bargain."

Aguirre let out a sullen sigh. He looked at the time and then gestured to the door. "Are we ready for this?"

"Yes, Mr. President. The question is whether you're ready?" He waited for Aguirre's nod. "Yeoh isn't here for this one. She headed out to Augustine to meet with Lieutenant Booker's family. We'll have one of her subordinates here and he won't ask too many questions. I'd say we should try to get the routine stuff out of the way first before moving on to the Scheherazade fallout to give you a breather—"

"I'm fine, David," said Aguirre, shaking his head. "This business is going to drive all of our other decisions, anyway." He paused thoughtfully. "Are we ready to move up the timetable?"

"Our people are on board, yes." Kiribati nodded. "Enough of them that the other relevant business leaders will join up when they see the contracts and the money flowing for the people on the inside."

Again, Aguirre gestured for the door. "Let's get on with it."

Kiribati turned and walked across the office to let everyone in. Aguirre could have buzzed for one of his secretaries outside the office to get the door. Instead, the president used the simple task to remind his intelligence chief who was in charge. It wasn't the sort of thing Kiribati missed, but they'd all come too far in this to let anyone's petty idiosyncrasies become an issue now.

He expected to see Yeoh's stand-in waiting outside, as well as Theresa Cotton, the defense minister, and all the usual aides. He didn't expect to see the smiles.

"Mr. President," Theresa said as she walked in, "we just got word. They're alive."

• • •

Operations Specialist: a versatile rating whose duties include astrogation, high-level helmsman duty, and coordination of shipboard operations. Applicants must qualify for Delta security clearance.

Signalman: Operates, maintains, and installs communications gear. Signalmen with qualifying aptitude scores may receive advanced foreign language training. Applicants must qualify for Epsilon security clearance.

"What'cha doin'?"

Tanner looked up from his holo screen to Sanjay. The pair sat in an otherwise empty waiting room of characterless chairs, couches, and small tables. Pictures of navy ships adorned the walls.

Both of them wore hospital robes. Wealthier civilians in such circumstances could get around in antigrav chairs and the like. For all the emphasis on high-quality medicine, though, the navy found some old-fashioned implements to be much more cost-efficient. Tanner's knee surgery left him on crutches for a couple more days. Sanjay sat in a wheelchair. The sleeve of his robe hung limply over his missing arm. Replacement growth and attachment surgery would take weeks.

"I'm looking at rating options," Tanner sighed. "Gonna have to make a decision pretty soon."

"What are you thinking?"

"Well, initially I wanted a science tech rating, but those all got closed up. After that, I thought maybe I could go corpsman or survival tech. I want to do planetary survey work when I get out of the navy, so I figured those might be good preparation, y'know?"

Sanjay frowned a bit. "Those are both combat arms ratings, right? I thought you wanted to get away from that sort of thing."

"I did. I do." Though anyone on a ship could wind up involved in combat, the navy specified certain ratings as more likely to face such exposure than others. Corpsmen frequently served as combat medics alongside marines. Survival techs were essentially search-and-rescue specialists, but their skill set could easily put them into combat as well. "Part of it is a process of elimination. I know I don't want an admin job. I'm not the technical sort, either, so none of the engineering ratings fit."

"And you're a terrible pilot," Sanjay offered helpfully.

"Yeah, I'm a terrible pilot," Tanner agreed with another sigh. He drew a circle around the operations specialist summary with one finger and then poked at it in the center to eliminate the text on his screen.

"So it's corpsman or survival tech?"

"Well . . . it was."

"What happened?"

"Conversations with a few people. Captain Kelly for one. Vanessa. And . . ." His voice trailed off as the door opposite their seats opened up. Several officers in dress uniforms filed out one by one. A few headed for the restrooms. A couple of others walked off in conversation with Lieutenant Booker, also in dress uniform, who managed only a glance and a nod toward the two younger men.

Two more officers walked directly to the crewmen. One of them was a tall, well-built man with a commander's bars. The other was Admiral Yeoh.

"Crewman Sanjay," said the commander, "we're taking a quick break, but your debriefing is up next. Are you ready to go? I thought we might get you settled in, unless you need anything first."

"No, sir." Sanjay shook his head. "I'm good to go."

Yeoh gave Sanjay the soft, reassuring but controlled smile that Tanner had seen at their first meeting. "This likely won't take long, crewman," she said. "Lieutenant Booker spoke very highly of you. This isn't an inquest. You're in no trouble at all. Quite the opposite. We want everyone's unvarnished impressions."

"Yes, ma'am. I'm ready."

The commander got behind Sanjay's wheelchair and pushed him toward the briefing room. Yeoh lingered, watching the pair leave. Tanner saw her smile fade. "Something bothering you, ma'am?"

"This would all be more complete if we could have debriefed Agent Rios."

Tanner nodded. Word came down for Vanessa to return to her own service headquarters within hours of their packet ship's arrival in the system. At first, Tanner presumed it was only to limit exposure of her identity and to preserve her ability to work undercover. It wasn't until now, hearing the tone in Yeoh's voice, that he suspected something else might be at work.

"She saved our hides out there," said Tanner. "And mine specifically."

"So I'm told."

Tanner waited for her to say something else. His thoughts turned toward his conversation with Vanessa in the packet ship. Not for the first time, he wondered if the debriefing might confront him with a choice of loyalties. He also noted that Yeoh had him alone out here. He'd been concerned with what she or one of the debriefing officers would ask him in the presence of others; now he wondered what she wanted to say to him privately.

"Lieutenant Booker mentioned that you handled the last communications with *Argent*."

"Yes, ma'am."

"Did you hear anyone on that ship identify themselves?"

"No, ma'am. I'm pretty sure I was speaking to a woman. That's all I could say."

"So you aren't sure if you spoke with the captain or a subordinate?"

Tanner blinked. "No, ma'am." He noted the slight darkening of her brow. Again, he thought back to his talk with Vanessa, and

Lieutenant Kelly's exchange with Booker and Chief Romita on *Joan of Arc*.

Yeoh doesn't know who's in command of that ship?

Movement in the waiting room caught their attention. Tanner noted the gradual return of the panel of officers to the briefing room. No one would rush the admiral, but she wouldn't keep them waiting. Tanner wondered if he should say anything about what he knew. For all the distance of rank and power between them, Tanner knew that Yeoh trusted him.

So did the woman who'd carried him away from a hail of gunfire.

"I am very glad you made it out of there alive, Tanner," she said softly. "When *Joan of Arc* came back without you, I . . . well. I wanted you to understand that your record up 'til now hasn't been a fluke. I also wanted you to realize you won't have to handle every crisis alone. That's why I put you on *Joan of Arc*. I just didn't realize how hairy things would become, or I'd have sent a hell of a lot more than one extra corvette."

"I'm not second-guessing you, ma'am."

Her smile made a faint return. "Thank you. I've got to get back in there. It'll be your turn soon enough." With that, she turned to go.

"There's a lot of secrets to deal with here," he said. "Aren't there, ma'am?"

She stopped and looked back to him. "What does Sun Tzu say?"

"That warfare is based on deception."

The admiral nodded. "Yes, it is. I'm glad you made it back, crewman." She disappeared behind the briefing room door, and then Tanner was alone. His holo screen remained. So did his concerns.

That ship took a shot at us, and even Yeoh doesn't know who's in command.

He didn't fixate on *Argent*. In the long run, Tanner figured, he might never run into that ship again. Its captain might get cashiered for nearly killing people with friendly fire, or perhaps it was a legitimate accident. Regardless, he would likely never know.

Non-rate crewmen didn't get the full rundown on every operation. Lieutenant Kelly's example aside, information didn't often trickle down that far.

Tanner brought his fingers to the holo screen. He keyed in several commands, calling up the ratings offering the highest security clearance. He eliminated the engineering and administrative groupings, knowing that neither appealed to his interests.

"Cryptologist." Tanner didn't bother. The job involved Epsilon security clearance, but it also involved spending a great deal of time staring at computer screens in a locked room on either a huge ship or a headquarters unit. He knew he'd go insane.

"Intelligence Specialist: collects and analyzes data on threats and strategic concerns across the Union and beyond. Assists in planning future operations. Applicants must qualify for Epsilon security clearance." He stared at the brief statements thoughtfully. In one of her last letters, Madelyn mused about shifting her focus at Annapolis from small unit command to intelligence . . . but that was the Union fleet, and she was in training to be an officer. Tanner didn't imagine he'd see much fieldwork as a junior enlisted man, and he wouldn't consider a second term.

"Master-at-Arms: provides law enforcement and security. Maintains order and discipline, conducts criminal investigations and some counterintelligence duties. Often involved in boarding team operations. This is a combat arms position. Applicants must qualify for Epsilon security clearance and provide character recommendations from their command."

This is a combat arms position, he repeated in his head.

Tanner sat back in his chair and stared at the text.

"Initial critical review of Operation Juniper shows a complete failure. No tangible objectives were achieved. The consulate staff escaped
capture after scrubbing the building clean of any data that might
have been of use. Several of our operatives were killed and others
injured.

"However, the tangible objectives were all secondary to Juniper's
ultimate goals. Primarily, Juniper was conceived as one of many
operations geared toward placing stress on Archangel's military and
political establishments to assess their capabilities and gauge the via-
bility of future operations. As such, Juniper was a success. The operation also offered field-testing of new equipment and procedures.
Further, all indications hold that the company may maintain full
deniability of involvement with the incident.

"Most importantly, Juniper may have exposed a critical information leak. Investigations are currently underway. Though leaks of
this nature are never to be taken lightly, Juniper was ultimately a
low-cost, low-impact operation. This incident presents us with an
opportunity to resolve information security concerns in advance of
significantly larger operations."

—Maria Pedroso, NorthStar executive VP
of Risk Management, Incident Report
(Maximum Confidentiality), May 2276

SIX

Maneuvering

"Applicants to the master-at-arms rating must provide three recommendations from active-duty personnel of NCO status or higher,
including a minimum of one commissioned officer. Please list recommending personnel with assignment/command below:
    Lieutenant Lynette Kelly, Commanding Officer, ANS Joan of Arc
    Colonel Daniel Figueroa, Commanding Officer, Ascension Hall
                Honor Guard
    Admiral Meiling Yeoh, Commanding Officer, Archangel Navy"
—Personnel File for Crewman Tanner Malone, June 2276

The first morning at Fort Melendez convinced Tanner that his rating school would be nothing like his time in basic at Fort Stalwart
or his still relatively regimented month with the marine recruits
in weapons and tactics school. The syllabus and all of his research
promised a fairly rigorous four months, with time set aside daily
for PT in addition to significant combat training. Yet most of the
schedule lent itself to classroom time.

He saw listings for lectures, examinations, and mock trials. Master-at-arms training would involve more than a little bit of role-play. Often enough, he'd just be himself. Sometimes he'd be called upon to be the bad guy. When Tanner checked in at the barracks and first started meeting the other members of his class of non-rates—along with aspiring intelligence specialists, survival-men, cryptologists, and the students of other ratings schools on the base—he even got the impression that he might have a good time with all of this.

The tables set out for Tanner's class of thirty on their first day reminded him of his first meeting with Everett and Janeka, but MA1 Hartford took to the front of the room and struck a decid-edly different tone. He didn't bark, nor insult anyone, or have to deliberately call the room to order. Students all quieted down and listened as soon as he stepped up to talk, mostly about base regula-tions and ordinary concerns. He joked and smiled.

Then, with his eyes flicking up beyond the assembled class to the door at the rear of the room, he called, "Attention on deck."

Everyone rose and snapped to attention. "As you were," said the newcomer. As Tanner and the others sat back down, they saw Hartford step aside for an older man in a crisp but standard gray navy service uniform—with blood stripes on his trousers and admiral's stars on his shoulders and collar.

"Morning, everyone," he said, offering a friendly enough smile. "Sorry to derail the class here, but the instructors tell me it's better to do this early rather than late. If you didn't see my handsome face on the wall with all the other base officers in the barracks lobby, I'm Rear Admiral Todd Branch, and I'm the CO of this base here." His accent immediately gave away his origins. He had to be from one of Archangel's asteroid mining colonies. "To be honest," he admitted, "I don't know why I introduce myself with my first name anymore, 'cause if any of you called me 'Todd,' military custom would obligate me to have you skinned alive."

Most of the class chuckled. Admiral Branch gave a shrug. "You'll probably only see me this once, and then at graduation. I'll give a nice, folksy speech about duty or patriotism or whatever. If you have family there, they'll get inspired after seeing how far a hick like me can go in the navy, and they'll probably project all of those hopes onto you, so you're welcome for that.

"I come down here on the first day of every new class of MAs because you folks have an exceptional degree of responsibility within the navy. You all passed through a pretty serious selection process to get here. And you're all part of the 'new guard,' too, so you've already come through a new breadth and depth of training. It's okay to be proud of that. The old codgers around here still have plenty to teach you. I'm more concerned about the responsibility of your rating.

"You're gonna spend a lot of time playing security guard once you get out of here. You'll babysit morons in the brig who did stupid shit because they were drunk or frustrated or whatever. You'll walk around a ship or an orbital station or a base and make sure doors are locked like they should be. Sometimes you'll serve on boarding teams and maybe someday you'll be part of real criminal investigations. But hopefully before you signed up for this, someone told you that the job is usually—*hopefully*—pretty mundane, and the most exciting thing you'll do is break up a brawl once in a blue moon.

"The thing is, you're part of a very powerful organization with the navy. And you may well find yourselves in combat someday. I'm here to tell you, both as a highfalutin officer and a combat veteran, that these are two things that will make people *lose their goddamn minds*, and that's gonna be the real test you face as a master-at-arms."

He paused and looked around the classroom as if to ensure he still had everyone's attention, but he needn't have bothered. Everyone knew when to shut up and listen.

"You are here to enforce the law. You are also here to enforce the chain of command. Ideally, these are one and the same, but there are times when it's someone above you in the chain of command who screws that up. People in power sometimes abuse power. People in combat sometimes just plain throw the law out the window once the shooting starts, and we actively teach you all to fight dirty—but there's a difference between fighting dirty and committing a crime. And it can also be difficult to know when the fight's actually over and it's time to pull back from the ruthlessness and return to what we ordinarily consider normal behavior.

"The most difficult challenge you may ever face isn't an enemy who's out to kill you," said the admiral. "It isn't aliens, it isn't pirates, it isn't bombs and bullets and nonsense lasers. The most difficult challenge you may ever face in this service is the prospect of having to face down your own shipmates, including an officer or NCO above your rank, because you know what they're doing is wrong. Everyone has that responsibility, from the chief of naval operations right down to the newest recruit showing up on the first day of basic. It's tough to swallow. It's tough to recognize that moment when and if it comes. And, to be honest, it isn't remotely fair given the way you're trained to fight dirty and obey orders without question or hesitation. But that responsibility exists. It never goes away.

"You men and women, who will be masters-at-arms, will carry that burden closer and more dearly than anyone else, because you aren't ordinary crewmen anymore. You're officers of the law. You will be taught here to keep vigil over your shipmates and their behavior. You will be educated in the laws and the ethics of military service, and anyone who says those things don't exist or don't matter has watched too many movies. Laws and ethics are what make an army or a navy something different than a mob of assholes with guns. We cannot let ourselves become that mob. That's where your real responsibility lies.

"You, even more than any of your other shipmates, must know when to say, 'Aye, aye, sir,' and when to say, 'No, sir. That's illegal, sir. That's *wrong*, sir.' And you may even, God forbid, someday have to say, 'You're under arrest, *sir*,' when you know that 'sir' holds the unquestioning loyalty of everyone around you.

"You are not commissioned officers. Chances are slim that any of you will make it beyond third class before your first term of enlistment is up. But when you leave here, you will not only be Archangel Navy crewmen, you'll also be officers of the law. You are invested with authority and a sacred trust . . . and that isn't done just for you to turn a blind eye or walk away from a confrontation."

• • •

"In a crushing blow to Archangel, StellarCast Communications has opted out of a deal to provide access to its communications drone network. With so many providers declining to carry Archangel traffic, the system must provide for interstellar communications on its own. StellarCast CEO Vikram Pandit denied rumors of pressure from Lai Wa and NorthStar regarding his decision. 'We simply felt that Archangel's low credit and other trouble made the deal a bad risk,' Pandit explained."

—Armstrong News Service, June 2276

"Yes, long-term occupations are . . . I'm sorry, did I call it an occupation again?" Brekhov sighed. His public affairs adviser nodded. Brekhov leaned back in his plush desk chair, waving one hand as if to banish the word from the air. "Peacekeeping operations, I should say, are inherently unprofitable in the short term, yes. We must look at operations in Hashem as an investment.

"Additionally, we're a neutral party in all of this. We contracted out ships in order to ferry troops, of course, but Prince Murtada assured us that the operation would be peaceful, and there is in fact substantial question as to who fired the first shots. There may have been provocateurs at work. At any rate, our troops and CDCs are coming in to create a buffer and restore the peace. Our jobs will be about reconstruction, law and order, and stability. Should Prince Murtada and Prince Kaseem continue to fight on through the rest of the Kingdom—tragic as that may be, and we'll naturally work to restore the peace—the ordinary people of Scheherazade and elsewhere will know we're there to protect them from that turmoil. In the end, they'll remember us as protectors regardless of the final political outcome. Good enough?"

"I think so," said his interviewer. "I'll give the language a polish and then get it back to you before it goes out to the shareholders."

"See that you do," Brekhov replied. "We want to speak to our shareholders' interests, but this is bound to get out into the open media. The troubles of serving two masters," he added, and then dismissed the aide with a polite nod.

"How sure can we be that Murtada won't turn on us?" asked Jon Weir. He glanced up from the screen of notes floating over his lap to take the drink offered to him by Brekhov's butler. Brekhov had a brilliant, well-appointed home overlooking the ocean, with sunlight streaming in through bay windows behind the CEO's desk. It made for a nicer setting than the executive suites in the city—especially with all of them still being scoured for bugs and other spying devices.

Meetings on matters such as this were never discussed in those offices, anyway.

"Because Murtada is dependent on us for guns and fuel," snorted Maria Pedroso. "Come on, Jon. This isn't exactly our first rodeo. We know his time lines. It'll take at least two years for him to pacify the rest of the Kingdom, and that's if things go swimmingly for him. The king still has loyal people, and they're only now getting fully mobilized. The king also has Prince Khalil, whom most of the population would rather see as successor. Kaseem's people are on the move and won't give up without a serious fight. Murtada will slow down as soon as he gets a bloody nose."

"He'll lean hard on his holdings for further resources and manpower," said Brekhov, "and then we'll intercede, publicly, as a matter of conscience. The people of Hashem will see it. And then, yes, Jon, they'll prefer us to any of their princes."

Weir shifted a bit in his seat. Maria looked perfectly relaxed, dressed in stylish but casual clothes for a vacation, just like their boss. Weir still wore his suit, having come from slightly more formal duties elsewhere on Fairhaven. "Still, the short-term expense of keeping the fleet engaged in the Scheherazade system and all the rest is a strain on the budget. Every day I get an earful from Donaldson about our cash reserves. We're stretched thin as it is."

"It's a gamble, I'll grant," Brekhov agreed, "but our exposure is limited. Lai Wa has seen fit to underwrite a certain degree of the operation, given that we're salvaging or protecting a good number of their assets with all this. And if we have to scale back our exposure further, we'll pressure the Union fleet to step up and take their share of the burden."

"You think they'll do that?"

"They will if we push them hard enough," said Pedroso. "We have more leverage on them than the guns and butter stuff. We own fifty-eight percent of all the personal debt among fleet personnel. If we dangle the right incentives, the fleet's leadership will be chomping at the bit for the Union Assembly to let them go in. That'll be all the political cover those assholes need."

"Mm. About that," Brekhov said, sitting up and putting his drink down on his desk. "Donaldson gave me a better analysis of our pressure tactics for Archangel. I think it's time to pull another tool out of the box."

"Excuse me, sir?" the butler interrupted. A small holo screen floated near the man's hand. "Mr. Donaldson just arrived. He's asking to see you immediately. Apparently he's on his way through the mansion now."

Brekhov received the news with a curious frown. "Speak of the devil. Is anyone with him?"

"No, sir. He's alone. I'm sorry I didn't catch this news sooner."

"It's fine. Have him shown in." The words had hardly left his mouth before Brekhov heard a knock at the door to his spacious home office. "Ah. He must be in a real hurry." With a gesture of his hand, Brekhov had the door open. "Terry, welcome. I take it this is something urgent?"

The tall, thin man in the suit hardly slowed his stride until he reached Brekhov's desk. "You're going to want to see this, Anton," he said. He tapped the ring on his finger to open up his own stylish holocom, a model so streamlined it wasn't yet on the open market. Screens opened up. Donaldson breathlessly input commands, opening up a larger screen for Brekhov's benefit. "You know about the stock drop for CDC over the last few weeks?"

"Yes." Brekhov's brow furrowed deeper with concern.

"Coughlin did an interview," Donaldson explained, and then opened up a video preset to a specific moment. Brekhov and the other viewers saw a woman journalist and a suited, distinguished if somewhat portly man whom they all recognized as the CEO of one of their rival companies.

". . . You're saying there's no truth to any of the rumors about CDC's cash reserves?" asked the journalist. "Rumors that seem to be driving your stock prices down?"

"Well, Anna, I can't claim to have heard every rumor out there." Jedidiah Coughlin shrugged, holding his hands out openly as if to concede a point. "But to address the overall point, no. There's no factual basis to any rumor that our cash on hand is low."

"He looks terrible," murmured Pedroso, who leaned forward in her seat to watch.

"Yeah," Weir said.

"Shh!" Donaldson cut them off.

"No truth at all, Mr. Coughlin?"

"None whatsoever. I couldn't tell you where that came from."

"You don't think that CDC's affairs in Hashem or the ongoing lockout from Archangel might have anything to do with it?"

"Oh, I'm sure people speculate. People speculate all the time. Heck"—he chuckled—"'speculating' is a long-standing profession here on Earth."

"Don't joke, Jed," breathed Brekhov, "you sound like you're covering something up."

"But no," Coughlin continued, "those matters are well in hand. The ships in Hashem are largely the same ships we had in Archangel space all along, so it's not like operating them in another system creates a new expense."

"Even when it's not part of a contracted arrangement for payment?" asked the journalist, her tone and mannerism perfectly calm and courteous. Her approach seemed friendly. Almost helpful. "How do you respond to sources at Lloyd's Financial who express privately that the firm is looking to reduce its exposure with CDC by pulling back from regular repurchase agreements?"

Coughlin blinked. "Again, A-Anna," he stammered, "I couldn't speak to a single source sharing a single rumor, but—"

"Damn. How old is this?" asked Brekhov with wide eyes.

"Six days," said Donaldson. "I got it off our internal express dispatch. The rest of Fairhaven won't have it before tomorrow morning. Anton, I got a transmission from a follow-up dispatch ship as I made it here. Dallas sent it about ten minutes after the one with this broadcast. CDC's stock fell another eight percent before this interview was over and it was still dropping."

Brekhov sat back in his chair and rubbed his eyes. "That stupid idiot never should have spoken up in the first place." He exhaled. "Now he looks like he's hiding something. And this is six days old . . ."

"What're they losing so much cash over?" asked Weir.

"Everything you'd expect," Donaldson grumbled. "Archangel, Hashem, a couple bad product rollouts, and then this rumormongering. CDC's overexposed. They should've seen it coming, and they shouldn't have gone in on Hashem with us like they did."

In the space of a few heartbeats, Brekhov's expression moved from breathless dread to rage. He swept his desk with one angry forearm, sending glasses, papers, and a small crystalline statue flying off to one side. Weir jerked back in his seat, still new enough to his position that he'd never seen the CEO's anger take physical expression.

Pedroso and Donaldson were not so surprised. They shared a long, wary glance while Brekhov fumed. Pedroso gave a nod, and Donaldson spoke again. "Sir," he said, "we should talk about our exposure if CDC actually runs out of cash."

. . .

"It's getting pretty bad out here, Tanner. Every night there are three different jerks on the news talking about how Archangel is pulling down the whole economy and they never tell any other side of it. Some of my instructors are repeating it, too. Hell, I got a snotty remark from the junior cohort commander about me wanting a free lunch because I'm from Archangel. If you see your ex, tell her she'd better punch up the PR, because we don't look good at all."

—Midshipman Madelyn Carter, Annapolis, August 2276

"This is why we never should have outlawed extraterritorial assassinations."

Patrick Shay's grumble broke the relative silence in the conference room, but no one replied right away. From her seat at the far end of the conference table, Andrea Bennett looked up and opened her mouth to speak, but Victor Hickman headed that off with a gentle hand on her wrist and a stern look. The president's chief of staff then jotted two words onto the paper notepad in front of him: "No politics."

Andrea made a face but nodded in consent. The leader of Archangel's religious conservative Heritage Party had offered her a wonderful opening that she would have to let slide for the sake of governmental unity. Nothing said here could be used to score points in the media. They'd all managed to agree to that before the briefings began.

A dozen senators sat at the table, but in practice only three of them spoke. Stewart Dempsey, leader of the liberal Foundation Party, was the closest ally President Aguirre had in the senate and in the room. The real heavyweights, though, were Shay and Diana Castillo of the Compass Party.

"Senator Shay, you're welcome to initiate legislation to change that," said David Kiribati. He sat beside President Aguirre at the center of the table, which was lined up with several of the president's advisers opposite the legislative leaders.

"No, he's not." Castillo scowled. As a younger woman, she'd spearheaded the newborn secular conservative Compass Party that made Archangel's drift from its religious roots into a lasting change. She'd also been president herself only two decades ago.

Aguirre was not entirely thrilled with her return to politics in the last election, but he couldn't complain now. He needed her. "Sorry, senator," he said. "Gallows humor. Anyway, assassinating them wouldn't matter. They'd be replaced practically overnight. We're not dealing with individuals here, we're dealing with a mindset. Someone will always step up to act like this until the behavior itself becomes unprofitable."

"And you say that your primary source for this information is no longer embedded within NorthStar, correct?" asked Castillo. "All of this has been vetted and verified already?"

"The officer in charge felt that exposure was imminent, so she pulled the source, yes," said Kiribati. "We've verified the info as best we can. A lot of that comes down to statistical analysis, but we spent the last couple months on it before coming to you. We're confident in our conclusions."

"So this represents a covert action that is no longer in progress?" asked Shay.

"Technically, yes"—Kiribati nodded—"so this briefing is therefore not subject to restrictions under Article Nineteen, if that's what you're asking. Regardless, I implore you all not to go public with any of this."

"That's why you asked us to come without any staff aides," noted Senator Dempsey. "And why you offered the PR gag on Andrea over there."

"You've got it," Aguirre confirmed, leaning forward in his seat. "Senators, about ten months ago, we all got together in this room and agreed to take back our schools from these bastards. I feel a bit silly saying 'take back,' when we never had control in the first place," he added with a grumble, "but that's neither here nor there. We agreed to hammer out a basic outline of a plan and we stuck with it, and because of that unity and commitment, the overwhelming majority of teachers and other staff stayed on. We had the schools back up and running in less than two months, and now they're *our* schools."

"They're our religious schools now," muttered Castillo.

"Ten percent!" Shay blurted. "Ten percent of social studies curriculum is dedicated to religious studies! A curriculum that specifically doesn't proselytize! It's cultural awareness!"

"And that's a compromise that we agreed to make," Aguirre counseled calmly, holding up his hands in a gesture of peace while giving Castillo a stern frown. "It wasn't the only compromise, either. But those deals got us where we wanted. We hammered that all out quietly, well in advance of the public debate. You got your parties in line, we offered cover, we went out of our way to share the credit, and we got it done.

"I invited you all here to ask you to do it again. Only this time we need to do it on a much bigger scale, and we need to be rock solid."

The senators glanced at one another curiously. Dempsey spoke first. "What is it you want to do?"

"Yesterday, we received an offer from the chairman of the Union Assembly to mediate a settlement. He's got NorthStar, Lai Wa, and CDC ready to sit down with us. They're ready to make concessions."

"They're ready to cry 'uncle,' huh?" Shay frowned. "Why now? CDC's hurting lately, but NorthStar and Lai Wa seem fine. We can't be costing them *that* much money, and they've fought tooth and nail on every front."

"The intelligence," Castillo realized. "You said your operatives believed that the source was already at risk. They know that we know?"

Kiribati nodded. "It seems likely, yes. We probably know more than they think we do, though. Our people on Scheherazade came back with a smoking gun. It's also possible that all this has hurt the other two big players more than they're letting on."

"But we're not going to give the school system back," Dempsey said. "We agreed to that. We didn't go through all of that for nothing."

"No," Aguirre agreed. "No, we didn't."

"So, what, then?" asked Castillo.

"That's what we're here to discuss, senator," Aguirre said. "We need to discuss our options, work out a compromise that we can live with, and then sell it—*quietly*—to our respective parties, and we need to do that in advance of accepting any offer to negotiate. I realize that could take weeks. Maybe a month or two. I'm willing to accept that. The Big Three may get tired of waiting for a response and start complaining about it publicly, and I don't care. If you'll work with me to ensure solidarity on our end, I'll take the heat." He looked around the room. "Can we do that?"

Dempsey nodded. "Sure," Castillo replied. Shay also voiced his consent, though most present knew he more or less had to agree once Castillo was on board.

"No leaks?" Aguirre pressed. Again, he saw unanimous agreement.

"So again," Castillo said, "what have you got in mind? I'm sure the Big Three will fall all over themselves to get us to stay quiet with this. We'll probably have to give some ground to let them save face and make it look legitimate to outside observers, but we could have much better terms than we've ever had."

Aguirre gave a slow nod. "That's one way we could go, yes."

"But that's not your plan, is it?"

"No. No, it's not."

• • •

"Dear Mr. Malone,

"Congratulations on your outstanding payment record with our Educational Investment Payoff (EIP) program. To date, you have paid off 16,500 credits of your educational debt, which exceeds the minimum payoff target.

"However, we regret to inform you that due to the debt defaults and failing credit of the Archangel system, NorthStar Corporation and its affiliates can no longer recognize the EIP payment-matching arrangement formerly held between NorthStar, the Archangel Navy, and the government of Archangel. Because of these unfortunate circumstances, your current educational debt remains at 53,974 credits, rather than the 37,132 credits we reported in your last statement.

"We understand that this may cause some disappointment, and we sympathize."

—Personal Account Statement, September 2276

Tanner held back as his boarding team leader stepped closer to the freighter's crew chief. He didn't like the look on the stranger's face, or the arrangement of crates and machinery in view. A couple of other freighter crewmen stood nearby, all lingering around and watching rather than working. That didn't seem odd. People stopped and watched boardings happen all the time. Yet as the usual routine progressed, Tanner felt something out of place. He saw less lollygagging and more tension in the body language before him.

The crew chief turned his back to the boarding team leader, reaching for something out of sight, and then spun around quickly to swing a huge wrench at Tanner's comrade. Tanner had his laser pistol out by the time the wrench connected with the team leader's shoulder. The world around him exploded into action; crewmen burst from their positions, many of them having hidden behind the plentiful cover offered by the freighter's myriad forms of cargo. Several rushed forward; others took off in different directions, but that only meant they were a lesser priority. Tanner put a blast straight through the crew chief's torso, shooting him even before his injured team leader fell out of the way. Then he turned his attention to all the approaching movement in his peripheral vision.

Freighter crewmen ran left, right, and away, ducking for cover or reaching for weapons. Tanner started shooting. With no cover in immediate reach, Tanner threw himself to the deck as he fired. He didn't hit with every blast, but he put down more than one of his targets in those first few seconds. Blast after blast shot from his weapon. People screamed. Men fell lifelessly to the deck.

Someone ran down the passageway up ahead. Tanner saw only shadows, but he didn't need more. He launched himself up from the deck to chase after the fleeing crew, knowing from ugly experience the importance of seizing the initiative and holding it. His priorities fell into place as he reached the edge of the compartment and dove through, ready to hit the deck and fire again as soon as he saw a target.

His leap took him right through the edge of the hologram. Tanner found himself in the dark margins of numerous other holographic training areas. Tiles marked out the edges of each, and in fact he found his left hand and wrist partially within another holographic cube, causing a disruption at the edges.

"Woah, woah, Malone," came a voice in his helmet, "what the fuck are you doing?"

Tanner blinked. He took a deep breath, making sure to calm himself before he spoke. His first few tries at judgment shoots after the loss of *St. Jude* had left him shaking. He'd passed a similar test on *Joan of Arc*, but given the restrictions of the cargo bay, it was easier to remember that the people were all holograms. *I'm fine*, he thought after another second. *I'm fine.*

"Malone, get back in here!" demanded another voice.

"Aw Christ," muttered Tanner. He holstered his weapon and walked back through the edge of the hologram—now just a flat blue projection—to face the music.

Two uniformed masters-at-arms stood behind a red line on the opposite end of Tanner's training "cube," both with holo screens in front of them listing his performance info, testing parameters, or whatever else they looked at while watching someone decide whether or not to shoot at holographic people. Both had a good fifteen to twenty years in service on him. Neither looked terribly pleased.

"What was that?" asked MA2 Divin.

"That was reflex. Sorry."

"Reflex?" scowled MA1 Hartford.

"Are you taking this seriously?" pressed Divin.

"Sure. Yes. Of course I am," Tanner answered sincerely.

"Then what the hell was that?" asked Hartford, pointing at the holographic wall behind Tanner. "You just shot every mother-fucker on the deck."

Tanner hesitated, but couldn't hold it back: "I didn't shoot my boarding team leader."

"You—" blurted Divin, but then bit off his anger.

Hartford was less restrained. "You mowed down everyone you didn't know, and then you charged off into the passageway! What the hell were you going to do?"

"I was gonna take engineering," Tanner admitted.

". . . What?"

"Well, I didn't know how far back the hologram went," Tanner explained, hoping that part sounded at least a little convincing, "and so I figured the test might still be running, and—"

"You were gonna take the engineering space of a hostile freighter. By yourself."

"Yes."

"You thought this whole test layout would take you all the way to a holographic engineering space?" asked Divin.

"Seems kind of silly now, yeah." Tanner scratched the back of his neck.

"Okay, whatever, forget that," Hartford decided with a wave of his hands. "You planned on taking engineering all by yourself? Without calling for any backup at all?"

"That was on my mind, yes," Tanner said, "I just hadn't spoken yet. But I can't wait on that when the suspect ship might take off." He paused. "It's happened to me before."

Divin's mouth hung open for a moment, but it closed with a snap as he turned to share a quick look with his fellow instructor. The other MA raised both hands in the air as if to relinquish the situation, turned around, and stalked out.

"Malone," said Divin, "I'm not used to saying this, but I think we're gonna have to dial you back a bit. I'm putting you back at the end of the line tonight. Head out into the waiting room and send in whomever is next. In the meantime, you open up your holocom, call up an incident report form, and fill it out to the best of your ability to explain all this like it was real. I want attention to detail. I want an explanation of your decision to escalate violence of action. I want descriptions of the suspects. All of it. From memory. Did you see anything that gave you hints that this was about to turn bad? Write it down. Doesn't matter if it would be admissible in court or not, write it down. Got me?"

"Aye, aye." Tanner nodded. He took off his gun belt and handed it to Divin, who accepted it without another word.

Out in the hallway, Tanner found Hartford coming back. Tanner stopped, unsure whether the older man would say anything. Instead, Hartford slowed long enough to pat Tanner on the shoulder and then continued on his way.

The waiting room held several rows of chairs, more than enough to accommodate Tanner's whole class. About half of his fellow MA students were in other training spaces within the firing range. That left fifteen or so in the room, most of them either playing with this or that on their holocoms or talking to pass the time. "Hey, whoever's next," Tanner spoke up, jerking his thumb over his shoulder, "Hartford and Divin are ready. Compartment Four."

A young woman rose and threw Tanner a concerned glance. "You're done already? You just went in there ten minutes ago."

Tanner shook his head. "They said to send in the next person." He looked for a chair in a relatively empty corner as his classmate went on her way.

"What happened?" asked one student.

"Did you wash out?" asked another.

"No, I don't think so." Tanner frowned as he called up the reports screen from his holocom. "I'm probably not supposed to say anything. They told me to put myself back at the end of the rotation and write up a report on the last test."

"Reports? Holy shit, they want us to do reports on this, too?"

"God, how many reports are we supposed to do?"

"They didn't tell me to write anything up! You think that means I failed?"

Tanner used the report as an excuse to turn his back on his classmates. In truth, he wondered if perhaps he should go hide in the bathroom while he calmed down. He'd managed to keep his hands from shaking this far. Isolated from the conversation, Tanner took in several deep breaths, leaned forward, and rubbed his eyes. He breathed some more. He could still feel his blood pumping. His shoulders remained tense. Yet he felt it slowly drain—thankfully.

The edge came off his fight-or-flight reaction as soon as he'd run out of the hologram on the testing floor. Tanner considered that a good sign. In the first months after *St. Jude*, he'd had to focus on things like the lights in the ceiling and the view out the nearest window to calm himself.

Therapy wasn't always this effective. He wondered how veterans in earlier times ever managed.

Tanner took another long, shaking breath before he actually focused on the screen in front of him. It had been a long day already, mixing classroom instruction with role-playing scenarios, PT, and a pop quiz on evidence rules. Yesterday had been much the same, and all the days before, though today was the first day-of-judgment shoot training rather than the much more structured marksmanship training on the range.

The instructors saved this for the evening hours on purpose. They wanted the students to be a little tired and stressed. No one could expect to make all their shoot-or-don't-shoot decisions early on a shift, just after breakfast, and while they were bright-eyed and bushy-tailed, whatever that meant. At first, Tanner wondered how much combat and defense training the school could pack in given all the other stuff on the agenda. Then he arrived and discovered that combat classes simply weren't included on the schedule, but they were very much part of MA training.

As the instructors said over and over, the life of a junior MA was mostly that of a security guard . . . but if they had to deal with a dangerous suspect, chances were that suspect would be a combat-trained Archangel crewman or marine. An MA didn't just have to train to take down the enemy; he had to be ready to take down one of his own.

· · ·

"Rumors are already circulating that NorthStar is having trouble finding enough cash to cover its weekly obligations. Company officials have laughed off these rumors, calling them clumsy propaganda at best. Yet some major shareholders complain that detailed answers have not been forthcoming since peacekeeping operations in Scheherazade placed a new strain on the company's security fleet. Many observers suggest that NorthStar may face the same weaknesses shown by CDC in recent months."

—"Weekly Rundown," *Union Business Review*, October 2276

"Seems like a crime to come all this way and not have any time to enjoy the scenery," Andrea muttered. "Almost two weeks in transit and this is as close as we get."

Men and women in suits and a handful of others in dress uniforms strode through the ornate halls, all of them presumably on important business. Through the arcing windows beyond them, Andrea could see the blue skies and white clouds of Earth looming above the station. Africa slowly passed by, lit and warmed by the sun, reminding her of holiday trips during her years at Harvard.

The planet and its people had survived all of the growing pains from the first uses of tools to spaceflight. Despite all of humanity's self-inflicted wounds, from slavery to genocide to the environmental damage that took such a toll while the reach of humanity barely stretched out beyond the orbit of its moon, the race had survived.

Yet even during the Expansion Wars, when humanity struggled fiercely against the Krokinthian and Nyuyinaro races for its place among the stars, those same aliens maintained all along that humanity was its own worst enemy.

Andrea couldn't argue with that. She never saw how anyone with a shred of objectivity could argue with it. And here she stood, wondering if she was part of another self-inflicted wound.

"Never cared for it," sniffed Abdul Shadid. Archangel's finance minister stood beside Andrea, looking up only because she drew his attention to the home world looming above. "I've been here a few times, but I've always been happy to go home."

"Really?" Andrea replied. Like Andrea, Shadid looked several decades younger than his actual age. In truth, he had a couple of decades on her. "All that history? All the places to go? I'd have thought you would be all about this."

"The history and culture are great, but I don't care for the day-to-day reality down there. I was as excited as anyone for the hajj, and it was a worthwhile experience, but everything else I found? Too depressing. I felt like everyone on Earth was either too poor to leave, too rich to care about anyone else's problems, or too religious to look beyond the ground at their feet."

"Speaking of too rich to care," broke in Theresa Cotton, her voice deliberately low. Standing just behind the pair, she drew their attention to the suited gentleman approaching their small clutch of staff. "Looks like it's showtime. Stick to the plan," she reminded her colleagues.

Andrea nodded. As foreign minister, Theresa technically held the senior position and therefore led the delegation, but the matters at hand fell more toward Abdul's role. As the junior partner on this mission, all Andrea had to do was follow their lead. She did exactly that in a literal sense as they were ushered into a well-appointed conference room, where they found both their Union Assembly hosts and high-level executives and negotiators from NorthStar, Lai Wa, CDC, and others waiting for them.

"Ladies and gentlemen, thank you for joining us," said Terrence Jackson from the head of the table. The vice-chairperson of the Union Assembly presented a genuinely welcoming face, gesturing to open seats. He and the other Assembly representatives—most of the rest standing near chairs somewhat removed from the table, on hand in case they were needed—gave off a more congenial mood than the stone-faced corporate suits opposite Archangel's side of the table. That much shocked no one, of course. The economic ripples of the dispute reached far beyond the belligerent parties. The Union wanted desperately to smooth all of this over.

So did the corporations, of course, but Andrea knew that urge came from a very different mind-set.

Everyone sat. Jackson went through perfunctory introductions, naming those present as if anyone didn't already know all the names and faces at the table. "Mr. Lung-Wei here represents Lai Wa, and Mr. Covington leads our CDC delegation," Jackson explained. Andrea tuned out the rest of it while her eyes scanned the group. She felt all too familiar by now with Maria Pedroso, NorthStar's head of Risk Management, and their chief administrative officer, Jon Weir.

As it turned out, Weir either wasn't as familiar with everyone at the table or he felt like playing coy. He tilted his head as Jackson finished his round of introductions with Andrea. "That seems a little surprising," he said, flashing a smile that might have been charming in other circumstances. "I wouldn't expect a press secretary to be part of this."

Andrea nodded slightly. "I can see how the title might give that impression, Mr. Weir. However, I'm a senior policy adviser to President Aguirre, I have some background in macroeconomics, and I've served two terms in the Archangel Senate." She offered a tight-lipped smile and added, "I also bake when the mood strikes me."

Weir blinked, shrinking back in his seat. He glanced up the table as Jackson cleared his throat to break in before the exchange went any further.

"Now that we've all been introduced," Jackson said, "we should move straight to the issues at hand. Archangel's reforms have caused considerable economic stress in recent months, reaching well beyond its own borders. Everyone here and the Union as a whole has an interest in reducing the current tensions."

"Listen, for two hundred years, relationships like ours have tied the Union together." Maria Pedroso smiled, holding her hands out and open in a gesture of reconciliation. "We understand that the government of Archangel isn't happy with how things have played out lately. Mistakes have been made. We can all concede that. But the very concerns where Archangel has focused its ire—areas like defense and education—these are the things that actually *unify* the Union. We have arms limits on warships with the express understanding that corporate security fleets will help fill the gaps without leading to an arms buildup among Union states. NorthStar, Lai Wa, and CDC all provide educational programs with differences, sure, but those differences are vastly outweighed by their commonalities, because we want to create a Union standard.

"Archangel has rejected all of that, with hardly any dialogue or discussion on how to address your system's concerns. This has led to tensions on all sides, along with a few genuine tragedies. We need to come together on this before it goes too far."

"We must resolve these differences and return to normalcy," agreed Lai Wa's representative. Lung-Wei's tone did not rise to the warmth of Pedroso's, but he, too, opted for a less confrontational tack. "We are all prepared to renegotiate security services, educational contracts, and a return of packet ship services. From there, we can address the issue of Archangel's credit standing on the broader Union stage and other large concerns."

"We're not interested," replied Theresa.

Eyes across the table blinked in surprise. "Minister Cotton," said Pedroso, "you haven't yet heard our offers. We have a number of specialists on hand to address the particulars. We'd thought you would bring a delegation of similar size, but regardless, I think you'll find our offers are to Archangel's benefit."

"Ms. Pedroso," Theresa began, "we didn't bring much of a delegation because there was no need. Edith, if you would?" she asked, looking to one of the staffers sitting behind her. A young-looking blonde woman activated the holocom mounted on her bracelet and keyed in several commands to the resulting holographic screen.

"Mr. Vice-Chair, ladies and gentlemen," Theresa continued, "we have just uploaded to the conference room network a series of files outlining numerous operations by NorthStar, Lai Wa, and CDC targeting Archangel. For the past several months, Lai Wa and NorthStar have both exerted considerable pressure on independent packet ship services to prevent them from engaging in contracts with Archangel. In April of this year, NorthStar agents on Edison tried to hire a pirate crew to raid ships moving into and out of Archangel space. In May, CDC security fleet personnel fabricated evidence of at least two incidents of smuggling that led to arrests and charges against Archangel merchants traveling outside the system. We also have solid material evidence that NorthStar enlisted the aid of Prince Murtada's forces during his invasion of Scheherazade in an attempt to kidnap Archangel consulate staff."

Reactions on the other side of the table were mixed, but this in and of itself spoke volumes. Many kept a calm poker face. Some merely raised eyebrows. Others looked shocked. Jackson opened a holo screen at his seat. Several more opened up at the conference table and among the seats behind it.

"In addition," said Abdul, quieting the murmurs within the room, "you will find a copy of the algorithm set for distribution for this year's Union Academic Investment Evaluation—the Test." At this, Pedroso's placid demeanor cracked. Abdul continued. "As one can see from the introductory text, from the footnotes, and from any in-depth analysis, the program reads a student's academic records, physical stress indicators, and performance during the Test in order to create an increasingly difficult experience. A small percentage of random students in a given cohort are offered a Test without these conditions in order to create a level of deniability. Notably, students in the Society of Scholars and highly gifted students are also not subjected to this extra difficulty. But for the vast majority of students, the experience is designed to take advantage of every vulnerability."

"This is—I'm not sure where to begin," said Pedroso. Her conciliatory demeanor faded. "This file proves absolutely nothing—"

"We don't have to prove anything, Ms. Pedroso," Andrea cut her off. "Not outside our own borders. Your company and its peers have gone out of their way to block or derail any attempt at interstellar regulation or oversight for the past two hundred years. There is no court with jurisdiction in matters like this, because you've made sure no such court was ever established. Archangel is well within her rights to rescind any and all contracts with NorthStar. As for Lai Wa and CDC," she said, looking to the other representatives, "only a fool would look at the student success rates and debt ratios of students from your programs and NorthStar's and suggest that you operate any differently."

Lung-Wei scowled fiercely. "Lai Wa provides a rigorous education—"

"All three of your companies take your students for a ride and then *mug* them on the way out the door," said Andrea. "You aren't interested in rigor. You're interested in profits."

"Ministers, ah—ladies and gentlemen," Jackson spoke up. "These are grave allegations."

"They're outrageous!" blurted Jon Weir. "Who cooked up all this data? Do you seriously think anyone will believe this?"

"Again, Mr. Weir, we don't have to prove this to anyone but the people of Archangel," said Theresa. "The leaders of the legislature, the system governors, and numerous other officials have already agreed upon our course of action.

"Mr. Vice-Chair, ladies and gentlemen," she continued, "if private companies within Archangel wish to maintain ties with your businesses, they will be free to do so under strict limits and government oversight. We have enough of a commitment to free enterprise not to stand in the way, but to be blunt, I wouldn't hold out much hope. However, Archangel's government will not renew any contracts with the companies represented here—not educational services, not security or relay ship services, not any material goods purchases. We'll manage all that on our own."

"What?" exclaimed Weir. Pedroso looked on in shock. Lung-Wei, too, watched with wide eyes.

"Per executive order issued before we set out for this meeting and effective as of today," added Abdul, "any and all Archangel government entities with investment capacity will divest themselves of stocks and bonds relating to your companies. The trades are likely being made now in the exchanges in and out of the solar system, give or take some timing issues."

"You're dumping our stock on the market?" Covington gasped. "That's—that's an attack!"

"No, Mr. Covington, that's the free market. Your companies represent an unsound investment. If your agents are concerned about your stock value going down, they could always buy up the shares themselves."

"Archangel will continue to pay taxes and maintain all other ties to the Union," said Theresa, focusing her attention on Jackson at the head of the table. "However, in the face of overwhelming evidence of fraud and malfeasance dating back decades, Archangel considers her outstanding primary debt to NorthStar, Lai Wa, and CDC null and void."

"Additionally, in light of this evidence," said Abdul, "members of the legislature have already drafted measures to free Archangel's citizens from any domestic laws enforcing educational debt to your companies. Those citizens may well choose to keep making payments in order to address any concerns outside of Archangel space, but they will no longer be under any domestic obligation to pay for an education designed to put them in debt from the very start."

With that, all three Archangel representatives at the table stood. Their staffers quickly did the same.

"You're out of your minds!" Weir blurted. "No one will do business with you! You'll be frozen out of the Union economy!"

"We would have to be insane to continue on as we have." Abdul frowned. "The rest of the Union will have to decide how they feel about it on their own. Regardless, Archangel has four inhabited worlds and several other settlements within our borders. I'm sure we'll get by."

"Minister Cotton, Minister Abdul," said Jackson, rising from his seat, "please, you *must* remain and discuss this. What you are suggesting—I can't begin to imagine the damage this will do to the economy of the whole Union."

"Again, Mr. Vice-Chair," Andrea replied, "if the Articles of Union provided a court with jurisdiction over interstellar commerce, we would take our case there. These corporations have managed to kill every effort at establishing such a court for two centuries. They have demonstrated time and again that they won't submit to an Archangel court for matters at this level. We're not talking about a lawsuit for a botched construction job here. This is systemic fraud and extortion impacting every one of our citizens. We're done with it."

"Mr. Vice-Chair, we thank you for your time," said Theresa. "We have a long flight back home and we'd like to make it in time for President Aguirre's Annual Address in two weeks, whereupon he plans to announce the bulk of these policies to the system and the Union at large."

"You mean you already decided to do all this?" Covington practically shouted. "Why in the hell did you even come out here, then?"

"The president decided that waiting until his Annual Address to inform you of this decision would be too much like an ambush." Andrea shrugged. "Now you have almost two weeks' forewarning."

"Two weeks?" Covington burst, becoming increasingly exasperated. "We'll all lose more than half of that time in transit back to our corporate headquarters! You know damn well how long it takes information to travel from one system to the next!"

"We've given you far more of a head start than you deserve. What you do with that is up to you. Spin it. Issue preemptive denials. We don't care. Our decisions are final. Mr. Vice-Chair, thank you again for your time. Good day."

Archangel's foreign minister led her delegation out of the conference room without another word.

Everyone heard Jackson slump back into his chair. It was the only sound anyone made in the room.

"I wasn't making some sexist comment before," muttered Weir. "I was just—"

"I know that!" snapped Pedroso. "Goddammit, Jon, everyone at the table knew that, including her! You opened yourself up for a cheap punch and she took it, and then she had you flustered right out of the gate. You just sat there like an idiot the whole time." Her fingers came up to rub her temples.

"Well, that could've gone better." Jackson sighed. His eyes were on the holo screen in front of him displaying Archangel's complaints and evidence.

"They must be brought to heel," said Lung-Wei.

Jackson favored Lung-Wei with a sour look. "Like the lady said, it's not like you can bring them to court. You people have all made sure of that. What a mess . . ."

"It is far worse than you know."

"Lung-Wei," Pedroso murmured, throwing her counterpart a warning look.

"We do not have time to shuttle back and forth to our superiors and our boards of directors, Maria," Lung-Wei said. "It will be at least nine days before you or this news can reach your headquarters at Fairhaven. You and I both know the implications of this, here and now, as do others in this room. We must contain the damage with all possible speed."

"He's right," groaned Covington.

"You don't think we can talk about this privately first?" she pressed.

"Maria," said Covington, "the markets will tank on this. You know it, and you know why. And then we will have a run on *our banks* and the markets will nosedive all over again."

"What are you talking about?" broke in Jackson from the head of the table. "You are the most powerful companies in the Union! How thin are your cash reserves, anyway? Archangel's economy isn't *that* big. Surely you'll be able to adjust. This has been building for months. Haven't you people insured yourselves for potential losses?"

"Mr. Vice-Chair," said Lung-Wei, "when the largest corporations in existence wish to purchase insurance, do you think they turn to the smaller companies for coverage?"

Jackson's answer caught in his throat. He quickly processed the uncomfortable expressions on the faces before him. "Oh, you've got to be kidding me," he breathed.

"It's all very complicated," Covington tried to explain. "We have insurance with smaller companies on top of all that, but it's not like they can provide everything we need. And if we did have to invoke all of those small-provider policies, we'd still see huge losses. So, naturally, we've learned to rely on each other."

"The web of bargains and agreements between us is tangled, yes"—Lung-Wei nodded—"but the end result is clear. We are all exposed. If the ninth strongest economy in the Union withdraws unilaterally from its relationships with all of us, the cascade of consequences will be disastrous for all."

"And for the Union," Pedroso concurred, turning to Jackson. "It's not just a matter of our profits. This is about more than our companies. The entire Union economy could crash."

"You didn't think about that before running these policies?" Jackson fumed, gesturing to his holo screen. "My God, how long have you run the Test this way? Your three companies alone service fifty-eight percent of the schools in the Union!"

"They can't prove any of that," Pedroso maintained, waving her hand as if to dismiss some annoying bug. "But if they go public—"

"They just *went* public!" Jackson snapped. "What do you think this meeting was?" He gestured to his Union Assembly staffers. "I'm not putting my people under a gag order to protect your dirty secrets!"

Pedroso inhaled sharply, closing her eyes just long enough to marshal an argument. "Sir, you must. If this . . . *propaganda* starts to sow doubt about our policies, we'll see a bigger crisis. The Union *runs* on primary and individual debts! If everyone sees Archangel get away with this, we'll get half the Union following suit, and that will lead to an economic collapse. We *can't* let Archangel walk away."

"What are you saying? Do you plan to use force?"

"Sir," Pedroso ventured, "for the good of the Union, if the fleet would—"

Jackson slammed his fist down on the table. "Are you out of your minds? The fleet exists to protect the whole Union, not to act as anyone's thugs!" His eyes swept the room once more, looking at the collection of dismayed faces before him. "Andrea Bennett was right. You're on your own this time."

He sat back down in his chair, looking again to the complaint laid out in front of him in soft-blue lights. "How could you all have been so stupid?"

SEVEN

Showmanship

"*We have seven dead and sixteen wounded, almost all of them from our site security force. The site has suffered material damage, but nothing that can't be fixed. They clearly weren't out to destroy the facility, because they had the run of the whole moon. It looks like they were just after the inventory, and most of it was chaff missiles. Lots of chaff missiles. We lost our whole stock. And honestly, we haven't a clue who hit us. It was a small unit, well coordinated and obviously with a lot of reach to hit us way the hell out here, but I couldn't tell you who. Maybe the investigators will come up with something, but right now I'd say it could've been anybody.*"

—Arnold Erlich, Echo-Two Munitions Facility Manager,
Internal CDC Communiqué, November 2276

"Docking complete. Boarding permissions granted. Welcome home to *Los Angeles*, marines."

Corporal Alicia Wong tilted her head back against her chair and let out a long, heavy breath. She felt more than ready to shed her combat gear and the stress of the last mission. For all the close calls and the stiff fight put up by the opposition, her team hadn't lost anyone this time like they had on the Edison job. It still left her with plenty of tension to shake off. She wouldn't be able to talk to anyone about it other than her fellow marines on the shuttle, and on board the Archangel Navy's sole cruiser, she likely wouldn't find the necessary privacy even if she tried.

Los Angeles offered enough other ways to blow off her remaining steam, though. She had friends on board. Easier duties and a familiar setting. Brent.

She smiled. *Mostly Brent,* she admitted silently. Military romances weren't easy. Regulations against "fraternization" were often vague and contradictory. Nothing in the military could be as simple as "no sleeping with a subordinate or direct superior." Yet even if a relationship could fit through the Byzantine regulations, simple things often became annoyingly complex.

Arbitrary judgments by superiors clarified the poorly written regulations regarding public displays of affection. Shipboard life meant that finding any sort of extended privacy required heroic feats. And getting caught in a compromising position, regardless of the harmlessness of it all, could still land a couple in hot water for inappropriate conduct if their superiors wanted to be jerks.

Alicia and Brent accepted all that. She'd transferred out of his platoon when they'd first started dating to avoid any disapproving glares. Her selection for repeated covert operations made for some tension between them—Brent didn't care for being left behind, nor could she blame him—but at least the frequent separations over the last year made for a little more leniency among their superiors. Sergeants were more apt to turn a blind eye or show a little more tolerance when a couple hadn't seen one another for several weeks—which, at the moment, described her situation accurately.

Gathering her pulse rifle, ammo bag, and helmet, Alicia rose from her seat and found herself behind Corporal Ravenell. She gave him a playful jab. "Haven't you ever heard of 'ladies first,' jerk?"

Ravenell looked over his shoulder. "Are there any here?" He endured another jab under his ribs with a chuckle. "Should've gotten up faster."

Rolling her eyes, Alicia let the issue drop and followed him out. She saw nothing but his back as they stepped off the shuttle's gangway and into one of *Los Angeles*'s two small hangars. Then her comrade unexpectedly picked up his pace. "Holy shit!" He laughed. "I didn't know you were transferring out here!"

Ravenell strode forward to clasp someone's hand and then hug him. Alicia saw a dark-haired scalp and arms in a navy vac suit return the hug, but nothing else at first. She glanced around and found the shuttle bay busy, but otherwise ordinary. The guys from the ship's armory were apparently a little late to collect her team's weapons, but that happened all the time. Her attention returned to Ravenell, wondering who he was so excited to see.

She blinked. "Tanner?"

"Hey!" he answered brightly. Alicia felt an immediate sense of nervousness and then relief when Tanner stepped forward but didn't throw his arms around her. "It's good to see you. I tried looking you both up when I came aboard the other night. I guess you were out," he added, gesturing to the shuttle.

Alicia had to force a smile, mostly to conceal her surprise. With a brief glance, she had enough clues to explain his presence. His gray navy vac suit bore third-class rank pips on the collar and sleeves in the style of his rating. The sidearm on his hip stood out, too, given that only so many people walked around *Los Angeles* armed. "Wow. Master-at-arms, huh?"

He quirked an eyebrow. "Yeah, they let me graduate from my rating school after all."

His expression made her blink again and shake her head. They'd been in touch through letters. She knew where he'd been.

"Sorry. Totally slipped my mind. It's been kind of far from my thoughts lately. Stuff going on." Alicia looked around. Naturally, Ravenell had already vanished, leaving her to handle this on her own.

"No worries. I only found out that I'd been assigned here three weeks ago. I guess you've been out at least that long, huh? What's been going on?"

"Training exercises," Alicia answered out of reflex. She wondered if she saw something in Tanner's eyes.

"Long exercise," he observed.

"Yeah, well, some of us gotta work for a living, poster boy," she said with a wink.

"Hey, I'm trying." Tanner shrugged. "I'm not down here lollygagging, anyway. I came aboard the day before yesterday, so I'm still getting acclimated. Just getting the tour from one of the other MAs right now, but he stepped off for a second. You need help with anything?" Tanner moved forward, his hand outstretched.

"No, I'm good. I've got all my stuff." Alicia didn't know whether to step back or not, or if she was acting naturally enough. She noted the curious way he looked her over and knew he couldn't be checking out her figure, what with all the combat gear. In fact, it was the combat gear that likely had his attention.

She had the same problem with Brent after the first mission. "Listen, I've got things to take care of."

"Sure," said Tanner. She couldn't miss the softening of his tone. He plainly realized this was awkward for her, though probably not why. "Hopefully I'll get to catch up with you later? It's nice to see a familiar face."

"Yeah, I know the feeling," she agreed, and gave a genuine grin. "There are a couple of them on this ship."

"Malone," said a firm, strong, and unmistakable woman's voice.

He winced involuntarily before slowly turning around. Unable to resist the opportunity despite her worries, Alicia managed to slip in a whack at his backside with the butt of her pulse rifle before walking away. "Have fun with that," she hissed before quickly striding off the flight deck.

That was stupid, she thought once she'd crossed into the nearby passageway. *He's gonna think you did that to flirt. And maybe you did*, she admitted, and then sighed.

No. You didn't. Stupid.

Alicia was perfectly happy with the relationship she had. About the worst thing she had to deal with were Brent's worries about her safety on missions she couldn't tell him about . . . and, now, the presence of the only other guy she'd ever slept with on the same ship.

It'll be fine. Tanner knows I'm seeing someone. Brent might not be the jealous type. We are all adults. We don't have to have any drama. It'll be fine.

And if it all goes badly I can beat the hell out of both of them.

• • •

"Master-at-arms," Janeka observed flatly after giving him a long, head-to-toe look.

Tanner nodded. She said nothing. *You're not in basic anymore,* he thought. *Be cool.* "Yep."

She quirked an eyebrow. He wondered if she meant it as a warning. "What brings you to *Los Angeles?*"

"I'm part of the crew now, gunny." He couldn't help but notice that his escort was still off doing whatever, leaving Tanner to face this reintroduction alone. He wondered if the rest of the crew of *Los Angeles* was properly terrified of Gunnery Sergeant Janeka.

"I see. You're here to keep my marines and all these navy types in line?"

"Beg your pardon?"

"Don't beg. Begging is pathetic."

Tanner swallowed. *Okay. Fine.* "Yes, gunny. Yes, I am."

She nodded, then looked him up and down again. The silence held for a long moment that grew more and more awkward for Tanner as it seemed to stretch into an eternity. Her tone remained flat as she said, "You never call. You never write."

"I'm sor—" He blinked in surprise, but bit off his response. "I didn't think you missed me."

"So it's not a matter of you being a famous big shot and us little people not being worth your time?"

He didn't look away. "That's nonsense, gunny. Little people like you are always worth my time."

Her eyes narrowed, but he thought he saw one corner of her lip twitch. She held out her open hand, and he managed not to flinch.

Tanner accepted her handshake. Unsurprisingly, she was still stronger, but she didn't squeeze so hard as to make a point of it. "I'm very glad to have you aboard, Malone."

"Thank you, gunny. It's nice to see you, too," Tanner replied, surprised by his own smile.

"I have work to do. I'm sure I'll see you later. Carry on." Janeka moved off. Tanner watched her step away and then noticed the shocked stares from most of the rest of the navy personnel in view.

Yup. Properly terrified.

Predictably, Tanner's escort and tour guide returned only after their conversation had ended. "Hey, you know Gunny Janeka?" asked MA1 Lewis.

"Yeah." Tanner nodded, shaking off the rest of his nerves from the encounter. "Yeah, she was one of my company commanders in basic."

"Holy shit." Lewis chuckled. "You did six months in basic under *her*?" He patted Tanner on the back, both out of sympathy and to direct him further along on their way. "Wow. I can't imagine what that was like."

"She's not so . . ." Tanner began, and then stopped. He opened his mouth again to offer another word of defense, but that failed him, too. Ultimately, he shrugged. "If it hadn't been for her, I'd be dead."

"Huh. Well, she does a pretty good job of keeping her marines in line. From what I've heard, she's pretty serious in the ring, sparring and stuff. Been on board for about a year now."

"Yeah, that's her." Tanner looked back to the shuttle as they left the flight deck. Ravenell and another marine offloaded a plasma repeater and its accompanying backpack of power cells, handing it over to the supply crew. Like Alicia and Janeka, Ravenell wore more substantial protection than the combat jacket and helmet that Tanner had used while on *Joan of Arc*—and, like Alicia's, Ravenell's gear looked like it had seen some serious use. "Like I said, I've been in touch with a few people from basic who're on the ship. Guess I'm surprised they didn't mention her being on board. What's she do here?"

"You'd have to look it up. I presume she rides herd on the marine detachment. I'm sure she has a formal position on the chain of command, but it's never been a concern for me."

"So you don't know what that was all about?" Tanner asked, jerking his thumb over his shoulder.

Lewis gave Tanner a sober look. He replied quietly, though they were alone in the passageway. "Nope. If they say it's a training exercise, then it's a training exercise."

Tanner's eyebrow rose. He caught the warning but pushed a little further anyway. "Don't we have enough clearance to find out?" he asked, lowering his voice to match his companion's.

The older MA shook his head. "There's clearance, and then there's need to know. They didn't talk to you about that in MA school? Or basic?"

"Sure, but the first thing I learned out of basic is that not every ship actually follows the manuals. Can't take stuff like that for granted. I can play by the book just fine, but I've learned to at least ask."

"Okay. On this ship, when it comes to security, we play it by the book. If we get wind that something suspicious is goin' on with the marines and their 'training exercises' that affects ship security or crosses a legal line? Then, yeah, we look into it, and we've got clearance. But until then, we take what they tell us at face value and leave it alone. Training exercise. Nothing more."

"Understood."

"You'll get to work with the marines enough, anyway," Lewis went on. "They help fill out shipboard security posts and sometimes boarding teams, too, which means a lot of crossover and shared responsibility. We handle the training for all that. Seems like less of an issue for you 'new guard' types, since that extended basic program has such a big boarding team component, but we still have to keep everyone up with standards and such. Plus if the marines have an incident that goes beyond a minor infraction, they have to call us in—which doesn't make any of them happy, mind you. Marines like to take care of their own, but rules are rules, right?"

"What kind of incidents?"

"Ah, it's like they tell you in school. Sometimes one of them snaps and punches a superior and it turns into a whole thing. Once in a while one of them turns out to be a real asshole—which I'm not saying is limited to the marines, 'cause there are a few gems among the navy crew here—and he'll steal something or sneak contraband on board. We pretty much only ever have drunken brawls during port calls, since nobody can have alcohol while underway. Still, there's always someone with a stash of booze or whatever, and there's always someone who's just being an idiot. Sometimes both."

"So it sounds like we don't often have much of the criminal stuff to handle?"

"Not yet, no. She's still a young ship, though, right? She hasn't been in service for two whole years yet. Give it time. Four thousand men and women in a tin can, lots of them trained to kill? Someone'll do something stupid. Unless we wind up dealing with bigger problems first."

"Like?"

"I dunno. You're supposedly the only one on this ship who's seen actual combat in the last ten years. I figured maybe you could tell me."

Tanner grimaced. "Am I gonna hear a lot of that on this ship?" he asked reluctantly.

"You might. I don't know. Like I said, there are four thousand people on board and sometimes other units pass through here for training. I can't speak for everyone." Lewis paused. "You see what I did just there?"

"No." Tanner blinked.

"I shifted subjects twice and made sure to push at least one personal button." Lewis stopped Tanner gently and leaned in. "So now that I've dragged you away from that first train of thought, what did you see back there?"

"Back . . . you mean the marines?"

"You're supposed to have your eyes open all the time. Show me what you learned in MA school, Malone."

Tanner considered it. "They were in combat kit. Looked like they hadn't gotten cleaned up in a day or two. Some of the gear was scuffed up and dirty. They looked tired."

"None of that's unusual for marines"—Lewis shrugged—"particularly if they'd been on a training run."

"I know two of them. Three of them," Tanner corrected, more or less thinking out loud. "Janeka, plus two from my recruit company. They look different now. Something in the eyes."

"What else?" Lewis waited for a response, raising one eyebrow as he saw Tanner's hesitation. "You aren't trying to work through a hunch. I can see that in *your* eyes. Work on that later. Right now, tell me. What else did you see? What did you just figure out?"

"They didn't have all their grenades," Tanner said. "Ravenell had three. Wong had only one. Janeka had two. Those don't get doled out randomly. If they were on a training exercise, they'd probably all have performed the same skill checks, right?"

Still waiting, Lewis said nothing.

A dark frown crept over Tanner's face. "I'm not the only guy on this ship who's seen combat in the last ten years."

"Need to know, Tanner," Lewis repeated. "In this job, you need to know everything you can."

"Okay, but what are they—" Tanner began, and then stopped. "Yeah. You wouldn't know that, either, would you?"

"No. But I've figured out what you've figured out. Maybe you'll take it further. But don't make noise about it unless you see something's actually wrong. That's the problem with covert ops. We're all on the same side, right? We have to assume it's all legit until we actually have reason to believe it isn't." He motioned for Tanner to resume their walk and patted him on the back. "You'll do fine at this job."

The beep from Lewis's holocom cut off whatever else he might have said. He answered the call without calling up a holo screen. "This is Lewis."

"Time to shift gears from whatever you're doing," said a voice. "He's in the lower wardroom now."

"Thanks. Lewis out." He ended the call and then gestured down another passageway. "Let's go. Best way is down here to the nearest lift."

"Where are we going?" Tanner asked. They still had a third of the ship to go before his initial orientation walk-through was finished.

"To take care of another part of your new guy checklist. The captain can be pretty busy, so we'll get this out of the way while we can."

"The captain? He meets with every third class that comes aboard?" Tanner hoped he wasn't about to be told he was someone special again.

"Personal meet and greets don't usually happen for third classes, no," said Lewis as they entered the lift, "but we have that whole 'power of arrest' thing in our rating." Lewis hit the button for the upper decks. "Can't blame a captain for wanting to personally meet everyone on his ship who has that kind of authority."

Their path led up through nine decks and a good quarter of the ship's length. Enlisted ratings and officers moved this way and that as Tanner and Lewis strode through the gray passageways. They stepped through an open hatch at least every thirty meters, an interval set by the ship's designers to minimize the dangers of decompression or explosion. In combat or any other sort of emergency, each hatch would close to compartmentalize the cruiser.

Eventually, Lewis brought Tanner toward the combat information center, but he didn't actually head inside past the two armed marine sentries. Instead, he made a right turn at the entrance, leaving the CIC behind for another destination. "Y'know, on some ships, the wardrooms are exclusively for officer dining only, and using it for anything else is like a cardinal sin."

"But not here?" asked Tanner.

Lewis stopped to turn around with a wry grin. "We don't have that kind of captain. Besides, I think 'multipurpose' might be his middle name. I guess you look okay," he said after a quick head-to-toe glance. Then he turned back to the door, knocked twice, and entered as soon as he heard a response.

Tanner followed him in, hearing Lewis's perfunctory greetings while he came to attention. The wardroom held a few small creature comforts that the enlisted galleys did not, such as actual glassware, a finely polished oak dining table, and a few paintings. Rather than place settings, though, Tanner saw half a dozen holo screens and a few hard-copy paper records spread out on the table.

There were two men inside. One of them, standing up from the opposite side of the table, was Captain Bernard. The tall, dark-skinned man's insignia marked him as a captain in rank as well as by virtue of command of the vessel. Blood stripes down the seams of his trousers attested to service in combat.

Beside him stood another officer, similarly tall but more muscular than the captain. Tanner winced. He should have remembered the name when he saw it on a few status boards upon arrival.

"Captain Bernard," said Lewis, "this is Master-at-Arms Third Class Tanner Malone, reported aboard yesterday."

"At ease, gentlemen," Bernard smiled, reaching out to shake hands. "Tanner, welcome aboard. This is the XO, Commander Sutton."

"We've met." Sutton smirked, then offered a handshake as soon as Bernard's was done.

"Oh?" The captain's eyebrows rose.

"Ah, very briefly, sir," Tanner stammered, noting the firmness of Sutton's grip.

"Malone here was on one of the recruit work details in the run-up for the commissioning ceremony. It was brief, but he made an impression."

"Fair enough," the captain said. "How do you like the ship?"

"We're not through with the tour, sir, but I like what I've seen so far. It's a far cry from corvette duty," said Tanner.

"I would imagine. She's a big ship with big responsibilities. Your department plays an important role in that."

"Yes, sir."

"Ironically, the less I hear from the masters-at-arms, the better I can feel about how things are going with the crew. I have a lot of faith in Lieutenant Commander Jacobson and the rest of your department, so I won't lecture you. But I like to meet all the MAs personally. Especially the ones just out of school. You have a lot of responsibility and professional authority contending with a relatively low rank. I know that can be a challenge."

Tanner nodded. "It looks like I have some good mentors, sir."

"You do. Lean on them. A lot of situations may not be what they seem on the surface, and like I said, it's a big ship and a big crew. Things can get complicated quickly. Follow the lead of the senior MAs, but if you're stuck on your own, trust your instincts and your training. I'd rather have to settle down an overexuberant MA than have someone just filling out the suit because he's too shy to do the job."

"Understood, sir."

"Okay, then. That's the speech," Bernard said with a faint, wry grin. "Not much more to it. I should let you get back to business. Except for one other thing." He turned to one side, looking down to a small stack of printed files and reports on his desk. "This got passed to me by my yeoman today. I realize you just got here, but the rest of Archangel doesn't exactly run on a naval schedule."

He drew from the stack of files a single embossed envelope, which he handed to Tanner. The young man immediately recognized the seal. "I'm fairly certain you don't get personal letters from President Aguirre," said Bernard, "but I don't even get paper letters from my own children, so I imagine this must be something special."

"No, sir," Tanner said, shaking his head. "I've seen this before. This is for the Annual Address. They told me I'd get invited every year. Part of getting the Archangel Star for, um . . . well." Tanner shrugged. He hadn't actually given the Address any thought since the last time.

"That makes sense. It's that time of year. I presume you have at least a couple days' worth of leave you could use for it? We don't have orders to leave the system in the foreseeable future, so I don't think it will be too tough to get you to Raphael and back."

"Oh no, sir, this isn't an obligation or anything," Tanner replied. "I don't actually have to go. They're going to send these every year . . ."

His voice trailed off. He couldn't think of much else to say to the serious looks of the captain and the XO in front of him. "It won't be any trouble at all, Malone," said Sutton. "We'd be happy to have you there to represent the ship."

Aw, you had to make it about the ship. Tanner swallowed. "Yes, sir. I'll be there, sir."

"Good. That'll be all, gentlemen," said Bernard. "Dismissed."

Exiting the compartment, Tanner held his posture and stride steady until he heard the hatch close behind them. Then he let out a tense sigh.

"What's wrong?" Lewis asked. "You don't want to go? I'd figure you'd jump at the chance. You were on the honor guard and all, don't you have friends there you'd like to see, at least?"

"Sure, I just . . . I wasn't thinking about going, and I just came on board, and . . . ugh!" Tanner groaned as the implications caught up with him. "Where the hell am I gonna find a date?"

• • •

"Listen, I'm in Salvation on Raphael right now 'cause I have to go to the stupid Annual Address, and I never found a date. You got plans tonight?"

"Oh fuck, did Ordoñez put you up to this?" asked Sanjay. The holo screen showed him lying on a couch in his barracks room in casual civilian clothes. "She's still pissed off that I saw that guy first? Man, I told her, I'm not usually into men, but *anyone* would have taken *him* home—"

"What? No!" Tanner's palm smacked against his forehead. He stood alone in his dress uniform while crowds of people filled up the other side of the wide street. Senators, celebrities, and other VIP guests—as if any guest at the Address was not, by definition, a VIP—made their way through a red-carpet gauntlet of journalists, lobbyists, and security in both uniform and plain clothes. The extra lighting and buzzing camera drones only added to the glitzy aura of the scene.

True to Tanner's expectations, he had yet to see anyone approach the steps alone.

Sanjay continued. "I mean, that's nothing against you, I just wouldn't have expected—"

"I'm not into men, Sanjay." Tanner sighed. *Way to put your foot in your mouth, Malone.*

"Then why are you calling me up asking me if I want to go to a fancy date thing with you?" Sanjay frowned. "You're weird, man."

"It's not a date, okay? I already ran through all my 'date' options and came up dry. I'd be happy to just have someone to hang out with at this point. Last year I had Andrea Bennett showing me around when I was a news story. This year I'm back to being nobody, which is fine, but I'm still stuck here. This place is crawling with celebrities and powerful people, but that also means it's basically a party full of strangers. Who wants to go to those alone?"

"Seriously? You couldn't find a date for that?" Sanjay snickered. "I know girls who'd murder their mothers for that ticket."

"Look, I reported aboard *Los Angeles* five days ago and the captain told me I had to come for the pride of the ship or some such. You wouldn't believe what a pain it is to find a date for this thing. Every woman I know from the honor guard is actually *working* here tonight, and every civilian I'd ask is either at a university on another planet or tied up with something else. The girl I took to my senior prom is on some geological survey for school, for Christ's sake."

"You're on a cruiser and you couldn't find one woman to take to a thing like that?"

"I just reported on board! They've been busting my ass with getting me qualified for this, that, and the other thing. You think I've had time to socialize with anyone? I haven't met half of my own department yet. And I'm not gonna take a blind date to the Annual Address. What if she gets drunk and throws up on the president? Or calls him a fascist?"

"You didn't ask Ordoñez? She'd go."

"I asked when I called the watch section on the ship. She's on leave."

"Oh yeah. Right."

"I'd have asked Lieutenant Kelly if I could, but that'd be fraternization, and—"

"Hah! I knew you had a thing for her."

"And I can't do anything about it, and I need someone to go with for this thing now."

"Wait, don't you mean *right* now? Isn't that supposed to start in half an hour?" Tanner saw Sanjay reach for the holo screen to open up a new window. "Yeah, they're already doing the preshow stuff. I think you're a little late, Tanner."

"That's just the speech. I'm not worried about that. They'll find a body to fill the extra seat, anyway. I need someone for the ball afterward. Look, it's a free dinner and drinks and you get to meet famous people. Throw on your dress uniform and your shiny new medals and hop on a rapid transport to the capital. You'll be here in time for the ball. I'll pay you back for the fare. I don't have to take an actual date. You're a shipmate and you got decorated on Scheherazade, that's more than enough reason to get you in the door with me."

"Are there gonna be single women there?"

Tanner sighed. "Probably not many, no," he admitted.

"Yeah, see, I'd help you out, but I think I might've accidentally glued my ass to this couch. You're on your own for this one, buddy."

"Fine," Tanner grumbled. He glanced over at the reception area. If his experiences in working security for such events on the honor guard were any indication, the best time to slip through quickly seemed to be upon him. "How's the arm?"

"It's okay," Sanjay answered. Tanner's attention turned back to the holo screen. Sanjay hesitated. "It hurts," he added.

"All the time?" Tanner asked with concern.

"Pretty much, yeah. It works fine. I'm still in physical therapy and it's weaker than my right arm, obviously, but it's getting there. The doctors say the pain has something to do with the new neural tissue interacting with the natural stuff. They say it should go away, but if it doesn't, there are drugs and procedures they might try. I'm still a little less agile than I was, too, but hell, I was right-handed in the first place, you know?"

"Yeah. I'm sorry, Sanjay."

"Hey, I didn't want you to think I was bullshitting you, so I figured I'd tell you the truth," Sanjay said. "You did the right thing, Tanner. I don't blame you. And don't make this weird with your accidentally not asking me out. I'm just trying not to laugh at you here."

"Sure you don't want to come out to this, anyway? The dinner's pretty spectacular. They only stock the good stuff at the ball and it's basically an open bar. Might help dull the pain in your arm."

"You're not gonna touch a drop tonight, are you?"

Again, Tanner sighed. "Not at a scene like this, no."

Sanjay made a face. "Why? Afraid you'll say something to embarrass your press secretary *ex*-girlfriend?"

"Y'know, I'm not all that bitter about her."

"Bitter, hell. I'm not saying you have to do anything to get back at her. But you should, I don't know, try maybe getting over her. If anyone needs something to dull the pain, it's you."

"Okay, I'm cutting this off now."

"That's fine. I've got the live feed from the media out front on another screen. I'll watch you walk in. Try not to embarrass the navy, okay?"

Tanner killed the holo screen. He moved across the street, watching both traffic and the people on the red carpet at the receiving gate. He'd waited for a thin enough line that he could slip through quickly. It had been five months since his name appeared in a media piece—he'd checked hours before, just in case. At least he wouldn't likely receive any media attention.

A year ago, he arrived with the best of all possible guides. He expected she was with the rest of the president's staff now, focusing more on his speech than whomever her date was for the night—if she was back yet from those negotiations on Earth.

He filed in behind a senator and her husband and a movie star couple ahead of them. *Important people jockey all year long for an invitation to this*, Andrea had told him at the ball last year. *Heads of state. Corporate presidents. Celebrities. Scientists. Royalty.*

Journalists, obediently minding an invisible line of courtesy to one side of the entrance, leaned forward to catch quotes and brief little exchanges. Even they were dressed in expensive suits and high-fashion gowns. Yet Tanner knew from experience that none of the journalists out here would actually get inside, or go to the ball. Their colleagues with the bigger names got to do that.

Hidden behind the pair of couples ahead of him, Tanner's eyes drifted across that line of journalists. He recognized more than one of them.

Fuck it, he decided, and deliberately fell behind Senator and Mr. Whoever.

• • •

"You might want to catch the Annual Address if you're not too busy tonight," said the message from Kiribati. It came directly to Casey's holocom, bypassing the usual routing of comms traffic since *Argent* was so close to Raphael. Transmission delays at this range amounted to only a few seconds. Anyone on the ship could watch media channels on a live feed.

Some of the crew would, indeed, watch the whole Address, depending on their duty schedules. Others would blow it off entirely, having little interest in politics. One could catch the media analysis at a later date without having to sit through the inspirational bullshit and political glad-handing that was always part of such a speech. Casey decided to turn on the live feed, watching in his quarters alone with *Argent*'s crew efficiency reports and a decent bottle of wine.

At least his restrictions didn't include alcohol. Though he felt little genuine loyalty to the ship or its crew, Casey's sense of self-preservation kept him from getting drunk while in command. He could have used a couple of good drunken nights—or a couple dozen of them—since coming aboard. Yet his current circumstances beat the alternatives. The ship was still a prison, but the captain's cabin of a converted space liner made for better accommodations than a prison cell.

The thought of prison drew his attention from the reports to the prespeech media coverage on the large screen on his wall. A year ago, he'd heard the Annual Address while in a holding cell awaiting trial. That same night, Kiribati had laid out his deal and his expectations. As much as Casey hated Kiribati, the government and people of Archangel, and pretty much anyone he could name in that moment, he couldn't turn down the deal. He accepted that until an opportunity for escape or an exceptional change of circumstance presented itself, Archangel's fate and her enemies were now his.

Casey still wondered where it would all lead. Kiribati's message hinted that he would gain some clue about that direction through the speech. He just had to sit through all the bullshit first.

"Senator, what do you expect to hear in the president's speech tonight?" asked one reporter as he leaned in to a passing politician and his wife. Casey rolled his eyes. *Blah, blah, blah, excuses and bad ideas and he doesn't do things my way*, the captain thought. *Like this guy's gonna say anything worth hearing? The fuck kind of question is that?*

He called up the viewer controls on his holocom and switched to another channel. This one picked up in the middle of a close-up of the broadcasting journalist herself. She was dark-haired and pretty. Her blue dress, cut to tastefully show off her figure while keeping her mobile as her job required, matched her eyes perfectly. Much of the sparkle in her earrings and her necklace was likely artificially generated from within to provide extra camera lighting. *Good enough*, Casey decided. He had no idea who she was or if she'd do real reporting, but at least she was nice enough to look at.

"The crowd seems to be thinning out a bit," said the journalist, apparently in some back and forth with a fellow correspondent at a different location. "We see Senator Murphy arriving with her husband, along with Uriel Shipyards magnate Stephan Alonzo and his fiancée."

Casey's mind tuned out while watching her. Dressed like that, she might well be more of a fashion and style reporter than a serious political journalist, but who could tell at an event like this? Ultimately, she was a reminder of a genuine drawback to his current circumstances.

He hadn't been with a woman since leaving Paradise. He couldn't leave *Argent*, and there was no way to get a prostitute on board without Hawkins or one of his other minders blocking the whole thing, and he somehow doubted he'd get very far with any of the women in his crew.

Still. They were his only real shot at getting laid for the foreseeable future. He'd never get away with using his position as leverage. Galling though it might be, Casey would have to jump through all the charm and romance hoops. Besides, sooner or later he'd get tired of whomever he hooked up with, and then he'd have to deal with that fallout. A jilted lover wouldn't cause him any stress, to be sure, but he'd still have to deal with it.

He stared at the lovely face on the screen. *Christ. How hard does it have to be to get laid?*

"Excuse me, miss?" someone said off to the reporter's side. Casey's eyes flared. "Rebecca Krause, right? Gabriel News Media?"

"Oh, you're Tanner Malone!" the journalist said after a beat, smiling brightly. The picture shifted, moving from the across-the-entrance view to the cameras mounted in her jewelry. Where the screen had once offered a head-to-waist image of a good-looking woman in a blue dress, now he had a close-up of Malone's face.

"Hi," Malone said, offering his hand with a pleasant smile.

The wineglass in Casey's hand broke at the stem.

"We met last year, briefly," he said.

"Yes, of course, I remember the interview, Mr.—is it still Crewman Malone?"

"You can call me Tanner, actually. Please."

"Thank you. I'd heard you were on the honor guard? Are you here on duty?"

"I'm on the invitation list, actually. Would you like to come inside with me as my guest for the speech and the ball?"

"Oh, why, um . . . that's very unexpected," she stammered, almost certainly waiting for instructions from her producer or whomever the hell coordinated these things from behind the scenes. Her surprise offered just enough cover for that, but within the space of a breath, she took his hand and said, "Yes, of course! Who wouldn't?"

Glass shattered and wine exploded all over the screen. The impact of Casey's bottle did nothing other than to leave wet stains. People kept talking and moving. The stupid fucking cow in the blue dress laughed and jokingly taunted her fellow journalists as she stepped out of their line and into the stream of guests. Casey jabbed at the controls on his holocom to cut off the whole insipid scene. The room fell silent.

It was a foregone conclusion, of course. Any reporter would've gone for it. The story angle was obvious. No way would any one of those assholes outside the red carpet stay on station when they could go inside instead.

None of that dimmed Casey's fury as he sat alone in his prison.

• • •

He couldn't help but look for her during the speech.

Tanner knew many of the visual cues one could find in the Annual Address. As the president entered and the event began, Tanner thought back to what he'd learned in school from his social studies teachers—only three years ago now, though it seemed like so much longer—and from his months on the honor guard. He recognized the formal etiquette and deliberate pageantry, the meaning behind certain seating arrangements, and the choice of décor.

He knew the whole scene before him was designed to emphasize domestic unity. Aguirre pulled out all the stops, walking to the dais with the leaders of all three major parties rather than walking beside his vice president. The opening prayer asked for strength in the face of tribulations and resolve against temptation in much more pious terms than Aguirre normally used. After more rousing applause, Aguirre was invited to the dais by the leader of the secular conservatives rather than his own party's leader, another clear signal of unity.

The order of topics held meaning, too. Aguirre led off by praising Archangel's domestic matters, acknowledging business leaders who'd worked to help the system through the economic harm brought by the government's dispute with the Union's biggest corporations. Tanner knew the president would then turn to less important matters, only to return to the core theme of his speech.

Tanner knew some of the president's favorite rhetorical techniques. Aguirre liked assertive language. Aguirre's most talented speechwriter preferred to offer solid statistics and use names rather than allusions. He would have known what to listen for, had his attention not drifted from the speech to thoughts of the woman who likely wrote a good deal of it.

From his seat in the second row of the balcony, Tanner couldn't expect to see everyone, but his eyes scanned the lower level and the spaces around the dais for Andrea. He could think of any number of reasons why she wouldn't be in view: she could be off in the wings handling media relations, or already on-site at the ballroom, or perhaps the media rumors had been wrong and her shuttle hadn't come back from Earth yet. Tanner recognized plenty of faces: cabinet secretaries, planetary governors, Admiral Yeoh. Yet he didn't see Andrea anywhere.

Am I not over this? He hadn't given her all that much thought until the captain all but ordered him to attend tonight. Tanner had deliberately stopped watching her press appearances after their split, rather than poke at his feelings. Yet here he sat, scanning the crowd instead of listening to the speech. *It's not like I don't miss her. Maybe this is natural? Why wouldn't I think about her right now? It's not like I can talk to Rebecca until Aguirre shuts up.*

He glanced to the woman at his side. She could have all the attention she wanted from him. He was at least far enough over Andrea to move on. Rebecca, for her part, seemed fully engaged in listening to the president. Her eyes were wide with awe.

Tanner looked back to the dais.

"This is not suspicion or conjecture," said Aguirre. "Analysts from the intelligence sector, academia, and a few select domestic firms have applied these metrics to test results from prior years and confirmed that the same pattern holds true. We don't know exactly how long this scam has gone on. But we do know that *it is a scam*—that our young people have been robbed by the institutions that claimed to prepare them for adulthood." His eyes were alive with righteous energy and purpose. "We know that the same patterns apply to students of programs run by Lai Wa and by CDC, and we know that the graduating students of 2276, despite the turmoil of change within their schools, have not fallen so short in their final exams. When called to perform on a fair and level playing field, our students succeed. Our teachers, likewise duped by the scam of the Test, also succeed. Our *schools* succeed—now that they are, in truth, *our schools*."

Holy shit, thought Tanner. *What did I just miss?*

"My friends, my fellow citizens: we have been robbed. Our *children* have been robbed of their futures. But I can tell you now that this crime has ended—for all of us.

"The leaders of our political parties in the Senate have agreed. We have already given notice to our former corporate 'partners.' Tomorrow, as the first item of the agenda, the leaders of all three parties will jointly introduce legislation to relieve Archangel's citizens of any and all legal obligation under domestic law to fulfill any outstanding debt for compulsory education."

Tanner suddenly felt something heavy within his chest. Loud applause burst from the audience as the entire Senate and most of the night's guests rose to their feet. Tanner remained seated. *How can they make that stick? What does any of that actually mean?*

"They will claim we have defaulted on our debts," Aguirre said, raising his voice to speak over the applause, which eventually quieted—but the audience remained standing. Tanner rose so he could see Aguirre. "They will shout from every mountaintop that *we* are destroying the economy of the Union, that *we* are bankrupting our children, that *we* have forced this situation. Yet we cannot turn a blind eye to corruption and greed of this magnitude. We will not be party to an economy based on lies at the expense of our youth.

"If the other systems and states of this Union are wise, if they are honest and true to their people, they will join us in this effort. We will bring these thieves to justice. Our stance will naturally force many to confront this crime, whether they like it or not. And when they face that confrontation, we will lend our voices and our support.

"We stand strong with the Union. We stand firm in our commitment to a common diplomatic effort toward our alien neighbors, and we stand firm in the common defense of humanity. But we will not pay for the privilege of being robbed!"

Again, the president's passion was met with thunderous cheering and applause. "Can you believe this?" asked Rebecca.

Tanner breathlessly shook his head. He couldn't believe it at all. His understanding of economics only went as far as the twelfth grade could take him. Tanner couldn't begin to know the implications of this.

How much will this hurt us? How much will it hurt them? This will go all over the Union. Can those companies even survive?

What will they do if they can't?

His eyes drifted over the crowd. Almost everyone clapped and cheered. Almost.

Admiral Yeoh stood, along with everyone in her section, but she didn't applaud.

• • •

"What's the live reaction tracking look like?" asked Andrea. She strode into a side hallway to the rear of the cathedral, dressed for the ball like everyone else, but she and her staff were all business. A dozen men and women stood with holo screens open before them, all watching and analyzing media reactions and live polls.

Not all were her people. Some of them were borrowed from Victor's department. They weren't all media experts, but they could watch and relay data, and they all shared a vested interest.

"We held at fifty-four percent favorable until the big reveal," answered an assistant to her left. "Then we jumped all the way to eighty-seven percent and stayed!"

"Jumped? Not spiked?"

"That's what I'm saying, Andrea. He jumped to eighty-seven and then leveled off."

"What are the media outlets saying? Jenny?"

"Holt News is already saying the president couldn't do any less," said a woman to Andrea's right.

"Warner Media has the Test script laid out on a split screen with their anchor," relayed another woman without prompting. "They're showing the same stuff you showed us and they're analyzing on-air. They started as soon as the data packet hit, so I guess they had someone on hand—"

"The *Trumpet*'s guy is asking if the Heritage Party sold out the system to the president," called out a young man down the hall.

"Of course he is," replied Andrea, not bothering to roll her eyes. "Dennis? You're watching Uriel Media, right?"

The somewhat heavyset staffer chuckled, looking up from his screen. "Yeah, it's pretty great. Sherman Deng might have a stroke. He's just saying, 'Ur, ur, ur . . .'"

Andrea smiled. "Excellent, put that in a clip and route it to me." With her voice raised to maintain an air of command, she said, "Unless anyone has something urgent for me, I think I can cut you all loose for the festivities. But remember the briefing points, because any one of us or anyone we talk to tonight might wind up in front of a reporter. We don't want to go off-page and we do not want to speculate. I don't want to read anyone's wild-assed guesses in the news, okay? Stay on message."

"Andrea?" asked her assistant as the group broke up. She moved in close enough to afford a little privacy. "Something you should know: Tanner is here."

"He has an Archangel Star." Andrea shrugged. "He gets to come to these as long as he's alive. Unless he showed up without pants or roaring drunk, I don't need to hear about it, okay?"

"No, no, I get it," Ellen said, having fully expected this. "That's not the problem. It's his date."

"Why? Ellen, I told you, we split, okay? He can come with a date. I'm here with a date. It's nobody's business. Nobody's gonna care who he's seeing after the bombshells the president dropped tonight. What's the problem?"

"He pulled Rebecca Krause off the red carpet line and brought her in," Ellen hissed. "Live. On the air."

That stopped Andrea dead in her tracks. "He did *what*?"

• • •

"Name three forms of art originating in the twentieth century that remain in widespread practice today."

"Well, that doesn't sound so bad. Let's see. Cinema, rock 'n' roll music, and . . . oh hell, I don't know. Wasn't graffiti a big thing in the twentieth?"

Several of the well-dressed men and women around the round table shared a chuckle at the answer, but Tanner didn't laugh. "Come on, Jim. Graffiti?" asked Jonathan Hartmann. "You don't think anyone wrote profanity on walls before the nineteen hundreds?"

"Gah. Well, no, but the elaborate paintings," said Jim Bowers, Chairman of Archangel's Independent Shipping Guild. "Isn't that the point where people started making it into real art?"

"It's not a bad answer," said Tanner, shaking his head, "as long as you get to justify it. But the Test never gives you that chance. You don't talk to the scorers." He glanced across the table of fine dinnerware and wineglasses to Bowers. "So that answer gets thrown out. And motion picture tech had its roots in the nineteenth century, with the first public showings happening in 1896. It might not be 'cinema' as we think of it today, but technically that means they get to mark you down for that answer, too."

Sitting beside him, Rebecca grinned and asked, "You knew that off the top of your head, Tanner?"

"I knew it because my answers on that question were rock 'n' roll, surrealist painting, and gangster movies." Tanner shrugged. "After the score I got on the Test, I looked up every single answer I could remember. That's how I know they could parse and throw out practically every answer that involved motion pictures."

"Surrealist painting?" Bowers wondered.

"My stepmother's an art teacher. I should've leaned on that for all three choices, but obviously rock 'n' roll is correct. Unless they want to argue what 'widespread' means, or if modern rock 'n' roll is the same form of music. All they need is one random 'expert' to claim it isn't, though, and then they've got a case."

"How much did that cost you?" asked Hartmann.

Tanner shook his head. "I don't know what individual wrong answers cost. Nobody does. That's part of the problem. But all together? I wound up owing them a lot. Or so my score said. Bastards."

"Was the whole Test like that?"

"A lot of it. I'll admit I got a few things wrong. I knew I goofed a couple of math questions. And I still don't know what score I got on astronomy, because they made me *draw* everything by hand, from memory."

"I don't blame you for being bitter," offered Jim's wife, Evelyn. Tanner knew her name from several famous High Court cases he'd studied in school. If anything, she was more famous than her husband. "Our daughter took the Test the same year you did. I gave her such a hard time for owing sixty-eight hundred credits." Tanner choked on his mouthful of food, but no one seemed to notice. "I feel awful about that now."

Swallowing hard, Tanner managed to ask, "Was your daughter in the Society of Scholars program?"

"Yes," said Evelyn brightly, "right from the start!" Then her brow furrowed. "Although I suppose that whole program was as dirty as the rest of this. We certainly paid enough for it."

Let it go. She's a nice rich lady. Her rich daughter is probably perfectly nice, too. It's not a crime to be rich. Let it go. Let it go. "Well, I think we all got a lot less than we paid for," Tanner agreed.

"Rebecca," said Bowers, "you won't go quoting me on that graffiti answer, will you?"

Another round of chuckles swept the table, though this time Jim plainly intended that. "No quotes," Rebecca assured him. "I'm not here to ambush anyone."

"Sure, sure," Evelyn scoffed.

"No, it's true." Rebecca laughed back. She gestured to Tanner. "Would *you* have turned down an invitation like this? I'll admit that I might find tonight extremely informative," she teased, "but I won't be naming names or even hints of names. I'm not here to pick a fight with—Andrea Bennett, hello! You look wonderful!"

Andrea rounded the table with a graceful stride, throwing Tanner a quick glance and a cryptic smile, but her attention focused first on Rebecca. "Coming from you, that's high praise," she said. "I haven't caught any of your entrance coverage yet, but you're never one to hold back."

Tanner looked Andrea up and down and felt his heart stop, just as he'd known it would. It was almost inevitable. At least the brief distraction offered by his date gave him a chance to process his emotions.

"Well, have no worries." Rebecca smiled. "I'm sure I'll get caught up on the fashion and style commentary soon enough once the ball is over." She pulled the cloth napkin from her lap and put it beside her plate. "Should we talk shop?"

"Only if you're still on the clock while you're here," answered Andrea.

"Hah! You bet your life." Rebecca stood. "I'll be back in a minute, Tanner."

"Yes," Andrea agreed, placing her hand on his shoulder as she passed. "Don't go anywhere."

Tanner watched them stride away and let out a sigh as he turned back to his dinner plate. If there was one thing he hated about his relationships with women, it was the suspense.

"So, Tanner," spoke up Hartmann, "I take it you didn't plan on a career in politics after you finish your enlistment?"

The joke almost flew past him, but Tanner laughed. "No, I don't think so. I'm not sure what I'll do, to be honest. Get out and go to a university, sure, but who knows what the job market will look like in three more years? Or the economy altogether? I mean, that has to be on *your* mind, right?"

"Sure. The government is taking a huge gamble here."

"You don't seem too stressed about it. Won't your firm be pretty busy?"

"We have offices all over the system and beyond," replied Hartmann. "A company like mine never sleeps. But to be honest, anyone in Archangel with investments in the Big Three should've pulled out over a year ago. The writing was on the wall when the security contracts were canceled."

Tanner considered his words. Plenty of voices had called for Archangel's citizens to pull out of such investments, of course— if not at the point Hartmann suggested, then certainly after the previous Annual Address and the takeover of the school system. Yet that seemed like a patriotic reaction. Tanner wondered if a financial firm would ever make its decisions based on patriotism alone.

Hartmann didn't seem concerned at all. Nor did Mr. or Mrs. Bowers, nor many others, whereas Tanner felt like he had just heard the most momentous announcement in his life. And Rebecca—a professional journalist, who for all her attention to "fashion and style" clearly kept up with politics—was just as surprised as Tanner.

The others at his table seemed interested but unsurprised. They were high-powered people, all of them, and probably accustomed to putting on a calm front in the face of sudden change. They had to be. Yet to accept all this so quickly and so easily . . .

He'd met these people before, when they came to meet the president. Months ago. In the case of Jim Bowers, visits to Ascension Hall happened almost monthly. And they seemed perfectly relaxed.

"Mr. Hartmann," Tanner spoke up, "what would people in Archangel have had to do in order to *make* money on this whole shift? I mean, not just avoid losing money, like you're saying. But are there ways anyone could have turned a profit?"

Hartmann blinked. "Well, certainly," he said, showing the first bit of consternation Tanner had seen from him all night. "People and companies who are ready to step up and fill the gaps in goods and services will do well. And, frankly, our credit with the rest of the Union has been in a nosedive for the last year because of all our disputes. The smart money is on buying and selling domestically. Businesses that bank on that strategy will probably see it pay off big."

"I guess that makes sense," Tanner said, but then another point caught up to him. "But that's about going forward. I mean, where would a person have had to be before tonight in order for this to really benefit?"

"Well, I wouldn't want to speculate too much," Hartmann slowly answered. "Hypothetically, some stocks and other financial plans will do better than others. That happens with every Annual Address, really."

Tanner watched and listened. He hadn't asked his first question as a probe, but he noticed how Hartmann's voice changed as he spoke in generalities. He shifted in his seat, fidgeting with his cloth napkin. His rating school, still fresh in his mind, had offered multiple classes about body language, interviews, and interrogation.

Is he hiding something? Why would he be hiding anything from me? It's not like Rebecca's still at . . . the reporter isn't at the table anymore, Tanner realized. *I'm just a kid to him. I caught him off guard. What is going on?*

"And," Hartmann continued, "I suppose folks who've paid only the minimums on their educational debt or were even behind on payments might come out ahead. The people who paid aggressively might be kicking themselves right now, though."

That hit home. "Yeah"—Tanner sighed—"I did that."

"A lot of people did," Hartmann sympathized. "Or tried to, but fell behind, and hurt worse because of it. These will be massive changes for Archangel, and they'll be pretty serious changes for other systems, too. The Big Three have a lot of explaining to do to the other planetary systems. With any luck, they'll cut their losses here and be glad to be rid of us before we cause them more trouble. Bad enough that they've lost so much here already, but people have other debts to the Big Three besides education. There's medical debt, financial services for business . . . if the educational system was so dishonest, what other dirty tricks might they have pulled in other fields? The Big Three don't want this mess to get worse for them. But it probably will."

Tanner nodded. "That's what I worry about."

Hartmann's eyes flicked up to something behind Tanner's shoulder. "You might want to worry about more immediate problems," he said meaningfully.

"Hey, Tanner, I'm back." Rebecca smiled as she sat down. "Had to talk about ground rules with Andrea. No big deal. But she's hoping you'll go speak with her."

"Right." Tanner rose from his chair. "Thanks."

"Tell me everything," Rebecca joked as he left. "Maybe take notes?"

With a sigh, Tanner slipped around more crowded tables and the occasional waiter on his way to the shimmering curtains that partitioned off the dining area from a service hallway nearby. Andrea stood at the edge of the curtain, her expression perfectly pleasant. None of the passersby who spoke with her lingered in a way that would delay this conversation.

"Hey," Tanner said as he drew within speaking distance.

"Hi."

He kept walking. She'd want this close enough to whisper, even with the band and the crowd. "You look wonderful."

"Thank you."

"You always look wonderful," he admitted with a shrug.

"So are you, by any chance, a little pissed off at me?"

". . . No?"

"And this isn't a giant stunt to get back at me for calling it quits?"

"No, this is a giant stunt because I came to this thing without a date."

"You have an invitation to the *Annual Address* and you couldn't find a date? I know it's not a sports championship, but you expect me to believe you couldn't find a date for *this*?"

"*No*, Andrea, I couldn't," Tanner fumed, though he kept his voice in check. "I hadn't planned on coming. I transferred onto *Los Angeles* less than a week ago, and the captain saw the invitation as a point of pride for the ship. I can think of a half-dozen women I'd have asked if they weren't tied up or living in another star system. Believe me, I tried."

Andrea frowned. "So you just walked up to a reporter *on camera* and asked her?"

"Seemed like I wouldn't have to worry about her doing anything crazy or embarrassing to the president if she was professional enough to be on that line."

"Embarrassing to the—you really had that in mind?" Andrea blinked incredulously.

"No," Tanner asserted. "Honestly, I couldn't care less about that right now. But I knew *you'd* care."

"Me? You didn't think about maybe embarrassing yourself? I thought you wanted out of the limelight."

"What, you think they won't want to use me for recruiting ads anymore?"

"No! But you knew she was broadcasting live! What were you gonna do if she said no?"

"I thought about that. I'd have moved on down the line to ask the next lady," Tanner answered readily. "And that would've probably been on camera, too. Sounds like comedy gold to me. Look, is anyone going to care about me and how I found a date after the bombshells you guys dropped tonight?"

Andrea crossed her arms across her chest uncomfortably. "No, I imagine not. Gossip writers need to fill their pages, but it's not like they'll be getting all the attention after this. But what did you mean you couldn't care less? You're angry about something. I can tell."

"What's NorthStar going to do about us canceling our debts, Andrea?" Tanner asked. "You were just out there on a negotiation. Did they only meet with you to stonewall? Did they not budge on anything?"

"You know I can't talk about that, Tanner, not right now. I thought you'd be happy about this," she said, her voice softening. "I was thinking of you while we were out there and when we made this decision. They *robbed* you, Tanner. You and everyone else. They've been doing it for decades. What else should we do?"

Tanner let out a breath, trying to ease off as Andrea did. "Do you know who Sanjay Bhatia is?"

"I don't. It rings a bell, but I'm sorry, I'm not placing it."

"He was with me on Scheherazade. I had to cut his arm off to keep some chaff from burning right on up into his chest and killing him," Tanner explained. He saw the note of recognition in Andrea's eyes. "Four marines died on Scheherazade, and Lieutenant Kelly put her ship in front of a blast from a laser cannon that could've killed a lot more. I had to cut off a guy's arm and his new one still doesn't work right. And all that happened because NorthStar wanted to let us know they were pissed at us."

"I know." Andrea nodded. "I didn't place the name, but I know what happened. But it's all part of this. What else should we do but slam the door and tell them to never come back?"

"You think they'll actually walk away?" Tanner countered. "They pulled all that shit on Scheherazade to give us a shot across the bow. They could've kidnapped or killed hundreds of our people if we hadn't been there. It was their idea of a warning. We've got one real cruiser. They have battleships.

"I'm not thrilled about going into another fight, but at least I've been there before. I'm scared for all the other people who are gonna have to face that."

Andrea reached out to take his hand. "You don't think other people feel the same way? You think everyone wants to hide behind you?" She waited for an answer, but he didn't give one. "There's a plan, Tanner. We had a plan going into this, and there are plans for the way out. They don't share the military stuff with me. But there is a plan. You have to have faith. In Admiral Yeoh, in the president. In me."

"I don't think people realize how bad this could get."

"I don't think *you* realize that," Andrea pointed out. "Nobody does. But you can't hide forever."

"Hey, I don't want to hide, I just . . ." His voice trailed off. Tanner glanced out toward the ballroom and its glittering lights and people in fancy clothes. "I had to cut his arm off. He saved all of us. He should be here tonight. They all should. I feel like an asshole for being here when they're not.

"And I didn't ask Rebecca to get at you. I don't have any hard feelings, Andrea. I'd have been more than happy to be your date tonight. No ambitions, just a date. But hell, I don't know if you're seeing anyone new, and I didn't know if you'd be back in time for this."

Beneath Andrea's frown, Tanner could see some affection. She tilted her head back toward his table in the ballroom. "She's number two in line for Gabriel News Media's seat in the presidential pool. I think their capital bureau put her on the red carpet to bust her chops. You might've given Cinderella her glass slippers."

Tanner smiled. "Well, everyone deserves a fairy godmother, I guess."

"My point is, if you want to make a friend, give her a good story."

"I thought we just established that the president and the Address were the story tonight?"

"They are"—Andrea nodded—"but there's no way she doesn't get at least a feature out of you asking her out right there on the carpet, and she's not just a fashion reporter. You were on Scheherazade. You want to talk? Tell her what you told me." She gave him a wink and added, "But I never told you to do any such thing."

EIGHT

Drums

"NorthStar, Lai Wa, and CDC clearly knew what was coming at the Annual Address. Representatives arrived with grim expressions and generally refused to engage with reporters. When the president began making his case, all three delegations, about a dozen people in all, stood up and walked out in an apparent show of solidarity."
—Bob Norris, Raphael Public Media, November 2276

Waking up in a real bed was nice. Waking up later would have been far better. The sky outside showed only the first hint of daylight. Tanner rolled over to silence the news broadcast set to wake him up. He allowed himself a brief sigh before rising, but nothing more than that. He didn't want to risk falling back to sleep. He didn't know how long it would be until he could sleep in something better than a bunk on a warship again, but he knew that he didn't want to miss his shuttle back up to *Los Angeles*.

Groggy and a little grumpy, Tanner staggered off into the shower, put on his service uniform, and collected his small bag of personal items and the bag containing his dress grays. He gave his civilian surroundings one last look before checking out via holo-com and heading for the transport depot.

In the hotel elevator, in the lobby, and while waiting for his taxi, Tanner passed multiple holo screens with men and women talking in breathless, excited tones about the announcements of last night. Tanner heard words like "revolutionary" and "rebellion," along with the names of ambassadors from other systems who could not yet make substantive comments. He heard about the "countdown clock" established by the governor of Gabriel for NorthStar and Lai Wa executives to get off the planet, lest they be arrested and charged, but Tanner didn't hear what possible legal grounds could justify such a stunt.

Though normally an avid follower of news media, Tanner felt little interest that morning. Political grandstanding was predictable. So was rampant media speculation. Events would play out as they would. Today, he preferred to savor the view of the streets and the skyline.

The rosy glow of the sunrise made it all look too much like the streets and skyline of Scheherazade.

Tanner tried to put that out of his head. He'd spoken his mind last night in his impromptu interview with Rebecca. As Andrea had predicted, Rebecca told him she didn't know when her piece on her experience at the Address would be run, how long it would be, or what sort of angle her producers would want. She seemed genuine enough, but the only thing anyone knew for sure was that human-interest stories would take a backseat to hard-core politics for the time being.

Nothing held Tanner up as he moved through the civilian shuttle depot to the facility's small military wing. He took up a chair in the waiting room, passed the time by plunging back into all the reading necessary for his new post, and eventually boarded his shuttle.

Other uniformed personnel shuffled in and took seats. None of them stood out, though Tanner did not give them much thought. He decided instead to close his eyes and try to relax. He'd only have half an hour or so, and then a long day ahead of him after a long, late night. Like pretty much every other ship in the navy, *Los Angeles* ran with her internal clock set to Salvation's local time zone. He'd likely have to rush to get back to his bunk and change into a regular duty vac suit and make it to the morning briefing. It seemed wise to take advantage of what little chance he had to doze off.

Someone took up the chair beside him. He glanced at her only long enough to ensure that he wouldn't be invading her space as she settled in, then closed his eyes again. Tanner felt the subtle shift from natural gravity to the shuttle's artificial gravity generators, and then the soft vibrations of the engines as it took off. Some of the passengers chatted. He heard the quiet beeps of a few bits of personal electronics here and there.

"I expected a master-at-arms to be more vigilant," said the woman beside him in a quiet, serene voice. Tanner's eyes opened and his heart nearly leapt into his throat, but he kept silent. "Or have you really become that indifferent to famous faces?"

Admiral Yeoh wore ordinary marine service blues, not too different from his own uniform, only that she bore only the rank of a staff sergeant. She held a small black messenger bag in her lap. "I'm sorry if I woke you. Couldn't help myself."

Tanner swallowed hard. He quickly processed the implications of the head of the military putting on a disguise to board a shuttle bound for *Los Angeles*. "Technically, you shouldn't still be wearing your cap," he observed. "Not once you're on board, unless you're under arms."

"Only sticklers and martinets enforce a rule like that," she replied mildly. "Unless I'm under arms."

He gave her another up-and-down glance. "You're hiding it well if you are. Except for the cap."

"I've had practice. You didn't say hello at the ball."

"You weren't there long. Can't imagine why."

"No, I wasn't," she conceded, "and you had a lovely date to entertain. How did that go?"

"Pretty sure I'll get an invitation to her wedding." Tanner sighed. "Can't say I'm shocked. Most of the time when you meet someone attractive, you find out they're already involved."

"Better luck next time."

He paused. "How do you do that? Think about casual stuff like that at a time like this?"

"I do not see a 'time like this' as different from other time. Change is the only constant. And I'm sure you do it, too." She looked at him sideways. "Crises come and go. Life moves on. Move with it."

Tanner chewed on her suggestion. His eyes flitted this way and that, taking in the faces and postures of the other passengers in the shuttle. Several of the others had to be Yeoh's personal staff, yet he saw only enlisted and junior officer uniforms.

"I take it they won't be ringing the ship's bell when you arrive?"

"No," Yeoh answered. "Nor will there be a side party. This isn't exactly a surprise inspection. The captain knows I'm coming, but he'll keep quiet about it. That means he won't be able to set his crew on a mad spree of cleaning to prepare for my arrival. He's probably beside himself right now."

Tanner looked back at her and found her lips closer to a genuine smile than he'd ever seen. He couldn't help but grin. "You think that's funny?"

"I do. There's likely a stain on the deck in the hangar bay right now that is driving him mad. It happens when you're the captain of a ship."

"Never thought I'd get to see your sense of humor."

"You should talk to my husband or my daughters. I'm hysterical."

Tanner bit his lip. "Are either of your daughters single? I'm probably gonna need a date for next year."

"At the risk of sounding overprotective, I don't think that's a good idea. They would both love to go, and they'll be old enough that I can't tell them what to do. But if you invited one, the other would likely hunt you down and murder you in your sleep. I have to look out for my subordinates."

• • •

The shuttle's arrival left Tanner with about as much slack time as expected. He felt self-conscious enough about leaving the ship so soon after arriving, even if only for an overnight trip. Being a little late to the morning briefing might be understandable in his circumstances, but he preferred to avoid it if only to make a good impression.

He didn't expect everyone to stand up and applaud when he walked in. He'd opened the hatch to find the two dozen or so MAs in the room lounging and chatting, but then one stood and started clapping and the others all joined in. Tanner froze awkwardly, looking from one to the other, seeing only grins and laughter. He blushed fiercely.

"What's the deal, guys?"

The applause and chuckles died off as people took their seats once more. "You were all over the preshow for the Address," someone explained.

"Okay, that was all planned out in advance, right?" asked another shipmate. "That was a media stunt? They set you up with her?"

"No," Tanner admitted, moving over to an empty seat a couple rows back from the front. "Turns out I was just desperate."

"So how did it play out?" asked yet another shipmate. "Anything happen?"

"Nah, turns out she's engaged."

"So what?"

"Okay, guys, quiet down," called out MA1 Lewis as he moved to the front of the room. "Commander Jacobson and Chief Lockwood told me to get this rolling if they don't make it back in time, so let's clear out the simple stuff first and see if they catch up before we're done. We've still got three guys in the brig right now: Staehely and Crall from engine two for that fight yesterday and obviously Finkbiner is still in there. We're down to three days left with him, but I imagine the other two knuckleheads will be let out once their department head deals with the situation. They haven't been a problem since they got brought in. Baldwin, how's the eye?"

"Fine," grumbled the petite third class sitting in front of Tanner. She'd been on an opposite shift from his upon arrival. He hadn't met her before now. "The swelling died down before I woke up this morning."

"Well, I guess the LT is gonna make the call on whether they get nailed for striking an MA or not. I know you said it was on the backswing while they were still fighting, but it shouldn't have happened at all.

"Now, that said, all of you," Lewis continued, his gaze falling over each of his peers and subordinates in the small audience, "remember, if you get asked what's gonna happen with those jack-asses, don't say you don't know. People should know better. At this point, we need to start pushing back. If you get asked by someone of higher rank, I expect you to respectfully refer the question to a higher authority, but if it's anyone your rank or lower, I want you to respectfully put your foot up his or her ass for asking in the first place."

Tanner heard chuckles and saw a few small grins. No one needed to write notes for that. His fellow MAs seemed like a good bunch: competent, levelheaded, and generally mature. He felt a sense of ease in the room despite the serious nature of their duties. Minor brawls, petty thefts, and disciplinary infractions were common matters for the MA force while the ship was underway. Tanner glanced at the training schedule and boarding team rotations listed on a bulkhead bulletin board. The routine was busy, but still routine.

He considered what he'd heard the night before, and the passengers on his shuttle, and wondered if he would have any time at all to get used to the routine.

Lewis continued. "So the ship's marines are going to play war in shuttle bay one for most of the day. I know it's fun to stand around and watch, but try to contain your curiosity and let them run the place until they're done, okay? Stay on your patrol rounds, but don't dawdle through there and look for reasons to hang— Attention on deck!" Lewis announced abruptly in time with the sound of the hatch opening at the rear of the compartment.

Ordinarily, Lieutenant Commander Jacobson gave the "at ease" order as soon as he walked into the ready room. This time he left them standing until he made it to the podium and the door sealed shut at the back of the compartment. The head of the MA force somehow always looked a touch sharper and cleaner cut than anyone else despite wearing the same uniform and adhering to the same grooming standards.

"This briefing is now classified," said Jacobson. "If you have your holocom running, turn it off. If you have something else on your mind, put it aside. We have a brief head start on some bad news and we need to take full advantage of the time we have. Take your seats, people."

He gave the MAs a chance to settle back in once more. Thus far, Tanner had only shared a standard "welcome aboard" conversation with Jacobson. He hadn't gotten to know the man at all, but he knew the other MAs seemed to respect him.

"*Los Angeles* will go quiet within the hour. The MA force is quiet as of *now*. No message traffic other than ship's business will be allowed. If you have a letter you hadn't sent or you planned on writing home tonight, I'm sorry. It won't be going out. I do not know how long this will last, but I'm told it may be months. On that note, all leave scheduled for the next four weeks is canceled, and that will continue as long as our quiet status. Family notifications and financial issues will be handled in the normal fashion. And that's just the start of it," he added with a grim smile.

"Sometime tomorrow, we will rendezvous with two specially chartered civilian liners from the AISG to take on the 7th and 13th Marine Battalions. Note that I said 'battalions' and not 'elements of.' A large number of additional naval personnel will be coming along with them. We're talking about more than doubling our current crew compliment, ladies and gentlemen, and they aren't here for a couple of days.

"They're bringing along a good deal more in the way of supplies, especially food and extra water, but this will still be a major strain on the ship and her personnel. We will have marines camped out in the cargo bays and every other available space. Beyond that, we're looking at a large portion of the crew having to hot rack with these guys. Everybody gets a buddy. You wake up and get turned out, and your buddy goes to sleep in the bunk until it's time to switch."

"Sir?" asked one incredulous voice, "*how* many people will have to do this?"

"Everyone below the rank of chief, I imagine. Senior NCO quarters might go far enough that they'll all be able to squeeze in together without actually sharing bunks. Same for officers. I don't know yet. You'd have to ask Lieutenant Meese how the deck department is handling all of that. However, he's got more than enough on his hands as it is, so let's not bother him if we don't have to.

"Like I said, this will obviously be tough on everyone. People all over the ship will have their watch schedules flipped. We're looking at cutting showers to two minutes per day. And I don't want to think about what a nightmare this will be for all those poor bastards who work in the galley.

"As you can imagine, there will be some very unhappy crewmen and marines when this news hits. Plenty of people will bitch and moan in proper military fashion, and that's fine. But we need to be ready in case someone throws a real tantrum . . . and that could happen at any time starting in about fifty-three minutes or so. Fortunately, our usual problem children are already under close eye or locked up in the brig, but I don't want us caught with our pants down in front of everyone if there's an issue."

Again, Jacobson let his gaze sweep the room, either to impress his degree of concern upon them or to search for objections. Tanner didn't know him well enough yet to know which. "I know this will be stressful and uncomfortable. We can't let that show, and we *cannot* take our frustrations out on our shipmates. The MA force needs to set an example. We need to *solve* problems, not just put people on report. We will keep order and maintain discipline, but we will also step up and help. Understood?"

"Yes, sir," came the unified response.

"Oh, and one other thing. Admiral Yeoh and a chunk of her staff slipped on board this morning while most of you were at breakfast or just coming off your watch. They'll be here awhile, operating out of the flag bridge. The captain is still in command of the ship, but obviously the whole wardroom will be very conscious of her presence, and that sort of thing rolls downhill. So let's go over our patrol routes," he said, turning his eyes to his holocom to call up a few briefing screens.

"Sir?" spoke up one of the junior MAs. Tanner looked up over to MA3 Farina, who seemed a bit pale.

"What is it, Farina?"

"Are we . . . Sir, that many people coming on board . . . Are we invading Fairhaven or something?"

Tanner wondered how hard Farina would be slammed for speaking out of turn, but Jacobson gave a chuckle and—subtly, but Tanner noticed it—glanced at Lewis and gave the tiniest of waves. He didn't want anyone coming down on Farina for asking a question like that. Tanner's respect for him grew.

"I'm not gonna speculate, Farina. They didn't tell me. But I will say, just between us and with the doors shut and all, that Lieutenant Meese had an awful lot of the logistics already worked out when I went into our meeting this morning, so this is something that at least a few people in the wardroom have had planned out for a while now. This will be a pain in the ass, but you don't need to feel like this is an emergency. For all I know, things like this might become an annual event."

Several of the old salts in the room chuckled. Farina seemed a bit mollified by the response. Tanner felt no relief from the answer, but the delivery and the general attitude in the room spoke volumes about his new department. As Jacobson noted, the MAs needed to be ready to set an example. Most of them were accustomed to that.

Jacobson instructed everyone to open up several notes on their own holocoms. As Tanner pulled the requisite projections up, Baldwin's head tilted back and over toward him. "Congratulations," she murmured.

"Hm?"

"You're officially the last guy on this boat who had a vacation."

• • •

"Archangel currently fields one cruiser, ten destroyers—one more than they are allowed per Union armament treaties, to be precise— a handful of aging frigates, and about forty-five corvettes. They also have a couple of orbital naval space stations and decent screening drones."

Commodore Eldridge of NorthStar Security Forces left the holo projection showing the naval profile sheets up, allowing the vice presidents and board members around the conference table to digest at least a little of the details. His neatly trimmed dark blond beard combined with his deep, confident voice gave him an almost fatherly demeanor.

"If that sounds like a lot, that's because it is—for a state that encompasses a single star system," Eldridge continued. "By comparison, the unified Hashemite Navy was four times that size before their current internal conflict, but they have considerably more real estate to cover.

"Additionally, much of Archangel's strength in warships comes with caveats. As I said, the frigates are older ships, notably older than anything we're currently fielding. A good third of those corvettes and destroyers, along with the cruiser *Los Angeles*, are recent acquisitions. Their crews have been together for less than two years. Archangel hasn't been in a hot conflict in over three decades, so while a number of senior officers and NCOs have combat experience, the vast majority do not.

"That said, we shouldn't underestimate their capabilities. We saw how good those corvettes can be during the invasion of Scheherazade. Archangel has always offered one of the better training programs among the Union's system militias. From what we've gathered, I'd say their basic training for new recruits may be the best in the Union. It's certainly lengthier and more rigorous than ours or the Union fleet's program. Archangel doesn't field a dedicated elite operations force akin to our rangers—they tend to handpick people for sensitive missions—but their average forces are a notch above most Union militias.

"They also have considerable depth in manpower. In fact, they've got more people qualified for starship service than they have ships to put them on. Our best estimates hold that they've been procuring noncombatant ships to ferry around boarding teams and such in order to plug the holes in their customs and inspection coverage created by our absence. Frankly, left to their own devices, they will actually do a better job on that score than we did. As on Scheherazade, we can expect at least some of their civilian starship crews to step up if asked. They might not be heavily armed or armored, but they can provide logistical support."

"So are you saying that our fleet will have a hard time with this?" asked Jon Weir, leaning back in his seat and tapping his fingers anxiously against the side of the table.

"I'm saying that if they decide to fight, it'll cost us," Eldridge answered. "I'll let Ms. Pedroso and the Risk Management team discuss the likelihood of a violent conflict, because that's a political decision on the part of Archangel's government. But if they give the order, Archangel's navy will fight. We will win but not painlessly. I've given my projections on casualties and materiel losses from a military standpoint. It's up to you whether those losses are acceptable."

"Best guess, Hector?" asked Anton Brekhov from the head of the table.

The commodore looked at Maria, who nodded. "Sir," he said, "I think the only way to go in is with overwhelming force. We have to make the fight pointless from the start. We cannot do this piecemeal, or they'll fight and we'll lose ships and they will only be encouraged to keep fighting. This has to happen all at once. We have to go in with everything we can, sir, and we can't give them time to consider their options. Our warning shot has to be our fleet crashing right through their screening drones."

Eldridge rearranged the holo projections. The naval display floated in the air to one side of the conference table while Eldridge brought back the three-dimensional holographic model of the star system.

"If it's a fight, they'll be massed near Raphael waiting for us," he explained. "If we're operating with the sort of strength I've requested, we'll meet them with twice as many ships as they have to offer, even without our battleships—and that figure doesn't convey the massive advantage we have in size and power on a ship-to-ship basis. Still, it's our battleships that will do the work. The rest are effectively screening ships. Neither their cruiser nor the destroyers will stand up to a battleship. The guns on those corvettes can't penetrate a battleship's ES-reinforced hull. Our ships will take damage, we'll lose people . . . but we won't lose the battle."

"Is that a worst-case scenario?" asked Weir.

Eldridge gave a bit of a shrug. "Depending on how you look at it, you could call it the worst case or the best case. My hope is that their fleet won't be massed at all because they won't expect this sort of intervention. Given that this situation is unprecedented, Archangel may expect us to focus only on diplomatic and economic avenues. In that case, they'll be spread out, conducting the usual patrols and inspections and training exercises. If that happens, there's a much lower chance of a serious battle. We'll have their capital and other strategic points before they have a chance to get organized.

"But if Archangel expects trouble, they'll be massed near Raphael, and there will be a reckoning as soon as we arrive. Either they stand down, or we crush them . . . and how quickly and efficiently we crush them is a matter of how much of a fleet we bring in."

"Well, Maria?" asked Brekhov as he looked to his left.

The head of Risk Management stood. "Mr. President, ladies and gentlemen, our assessment is in line with the commodore's. Archangel has some advantages. The honest truth is that for the past year or more, we have underestimated the abilities of their intelligence network. They had a mole concealed within the top ranks of our company. They knew that the onset of destabilization within Hashem provided them an opportunity to make provocative moves. They may well have known about the financial vulnerabilities of the CDC and the ripple effect that could have with our own concerns and the rest of the Union economy. Their timing could not have been worse for us.

"Perhaps most worrisome is our inability to establish equally productive intelligence sources within their establishments. We have certainly had our sources in their business sector for years, but we have had little success in penetrating the top levels of government or defense. We're not blind, but the edge, I have to confess, has gone to them," she admitted.

She paused for that to sink in. "It's reasonable to assume that Archangel has a few more tricks up their sleeves. As the commodore points out, they have a significant navy, but it shows the signs of more flash than substance. The militia touts its people as its greatest strength, which is good for PR, but all those people don't do them much good in a starship battle. You can see much the same angle in their political rhetoric and their economic ideology: lots of reassurance and emphasis placed upon lofty ethics and morals to distract from pragmatic concerns.

"I'll put this in the simplest of terms, though my position is backed up by considerable research done by my department. The tactics and rhetoric of the Aguirre administration reveals a deep-seated persecution complex. They see themselves—Archangel as a whole—as the victims of protracted bullying. They see us as the primary bullies. As many of us know, the classic thinking with schoolyard bullies holds that the victim only needs to turn and fight once in order to stop the bullying. The victim doesn't need to win the fight, although that's obviously the fantasy. As long as the victim puts up a fight and causes a little bit of pain, the bully will move on to a more vulnerable target.

"Now, let's look at the time line," Maria continued. "The Aguirre administration has spent the last two years psyching up the populace for that moment where they fight the bully. They waited for us to be distracted and invested in a major operation before making their move. And when they did, they did so with intensity. They caused us multiple problems: PR issues with other systems across the Union, a revenue crunch, even the negotiations themselves were a fake-out to keep us off balance.

"The rest is not entirely schoolyard psychology, but it's still pretty simple. We know that President Aguirre is an adherent of Sun Tzu. This is something he shares with the head of Archangel's navy, Admiral Yeoh. It's one of the reasons he appointed her. The philosophy is visible throughout their strategy."

She raised one finger to point at the display of naval strength still floating in the air off to one side of the table. "Sun Tzu advises a leader to appear strong when he is weak," she said. "Maximum legal naval strength. A militia with a visible abundance of personnel. Training designed to build up confidence.

"Sun Tzu also says, 'Thus, what is of supreme importance in war is to attack the enemy's strategy. Next is to disrupt his alliances. The next best is to attack his army.' We haven't seen them do the last, but Archangel has certainly attacked our strategies and our alliances. That brings us to another key point of their strategy: 'To subdue the enemy without fighting is the acme of skill.'

"Archangel punched us as hard as they could in the form of Aguirre's revelations. In their attempt to disrupt our educational system across the Union, they tried to disrupt our position and to threaten us through implication that they would do worse if we don't back off. I don't believe they can. If they could have hit us harder, they would have done that. They've taken their best shot. They're hoping it scares us away.

"But we aren't a schoolyard bully. We are a sophisticated, modern organization, and we are the very backbone of the Union. We hold humanity together. And as unpleasant and unfortunate as this might be, we cannot allow a single system to cause such chaos.

Whatever their complaints, Archangel's tactics are unacceptable. We have to resolve this before the damage gets worse. When it's done, we can resolve whatever political ramifications this has with the Union Assembly and our individual state clients."

Brekhov snorted. "Better to beg forgiveness than to ask permission."

"Yes, sir," Maria replied.

"That doesn't answer the question of fleet strength," noted Jon Weir. "What's your assessment?"

"I think we listen to our expert," replied Maria. "We go in with overwhelming force. We pull our fleet from its current engagements in Hashem and elsewhere. We don't need their full strength in Archangel on a long-term basis, but we certainly need the full strength to open our intervention, hopefully without bloodshed."

"How long will it take to assemble the force you have in mind, Hector?" Brekhov asked.

"We can be assembled and ready to hit them within three weeks," said Eldridge. "If we do this, we need to assemble and move in as a single continuous operation. If we assemble the fleet and then sit and wait for a go order, that gives Archangel and other parties time to catch wind of our ship movements and put the puzzle pieces together. Additionally, we won't be able to have all of those ships tied up in this operation for long. Many of them will be needed elsewhere in the long term."

"But wait a second," Weir countered, looking to Brekhov and Pedroso. "Eldridge already said that an engagement will also cost us. If that's the case, shouldn't we try to ascertain the minimum force to accomplish this, so we don't leave ourselves exposed on other fronts any more than absolutely necessary?"

"Jon," spoke up Brekhov again, "you don't pull a gun on someone unless you intend to use it. We go in with the intent and expectation of destroying their fleet and occupying their cities. Don't worry about covering our losses. We'll deal with that when it's time to assess indemnities and reparations. If they are sensible and they stand down before it comes to violence, then so much the better. I hope that is what happens, but hope does not make for good policy.

"Once we have control of the situation in Archangel, we'll be able to provide all the confessions and all of the material proof we'll ever need to show the rest of the Union that Archangel fabricated all of their evidence," said Brekhov, making clear with his gaze that he didn't want to have to elaborate on his euphemisms. "Nor will anyone want to press the issue afterward. We will hear far fewer objections to our success than our failure, and so we must not fail. And on that note, we'd best make sure CDC and Lai Wa are on board with us."

• • •

"Let's consider the economics here. Archangel has four terraformed planets—four! Michael, Raphael, Gabriel, and Uriel, all named for archangels, of course. They also have settlements on another planet, Augustine, and several asteroid mining colonies. All that diversity, all that development, packed into a single star system, with the ninth strongest economy in the Union. And what's their answer to their debts and economic problems? Default followed by propaganda. Look at the markets! We're all suffering for it."

—Union Assemblyman Warren Markinson, Edison,
Union Assembly Floor Speech, November 2276

"This is such bullshit. Same fuckin' food as yesterday and the day before. All they care about is mass production. Look at this, it's all red beans and rice or assembly-line hamburgers. Or I could have what's left of the chili and pasta they didn't shell out yesterday. Great."

Tanner heard the burly marine's complaints over the rest of the conversation in the passageway. Half of the available space was taken up by the single-file line of people waiting to get into the galley. Walking past the line, Tanner slowed his stride, taking notice of the man's volume.

"What, you got the menu open there?" asked another marine.

"Yeah, right here," said the first, gesturing to the screen projected by the holocom on his wrist. "Oh, wait, I could go vegetarian and have whatever they poured into a muffin tray. Bet'cha the officers in the wardroom are still getting steaks grilled to order, though."

Tanner stopped and turned around. Talk like that could get a guy in trouble. "Hey, they're supposed to get the fryers up and running again tomorrow," he offered. "The galley had to more than double their output, so right now they're just trying to keep up, but they'll hit their stride soon, y'know?"

The marine glared. Tanner read his uniform tags and insignia quickly: Private First Class DeLeon, fleet marines, fully qualified for zero-g ops and infantry. The guy probably graduated from the same sort of extended basic training Tanner went through. He should be able to handle these sorts of inconveniences. Yet he seemed decidedly aggravated and unfriendly. "Yeah, that's great, pal. Who asked you? And shouldn't you have a buddy with you if you're doing your little walk around the boat looking for people to hassle?"

"DeLeon, ease up," said one of the marines. A couple of others looked on with concern.

"Woah, there's no hassle." Tanner held his hands up. He was under arms and therefore had the look of an MA on patrol, given the black beret and the sidearm on his hip. In truth, he was simply on his way to relieve the watch in the brig for lunch. Still, as Jacobson had decreed, the MAs were always on duty. "Listen, I get the same menu, too. It's only been three days. This will get easier, we just need to be patient."

"You need to get out of my face!"

Something about the marine's warning seemed too absurd to take seriously. "Or what?" Tanner chuckled. "C'mon, let's—"

The marine's uppercut caught Tanner squarely on the jaw, knocking him back until his skull struck the bulkhead behind him. Disoriented and surprised, Tanner slid to the deck with his eyes wide. He recovered his senses right away, but by then the other marines had DeLeon tied up in a mess of arms and legs.

Another marine leaned in toward Tanner with his hand outstretched. "You okay, buddy?"

"I'm all right." Tanner opened and closed his mouth to ensure he had all his teeth. He was a bit surprised that such a solid punch didn't dislocate his jaw. "Okay. I may have escalated there when I didn't mean to."

The marines pulled Tanner to his feet. One of them returned his helmet, which had tumbled away off its shoulder mount during his fall. "Goddammit"—he sighed—"this is exactly what I *didn't* want." With DeLeon largely under control but still swearing up a storm, Tanner pushed into the scrum and set to getting the irate marine in cuffs. "You're under arrest for assault," Tanner declared over the raised voices. "Relax, or it becomes resisting arrest. And shut up before you make it into something worse!"

"Relax, DeLeon!" agreed several other marines. "Relax! Don't be stupid!"

Within seconds, DeLeon understood the futility of struggling. Tanner had one wrist cuffed already and had two other guys helping him. Surrendering to the inevitable, DeLeon let his other wrist get cuffed and stood with a dark scowl.

"What's your unit?" Tanner asked, hoping for the marine's sake that DeLeon wouldn't answer by spitting on him or making some dumb threat. He stepped behind his prisoner and confiscated the marine's standard-issue survival knife, vac helmet, and military-issue holocom, then began the normal pat down for any hidden weapons or surprises. He found nothing.

Another marine answered for DeLeon. "Third Platoon, Bravo Company, ship's detachment."

Tanner let out a breath. "Shit." He'd expected the problems to come from the visiting forces, not the ship's own. But suddenly it clicked into place: it was the marines who'd already become used to routines on *Los Angeles* who felt the disruptions most acutely.

"We'll let his platoon leader know," said a third marine. She and the others looked embarrassed more than anything else, perhaps even ashamed. "You want a couple of us to walk him down to the brig with you?"

Oh God, they feel bad about one of their own picking on a little navy guy. Marines. Wow. "No, I got it. I'm fine," Tanner said. "We'll send out the usual notifications, but if you want to tell his sergeant or whoever, that's fine." He gave DeLeon a glare. "Are we done?"

"Yeah, whatever," DeLeon grumbled.

Tanner took a firm grip on the chain linking the cuffs with his left hand, staying behind DeLeon but affording himself a good level of control. Standard procedure held that he should call in and wait for backup before bringing a prisoner to the brig rather than doing it by himself. Tanner's first inclination was to end the disruption as quickly as possible, and there was no nearby compartment where he could hold DeLeon until the lunch line died down. If the last two days were any indication, that wouldn't happen for another ninety minutes.

DeLeon seemed resigned to his fate. Tanner opted to walk him down to the brig on his own. He noted that a couple of the marines fell out of line and followed a short distance behind, but their motives were obvious. They didn't want DeLeon making any more trouble.

The route to the brig required some odd detours to avoid crowds, maintenance crews, and training ops. Always a busy ship under normal circumstances, *Los Angeles* now hosted a carefully managed swarm of activity. Much of deck ten's passageways served as a running circuit. The shuttle bay saw constant use. Outside the ship's hull, two platoons from the 13th conducted zero-g training and certification for newer marines, with ANS *St. George* and a freighter from the AISG providing assistance. The gym, the shooting range, and the rec rooms were packed around the clock.

Yesterday, the ship had gone through two modified emergency drills for the sake of establishing basic safety procedures while so many people were aboard. Both drills had turned into complete fiascos, doing nothing to diminish anyone's discomfort. Tanner hoped to keep the incident with DeLeon quiet and resolve it quickly, lest the image of marines being hauled off to the brig add to that stress.

They made the trip in silence, and though they encountered a few people on the way, no one held them up. Tanner felt his holocom buzz and noted on the display that the call came from his destination, but by then he was only seconds away.

Lewis and Baldwin both awaited him at the front desk area, as well as a marine corporal. Lewis came up with Baldwin to take DeLeon by either arm. The corporal simply gave DeLeon a look of disappointment and stayed out of the way, but Tanner figured that look was the best control method anyone present could use on the big marine.

"You're supposed to call this in immediately," Lewis said to Tanner as he guided DeLeon around a corner behind the desk to one of several open cells. The brig was, fortunately, not a busy place.

"Yeah, sorry," Tanner replied. "I know. But it was over as soon as it began and he cooperated. I just wanted to get him down here before it became more of a spectacle."

Lewis didn't respond right away, concerned first with getting DeLeon settled. The marine followed every instruction and soon sat on the cell's bunk with his hands freed from Tanner's cuffs. The MAs then stepped outside and the transparent fourth wall of the cell slid into place, sealing DeLeon in. Lewis guided his subordinates back around the corner.

"I don't care if he manages to cuff himself for you and I don't care if the whole world's watching. Call it in before you transport. Every time. Got me?" Lewis admonished.

"Aye, aye," Tanner answered. "Won't happen again."

"Yeah, so on that note, what *did* happen? All I know is this guy knocked you on your ass?"

Tanner frowned. "He was in line for chow while I was on my way here, bitching up a storm about the menu and whatever else. I tried to talk to him all friendly like, I didn't come down hard or try to shut him down or give him a dirty look . . . but he told me to get out of his face, and I didn't take that seriously. I said, 'Or what?' just like I obviously shouldn't have said, and so he tagged me. Then his buddies jumped in and restrained him and here we are."

"'Or what?'" Baldwin repeated. "You said that?"

"I don't respond well to threats." Tanner shrugged defensively. "It was dumb, I know. I feel a little responsible for this. I should've known better than to impugn his manly might or whatever. I didn't think he could be serious."

Lewis ran one hand over his scalp. "No, you shouldn't have said that, but he shouldn't have hit anyone."

"Well, yeah," Tanner agreed.

"Baldwin, go ahead and grab chow. No sweat if you're a little late getting back, 'cause your relief here has work to do now, anyway. Malone, stow this guy's stuff and get to work on your report right away. I'll let Chief Lockwood know what happened. Then I'll talk to this guy after he's had time to cool down."

"Aye, aye." Tanner nodded again, but he heard Baldwin simply say, "See you later." He wondered if he didn't need formal responses like that aside from talking to the officers. With that, Tanner went into the evidence locker, pulled out one of the many small metal baskets for collecting personal items, and then headed back out to the front desk to take over for Baldwin.

"Nothing to pass on," she said, collecting her helmet from the desk as she headed out. "You know how to find the arrest reports and stuff?"

"Yeah," he said, then paused. "How long was it before you made your first arrest?"

Baldwin rolled her eyes. "I've been here seven months and my first arrest was the other night. Only time I've been hit, too, but it was an accident. Guess I'm just more likable than you."

"Can't argue that." Tanner took his seat while she walked out. The brig's front desk was a semicircular affair, with hardened screens and embedded, physical controls like one would find on the bridge and other vital compartments. The suite offered holo screens as well, but the brig was one of several areas where designers opted for clunky but reliable technology over delicate modernity.

That left Tanner alone in the front office with the marine corporal, who waited until Tanner looked up at him to speak. "You okay?" the marine asked. He looked perhaps a little older than Tanner and had a friendly face. At his rank, Tanner guessed his age was natural rather than affected by longevity treatments. He seemed a bit taller than Tanner, his red hair buzzed down to a fine stubble on his scalp.

Tanner let out a heavy breath. "Yes. I'm fine. It was one punch. And, y'know, my skull against the bulkhead, but I'm fine."

"DeLeon hits pretty hard. I've done some sparring with him." He paused. "I'm his squad leader. He normally isn't the type to get into problems like this. I came down as soon as I heard, obviously.

I'd like to apologize on behalf of him and the squad. The platoon, too, though I probably shouldn't speak for the lieutenant . . . but he'll be down here shortly. Stuck in a meeting."

Though he nearly repeated that he was fine, Tanner bit back his irritation. The guy felt bad. He stood from the desk again and held out his hand, noting the marine's name tag. "I'm Tanner Malone. You're . . . Corporal Collins?"

"Yeah." The marine stepped forward to shake hands over the desk. "I know who you are. Everyone knows."

At that, Tanner sighed. "Guess I should be used to that. Hey, you're in Third Platoon . . . you wouldn't be Brent, would you?" He saw Collins nod and added, "Alicia's boyfriend?"

"That, too."

"She's told me a lot about you," Tanner said. "Until I came on board, anyway. Hasn't responded to anything since. Is she pissed off at me?"

"Yeah, she is," Collins confirmed with a casual, matter-of-fact shrug. "I wouldn't sweat it. She'll let you know why when she figures it out for herself. Anyway, believe it or not, this is my first, um . . . squad fuckup," he went on, gesturing back toward the cells. "What happens now?"

"Well, we give DeLeon a little time to sit there and wind down. Then one of the senior MAs talks to him, and we figure out whether this is a captain's mast or a court martial. There were a dozen witnesses and all, so if he's smart he basically pleads guilty and we have the captain's mast. Most of the punishments for that are things like extra duty and loss of privileges and maybe some pay, but it doesn't lead to prison or a discharge. If he wants to fight it, though, someone gets to be his lawyer and we go to court martial. When he inevitably gets found guilty, they'll throw the book at him." Tanner frowned. "I think they get grouchy for having to set up a court martial in the first place."

Collins shook his head. "DeLeon is usually a stand-up guy. I can't imagine he'll want to fight this. It isn't like he can say it was someone else. You, uh . . . you guys might want to talk to him sooner rather than later, though. Sitting in that cell wondering what's gonna happen will probably spin him up, not wind him down. He's had too much time to think as it is."

"Gotcha. I'll let the bosses know. Sounds like he's been boiling for a while, then? I didn't think the food in the galley was what had him so angry."

"Nah, he . . ." Collins paused, clearly debating with himself how much he should say. "His wife is gonna have a baby in a few weeks."

"Oh." Tanner winced. "He had his leave canceled?"

"Yeah, and that was bad enough, but he's also one of the guys who enlisted in the first place because he wound up in major debt from school and he needed the payoff benefits. Then the president comes out last week and says 'no more educational debt,' so DeLeon is . . . kinda pissed."

Tanner swallowed hard. "You don't say."

"Kinda like everyone else, right?"

"Kind of."

"Well, like I said, he doesn't have any excuses, but that's where his head is at."

The suggestion seemed reasonable. Unless DeLeon had some history of screwing up that Collins didn't know about, his rank implied that he was still very new in the service. Tanner wondered about his age. The thought of trying to have a family while still in the lowest ranks of the service seemed crazy to him, but he didn't consider the military his career, nor did he have any thoughts of children in the first place. Some communities within Archangel encouraged starting families at a young age.

"Thanks for the advice," Tanner said. "Anyway, I don't want to give you the brush-off, but he's here and he isn't giving us any more trouble. I have to write this report and log in his personal belongings. He doesn't talk to his chain of command until he talks to a senior MA, and they figure out whether to release him back to your unit and under what conditions."

"Gotcha. And thank you. Again, on behalf of the platoon—"

"Really, don't worry about it," Tanner said, trying to wave it off.

The hatch opened once again. A marine sergeant entered the compartment. "I'm told one of my people is in here? Who'd DeLeon hit and is he okay?"

"Private DeLeon is fine, sergeant," Tanner began.

"I'm sure DeLeon is fine. I want to make sure he didn't break some poor navy kid in half!"

Tanner took a deep breath. *Marines*, he thought.

Half an hour later, with Collins, the platoon sergeant, the platoon leader, and Bravo Company's first sergeant all personally assured that DeLeon had not, in fact, punched anyone's head clean off his shoulders, Tanner had the prisoner's personal gear cataloged and his helmet returned to him in case of emergency. He sat back down at the front desk, calling up the forms for arrest and incident reports.

The hatch opened once again. Tanner glanced up to see Baldwin return, and then did a double take as she placed the galley tray on the edge of the desk. He saw several large cookies, a couple of brownies, and three small bowls of soft-serve ice cream, all standard desserts still available despite the current strain on galley services.

"Second squad, Third Platoon of Bravo Company wants you to know that they're extra super sorry their squad mate picked on you"—Baldwin sighed—"and they will make sure the big, bad marine never hurts you again."

Tanner stared at the tray. "They gave me their desserts?"

"In their defense, I don't think they're sucking up to you because you're famous. I'm pretty sure they didn't realize who you were."

He didn't know what to say. "Is this a joke?" he wondered aloud.

Baldwin scowled at him. "I'm taking your ice cream," she declared as she claimed one dish from the tray and took up the other seat behind the desk. "Have you not started writing your report yet? It's not that hard. Do you want help?"

NINE

Personnel Concerns

*"I know someone out there will jump on me for raising old stereo-
types, but let's think critically here. The Catholic Church only shaped
up on issues like gay marriage and its institutionalized child abuse
because it had to in order to survive in the twenty-first century. And
beyond that, the Church talked and talked about charity and gen-
erosity and lambasted greed, but when privatized space exploration
became a thing, who was it that had the money to fund a colony
tucked away underneath the Vatican? All I'm saying is we shouldn't
look at Archangel as if they're Christ turning over the moneylenders'
tables."*

—Mars Governor Reverend Harry Tidewater,
Monthly Press Conference, November 2276

Life on *Los Angeles* quickly became an exercise in mass stress
management.

Like most other third and second class ratings, Tanner found
himself hot-racking with not one but two other men, each of
whom got to use Tanner's assigned rack for exactly eight hours.

Given that most such individuals, including Tanner, had to set their wake-up calls to slightly before the eight hour mark and that hardly anyone ever actually made it to bed on time, that naturally ensured that no one ever got even seven hours. Nor did this leave the bunk in a very good state. Tanner found himself devoting fifteen to twenty minutes sorting and replacing linens every night rather than trying to sleep in the mess left behind by the two "guests" he never met. Nor did he complain, knowing that the non-rate berths were probably more cramped and uncomfortable than his.

Though variety in the galley improved, the lines did not. Frustrations mounted as people spent most of their chow breaks standing in line. Workspaces were often cramped as well, with more than a few departments expected to host "refresher classes" and "job shadows" for the sake of cross-training, along with the mandatory calisthenics workouts imposed on virtually everyone. Between that and the drills, Tanner and several of the other MAs suspected that all the activity was meant to keep everyone busy. Overcrowding was bad, but overcrowding with excessive idle time would create serious problems even among well-disciplined professionals.

After a few days, once people figured out their schedules and started to connect with their social networks among the crew and the guests, one bright spot emerged. Ejected from his rack with seven hours to go before his shift on watch in the brig, Tanner learned of the impromptu reunion of Oscar Company in a rec room on deck ten.

"Naw, that boat was terrible, guys," said Sinclair, once Tanner's squad leader and now a signalman third class. "I don't know where to start. We worked for this BM2 who said, 'When we're in port, you non-rates have two days on the duty rotation: yours and mine! I don't care if the whole boat is on liberty. If I'm working, you're working.'" For all Sinclair's legitimate complaints, Tanner noted that his old squad leader was at least still smiling. Reminiscing turned to grousing, but it stayed good-natured.

"Wow, are you serious?" Corpsman Third Class Matuskey blinked. He'd snagged one of the last few chairs in the rec room. Most people either sat on the pool tables or just stood. "Didn't anyone say anything to *his* supervisor?"

"What would we say?" asked Baljashanpreet, another Oscar recruit who now bore the hard-won rating patch of a survivalman. "He told us that right in front of his department head! That was our first day on the ship, straight out of basic. He worked us like dogs."

"Ramos actually did say something once," added Sinclair. "Tried talking to the first lieutenant about the whole thing, and the lieutenant believed him and talked to the BM2, but it didn't fix anything. And you don't see Ramos here, do you? That's because his promotion to crewman got delayed, and he's only now going through his rating school." Sinclair shook his head. "Fuck *Belfast*. Leaving for my rating school was probably the happiest day of my life."

"Yeah. Fuck *Belfast*," agreed Baljashanpreet. "Seriously, I thought I was gonna go nuts on that boat."

"What," said Huang, "you thought you were gonna pull a Gomez?"

A good portion of the young men and women crowded into the rec room shared a groan and a laugh that Tanner didn't understand. "Wait, what about Gomez?" he asked, and naturally looked—like everyone did back in basic—to Other Gomez, a habit that neither young man did anything to invite.

"Oh God, don't ask me," groaned Other Gomez.

Alicia laughed. "No, you gotta tell it now." She stood among several other Oscar grads. Tanner couldn't help but notice that his best friend from those days seemed inclined to keep her distance from him.

"I wasn't there!" Other Gomez protested.

"Doesn't matter, you've gotta tell the story. He's your brother."

"We're not related at all! His family came over from Argentina! Mine's from Texas!"

The ship's bell rang twice over the PA system. "Now, *St. Francis* arriving," announced a voice from somewhere on the bridge.

"Wow," said Other Gomez, "is *everyone* coming on board today?"

Tanner wondered the same. Ever since the first arrival, he kept one ear toward the announcements. One particular ship's captain was worth listening for. Everyone else in the rec room, however, seemed to know Other Gomez just wanted to change the subject.

"Seriously, though, what happened?" asked Tanner. "He always said he only ever wanted to be a science tech. That rating's impacted, so I figured he'd still be here as a crewman, right?"

Other Gomez shook his head. "Look, it's not like he and I talked a ton, but I knew he wasn't happy to find out he'd have to wait another whole year before he could go to his rating school. And, yeah, the guys in charge of our section of the deck department could be dicks, too, but nothing like you're talking about," he said, nodding to Sinclair and Baljashanpreet. "Mostly I think it was the workload for the ship in general and Gomez knowing that it wasn't gonna lighten up anytime soon.

"Anyway, one night he's on watch on the bridge while we're heading into port at Bethlehem Station, orbiting Michael, right? Commander Manyara's the OOD. It's the middle of the night, and Manyara says to one of the other officers, 'You know, I'll bet the ship isn't ready for an unplanned drill right now. They probably all think the workday is over since we've got a port call right around the corner.' It's almost time for Gomez's watch to be up, and Gomez says, 'You want to run a man overboard drill, sir?' And Manyara laughs and says, 'Oh, sure,' but he's *clearly* joking, right? Everyone knows he's joking.

"Only Gomez, he gets up from his station with his helmet, like he's about to visit the head or something, and then he walks past the command chair and goes straight off the bridge without any sort of permission or the usual formalities. But by the time Manyara asks, 'Hey, what the hell?' that fucker had walked right into an escape pod and launched himself off the ship."

"*What?*" Tanner blurted, along with several friends who hadn't heard the story yet. Others laughed.

The ship's bell rang once more. "Now, *St. Catherine* arriving."

"Like I said. One of the smaller ones, not the lifeboats. He didn't put in any directional commands or try to land on Michael. He just jettisoned the pod and floated there. Then we had to turn the ship around and run 'man overboard' for real."

Tanner didn't laugh. "What happened to him? Did anyone give him a psych eval or counseling? He must've been desperate to do something like that."

"Oh, he was desperate," chuckled Fuller, another Oscar grad who'd come to *Los Angeles* as a non-rate. She'd been put into engineering and had made good on her experience by moving on to become a damage controlman. "I talked to him before he got thrown off the ship. He was super unhappy and he really didn't like Manyara. He decided he wanted out, right then and there. Literally. He wasn't crazy, he just didn't want to do any of this anymore.

"I'm still in touch with him a little," she continued. "They discharged him, but he knew he could get a job with his family's business. It's not a lot of money and he's in debt like most people, but at least the discharge didn't leave him unemployed."

"Yeah, but to come all the way through basic with us and then do something like that . . ." Sinclair shook his head. "I feel kinda bad for the guy."

"He's fine." Fuller waved her hand. "Leave it alone. Besides, he got the last laugh on Manyara. Does that guy even get a turn in the OOD rotation anymore? I mean, obviously everyone knows it wasn't his fault, but it still made him look bad just because it happened on his watch."

Once more came the ship's bells. "Now, *Joan of Arc* arriving."

Tanner's head fairly snapped up at the announcement. "Hey, I'll be back," he said, slipping out of the crowd.

"Where are you going?" asked Sinclair.

"I've got another reunion to catch!" Tanner called back from the exit to the rec room. As soon as he broke free from the crowd and into the passageway—which was never exactly empty anymore—Tanner took off running.

The moment tested Tanner's familiarity with the ship. He hustled through passageways and all but vaulted up a couple of ladders—he hardly ever called them stairs anymore—and hauled ass for the wardroom. All that he knew from the ship's Plan of the Day was that a meeting of other vessel captains would be held there. Even the MA's security-privileged version of the Plan didn't specify which ships or a time line.

Tanner made it to the wardroom quickly, but didn't find familiar faces outside the door. His search didn't end before he'd checked all the approaching passageways. Plenty of people moved about, but not the ones he was looking for. He no longer paid attention to the ship's bell. Other ships and captains meant little to him.

Coming back for another sweep starting out from the wardroom door, he spotted a man and a woman in gray navy vac suits. The woman wore her deep-red hair boyishly short, walked with a confident gait, and bore a lieutenant's pips on her shoulder. Both she and her companion had blood stripes down the outer seams of their pants.

"Captain Kelly!" he called out, walking quickly to catch up.

The pair paused and turned. He saw quizzical looks brighten up as they recognized him. "Oh, hey, Tanner." Chief Romita smiled. "You stationed here now?"

"Sure am." Tanner accepted the offered handshake as he joined them. "Got here a little over a week ago. I hear things are good with all of you?"

"Yeah," Kelly answered. "Sanjay mentioned that you called while you were on Raphael. How's it going here?"

Tanner held his arms out to gesture around them. "Busy, ma'am. Obviously."

"*Joan* is linked up over at airlock four if you want to go say hi to everyone else," Kelly offered.

"I might. They didn't tell us how long you'd be on, though. I wanted to catch you before you got tied up."

They heard the bell once more. "Now, *St. Sebastian* arriving."

The captain's smile tightened. "People still coming on board. We've got a few minutes, I'd imagine."

"Oh good," Tanner said, then hesitated. He realized then that he didn't actually know what to say. Not given her rank and the distance mandated by regulations and custom. And even without all that . . . *I'd have to stand on a chair to reach that high.*

"Chief," Kelly said after a pause, "would you mind heading in and saving us a couple of seats?"

"Not at all." Romita slapped Tanner on the shoulder before leaving. "Good to see you."

"You, too, chief."

Kelly waited for a beat or two before turning back to Tanner. "Are you on duty?"

"On duty, but not anyplace specific. All the overcrowding means if I'm not in my rack, I'm on duty, if only to be a visible presence."

"Did you run from somewhere to meet us?" she asked.

"Maybe a little," Tanner admitted. "Wouldn't run for just anyone."

The amused captain couldn't help but mirror his smile. "Then I'm flattered. On behalf of the ship, of course."

"Of course. She's a good ship."

"How's this one?"

"Not the same. It's a good ship, too, but not the same."

"Hm. 'It.' Not exactly the parlance the navy expects."

"To be fair, I've been here less than two weeks, but . . . not the same." He paused. "I wasn't exaggerating. I've missed you. And *Joan* and everyone."

"It's mutual. For all of us," she added with a knowing emphasis. "I saw your dating stunt the other night. Sanjay saw it happen live and sent out a call for the rest of us. That was pretty creative. To be honest, I forgot all about it after the president turned the whole economy upside down, but you had us all in stitches for a little while there."

"Well, like I told Sanjay, I didn't know I was going until the last minute, and then I couldn't find anyone special to go with." Tanner shrugged. "Most of my first ideas were either impractical or inappropriate."

The amused glint in her eye remained. "Like this whole conversation."

"I've missed you, ma'am," he said, nodding as if to concede the point. "That's all I wanted to say."

"You could stay in touch. Maybe write once in a while."

The suggestion caught him off guard. He heard no flirtation in her voice. Nothing that anyone could construe as out of line. Perfectly professional. "That's not inappropriate, too?"

"Maybe, but as long as the letters themselves aren't inappropriate, I'll bet the captain of my ship won't give a damn. She'll only be in the service for a few more years, anyway." She paused again, looking at him thoughtfully. "People come and go from your life all the time in this line of work . . . shame to let rank dictate who you can be friends with once you get out, you know?"

Tanner nodded slowly. "I might have to try that when *Los Angeles* comes off 'quiet mode,' then."

"About that—any chance you know what this briefing is about?" she asked, her mind coming back to the business at hand.

"I honestly don't. But I wouldn't be surprised if the lady running it is the same lady who put me on your ship."

"Ah," Kelly understood. "Then I won't be surprised, either. Thank you for that. I should probably get to it. Good to see you, Tanner."

"Good to see you, too. Captain."

She pursed her lips. "That might be a little more appropriate."

"Might. I dunno. 'Ma'am' does make you sound old."

Kelly bit back her laughter before it escaped. She shook her head, turned, and continued on her way, but Tanner caught a glimpse of her face as she disappeared into the wardroom.

She was still smiling.

. . .

"I'm just saying, you made this whole big deal about looking for a date. I was right here the whole time," Baldwin explained. Neither she nor Tanner could help but notice the increasing number of navy crewmen and marines heading in the same direction as they walked through the corridor. "I'm not trying to give you the wrong idea, but you didn't want to go alone, and who wouldn't want to get off this boat for a couple days?"

"Okay, but I hadn't met you yet. You were on opposite shifts from me the entire time."

"Weren't you asking people you'd only just met? You didn't think to say, 'Hey, guys, isn't there anyone in the department I could ask?' Nobody said anything?"

"Well, not really, no," Tanner answered, doing his best to keep up as Baldwin weaved between slower walkers. "To be honest, I think people liked seeing me twist in the wind."

Baldwin looked over her shoulder skeptically, yet managed to maintain her pace without bumping into anyone. "You're serious?"

"New guy steps on board and immediately gets sent on shore leave for a ball full of celebrities? You don't think anyone would want to fuck with me for that? I'm lucky they didn't set me up with someone's grandmother or a goat or something." He paused and added, "Although plenty of people knew I was looking for someone to go with. Nobody mentioned you."

He noted the look of displeasure on her face before she turned her attention forward again. "I hate everyone," she fumed. "Still. You didn't maybe look at a roster?"

"I did!"

"And?"

"And the roster says your name is Jesse. That could go either way."

"It's short for Jessica! I'm a girl!"

"I noticed!"

"I could've worn a dress for once instead of a stupid uniform! My family's on Raphael. I probably still fit in the dress I wore to prom and it's still in my closet back home. That would've been fine. Jesus, a girl signs up for the navy, you think she doesn't want to get dressed up once in a while?"

"You own dresses?" asked a random machinist's mate as they passed by.

"Oh, for fuck's sake," she replied sourly, "who asked you?"

"Well, to be fair," Tanner ventured, "that kind of swearing wouldn't go over well at Ascension Hall."

"I know when to talk and when to shut up," she grumbled, then glanced around at the growing flood of bodies. "Seriously, is *everyone* going to this? Who's still on watch?"

"Well, we are kind of overstaffed at the moment."

"Gangway!" Baldwin called out, impressing Tanner with the volume of her voice. "Masters-at-arms coming through! Gangway!"

To Tanner's surprise, her tactic worked. Most of the crowd ahead shuffled and squeezed to the right to let them pass on the left. Baldwin broke into a jog, which Tanner followed mostly to back her play. In truth, while they were theoretically on patrol, neither of them had been called to hangar one because they were needed for crowd control or some other rating-related duty. They'd simply been directed there, like the masses of shipmates, by a message over their holocoms and simultaneous instructions from the duty dispatcher.

Thanks to Baldwin's shouting, they managed to arrive roughly halfway through the assembly period. Numerous members of the deck department handled issues of crowd control. Baldwin tugged Tanner over to one side and away from the crowd as soon as they were in the hangar bay. The pair remained on the outskirts, doing a decent job of looking semiofficial while really just being two more faces in the crowd.

"They're all *Los Angeles* crew," Tanner noted as they got a better look. "Everyone's wearing the ship patch on their shoulders. Marines, too."

"Yeah, I caught that," Baldwin murmured. She glanced around. "Notice the shuttles are all out to make room? There have to be at least a thousand people in here."

"Going on two thousand," said a bo'sun from behind them. "Standing room only, going to get a bit tight in here."

"Jesus," breathed Tanner, "why didn't they send out an all-call? This isn't on the Plan of the Day or on any schedule I saw."

The bo'sun shrugged. "Hey, they don't tell me, so I couldn't tell you."

"They woke people up for this," Baldwin observed. "I know some of these people. They should be asleep right now. What is going on?"

Tanner looked around for some better vantage point and found two low storage containers. He climbed up onto one of them and swept the hangar bay with his gaze. "I think we're about to find out," he said as he helped Baldwin up. Seconds later, they could see the XO of the ship along with several other officers near a mobile loading platform.

"I don't recognize all of those people." Baldwin frowned. "And I should."

Soon, the flow of bodies into the hangar bay slowed to a trickle, then seemed more or less over. As the bo'sun had warned, space amounted to standing room only. The deck crewmen and several hangar bay engineers maintained a perimeter of sorts to keep people from leaning or sitting on mobile equipment and machinery lining the bulkheads. The loading platform up toward the center of the bay rose, with a couple of officers riding it as if to give everyone someone to look at. Then one of them called out the order, enhanced by the hangar bay's public address system: "Attention on deck!"

Everyone stood rigid. The bay went silent. Soon, they all saw one more officer, wearing her vac suit like the rest of them, ascend the loading platform.

"Thank you for your rapid assembly," said Admiral Yeoh. "I have a few things to explain, and I wanted to do it personally. Stand at ease." She paused for a breath, long enough to make sure everyone's attention remained focused, and then began speaking.

"I want to thank you all for putting up with all of the stress and inconvenience of the last few days. I must ask much more of you in the near future. Yet I know you will live up to every challenge, as you lived up to this one and all the challenges before it.

"Most of you here are 'new guard.' You've risen to an enhanced level of training and readiness. You either passed through our new basic training regimen and then came into the fleet, or you met new rigorous standards and fulfilled numerous qualifications suited to the Archangel Navy's new philosophy. You marines are trained and capable of filling out any number of navy crew billets if the situation demands it. You navy crewmen stand ready to shoulder a weapon and go into combat with your marine comrades. The new guard of the Archangel Navy is the best-trained and best-prepared militia force in the Union. I don't tell you this to make you feel proud of yourselves or justify all these new standards," she said, gazing levelly at the hundreds of young men and women before her. "I made sure you would be the best in the Union because Archangel *needs* you to be the best.

"By now, you're all aware of the news from the president's Annual Address. You know we have severed our ties with NorthStar, Lai Wa, and CDC. You know the legislature is united in this decision, and you know why. You know what those companies have done to you, to your family and your friends. And as you can imagine, the Big Three are *not happy* about that revelation."

A few people in the audience chuckled. The admiral did not.

"Ladies and gentlemen, those corporations may not let us go. They may well come after us. They may feel their survival is at stake, and they may feel the need to make an example of us. If that happens, and I believe it will," she noted, "they will not come to make a token show of force. They will come with a navy greater than any in human space save for the Union fleet. They will bring battleships and cruisers and assault carriers with the intent of occupying our homes. They will have considerably greater numbers and greater firepower. And still, it will fall to us—to you and me and the rest of the Archangel Navy—to throw them back out on their asses."

Her calm, firm demeanor did not invite cheers. Indeed, Tanner looked around and saw more than a few worried faces in the crowd. Admiral Yeoh, as always, looked serene and sure.

"If they come, it will likely happen soon. Weeks but probably not months. We have time to prepare. That's why you're all here now, packed in on *Los Angeles* like a good many of your comrades are packed on board the frigates and destroyers nearby. I've spoken with their captains. They know their roles. It's time you knew yours."

Yeoh touched a button on the holocom attached to her wrist. Large screens, likely routed through powerful holo projectors mounted in the shuttle bay's bulkheads, lit up to either side of her. The screens showed a tactical layout of the fleet of ships around *Los Angeles*—most of the destroyers the navy had, along with all of its frigates and more than half of the corvettes. The other showed a projection of the star system, noting key military points from Michael to Augustine.

"Ladies and gentlemen, this is Operation Beowulf."

From his spot on top of the crates with Baldwin at his side, Tanner watched Yeoh bring up more projections. His mouth slowly fell open. "You've gotta be kidding me."

. . .

"It's a *job*. You ain't here defending your homes, and this whole fiasco isn't some mission to save the Union." Harris's glare moved from one member of the ten-man assault team to the next. Street lighting and the illumination from various electronics gave him a look at their young, tense faces. The rest of their bodies were covered by black recon armor. Though they ranged anywhere from raw recruits to five years in service, almost all of them were on their first combat tour.

Each member of the team underwent a tough training regimen to get to this point, but the selection process wasn't finished until they'd completed a combat tour under the guidance of fully qualified NorthStar rangers. To Harris's thinking, that was about the most useful thing he or anyone else in the NorthStar fleet would get out of Scheherazade. Peacekeeping ops made for decent live-fire on-the-job training and not much else.

"These fuckers killed Cunningham," grumbled one of the riflemen. Finch was a big guy, which had its advantages. The recon armor didn't offer the level of powered assistance found in other models, but it still gave the wearer's strength a significant boost. That on top of Finch's native strength made him a natural choice for door kicker if the job called for it. "You saying they aren't up for some payback?"

"I'm saying that payback will come one way or the other. Don't get *yourself* killed making it happen," Harris replied. His tone made plain his lack of patience for any further argument. "Cunningham went out like a soldier. He called out that ambush to keep the rest of you alive. That was the right thing to do. But he chose to be out here, just like you. He thought combat would be a thrill, and he wasn't wrong. He wanted the right to say he was one of the best and he wanted the paycheck to go with it. You all feel the same way, or you wouldn't be here.

"But people die in combat, on both sides. Don't get bent out of shape when someone else who feels the same damn way you do buys the farm. Not if you want to do this for a living. He wasn't a victim, he was a volunteer. This war ain't a cause for you. It's a job."

Several of the men and women around him nodded. Others would not let go of their scowls. Harris wanted to make sure his point got across. "You wanna be rangers? You wanna impress me? Then do this job like getting it done and living through it is more important than what the evaluator thinks. You had to be a cut above the rest to make it this far. You're motivated and you're skilled. Time now to show me you can keep your heads. Cunningham won't be the last buddy you bury in this job. It's time you learned to manage that. Stay cool. Get it done."

Harris gave the hand signal to mount up. The team donned their helmets and walked past him to take their seats on the assault shuttle. Harris walked on last, looking over each trooper to make sure they would be ready to go when their seats fell out from under them. They needed each weapon loaded and ready, their armor amped up and secure comms assured. Most of all, they needed cool heads. Rage and indiscriminate destruction were for amateurs.

Satisfied with the team's readiness, Harris gave the team leader and the shuttle's crew chief his nod of approval before moving into the cockpit. The port-side operations chair remained open for him behind the pilot and copilot seats. The starboard station already held his co-trainer.

"You give them the speech?" asked Soldan.

"Yeah."

"Think any of them got it?"

"A couple, which is about all I can hope for. Some of them will figure shit out before too long and they might remember what I said. You can't win 'em all."

"I'm surprised you haven't been told not to say things like that," Soldan commented as the shuttle lifted off into the night. Powerful antigrav engines all but negated the vehicle's weight, allowing for quiet propulsion through the night sky. The atmosphere within the cockpit encouraged Soldan to keep his voice low, as if someone a thousand feet below might hear him. "Isn't 'real talk' like that bad for morale? For the esprit de corps of the rangers?"

"I *have* been told not to say things like that." Harris shrugged, his eyes on the map of the city and their target zone on his screens. "And if I thought I had a chance of getting promoted again, I might give a fuck what some jackass from Human Resources or Risk Management thinks of my attitude."

"You think you won't be promoted again?"

"Nope. Because I've got a piss-poor attitude and I encourage the same in subordinates." He keyed a control on the comms panel. "Security team, we are one hundred seconds out."

"Assault team," a voice replied, "still all quiet here. Exits are covered at street level and below. Flush 'em out and we'll take 'em."

"Understood." Harris keyed the mic off. "I mean, I put operations on hold at the last second to give a pep talk on how they should separate their personal feelings from their work. It's not exactly something the HR people like to hear. Those assholes think you should be emotionally invested in all of this because you should love the company so damn much."

"And then you bitch about it on the way to the drop," Soldan concurred. "Classy."

"Hey," spoke up one of the assault team members sitting just beside the cockpit partition, "you know some of us can hear you, right?"

"Well, yeah." Harris snorted, leaning back to look at the team. "Like I said, it's a job. People talk at the office. Show me you can handle it. Twenty seconds to drop. Remember, there's no bonuses for shooting noncombatants. Three strikes and you're out."

He turned back to his tactical display, activated a series of screens to show him the feed from each team member's helmet and rifle cameras, and waited for the pilot's cue. "Dropping in five . . . four . . . three . . ."

Arriving over the rooftop of a seven-story apartment building, the assault shuttle came to a sudden stop in midair and instantly switched from antigrav to the vertical thrusters built into its wings. Natural gravity reasserted itself, and the pilot activated the drop switch that pulled the assault team's seats out from under them. Each of the ten armored men and women fell through the shuttle's floor and onto the roof. This, along with the thrusters, made for more than a little noise, but the insertion was complete. The shuttle flew off, leaving its passengers to blast and tear through the roof with a combination of weapons and their armored hands.

Harris watched and listened for callouts over the comm net while Soldan reported the insertion to the guys at street level. The assault team broke into smaller groups, everyone sticking close to their partner like they'd practiced. With the optics offered by their helmets, they didn't need to flash around much light to move through the building, and given the strength enhancement offered by their armor, most of the doors wouldn't be a problem, either.

The apartments at the top corners were priorities, as they likely contained lookouts. Harris watched Finch kick a door right off its hinges, flanked on either side by team members whose gaze and aim swept the entry room. Finch kept low as he entered, his teammates following his lead, and at first it seemed as if there would be no trouble.

Blue bursts of light changed that. Someone opened up on the team with a pulse rifle, which only resulted in four guns coming back on the shooter in quick succession. The apartment furniture offered poor cover; it broke lines of sight, but it didn't block high-powered slugs. Harris saw the gunman fly back in an explosion of blood.

The team split into pairs and checked each bedroom. They found a screaming, terrified boy, whom one of the other troopers— Clark, Harris noted—hit with an electrical stunner to shut him up. Someone else thought to grab the pulse rifle and break it. The chem sniffers in their armor led them right to the antivehicle rocket launcher lying against one corner and the pair of rockets with it. One team member collected the weapons. Another covered the door, while a third quickly put restraints on the kid. They would be ready to move on in seconds.

The other teams encountered much the same. Unable to watch three firefights at once, Harris relied on the computer-assisted analysis to evaluate their performance. Another team recovered an additional rocket launcher. Bishop blew away some woman who had no firearm in hand, which would be a strike against him; two more and he'd receive failing marks for this evaluation.

"Jesus, look at the weapons these people are using," scoffed Soldan as the team moved on through the floor and down to the next. More flashes of lasers and pulse weapons split the darkness, most of them poorly aimed but a few striking home. Wilbourne caught a blast against his shoulder, but his armor deflected most of it. He went down and called out for a medic. He surely had nasty burns and perhaps a serious injury, but Harris guessed he'd live. Evans wasn't so lucky; the laser that lanced through his helmet put him down instantly. Soldan didn't get upset by the casualties. "That building is all wood and plaster on the inside, plus all the furniture. What do they want to do, set the place on fire?"

"These aren't exactly professionals, Soldan," Harris pointed out. "Smart enough to bar the doors, though. You see the one that Finch kicked down?"

"You'd think if they knew they were gonna get hit, they'd have cleared out the families." Soldan's disdain was evident. "Shit, then they could've trapped up the place without worrying about anyone's kid setting off a bomb while chasing his ball or whatever. Patrick just wasted a grandmother, by the way."

"Shit." Harris keyed the mic. "Assault team, this is Harris! Check your fire, dammit!"

A buzz on Harris's wrist indicated a priority message. Harris checked the sender info and then disregarded the rest. Traffic from HQ could wait until the shooting stopped. If they needed him to rush his team to another zone, they'd have gone through the pilot with a voice message. Harris turned back to the action.

Most of the team did fine. Within another minute or two, Harris ascertained that the insurgents within the building outnumbered his team, though those numbers rapidly dwindled. The room-to-room fighting briefly intensified, and there Harris saw signs of growth. Narendra charged right into a guy firing a light pulse pistol, trusting her armor to deflect the blasts as she clobbered him with a solid elbow to the chest. She left him practically embedded in the drywall, not only neutralizing him but saving her from having to hose down the room and hit the unarmed people inside. Finch learned to shoot through the furniture in another apartment, ending a firefight just as it began. Back upstairs, Wilbourne managed to self-medicate and reported himself stable without any prompting from anyone else.

"Woah, get a load of number nine," said Soldan. That drew Harris's eyes to another screen, where he saw the group's other designated door kicker hoist a combatant up over his head and pitch the guy down the center of the stairwell. The falling man's head hit one banister on the way down, bounced off, and fell against the next one. The view then shifted as trooper nine turned back toward the hallway.

"What the hell was that?" Harris demanded irritably over the comm net. "You showin' off for someone?"

"You said to check fire, sir," came the response. "The guy had a gun, but you gave an order."

"Which one is that?" Soldan asked.

Harris flicked off the mic. "You know exactly who that is." He sighed. "Two strikes, every time. I'm half-tempted to wash the kid out on general principle, but he gets shit done. Might be better off as a shock trooper, but I think he knows he wouldn't see as much action that way. Or make as much money." He checked the tactical boards again. The team had only two more floors to go. Nobody on the street-level security team reported anyone fleeing the building. Harris flicked the mic back on. "Eickenberry, we're gonna have another talk later."

"Yes, sir," the tall young man acknowledged.

"Well, he's got the chops," said Soldan. "Can't argue that. What's his story, anyway?"

"Ah, he washed out of basic in his home system militia a year or two ago," Harris said. "Dunno why. I don't really care. Probably looking to salvage his pride in the rangers, but he obviously likes combat. And he's in debt up to his eyeballs like the rest, so he needs a job like this to take care of him. This is who we pick up these days."

"How were we any different?"

No answer came to mind right away. Harris scowled, watching the team move through the last few rooms. He heard his people call out, "Clear," one by one. The security team stationed at street level sent in a couple of squads to help with mop-up.

Harris turned his attention to the message from HQ. "Cease any further operations immediately and return to base for redeployment," read his instructions. "Route any questions from local forces or client authorities to HQ. Engage in combat only to protect company assets on an emergency basis. Instructions for handing off operations will follow. Personnel and gear will be collected and ready for transport to NSS *Hercules* within twenty-four hours."

The message surprised him. The battleship *Hercules* was the flagship of NorthStar's fleet. A rapid pullout like that could only mean that some higher-priority mess awaited. Harris glanced up at the message routing instructions before continuing further. The note had gone out to a majority of combat units in his area of operations. It looked like a full-scale pullout.

Below the first paragraph, Harris found further instructions specific to his unit—which, given the familiar text, had gone through an automated filter. "Advise personnel of optional transfer: Eickenberry, Kevin P.; Wilbourne, Theodore J."

Harris pulled up their personnel files. Instructions like that held to a company standard: no security fleet personnel were ever ordered to go into a combat action targeting their homes of origin. Rangers were something of an exception. As an elite unit, Rangers were held to a higher standard of loyalty. They could participate in such operations on a voluntary basis.

"Archangel," Harris murmured, sinking back into his chair. The implications fell into place right away. Harris hadn't caught any news recently, but he knew there was supposed to be some sort of negotiation back on Earth with NorthStar and the other big companies. If things had been smoothed over and the security fleet was going back on the job in Archangel, there would be no need to screen out anyone. The more native sons and daughters sent in to patch things up, the better. These orders implied that the negotiations had not gone well at all—and that the situation was worse for the company than anyone knew.

That was all far above Harris's head. He had only his people to worry about. Wilbourne was hurt and might well end up transferred. Harris wouldn't know until the docs saw to him, but the prospect left some concern as to the team's numbers. Harris needed to have a chat with Eickenberry sooner rather than later.

. . .

"Ease up, folks. The passageways out of here can't handle more than three abreast," Tanner called out over the crowd. Marines and navy crewmen shuffled past or stood waiting for a chance to head out, their conversations creating enough volume that no one could hear announcements over the PA system. Though none of the men and women shoved or pushed, the mood leaned toward a grim sense of urgency.

People had watch stations and department quarters to get to. Officers and NCOs had to work up any number of special-task groups, requests for gear, and refresher training sessions. Most of all, for Beowulf to succeed, many of the men and women present would have to work with new teams and unfamiliar stresses. Tanner hadn't actually opened up the message on his holocom outlining his specific place in the Table of Operations & Equipment; he was still trying to digest the bigger picture.

Given the grim faces he saw before him, he figured he wasn't the only one.

"Hey!" belted his partner beside him. "Hold it up! Yeah, you guys! Just stop a second!" Baldwin held up one hand to halt the surge of people to the right of their perch and then waved with the second. "It's okay to bark at 'em when you need to, Tanner," she said off to her side once she saw the crowd follow her traffic directions. "Don't worry about stepping on some chief's toes when you're on the job. It's all part of being an MA, y'know?"

"Right. Sorry." He watched Baldwin work, surmising that the hangar bay would empty out within only a couple of minutes. "You have experience with this?"

"I worked in an amusement park before I enlisted. Try sending mobs of tourists home when they don't wanna leave. That's a real challenge." She watched the crowd, making sure it did as she wanted. "You think it'll actually happen?"

"Think what will happen?"

Baldwin gestured toward the platform where the admiral and her staff had stood minutes before. "That whole scenario. The Big Three coming to get us."

"I dunno," Tanner said. "We've hurt them pretty bad. The things that Aguirre revealed can't have been good for their business in the rest of the Union."

"Yeah, I know, but . . . they were screwing us. They're screwing everybody. You think they'll actually invade because we caught 'em and told on 'em? I mean, they'd really go to war?"

Tanner snorted. "Ask the East India Company."

"The who?"

"Nineteenth century. Britain sold opium in China even though it was illegal to sell in Britain. When the Chinese decided to outlaw the trade, Britain went to war over it. You could nitpick the details and who said what to whom, and if you asked the British, they'd have said it was about free trade. But in the end, Britain went to war over the chance to sell an addictive drug that they didn't want on their own turf. And they won. They got their 'free trade' and then some."

Baldwin didn't respond. Tanner looked over his shoulder at her. "How do you know all that?" she asked finally.

"I read a lot."

"Apparently."

"You want other examples? Britain's not the only country to pull something like that."

"No, I'm good. I'll take your word for it."

Tanner just smiled. "At this point, I'm never surprised how far people will go for the chance to make a whole lot of money off someone else's misery. There's usually a lofty excuse to justify it, too. Think the crowd's dying down."

"Think you're right. Don't go anywhere on me, though," she added.

"I'm good. No place else to be right now, anyway."

"You sure?" Baldwin asked. "Did you look at the lists? Who'd they put you with?"

He opened his mouth to dismiss her question but saw a familiar face in the crowd as it grew thinner and less needful of management. "Alicia!" he called, waving and then jumping down from their crate.

"Way to stick with your partner," Baldwin grumbled.

Tanner slipped through a couple of bodies to meet Alicia and found her coming toward him but with greater purpose. He noticed a couple of familiar faces beyond the young marine, but he hadn't so much as waved hello to Ravenell or thought of something suitably polite to say to Alicia's boyfriend before Alicia hooked her arm around Tanner's and tugged him backward. "Okay, we need to talk now," she declared.

"What?" Tanner blinked. He saw both Ravenell and Collins look on with surprise as Alicia dragged Tanner over toward the bulkhead rather than the exit. Without the least bit of ceremony or commentary, Alicia brought Tanner to the nearest damage-control locker, threw open its hatch, pushed Tanner inside, and followed him in before pulling the hatch shut behind them.

Though they followed curiously, Ravenell and Collins both came to a halt outside the hatch. Collins raised one finger to point at the locker, opened his mouth, and then closed it. He scratched the reddish stubble on his head. "Um," he opined.

"Hey, Brent," piped up another marine nearby, "isn't that your girl—"

"Shut up," Collins warned, holding up one hand but not looking away from the hatch.

"Yeah, this isn't awkward," muttered Ravenell.

"Is it?" Collins asked.

Then it was Ravenell's turn to scratch his head while trying to form words. "Uh, well . . ."

"Hey! Jarheads!" Baldwin called from atop her crate. "What the hell was that?"

"Lights?" Tanner asked. His head turned this way and that, but the locker full of damage-control gear was pitch black. He already felt a shelf full of tools and emergency kits against his back, and soon his right shoulder. Then Alicia hit the light on her holocom, which flashed right into Tanner's eyes. "Aw, dammit, now I'm blind!"

"Oh, shut up," said Alicia. "You're fine."

"Still," Tanner winced. "What's going on?"

"I don't want everyone listening in on every little conversation, and there's hardly anywhere on this stupid ship that isn't crawling with people anymore. Plus I've had Brent on me to talk to you, so, thanks for that." She frowned. "I figured I'd just take care of it now. Figured I'd *better* take care of it now."

"Okay?" Tanner ventured. "Why are you mad at me?"

"Who said I'm mad at you? Did Brent?"

"Like I need someone I don't know to tell me? Jesus, you brush me off like you're annoyed to see me when I get here, you don't respond to a single message on the comm, you avoid me at the reunion, and the couple times I've seen you in the passageways you barely even nod or wave."

"Did you come here to win me back?"

"I—*what*? You made it pretty clear all along that there wasn't a 'winning' to be had," Tanner said. He tried to throw his arms out in a gesture but only banged his gloved hands against the racks. "Ow."

"Yeah, right from the start."

"Well, more like *after* the start, but whatever," Tanner corrected with a mutter.

Alicia kept talking. "And I've told you about Brent all along, too. I'm happy with Brent. Happy as you can be dating someone on a ship, anyway, which isn't much, but—"

"I'm not trying to break you up!" Tanner snapped in exasperation. "I missed you! I missed you and Rav and—for Christ's sake, they sent half our recruit company to this ship. I didn't know how many might still be here, but I figured it was a safe bet that I'd at least be able to find a friendly face or two! You don't know what it's like to serve on a ship and have no one to talk to!"

The retort took her aback. He lowered his voice as soon as he saw her blink. "I'm fucking *lonely*, okay? It wasn't so bad once I got off *St. Jude*, but I had to take another underway billet after MA school and I figured this was my best bet. I didn't want to wind up stuck trying to pretend I'm more interested in reading than having a conversation with people at every meal, three times a day, all over again. I'm not trying to get you into bed again. I missed my friends. I've missed *having* friends."

She didn't know how to respond at first. "You're a good guy, Tanner." Alicia shook her head. "You make friends all the time. I know you had it rough on *St. Jude*, but those guys were assholes. It hasn't been like that since, right?"

"No, it hasn't," he agreed, "but I didn't want to take any risks when I was looking at the list of open billets. I figured I had a decent shot of getting what I asked for, so I asked for this. I thought you'd be happy to see me. I mean, I know it's not like we're going to see all that much of each other, and maybe you and Rav and the others from Oscar will rotate out before too long, but still. Better than coming in cold."

Alicia frowned. "Okay, whatever. You wanna know why I'm mad at you? If you knew they'd send you wherever you asked, why didn't you ask for shore duty?" She gestured up and down at him with one hand, as if to indicate his sidearm and the beret on his head. "Why'd you go master-at-arms? What the hell were you thinking?"

"You don't think I can handle it?"

"*You* don't think you can handle it," she asserted. "You get torn up about combat. You've said so yourself, more than once. God, you could've had any number of jobs, why'd you take the one rating that might even have you fighting with some of our own guys?"

"Hey, that thing with DeLeon was stupid. I don't think that's a regular occurrence."

"No, but you picked the one job where it's most likely to happen. Not to mention boarding teams and ship's security postings and this crazy shit they want us to do now," she added, jerking her thumb at the hatch.

"Yeah, well, given everyone they brought onto this ship, I have a feeling I'd be here anyway," Tanner thought aloud.

"That's not the point. You don't have to prove anything to anyone, Tanner. You of all people. And you know it. You're too smart *not* to know it, and you don't go for the gung ho bullshit. So why in the hell are you here?"

"You're mad at me because I went MA?"

"That, too. I'm complicated."

"Apparently."

"Well?"

The answer didn't come right away. He wasn't sure all of his reasons would sit well with Alicia, nor did he think he could do them justice in two minutes inside a closet with people likely waiting on the other side of the door. But even a partial answer was still truthful: "I don't want to leave other people to deal with the mess when things go wrong. I don't enjoy combat, no. I doubt very many people do. I don't think *you* enjoy combat, either."

"I—" Alicia began, but promptly stopped herself. The two stared at one another. "That's the *other* reason I'm pissed off," she admitted, almost speaking through her teeth. "Don't say anything," she warned, holding one hand up. "I'm just . . . I walk off a shuttle, and there you are, and I can see the wheels turning inside your head, and yeah, that was a little frustrating."

Tanner nodded slowly. "Are you okay?"

"I'm fine. I've dealt with it, probably better than you have, and that's what bothers me. I don't want to see you tear yourself up again, Tanner. Do you get that?"

"I get it," he answered. "I'm okay. I wear it on my sleeve. It's how I cope. When things go crazy, I'll be fine."

Alicia sighed. "You'd better be, because you're on my team for this one."

"I am? I didn't look yet."

"Yeah, I looked at my orders already, and I figured we'd better straighten ourselves out before we're in the middle of combat wondering what we should've said."

"You normally think about your personal drama when people are shooting at you?" he laughed. "I'm usually stuck on, 'Oh God, please don't let me die.'" Alicia slugged his arm but grinned. "Are we okay?" he asked.

Alicia brought her arms up and hugged him tightly. "I missed you, too," she sniffed.

Tanner held her close. Eventually, he had a thought, and opened his mouth.

She cut him off before he spoke. "If you ruin this by hitting on me as some sort of joke, I'll break your collarbones again."

He kept it to himself and just appreciated the hug.

Coming out of the locker, the pair found Baldwin and Collins waiting for them. With no one of rank watching closely, Alicia slipped her hand in Brent's and walked away with him. Tanner took in a long breath and let it out, feeling better despite the impending crisis.

"So," Baldwin began slowly, "you're gonna tell me all the dirt, right?"

Tanner made a face. "Don't we have an invasion to worry about?"

"Yeah, in a couple *weeks*. What's going on now? C'mon, this ship is boring without any drama!"

TEN

Fight Like a Pirate

"We will not bow, and we will not break. We will not take back what we have said, for we have both the evidence to back it up and the fortitude to withstand the inevitable backlash. My friends, it does not matter if they come at us with trade sanctions and boycotts. It does not matter if they tarnish our good name in the Assembly or in the media services they own. They can try all the shady, bloody covert actions they want, for we will know them for what they are. We know the truth, and the truth has set us free."

—President Gabriel Aguirre, Uriel Town Hall Speech,
November 2276

"Nice of him to come up and deliver the news in person, I guess." Casey watched the shuttle exit *Argent*'s bay on one of the monitor screens at the captain's chair.

Hawkins stood by, looking over his shoulder. "Is that resentment for the rear echelons I hear?"

"Well, the fucker never served a day in the field, I'll bet. Oh, sure, he's probably been *near* a crisis or three. Maybe he carried a gun a few times because regulations said it was appropriate. But he's smart. Too smart to be that damn arrogant if he'd ever been staring down the barrel or at least gotten a solid ass-kicking once or twice in his life.

"But no, I'm not callin' Kiribati a wuss for being a career bureaucrat or a politician. That just makes him a different kind of predator. He's risked as much here as anyone else," Casey said. "When it all falls apart, he'll either eat a bullet before the goon squads get their hands on him, or he'll wish he had. Oh, the corporate types won't torture him. They're not amateurs. He knows that. But he also knows it'll still be hell and they'll get everything they want out of him in the end, anyway, so I'm betting on the bullet." He glanced up at Hawkins and saw a disapproving glare. "What?"

"Torture is something we don't do, either."

The captain rolled his eyes. "Oh, fuck your morals. It's a matter of efficacy," muttered Casey. "They'll play as dirty as I ever did. Only difference is, I never had a trained interrogator in my crew, or at least nobody ever stepped forward."

"Shuttle bay secure," called out the helmsman. "Visiting shuttle is outbound for Raphael."

"Thank you, Schlensker. Bring us two-zero-zero by zero-fifteen and start cruising. We need some clear space for privacy, 'cause we're gonna be running drills. Renaldo," he said, turning to the woman at the comms station, "I need you to call the department heads into the wardroom for a briefing in ten minutes. Have all four of our duty shuttle pilots there for it, too."

"Aye, aye, captain," came simultaneous replies.

"Here's where it starts feeling like work again," Casey grumbled.

• • •

"We're on picket duty for the foreseeable future, and that future is a matter of days, maybe a week or two," the captain explained to the officers at his table. "Whatever back-and-forth diplomacy Aguirre's people run should be able to give us a better read on the situation, but until that catches up with the time lag between here and Earth and Fairhaven and New Shanghai, we've gotta expect the sky to fall on us. It's drills and training until then."

"So, business as usual?" asked Chief Engineer Okeke. His dark face held a stony but calm expression. Given his decades of experience, he had a talent for setting a good example for the younger officers and crew. It was a contribution Casey appreciated.

"Yeah, but now we've got a role and some idea of what to expect, so I think we can narrow down the specific drills we run. Still, we took on some new people with that last shuttle run, so we'll need to get them all up to speed. Nobody gets to pull the 'new guy' excuse once the real thing happens."

Casey called up a holo projection of Raphael and its moon. He then added a net of icons in a sphere outside the lunar paths. "In about a week, the navy will deploy the drone net. It's too expensive to run indefinitely, but they can't wait until the last minute, either, 'cause nobody knows what that last minute is. The enemy knows we've got a drone net, naturally, so they'll have to drop out of light speed farther out to avoid the risk of a catastrophic shift out of FTL. The drones have guns and shields, but they won't mean a damn thing against a serious attack force," he explained for those officers without military experience, "so they'll crash right through it. Ships like ours will be on the outside of the net—we'll be right here—pretending we're doing a shakedown cruise or whatever.

"If they come through near our position—and that's a huge if, when you consider the volume of space we're talking about here—they'll order us to hightail it out of the combat zone. I suppose it's possible that they'll let one ship break off from their force to board and commandeer us, because a liner like this would be a nice little prize, but that'll only happen if they show up with ships to spare on chores like that. They might not want to divide up right away.

"Regardless, it's our job to *make* them split up. The goal is to throw off their game plan from the start. We play innocent civilians long enough to let them think they've got their bearings, and then we hit 'em."

Silence followed. The assembled officers waited for Casey to continue, but after a beat, they realized he wouldn't. "I'm sorry, captain," spoke up Dr. Stanwood. "We 'hit 'em?' You mean as a hit-and-run, or . . . ?" He held out his hands questioningly.

"Depends on how they react." Casey shrugged. "If we see ships break off to deal with us, it comes down to how big and how many. That's a judgment call. If they don't take us seriously enough to send a significant force after us, we dive in until we bite off a bigger detachment. We need to push them into a real fight. We don't just throw a couple punches for a token effort and then bail out."

"So it's a suicide mission?"

"I don't do suicide, doc," Casey said levelly. "Look around on your way back to sick bay. This crew is made up of *survivors*, not quitters. Nobody would be on the *Argent* if they wanted to take the easy way out. We're gonna fight our way through this. Any other questions? Don't be shy. All right, then. Dismissed."

Hawkins lingered until the room emptied out. "Nice pep talk," he commented.

"I know how to motivate a crew, Hawkins. I could do it better without you running interference."

"You command the ship, I manage the crew," Hawkins replied in a calm tone. "That's the XO's job on any vessel I've ever been on. They'll perform. I'll make sure of that."

"You guys in the Intelligence Ministry screened this crew to make sure you didn't have any mutineer types on board," came Casey's dry response. "And it ain't like I'm going anywhere. I don't know what you're worried about."

Hawkins offered a tight, insincere smile. "Just doing my part to share the load, captain," he said as he stood and headed out.

Casey sat back in his chair and let out a long breath. "God, I miss Lauren," he grumbled.

. . .

"Dominguez, I'm putting you on Damage Control Team One. That team is closest to the bridge. Baumgartner's on there with you as a medic. She's one of ours. Grosser, you're in with security. The department lead knows you're coming. Szweda, you'll be in engineering . . . far as I can tell, things are solid down there, but keep your eyes peeled." Sitting at his desk, Hawkins killed the holo screens before him. He checked a small indicator on his desk to ensure that none of the three new crewmen before him had any of their own devices broadcasting.

"You all came up together?" he asked. The three newcomers, two men and one woman, all nodded. "Then you're all in the know? Repeat the protocol for me, please."

Grosser and Szweda glanced at one another. Dominguez spoke without further prompting. "Keep an eye out for mutiny or misconduct. Bring any concerns directly to you. If the captain tries to leave the ship without code-word authorization from you or the minister, we stop him. At all other times, follow orders per normal."

"What do you do if he gives the order to abandon ship?"

"Put two shots in the back of his head," Grosser answered, her voice calm but assertive. "Same as we do in the event of capture. Preferably, we make sure there's nothing left to identify, but top priority is to make sure he isn't breathing."

Hawkins nodded. "Correct." He frowned darkly. "He knows what he's doing in command of the ship, but we're coming up on the real moment of truth here, and I don't know what's gonna happen. In the end, we still have to follow the protocol. We're on this ship to make sure the captain doesn't escape. We make sure he doesn't fall into the wrong hands. Aside from that . . ." Hawkins trailed off, shaking his head in pensive thought, then continued, "we have to let him be the captain. Any questions?"

"How is the rest of the crew?" asked Dominguez.

"Solid enough. I had my doubts, and I'd rather be going into battle with a uniformed navy crew, but the Scheherazade op gave us a good trial by fire. We shook loose some dead weight after that, and the rest have had a chance to master their jobs since then."

"And their loyalty?" Grosser ventured.

"They'll hang together in a crisis. They'll follow the captain's lead. He's gotten them through tough spots before, so they should trust him to do it again."

Grosser's eyes narrowed. Hawkins did not answer her real question. "And if we have to put him down?"

"I don't know," Hawkins admitted. "Doesn't matter regardless. We follow the protocol, come what may. But I hope to God we never have to find out."

• • •

"Government authorities in seven systems, as well as numerous governments on Earth, have promised a full investigation into Archangel's accusations. Numerous other system governments have already decried these claims as a desperate stunt, while grumbling both on the street and in the financial houses of the Union continues to grow. Many observers say that the fallout is simply a matter of where a given system's loyalties lie and how much they can afford to bite the hands that feed them. In the end, the question is: What can the Big Three do to regain the Union's trust?"

—Gibril Coleman, *Solar Herald*, December 2276

The general quarters alarm woke Casey from his dreams. Its jarring urgency erased any emotion those dreams might have left behind, pushing him upright on his bed. He slapped the personal comms panel on his headboard, then reached for the vac suit he'd left on the chair beside the bed. "Bridge, captain. Report."

"Multiple contacts dropping out of FTL outside the picket line, sir," came the answer. Casey threw on his suit with a rapid efficiency borne of long experience as the voice continued. "Roughly one hundred seventy thousand klicks out from our position, bearing zero-seven-one mark zero-three-zero relative to us, sir. We're only twenty-two thousand klicks from the line." The speaker paused long enough for Casey to grab his helmet and get to his feet. "NorthStar Security Forces identifiers."

"How many ships?"

"Still acquiring new contacts . . . I think they brought all of them, sir."

Casey let out a pensive breath. "Well, fuck," he muttered. He looked down at himself to make sure he was good and sealed in, then headed for the bridge. His stateroom was only twenty meters from there. He saw other officers and designated bridge crew headed the same way. Routine drills paid off in response time, at least.

"Captain on the bridge," someone called out as he arrived, but no one popped to attention or looked up from their stations. The duty bridge crew kept at their work. The captain's chair was empty only because the ops boss, serving as the current officer of the deck, was over by the astrogation table. Casey moved straight for him.

"Signal incoming," announced Renaldo at comms. "They want to speak to the captain."

"Tell 'em the captain is on his way," Casey answered over the voice of his ops officer. Quentin looked up from the astrogation table with an obvious question. "We're a space liner," Casey explained as he took in the tactical info on the sensor bubble. "Nothing strange about a slow response. Jesus Christ, they really are right on top of us."

. . .

"*Telesto* and *Pallene* confirmed . . . *Cascia* confirmed . . . *Werrengo* arrived and . . . confirmed safe arrival, sir. Battle Group Hercules on scene and in proper order," the ops specialist finished. He turned from his station to look across the flag bridge at the commodore. "Command bridge reports they'll be ready to launch in one minute."

Commodore Eldridge didn't look up from his screens. Standing on *Hercules*'s flag bridge, he could see the battleship's condition and that of her escorts for himself. Announcements were a matter of routine. He pressed a button on the table to speak with the battleship's captain on the command bridge. "My compliments on the smooth ride, Captain Wagner."

He didn't listen for a response. Captain Wagner ran *Hercules* from the battleship's command bridge. Eldridge had command of the fleet as a whole: three battle groups, each centered on a battleship, along with three expeditionary groups and several destroyer squadrons, all with *Hercules* as the flagship. An image of *Hercules* floated above the center of the table. A faint sphere of yellow light extended farther and farther outward as the ship's sensors established the customary two light-minute sensor bubble.

Verbal reports continued across the flag bridge. "Battle Group Andromeda reporting in with all ships accounted for," announced another specialist. "No damage or disruptions. Moving into formation."

"Battle Group Ursa still assembling . . . *Irrawady* and *Daphnis* arriving."

Status reports for the expeditionary groups centered on the assault carriers offered similar positive results. With arrival going according to plan, Eldridge focused his attention on the ships and other contacts already in the area when his fleet dropped out of FTL. The sensor bubble around *Hercules* was still growing but would reach its full extent of two light-minutes soon enough.

He could already see multiple picket drones spread out in a circular net around Raphael and her moon. A cruise liner lay a few thousand klicks outside that net. For the moment, *Hercules* couldn't see any other contacts, but that could change in a heartbeat. Unless Archangel genuinely didn't expect a military incursion, the bulk of their navy would be within two light-minutes of Raphael. The presence of that drone net indicated the navy most certainly did expect unwelcome guests.

"Mr. Shabolov," Eldridge called out to one of his aides, "contact that liner and have them pull aside. We'll send over a boarding team to direct them out."

• • •

The three-dimensional display and its flat screen supplements explained everyone's apprehension. *Argent* lay close to the perimeter line created by the drone net, put in place to generate artificial gravity waves that would make FTL travel excessively dangerous. The absolute minimum safety line for FTL travel to a given planet typically matched the orbital path of its farthest moon, which for Raphael was not quite four hundred thousand kilometers. The drone net couldn't offer viable coverage further out than another two hundred fifty K, but that still provided a significant extension of Raphael's perimeter.

The arriving force couldn't have known the position of the drone net in advance of their arrival—not when NorthStar clearly set planning and fleet assembly in motion as soon as they knew of Aguirre's intentions—but they surely knew the basic layout of the Archangel star system. Someone in their planning section had doubled the distance between Raphael and its moon, Azarias, as an educated guess.

Apparently, the Big Three had made some advances in FTL safety that they hadn't shared with the rest of the Union yet. FTL transit within a system was always dangerous, even at this distance from any large source of gravity . . . but Casey saw dozens of contacts, some of them huge, and yet he saw not one sign of distress among any of them.

Within seconds, Casey had a straightforward grip on the situation: Raphael lay six hundred thousand kilometers to his rear. That was only two light-seconds. The capital was fully aware of this development by now. The navy was clear on the other side of the perimeter. One hundred fifty thousand klicks ahead, beyond a net of drones much too far apart to be seen with the naked eye, NorthStar's fleet of ships got themselves in order.

"So many," breathed a familiar voice beside him. Casey glanced up to see Hawkins looking wide-eyed at the projections.

"Yup." Casey nodded. "Three battleship strike groups, expeditionary groups behind them with some other loose change, and . . . heh. Look at that. One of those destroyer squadrons is all CDC ships. That one expeditionary group is Lai Wa vessels, too. Must have decided everyone had to put some skin in the game."

Contacts representing each of the ships drifted into closer formations. Each of the battleships was escorted by a companion cruiser, a pair of destroyers, and several frigates. New contacts appeared as all three of the battleships released a corvette from their launch bays. The assault carriers arrived in pairs with about as many escorts as the battleships, each of them a mammoth vessel holding thousands of troops, atmospheric flyers, and landing craft for an occupation.

"Helm," Casey called out, "get us drifting backward toward Raphael like we're nervous. Quarter speed, nothing more."

"Like we're nervous?" Hawkins repeated. He gestured toward the dreadful picture on the astrogation display. "What the hell are we supposed to do against that?"

"Nobody said we had to take 'em *all* on." Casey winked and slapped Hawkins on the shoulder. Their grim circumstances made it all the more amusing to fuck with his first officer. "C'mon. They want to talk to the captain. Unless you want me to take the call, that's gonna have to be you."

Hawkins swallowed hard. "The plan isn't going to work," he hissed. "Nobody expected a fleet of that size!"

"Could'a told them it wouldn't work if they'd ever asked my opinion," Casey agreed.

"We can't fight against that!"

Casey stopped and turned halfway around to look at his first officer. "Y'know what? How about you stay over there until you get your act together. I've got this. OOD, I have the conn," he said, officially taking over command of the bridge from the watch officer. "Comms, give me audio only and make sure the voice mask is running. Who am I talking to?"

"NSS *Hercules*, sir," Renaldo answered. "She's one of the battleships."

"Of course she is." Casey rolled his eyes. "*Hercules*. Fucking egomaniacs."

"Voice mask confirmed. Audio open on your station. Captain on comms," Renaldo added with a raised voice to tamp down on the ambient chatter on the bridge.

Casey took a deep breath and then hit a button on the side of the captain's chair. "NSS *Hercules*, this is, uh, ASG *Argent*," Casey said, sounding noticeably shakier than he actually felt. He called up several of his own holo projections to match those at the astrogation table, then set to eliminating the less relevant info on the displays as he spoke. "We're on shakedown cruise. Just Independent Shipping Guild standards."

"*Argent, Hercules.* Please open visual communications," came the response.

"Uh, negative, we—we can't do that just, um, just y-yet," Casey stammered. "We're working on it. Sorry. You kind of made us nervous showing up like this. Operator error, we're rebooting the system, sorry. Give us a second."

Nerves aside, Renaldo at the comms station threw a skeptical look at the captain. Casey released the transmit button. "Who cares if they believe it or not? We need to look a little sketchy here." He glanced at the tactical display. The closest of the enemy ships remained 135 K out, which was 15 K beyond the most extreme beam weapon range for anything he'd ever heard of on a starship. *Argent* drifted farther away, only a thousand kilometers every few seconds, but the distance would help.

Casey checked the other status boards. Air in the promenade, observatories, and other compartments of no use in combat would be drawn back into emergency compression tanks within the next thirty seconds. Every battle station reported its readiness.

"Helm," he said, "ease off now. Turn us one-eighty by zero, slowly. See that line from Raphael to the bad guys there? Go perpendicular from it. Let 'em think we're backing out of the line of fire."

"*Argent, Hercules,*" the voice on the comms speaker broke in. "Stand by. Maintain your current position."

Casey frowned. "Well, shit. Better do as he says. Helm, cut thrusters. I don't mind if we drift a bit."

"What's happening?" asked Hawkins.

"Well, Raphael's within a couple light-seconds of the fleet, so Salvation might be talking with them right now," Casey considered, "but I'm betting the fleet's making sure they're all in good order before they push on with their plans."

Eldridge turned his eyes to the status boards again. He still had no other sensor contacts on the far side of the drone picket line. Behind and around him were nothing but allied ships. He keyed a hard-point button on the command table. "Group Hercules, establish firing solutions on the drone net. Squadron Two, stand by for dispatch to secondary targets." He released the key and looked over to a senior aide. "Commander Gordon," he said, "send the message to Raphael. If they're not awake in Salvation by now, they will be soon enough."

The message flashed across several screens in the flag bridge as it was broadcast. Neither the ops specialists nor any automated system read it aloud. Most of the personnel present were familiar with its contents:

> *To all civil and military authorities of Raphael: Pursuant to Union Assembly Resolution Thirteen and related security and peacekeeping authorities granted to NorthStar Corporation, Lai Wa Corporation, and CDC Enterprises, you are hereby ordered to comply with any and all instructions from Task Force Intercession.*
>
> *Military forces are ordered to establish contact and stand down from all security and patrol operations. Failure to comply will result in the use of force.*
>
> *The President of Archangel, Speaker of the Legislature and Governor of Raphael are ordered to contact Task Force Intercession immediately. Failure to comply will result in military action.*

The sensor bubble around *Hercules* grew. A new contact emerged, far behind the fleet, representing a single civilian yacht. Elsewhere, drifting into the drone net from farther out into the system, was a lone freighter. A single navy corvette turned up orbiting Azarias, Raphael's sole moon.

Nothing resembling a defensive fleet appeared within the two light-minute bubble.

"Come on, Yeoh," Eldridge murmured as he watched and waited. "Don't be a fool."

• • •

"Did they—are they here with Assembly authority?" Hawkins choked.

"Are you kidding me?" scowled Casey. "They'd be here with Union fleet ships to fly the flag if they had that kind of backing. Resolution Thirteen just gives the Big Three the authority to have an armed fleet at all, and that's to defend against aliens and pirates and bullshit like that. Christ, don't you know anything? I thought you were an academy grad."

Hawkins swallowed hard. He knew that, of course. It was the sort of thing a ship's officer could rattle off at a whim. His duties on *Argent* aside, though, it had been awhile since Hawkins had served on a starship. He was more of a spook than a spacer anymore . . . but he knew that Archangel's militia couldn't handle a force like this in a straight fight. Just one of those battle groups could outlast the whole navy.

Seconds ticked past. No reply came from Salvation, nor any militia authority. No reply came at all.

Casey's tactical displays grew considerably more active. "Fleet ships firing!" announced Quentin from the ops station. "Beam weapons—they're blowing up the closest drones."

"Yeah, I see that," said Casey. Several contacts, identified as a couple of corvettes from deeper inside the mass of larger ships, split off from the main group, presumably to blow a wider hole in the net. The drones carried chaff rockets, signal scramblers, and a couple of light laser turrets for self-defense, but they couldn't stand up against the sort of firepower that real military ships offered. The net was a deterrent, not a fortified defense.

Casey recognized the opportunity. He hit the comms button again. "*Hercules*, what's going on?" he asked with deliberate fright.

"*Argent, Hercules*. Hold your position and stand by. Power down your engines." Contacts on the tactical board broke off from the main body. *Argent's* systems recognized them as destroyers. "*Argent*, you are ordered to heave to and prepare to be boarded and then guided out of the area. You will not be harmed. Please confirm."

"We've got us a ballgame," Casey muttered. "*Hercules, Argent*. Please explain."

"*Argent, Hercules*. Sit tight. Stay out of the way and you will not be harmed."

"They won't even say it," observed Hawkins.

"Of course they won't."

"Why are they all here in one big group?" Hawkins wondered nervously. "Shouldn't they . . . shouldn't they come in from more than one point?"

"Are you scared?" Casey looked over at his first officer but knew he wouldn't get an honest answer. "That's why. Intimidation value." His attention turned back to his tactical displays. "Oh good. It's all CDC ships coming out to us. Probably glad to give them something to do out of the way while the NorthStar boys do all the heavy lifting."

"That's two destroyers and a frigate," said Hawkins.

"Well, yeah. We're kinda dodgy here, sitting out on our own, not offering visuals . . . Guns, how do we look?"

"Waiting for orders, cap'n," answered his chief gunner.

"Keep the beam weapons cool. Don't want to tip our hand. Ranges?"

"Eighty thousand and closing," replied Quentin. "Contacts are splitting up. Destroyer *Norfolk* approaching off to starboard, destroyer *Colombo* drifting to port, frigate *Gwendolyn* trailing up the middle."

"They wanna box us in," Casey surmised. "Outstanding."

"How is that a good thing?" Hawkins asked.

Casey threw him a quizzical look. "We're out here to buy time. You want us to surrender?"

Though momentarily tongue-tied, Hawkins managed an answer: "We haven't heard anything from Raphael or the navy." He pointed to the astrogation table. "There's no way anyone expected that many ships to show up at our doorstep! For all we know, Raphael's already negotiating a surrender!"

Casey gestured for Hawkins to step closer, and then leaned in. "Ask me if I give a shit," he hissed, and then clapped Hawkins on the shoulder. "You might wanna get strapped in. Ops! Ranges?"

"Drawing within forty K and decelerating," Quentin announced.

"Guns, you got an optical lock?" Casey asked. "No bouncing signals off these guys. Might give them the wrong idea. You gotta do this on manual."

The gunner's mouth twitched with a nervous grin. Even manual targeting relied on considerable aid from the computers. "Yes, sir," he answered.

"Engineering, how are we doing?" Casey asked over the internal comms net.

"We're ready for full burn whenever you need," came the response.

"*Norfolk's* at twenty K . . . *Colombo* at eighteen K," Quentin reported. "*Gwendolyn's* closing to fifteen."

"We're receiving instructions from *Norfolk*, sir," spoke up the comms officer. "Come about and roll seventy degrees to receive shuttles."

"Let's oblige 'em. Helm, seventy-degree roll. Guns, on my mark. Engineering, hold steady. Quentin, you got your finger on the ES system?"

"Electrostatic reinforcement ready," Quentin confirmed. "Say the word."

"Not yet," Casey advised. He stared at the tactical boards, with each of the ships now coming in close enough that the computers kicked over to enhanced visuals. Within seconds, the almost leisurely pace of the ships halved the distances of Quentin's last report. The main fleet began drifting through the hole they'd made in the drone net. Nothing came from Raphael or from the Archangel Navy.

Casey adjusted the solid screen to his right. In its reflective black border, he saw Hawkins standing nearby. He routed targeting instructions via the screen, prioritizing silently between *Argent*'s systems.

"*Gwendolyn* and *Colombo* are launching shuttles," said Quentin. "*Norfolk* has us in weapons lock."

"Sure she does." Casey looked over his right shoulder and then his left, his eyes sweeping the bridge in one last check of his crew. Hawkins remained close. His hand rested on the holstered pistol at his side.

"*Gwendolyn* at two K and holding. *Colombo* at three K to port and decelerating but still closing. *Norfolk* is at rest at five K to starboard. Shuttles closing."

"Don't worry, Hawkins," Casey said. "There's no way I'd ever deprive your people and these motherfuckers a chance to murder each other."

Hawkins blinked. "What?"

"Hit 'em now!" Casey roared, stepping out of his chair. Hawkins blinked again, both at the sudden commitment to battle and Casey's unexpected movement. Weapons systems all across

Argent's length fired at once, engaging each of the approaching ships with a torrent of fire.

Gwendolyn suffered the first and worst of *Argent's* punishment, lined up as she was within the main gun's field of fire. *Argent's* computers had all the time they would ever need to line up the shot. Twin laser cannons tore into the bow of the frigate with greater power than any ordinary starliner could put toward her weapons. Though *Gwendolyn's* hull enjoyed the same sort of reflective coating and electrostatic reinforcement as *Argent* and most other warships, none of that was enough to withstand such a blast at this close range. Wide red beams blasted straight through the center of the ship, setting off a cascade of explosions within her hull.

The frigate was not the sole recipient of *Argent's* wrath. False panels along the liner's hull flew away, sent flying into space by high-pressure charges at their joints to reveal missile pods and laser batteries on both sides of the ship. Flashes of light crossed thousands of kilometers instantly. Missiles followed only a heartbeat later.

False airlock hatches opened to extend defensive gun turrets. Though their short-range explosive projectiles normally served as a last line of defense against incoming missiles, the turrets devoted their first few thousand rapid-fire shells to all but shredding the approaching shuttles.

Even with their crews vigilant and their combat systems ready, the sudden assault at such close range hit the destroyers hard. Facing the liner's "belly," *Norfolk* suffered less damage, but she still felt the unforgiving heat of lasers that dug ugly scars into her reflective hull. External protrusions like turrets and scanning domes shattered and burst, but the destroyer held together. Her defensive systems reacted in time to stave off death, intercepting and detonating incoming missiles just outside the deadliest edge of their impact zones. Yet those close calls sent *Norfolk* reeling sideways.

Colombo fared worse. With *Argent's* dorsal side facing the destroyer, more of those concealed weapons had a clear shot, and *Colombo* had dared to come closer than *Norfolk*. Lasers struck with greater accuracy, eliminating defensive turrets that might have protected *Colombo* from the three incoming missiles that spread themselves almost evenly across her length. Any one of the blows would have been critical, but the one that smashed through her engine room instantly set off every one of the destroyer's solid-state fuel cells. *Colombo* died in a sudden burst of fire and light, leaving behind a mess of splintered debris.

"Back out!" Casey ordered as his ship's scanners and computers assessed the damage they'd inflicted. "Full reverse! Chaff missiles toward the fleet! Fire! Don't wait for targets, just fire!"

Hawkins looked on with horror as he realized the gravity of *Argent's* actions. She'd lured in and all but assassinated two ships and crippled a third in full view of the biggest armada the Union had seen in his lifetime.

And his captain sounded ecstatic.

• • •

"*Argent* is firing!" blurted one of the ops specialists. She nearly rose from her seat, but the intensity of the liner's attack kept her riveted for the few heartbeats it took to assess the damage. "We've lost contact with all three ships!"

"Report!" Commodore Eldridge demanded, but then corrected himself rather than wait. "Gordon, send the other CDC ships in there to—"

High-pitched alarms, flashing lights, and the shocked voices of several other men and women on the flag bridge coincided with the bright flash of red light that cut through the space between *Hercules* and the frigate *Cascia* looming ahead of her. More such flashes followed, concentrating on the much smaller frigate rather than the battleship.

Eldridge's eyes darted to the command table, which had already processed the information. As the young ops specialist warned, none of the three ships remained on the comms net. *Colombo's* icon went from blue to a faded gray to indicate her destruction. *Gwendolyn* flashed in a rapid sequence to denote her suspected neutralization. *Norfolk*, too, bore similarly grim designations, but at least spat a couple of missiles at *Argent*. The liner now backed away, firing chaff missiles that confused the computers on *Hercules* and, likely, anyone else tracking her.

"She's firing at us!" another voice on the bridge reported needlessly.

"Gordon!" Eldridge called out.

"I'm on it, sir!" Commander Gordon replied. "Destroyers *Helene* and *Janus* dispatched. CDC destroyer *Devonport* is already moving in, too."

Eldridge nodded, maintaining his focus on the bigger picture but considering this development within it. He looked at a replay of the last few seconds. No cruise liner should have been able to do something like that to *Gwendolyn*. Even if one were heavily modified after she'd left the shipyards, the power draw alone wasn't something that civilian ships were built to handle.

Except, of course, for certain cruise liners built by NorthStar and presumably some built by Lai Wa.

"Inbound contact!" another voice announced. "Civilian yacht bearing one-eight-niner mark one-five-seven, moving fast!"

"She's not coming for us, she's moving for Expeditionary Group Alpha," Eldridge warned. "Tell them to close ranks; she'll be there in seconds!" He glanced back to the fight with *Argent* and saw missiles and beam weapon fire already flashing between the liner and his own forces.

Eldridge fumed. *These are just the stalling tactics. They're going to fight.* "Dammit!"

. . .

She was a comfortable ship: sleek, welcoming, efficient. She was fast, too, and well armed.

Seated beside the helmsman on the four-person bridge, where her original plush seating and user-friendly consoles remained, Chief Everett hoped the former *Guillotine* would hold under fire, too. This particular run wouldn't come without cost. "Seven seconds to weapons range."

"Mohamed, when I tell you to bank, go thirty-by-thirty and keep going, understand?" asked the man in the captain's chair behind Everett. Like everyone else in the crew, Lieutenant Alvarez was sealed in his vac suit with the faceplate of his helmet down and locked. Formerly the supervising officer of recruit training at Fort Stalwart and a solid performer, he'd been handpicked for this job.

Alvarez knew full well that Chief Everett made the call, regardless of the officers who sent Alvarez his orders. Even in the navy's traditional chain of command, a chief's word carried great weight.

"Aye, aye, sir, thirty-by-thirty," replied the young helmsman. "Still accelerating to maximum sublight."

"Three," said Everett. "Two. One."

"Fire at will, chief."

Three more seconds elapsed before the first beams of laser fire appeared, working in vain to catch the yacht. The brief gap in response time offered proof of concept: the invading fleet was still getting itself together, and *Guillotine*'s speed gave her the chance to take advantage of a sluggish reaction. Three seconds was not a long delay, but it allowed her to halve the distance to her targets.

The hail of defensive fire from the enemy ships intensified in a single heartbeat as escort ships all around the yacht's target joined in. *Guillotine* tilted, her thrusters deliberately sputtering to alter her speed and fool the enemy's targeting computers. Chief Everett waited one more crucial second before firing off four missiles from the launchers concealed in the yacht's wings. It left the assault carrier ahead of them only two seconds to intercept his shots.

A torrent of solid-projectile fire blocked one of the missiles. A late-firing chaff missile managed to destroy a second. The third and fourth made it through the defenses and smashed against the aft section of the assault carrier *Waterloo*.

Guillotine didn't stay to assess the damage. She banked according to her captain's orders, hard to the right and "up" from her previous course, burning at full speed to escape the wrath of *Waterloo*'s escorts. The yacht shook from multiple explosive shells impacting against her reinforced hull.

Everett heard a sudden, loud pop behind him, then saw a brief flash of heat and heard the rush of pressurized air against his vac suit. Then, just as suddenly, he heard nothing at all. He looked over his shoulder to see blood and debris against the overhead. A fountain of sparks erupted from the shattered command console. His friend slumped back in his seat. "Captain?" Everett shouted. "Alvarez! Shit!"

He glanced at the tactical screens. *Guillotine* would be back outside weapons range within two seconds. Mohamed had it under control. Everett popped his seat-belt buckle and climbed over to check on the captain, but he saw immediately that it was too late. The shell that burst straight up from under the captain's console had taken a good deal of Alvarez along with it. A half-meter hole in the deck beneath him provided an unobstructed view into the void outside the ship.

"Captain Alvarez is down," Everett announced over the ship's comm net. "Chief Everett assuming command. Is everyone else all right?"

"Engineering is fine," came one answer.

"Turrets one and two are good here," offered another. "That was too fast for us to get a couple shots off, but we're okay."

Everett turned back to his station. "What are they doing?"

"Nothing, chief," said Mohamed. "They're holding tight. Think we got that assault carrier good, though. She's moving slower than the others now."

"Then we go back for another run. Turn us around while I pick a new target."

. . .

Shockwaves rattled *Argent's* bridge as her screen of defensive fire detonated missiles just short of their effective blast radius. The sensations gave her crew a visceral reminder of their tenuous position.

"This is why you don't shoot your missiles off too soon, people," said Casey as he moved over to the command table. "Comms, any word from Salvation or the fleet yet? Or anybody?"

"Negative, sir!"

"Fuckers," Casey grumbled. The command table laid out his position plainly: *Argent* continued to pull back from the invasion fleet, but she now had three pursuers, all of them destroyers. She would not be so lucky as to take anyone by complete surprise a second time. *Norfolk* drifted helplessly where she'd first been engaged, occasionally throwing out a missile or a laser blast but at a slow pace that suggested she was sorely wounded.

"We might be able to outrun all three of them if we came one-eighty and burned at full speed right now," suggested Hawkins, who leaned on the table as the ship lightly shook again.

"Might," grunted Casey. "Might not. It'd be a good chase either way."

"Well, we're supposed to draw off escorts, right?" Hawkins pressed. "We've taken out three already and we've got three more in pursuit. Isn't that good enough?"

Casey snorted. "No."

"We can't take on three destroyers by ourselves!"

"I'm sorry, which one of us actually knows from experience how much punishment this ship can take from a destroyer?" Casey turned back to the table. Fortunately, the enemy's ships had all arrived with their basic transponders broadcasting, freely identifying themselves as a nod to their claim of legitimacy and willingness to act peacefully.

Devonport, another CDC ship, had at first moved in at full speed, but someone had clearly reined her in. She now approached at the top of a triangular pincer formation, coming at something of an arc with *Janus* to *Argent*'s starboard and *Helene* to port.

The distance between *Argent* and her opponents quickly shrank. *Devonport* fired missiles once again in a vain attempt to land an early blow. Casey suspected her captain might have reason to be a touch angrier than anyone on the two NorthStar ships following her.

Angered and accompanied by tenuous allies, *Devonport* was the weak link in this chain, and therefore the likeliest place to strike. The sensible thing to do, other than turning and running, was to do enough to keep *Janus* and *Helene* off balance while focusing on *Devonport*, taking advantage of her aggressive behavior and watching for her to overextend or to run her cannons and tubes into an overheating problem.

He'd faced a fight like this before, only it involved two destroyers instead of three, and they were older than these. But unlike his previous ship, *Argent* could afford to shed some of her bulk, and her crew performed to a higher standard.

"Helm, I'm gonna need some quick moves here," Casey began. "On my mark, hit a full forward burn for *Janus* at starboard there and put us in a spin. Like a bullet, right? The other two fuckers are gonna unload on us and I don't want them to concentrate fire on a single side of the ship. Keep us rolling. Make like you're gonna ram that bastard, but when I give the word I want you to pull a full turn and head for *Helene* instead, okay? We're gonna shift targets at the last second. Got me?"

"Aye, aye, sir!"

"At this range and at their speed, it'll happen fast. Be ready. Guns! Unload every beam weapon you got on whoever's directly in front of us. Don't bother with the other two bastards. Defensive volleys only if they fire missiles. And pass control of chaff four and five over to me. Understood?"

"Yes, sir!"

"Engineering! Damage-control parties! Stand by—this is gonna hurt. Helm, execute now!"

Spun up and ready to go for several minutes now, *Argent*'s main thrusters overcame the backward momentum of the ship almost instantly. Given the pursuit speed built up by the other three ships and *Argent*'s own rapid acceleration, the distance between her and her foes collapsed in seconds.

The enemy destroyers were ready for such a shift. *Argent* gained no particular benefit of surprise as fire rained down on her from three different angles, one of them dead ahead. Laser turrets blasted away at her hull, burning scars across metal and straining the electrostatic reinforcement that kept the metal together under such extremes. Missiles detonated ever closer, causing *Argent* to shudder violently and knocking crewmembers off their feet. One missile made it through her defenses, blasting *Argent* open midway across her frame. The entire promenade at her center exploded, sending furniture, glass, and décor out into space.

She lost a secondary laser turret, disguised as an observatory compartment, when *Janus* clipped her with its main laser cannons. Men and women died. Alarms screamed on the bridge.

Casey accepted the losses.

Argent gave almost as good as she got, though she was not an obvious match for *Janus* in a head-to-head battle. *Janus* turned to bring the batteries and defensive guns on her broadside to bear in the face of *Argent's* charge. *Helene* and *Devonport* continued to rain down a murderous torrent of fire. A single laser breached one of the bridge bulkheads, cutting from one corner at port and straight out again into the overhead. Atmosphere quickly vented out, and with it went most of the sound. Everyone could still hear one another over the comms nets provided by their helmets, and vibrations felt through the ship's decks and crewmen's seats still offered some of the same sensations, but the environment felt dramatically different.

"DC one to bridge now!" demanded Hawkins over the ship's comm net.

"Guns, fire missiles one and two! Helm, turn and burn on *Helene!*" Casey ordered. He fired off the chaff batteries under his personal control, directing them in an arc around *Janus* in the wake of the two missiles *Argent* sent loose.

Janus intercepted those missiles with her own chaff tubes, but the series of explosions around her in so many directions at once played havoc with her sensors. For the moment, *Janus* lay blinded. *Devonport* was slow to react. *Helene*, once lined up for a back-stabbing shot and now the primary focus of *Argent's* wrath, was suddenly on the wrong foot.

"All weapons on *Helene!*" demanded Casey. "Don't let up! We've got three seconds at this! Go! Go!"

Another nearby explosion shook *Argent* once again, causing a further minor breach in the bulkheads of the bridge. *Argent* gave everything she had in her headlong charge. Her laser cannon hammered away at *Helene*, straining the destroyer's hull. Secondary batteries scored hits. Missiles flew in through a brief gap in *Helene's* defenses and detonated right against her hull to catastrophic effect.

"Helm! Fly right into her! Go!"

The ships closed at a terrifying speed, but the tactical screens all around the bridge offered up clear visuals of a destroyer already undergoing a cascade of ruptures and explosions. *Argent* kept firing as she rushed in. A heartbeat before impact, *Helene* suffered one more devastating missile strike, one that flew across such a short distance that *Argent* felt some of the resultant explosion.

Crewmen on the bridge felt a terrifying, silent shudder as *Argent* charged straight through the cloud of burning gases and debris. Systems shorted out and lights flickered. Numerous holo screens died. One of the ship's internal monitor stations all but exploded, eliciting a shriek from the tech seated in front of the screens.

Casey looked over his shoulder. He found Hawkins there, waving his hands and gesturing to the four damage-control techs who rushed in . . . accompanied by a ship's security team.

"*Devonport* is turning to pursue!" warned Quentin, standing on the other side of the command table from Casey. "*Janus* is clearing that cloud!"

"Full defensive!" Casey ordered. He didn't pay any attention to the tactical boards now. His eyes scanned his surroundings desperately until he found something useful. *Argent* shook again under the force of a missile exploding not far behind her engines. Casey bent over with the blast, reaching down to the deck to grab the shard of metal that slid past his foot.

"Orders, captain?" pleaded his helmsman. He'd read the writing on the wall right away; *Argent* couldn't hold this course for long.

Casey's eyes swept the bridge again. The damage-control techs moved to the obvious trouble spots, but one in particular kept looking back to the command table. The security team spread out to cover the exits. Hawkins remained nearby.

His right hand was once again on the holstered pistol at his hip.

Casey watched the boards. *Devonport* sent more missiles after her, firing as if she had an endless supply. He held his tongue and waited as crewmen voiced warnings and reports over the comm. With no commands coming from the captain, fear and chaos grew.

Argent shook violently with another near hit, one that did real damage to the hull just past her engines. Again, lights flickered and crewmen fought to hold on.

The distraction was all Casey needed. He spun around in the brief darkness with his improvised dagger clenched in his fist, driving its pointed edge straight into his first officer's neck under his helmet.

Hawkins didn't scream. He couldn't. The magnets in his boots and at the joints of his vac suit kept him from tumbling far from his position. Casey recovered his balance and dragged himself back to the table. "Helm, hard to zenith!" he ordered. "Straight up! Go! Guns, return fire on *Devonport*! Let 'em have it!"

The motion gave *Argent* the extra space her defensive turrets needed to blast away another of the missiles that threatened to take out her engines. As Casey surmised, the CDC destroyer had already been too exuberant with her guns to put up a full screen of defensive fire. *Argent*'s batteries hit a number of spots against *Devonport*'s sides, but her missiles came all too close for comfort. *Devonport* emerged from the resultant explosive cloud to find *Argent* turning face-to-face on her.

The next shot from *Argent*'s main cannons struck a lethal blow straight through the weakened armor plating over *Devonport*'s bridge. Though the destroyer did not snap or explode like her fallen comrades, the results were clear and immediate. She turned slightly from her course while her guns fired blindly and then sputtered, drifting like a shark suddenly struck blind.

Argent now faced only a single opponent, and though wounded, she still held together with most of her weapons at the ready. Casey let out a breath. He'd whittled down the numbers arrayed against him. He could handle any single opponent.

The security teams remained at their posts. The damage-control team focused on their jobs. Quentin rushed over from his spot at the table to check on Hawkins, calling for a corpsman.

Hawkins didn't speak. He couldn't. Casey saw that plainly. Hawkins couldn't breathe, let alone give any last orders to whomever on the security or damage-control teams might be part of his plans. His eyes turned up toward the captain.

Casey couldn't speak any last parting words, either. Not with the comms net in full swing, recording every statement. He contented himself to flashing his middle finger at his first officer.

It was the last thing Hawkins ever saw.

ELEVEN

And Thousands More Like Him

"Civil emergency warning: This is not a test. The Civil Defense Force has declared a military emergency for the planet of Raphael. All emergency responders must report to their duty stations. Civilian air and space traffic is suspended. Citizens are advised to take shelter. Repeat: take shelter immediately."

—All-Media Emergency Override Message,
Raphael, December 2276

"So Freeman says Miller has been a good gunner's mate lately. Reliable guy except for this one little case of missing movement, does his job well, blah, blah, blah," Tanner said, his disagreement with that particular assertion plain in his tone. He shifted in his seat at the front desk in the brig. "Stevens listens and nods. He doesn't ask anyone else to make statements. Doesn't ask me anything about the calls that night. He sits behind his table with Miller standing there in his dress uniform lookin' all puppy dog–eyed and asks if Miller wants to make a statement.

"And Miller goes, 'Sir, I want to say that the cause of my downfall was the same thing that caused the Trojan War and the expulsion from Eden. I was in the clutches of a woman.'"

Seated beside him, Baldwin choked, then laughed. It was the only sound in the compartment apart from the soft hum of the ventilation. The two young MAs were the only ones on watch in a brig that had grown thankfully empty. "Wow, he actually said that?"

"He did."

"Fuckin' gunner's mates. What'd the captain do?"

"He sat there with his jaw hangin' open for a couple seconds and then said, 'I agree,' and threw the book at Miller. Temporary reduction in rank, thirty days confined to the ship, forfeiture of half his pay for three months, and extra duty shifts."

"That's pretty usual for a captain's mast," said Baldwin. "That sounds like the maximum for an offense like his, but those are all standard measures of nonjudicial punishment."

Tanner nodded. "We lost a guy while Miller was passed-out drunk. Almost lost two others on account of injuries on board the ship, and then there's the whole bit with the pirates taking off with me and two other guys still on board. Three, counting the one who died." His voice, already a bit subdued by weariness, turned sober as he recounted the casualties. "The captain felt like an asshole for being on leave when it happened. I mean, that wasn't his fault. Wasn't anyone's fault. The guy had leave days to burn and we weren't in any sort of crisis mode. But he felt awful, and there's Miller being a fuckup."

"You think he was taking it out on Miller, then?"

"I dunno. I never figured that out. The captain never talked to me, anyway."

"Well, if shit went sideways while I was away on vacation, I imagine I'd feel pretty bad, too. You guys wound up in a fight and the guy who had 'gunner' in his *job title* wasn't there."

"I guess. It's ancient history now. I just still think what Miller said was pretty funny. I mean, at a captain's mast, he said something like that. I'll never forget it as long as I live."

Baldwin smiled. "No women on that ship, I take it?"

"No. Not that one. For all I know, Miller would've said that, anyway. Guy was a piece of work."

"You don't sound too fond of any of them."

The observation gave Tanner pause. He liked Baldwin. She showed every indication of liking him. Yet she was also a genuine gossip, or at least interested in prying juicy details out of Tanner and presumably plenty of other people. He wondered what he could say.

He didn't feel the weight of the dead anymore, but he still felt the weight of their reputations.

"They died before I could settle everything that I needed to work out with them."

"You ever lose anyone close to you?"

Tanner blinked. *She really does just go for it, doesn't she?* "My mother died when I was fifteen. We were close. No teenage rebellion angst. But she got hit by a car, and . . ." He shrugged.

"I'm sorry. Shouldn't have asked."

"Nah, it's okay. But I think about everything that's going on, and she was all in favor of Archangel doing something like this for as long as I can remember, and here we are, y'know? Only my dad and my stepmother aren't in the system anymore, and I know the media propaganda was getting bad before Aguirre made his announcements. Here we are in quiet mode. I can't imagine what they're thinking now."

"You know they're proud of you, right?" Baldwin offered. "Your mom, too."

"Yeah. Yeah, I do. What about you?"

"Ugh. My parents were shocked when I enlisted. They didn't have the money to put me through college themselves, but past that, things were okay. They figured I'd stay home and dive right into all the extra college debt like everyone else. God, when I went off to basic, they cried and cried and cried."

She spoke of it easily. Casually. It didn't sound like a touchy subject at all for her. Tanner considered the implications. "Felt like you had nowhere else to go, huh?"

"I wouldn't say that, but . . . nowhere else that'd let me feel like I was standing on my own two feet."

Tanner smiled. "That's kind of how I felt."

"Anyway," Baldwin said. "Back to captain's masts. Captain Bernard will stick close to the book. It's practically his script. It'll be like the mock procedures from MA school. You wait until—"

The battle stations alarm interrupted her. Red lights flashed in the overhead fixtures. "All hands to battle stations!" announced a voice on the PA. "Operation Beowulf is underway! *This is not a drill!*"

After two weeks of practice drills and rehearsals, with response time and precision meaning everything to the operation, crewmen and marines found themselves lugging around all relevant gear to whatever duty station they might have. People slept in their bunks with combat jackets on top of their blankets. Rather than relying on emergency stations to provide oxygen cartridges for helmets, everyone carried at least four of their own in their pockets. Baldwin leapt out of her seat to grab her combat jacket from its resting place on the back of her chair.

Experience still held firm for Tanner. Before he did anything, he threw on his helmet and activated the seals. Then he hit the comms net button. "Lewis," he said, snatching up his own combat jacket and quickly assembling the buckles, "the brig is empty right now. No prisoners, just me and Baldwin."

"Go!" replied Lewis over the department channel. "Seal it up and get to your station. We'll handle the rest."

Per their most successful drills, the pair only had twenty seconds. Helmets were secure. Indicators glowed in green. Tanner hefted up his damage-control bag. Baldwin slung a field comms unit backpack over one shoulder. "You good?" she asked. He nodded. "I'll get the door. Let's go!"

Tanner rushed out of the compartment, where he found the passageways filled with crewmen going this way and that in a carefully rehearsed traffic plan orchestrated by the deck department. As people made it to their individual stations, the passageways would clear up, but for these first few seconds the focus was simply on avoiding bumps and jostles while moving as fast as possible. Tanner paused only long enough to seal up the brig before turning to follow his predetermined path.

Most of the crewmen he came across were suited up and ready to go. Some weren't. "Put your fucking helmet on!" he growled at several as he passed, caring little for rank or seniority. The sight of shipmates leaving themselves vulnerable like that made him genuinely angry. Didn't they know how dangerous this would be?

He moved on. Tanner and Baldwin crossed over to the other side of the ship, almost vaulting up a ladder well from one deck to the next, and soon came to their destination.

A vac-suited crewman stood inside airlock four. Given the combat jacket that covered up his name tag and the helmet that obscured his face, he'd have been all but unidentifiable to most of the people on *Los Angeles*. His only defining trait was his significant height.

Tanner slapped hands with the tall crewman on his way through the airlock. "Sanjay," he said.

"Good to see you, Tanner," came the reply. As Tanner passed through the airlock, he heard Sanjay say over his own ship's comms net, "Two more aboard, three left to go."

The lurching sensation of going from one ship's artificial gravity system, through a low-gravity tube and into another field of gravity still played havoc with Tanner's guts. He accepted this and put it aside in favor of stressing over the mission that lay ahead. Throwing up wouldn't get him out of this.

. . .

"*Argent* just engaged. Repeat: *Argent* has opened fire . . . holy shit," stammered the disembodied voice from *St. George*. Though Lieutenant Kelly and the others on *Joan of Arc*'s bridge listened with natural interest and tension, none of them paused in their work. Chief Romita drew up numerous contingency courses. Stan busied himself clearing the bridge of any coffee mug, hand tool, or papers that might go flying around in the course of combat. Kelly sat at the captain's chair watching *Joan*'s internal status boards as they signaled increasing readiness in engineering, her turrets, and her cargo bay. The voice of *St. George*'s ops specialist elaborated after a few seemingly endless seconds: "*Argent* has neutralized two targets! One frigate listing and silent, one destroyer KIA, one destroyer damaged!"

That declaration briefly stopped work on the bridge. Kelly, Romita, and Stan shared an instant of surprised glances, but no more than that. The situation left no time for commentary. They got back to work.

"Captain, this is Sanjay," the ship's comm broke in. "That's a full house. I'm sealing up the airlock now. XO and Ordoñez are getting everyone squared away."

"Acknowledged," Kelly replied. "Take over for Ordoñez as planned. We need her on the cannon right away. Command, this is *Joan of Arc*," she said, keying over to another designated channel. "We are go for Beowulf. Ready to launch on your order."

"*Joan*, command, understood. Stand by."

Kelly released the key. She looked up through *Joan of Arc*'s bridge canopy. Raphael floated above her—or perhaps beneath her, given *Joan*'s orientation in space—with the bright light of the star of Archangel falling across the planet's polar region. The scene offered a good deal of natural light within the bridge. *Los Angeles* and the rest of the fleet hovered near the edge of the planet's atmosphere, hoping to take advantage of Raphael to conceal the fleet's presence, or to at least have the world to their backs while defending it.

The enemy force arrived almost on the opposite side of Raphael from the fleet, which, depending on how one looked at the situation, meant that Yeoh had gotten either lucky or unlucky. Only *St. George*, sitting near Azarias, had a direct view of the action, which her bridge crew relayed with breathless tension.

"Three more ships breaking off from the main fleet to pursue *Argent*," reported the voice. "Decoy two is making a run now."

"The tension's gonna kill me before the bad guys do," Stan muttered. His workstation was now clear of any possible debris. All he had at the astrogation table were holograms and hardened screens.

"Take a look outside, Stan," Kelly offered. "It's a pretty view."

"I'd rather get on with this, ma'am," Stan confessed politely.

Kelly didn't quite smile. "Can't blame you." She noted one more green indicator on her status board. Ordoñez was at the main cannon now, which was already powered up and good to go. About the only battle stations system not in effect was the electrostatic generator, which couldn't activate until *Joan of Arc* separated from *Los Angeles*. The cruiser and her other exterior "passengers" all had the same problem.

"XO, how are we doing?" she asked over the comm.

"All secure, ready to move."

Another indicator on her control panel lit up, warning of a transmission from the flag bridge on *Los Angeles*. Per the comm system's prioritization protocol, the signal stepped on anything else incoming on *Joan*'s systems. "Alpha wing, command. Attack vector set and confirmed. Stand by."

Joan of Arc vibrated as *Los Angeles* gunned her thrusters, carrying the docked corvette along with her. Most of the other fleet vessels were close enough to be seen with the naked eye: all five of the navy's frigates, six destroyers, and a half-dozen freighters from Archangel's Independent Shipping Guild, all of them volunteers with a brief but important role in the operation. Each of the ships involved had corvettes piggybacked to their hulls; the destroyers all had three each, while every frigate held two, and the freighters carried one apiece. *Los Angeles* carried four. Only a handful of others flew freely among the group; unlike the rest, they had no last-minute payload to pick.

The fleet represented the vast majority of Archangel's naval strength. Admiral Yeoh banked on their enemies focusing on a swift decapitating strike at the capital on Raphael, and by all appearances, she was entirely correct. Her strategy left only token forces at Archangel's other populated worlds, but Kelly saw the necessity of it. A more even defense would have left each target without enough strength to win against their opponents. Archangel had the benefit of having a slightly larger navy than she publicly declared, even beyond the disguised civilian ships already engaged with the invaders . . . but that only amounted to a handful more corvettes than were normally listed on paper.

Any rational gambler would bet on NorthStar.

Los Angeles and the rest of the fleet built up speed, coming out from behind Raphael and arcing into a dive straight for the invaders. Kelly analyzed the data from her scanners. *Argent* was plainly in trouble, fighting for her life against three more ships. The invaders moved through the hole they had blasted through the picket line. Beyond that mess, to the rear of the invading fleet, that disturbingly well-armed yacht veered back and away from an attack run.

The enemy could clearly see Archangel's defenders now. They were less than two light-seconds apart. It was more than close enough to track, but not to provide detail. That was another part of the plan.

Dozens of missiles shot out from temporary mounts attached to the civilian freighters, streaming across the space between attackers and defenders. They were much too far out for accurate fire, but that was not their purpose. Less than one hundred thousand kilometers out from the launchers, each missile detonated with chaff and ECM flares that blotted out both active and passive signals across dozens of kilometers. The enemy would know the navy's general direction, but they wouldn't be able to determine accurate distance or formation. It would only last a few seconds, but seconds always mattered.

The flagship signaled once again: "Commence launch. You are weapons free. I say again, commence launch. You are weapons free. Transmit in code word only from this point on."

Kelly keyed her comm twice to confirm instructions. "Chief, take us out. Stan, activate ES systems as soon as we're within one light-second of the bad guys. No sense burning energy on it too soon." Hearing and seeing her orders followed, Kelly double-checked their course. *Joan* set out on the broad, curving line laid out by the flag bridge under Chief Romita's steady hand. Thirty-two other corvettes did the same.

Los Angeles and the other large warships picked up their pace, heading straight for the enemy fleet. The freighters dropped back but kept firing, maintaining the broad umbrella of chaff between attackers and defenders. The corvette force, as planned, flew out and away from their bigger comrades, spreading out for the sake of safety and pouring on the speed. They had to get around to the rear of the invaders, and that meant covering a lot of space while the rest of the navy held the line.

Everyone knew that line wouldn't hold for long.

• • •

"Bogey Two is making another run on Group Alpha!"

Eldridge scowled at the report. Any instruction he sent to the expeditionary group wouldn't get to them to be implemented in time. He had to let the pair of assault carriers and their escorts handle it themselves. He watched the info on the tactical boards, particularly the fight with the well-armed and armored cruise liner farther out.

"*Janus* reports minor damage," warned Commander Saraff. "*Devonport* . . . we're getting emergency signals from her. I think she lost her bridge, sir."

"Tell *Janus* to stay on it, that bastard's wounded now," Eldridge growled.

"*Thermopylae* is hit!" called out the ops specialist watching Group Alpha. "Two missile strikes to her aft quarter. Bogey Two is on her way outside the field of fire again. Minor hits . . . *Thermopylae* says she's okay, but it's gonna slow her down."

Again? Eldridge thought. The news made him groan. Now both of the carriers in Group Alpha were damaged. Her escorts were fine. The only sensible thing to do would be to let them hang back from the rest of the fleet and make repairs. The battleship groups needed to press on and crush through all of Raphael's orbital and planet-side defenses, but delaying landings from one expeditionary group—one of three, plus the troops in the other ships—wouldn't be too much of a problem.

That conclusion brought another realization: now Eldridge understood some measure of the enemy's plan. Two ships, both ostensibly civilian, taking shots at the fleet in order to slow things down . . . and perhaps offer a measure of deniability if the ploy failed? They could always be written off as fanatics or foreign provocateurs if they did no real damage. Yet he still hadn't actually heard anything from the Archangel Navy or the government, though at least one corvette lay within line of sight on the whole scene from Azarias.

Still. He couldn't let the harassing tactics continue unanswered. "Commander, dispatch *Chatham* out toward *Janus* to help finish off that son of a bitch. Mr. Mwangi, release *Foxhound* from our group to run down that yacht. Tell *Andromeda* and Group Alpha to send their corvettes to do the same. She clearly wants someone to chase her, so let's oblige."

"Commodore?" asked Saraff.

Eldridge looked over toward his assistant and caught the development on the "bubble" projection. "I see it," he said, walking back over to the table. Archangel's fleet ventured out from behind Raphael, moving in a tight formation but still betraying their numbers. It wasn't the whole navy—most of the corvettes had to be missing, and it looked as if there were slightly more midsize ships than any intel estimates suggested. Yet even if all those other corvettes appeared from, say, Raphael's surface, he still had more than a two-to-one advantage in simple numbers, and a far greater advantage in the size and power of his individual ships. Archangel had one cruiser; Eldridge's force had five. Nor could Archangel field anything that would match his battleships.

The navy's appearance seemed to confirm his initial assessment from the first shots: Aguirre and Yeoh meant to fight. Eldridge had already processed the implications of that tragedy. Now he had to carry out his duty. "Signal Group Alpha to hold back and allow for damage control. Everyone else, alter course to move in on the enemy fleet. Let's get this over with."

He saw the swarm of new signals speeding out directly from the opposing fleet. "Missiles!" some specialist warned needlessly. They were much too far out to present any serious threat. At this range, each would be tracked with complete accuracy and shot down well outside their danger zones.

Eldridge frowned thoughtfully. He had a few seconds to think. The missiles couldn't harm his fleet. What the hell was the point? The incoming missiles flew on, spreading out as Archangel's fleet followed behind them, but the gap between the ordnance and their launchers quickly grew.

Then the missiles began to detonate more than a light-second away from the NorthStar fleet, spreading their signal-scrambling contents out over broad spheres in an arcing curtain between Eldridge's position and the enemy's. Eldridge opened his mouth, his first thought one of aggressive reaction, wanting to charge right through that mess rather than letting it slow his plans or his fleet. Then he remembered the examples of *Argent* and that yacht; the enemy had to rely on petty tricks. Yeoh couldn't remotely match him ship to ship.

"That's an awful lot of chaff missiles," observed Commander Gordon. "How many do they have to spare?"

"Hold position," Eldridge ordered. "It'll clear up in a minute or so. Let them come to us."

"Sir?" asked Saraff.

"What are they going to do?" he asked. "Increase speed? Separate and try to flank us? Run away?"

As predicted, the cloud of chaff and scrambling agents soon cleared. Eldridge was right in two of his guesses: the fleet both increased speed and separated. Now he knew where the rest of the corvettes had gone. He could also see that a good number of those midsize ships were merely freighters. "Who do we have left from the destroyer squadrons?" he asked.

"*Daphnis*, *Calypso*, and *Hyperion* from Squadron One. With *Chatham* dispatched from Squadron Two, the only CDC destroyer left is *Hanjin*."

Eldridge considered it. The corvette wing moved fast in an arc that seemed drawn to keep them out of weapons range as they covered the distance. Already several other ships from the main body, which *Hercules* could now identify as civilian freighters, were well behind the rest. "Tell *Hanjin* and *Calypso* to fall back and form up with Group Alpha to increase their defensive screen. That'll provide some extra cover in case the corvette group focuses on the carriers. Keep the other two with us. Let's get moving forward again. Watch those corvettes, but we'll focus on the main body. I want that cruiser off the board in five minutes."

. . .

"Shit, they've put three corvettes on us now," Everett grunted as the trajectory on his screens became clear. "Mohamed, you're gonna have to stay in evasive for a while. Let me find a course. Garcia, how do we look?" he asked over the comm.

Guillotine shook violently from a blast off to her port side before the answer came. "It's ugly, but it won't slow us down yet. That last run cost us some living space and the cargo hold has a big hole going through the middle. Plumbing's shot. Hope nobody needs to use the head before this is over."

"Nothing vital?" Everett asked to be sure.

"We're at full power and the guns all still work, right? You got any problems at helm?"

Everett looked to Mohamed, but the much younger bo'sun concentrated mostly on flying the ship. He couldn't fault the choice of priorities. "Think we're okay," Everett confirmed.

"Almost like this ship was secretly built for combat rather than joyrides. ES system is running a little hot. Might have to draw the power down a bit in case it overloads, but I don't want to jump the gun on that."

"You and me both, Garcia. Thanks."

The ship rolled hard again, curving off to one side to dodge a pair of missiles, but *Guillotine* couldn't dodge a blast from one of her pursuer's turrets. Everett counted it as a blessing that it wasn't from a corvette's main cannon. "Gunners, listen up: don't worry about focusing fire now. Your job is to keep these assholes dodging us. Don't worry about hitting, just get them to drop back to a safer distance. Mohamed, our course is . . . shit," the chief grunted. His helmsman had put *Guillotine* through far too many rapid turns and curves to give him a course relative to port. Everett opted instead to key in destination coordinates and let Mohamed find his way there however he felt best. "Head for this point. Don't bother hugging close to any sort of lines, just keep dodging all the way there."

"We're running?" Mohamed asked.

"Runnin' for help," replied Everett. "We've got some of those bastards slowing down for repairs and now we've drawn off three corvettes. That's mission accomplished. *St. George* is done playing lookout, so let's see if they're ready to give us a hand."

"Aye, aye, sir. Er, chief."

Everett could hear the younger man's heavy breath every time he spoke into the comm. He didn't bother to correct his helmsman, but the mistake in titles said more than enough for his mood.

Mohamed put *Guillotine* through a sharp dive and turned hard to port, then all but reversed his new course with a corkscrew-like motion. All three of their pursuers overshot, giving the yacht a bit more space. The missiles stopped coming, but the blasts from the corvettes' turrets resumed.

"Lieutenant Alvarez is dead, isn't he?" Mohamed asked breathlessly. "You couldn't help him?"

"He's gone, Abdul," Everett said. "He's gone. You can't worry about him now. Last thing he'd want is for you to let that slow you down. Focus."

Mohamed went quiet. Everett looked at him warily. The helmsman shook his head. "I'd love to wipe all the sweat off my forehead right now," he confessed.

Everett nodded. He saw the main body of Archangel's fleet drawing closer to weapons range with the invaders. "Me, too, Mohamed. Me, too."

• • •

"Signal the battle group: half speed. Guild ships, maintain fire but fall back to the rear of the formation." Yeoh's tone betrayed none of her stress or turmoil. She'd mastered that long ago.

Mastery only came from acceptance. She'd always feel this way about combat. People would die—many people, on both sides, most of them all too young. Even the thrill of victory, which she couldn't deny any more than the fear and trepidation of going into combat, failed to erase the sense of loss. The only good victories were the bloodless ones.

"Commands confirmed, admiral," reported a young officer at ops. Yeoh glanced over at him. He was young and darkly tanned like so many of the people of Michael, with something of a baby face that gave him that much more to contend with as an ensign. Blair, she remembered. A newer addition to her staff. She didn't know much about him yet.

"Thank you, Ensign Blair," Yeoh said, making eye contact and nodding. At some point, she accepted that people looked up to her. Just being acknowledged by someone of her station could mean a lot to a young person like Blair. She saw him do a double take, but like any good officer, he set his surprise aside and continued on with his job. It still seemed a little absurd that her approval could mean so much, but it was more a matter of the rank and the uniform than the person wearing it. She told herself that all the time.

At almost every step in her career, she wondered when they'd all figure out she was just faking it. She faked being an adult, being an officer, being a leader. A good wife. A mother. Then she accepted that planets turned on the actions of people who felt like they were faking it. Men and women on the bridge called out orders and updates, drew up course corrections and targeting data, driving into the biggest battle their home system had ever seen, and many of them probably still felt like they were faking it. The best would learn to accept that.

She only truly came to any sort of peace with the turmoil when she accepted that these things would happen, anyway. She couldn't affect the politics—she'd understood that back when Aguirre and his advisers first made it plain that they would be on a collision course with the biggest powers in the Union. The only way Yeoh could have altered that course was to ensure that the navy was too weak to even consider it . . . but that was unacceptable. So she built up instead, as quickly and effectively as she could.

She also accepted that she would have to see the destruction of a great deal of all she'd built today. In defiance of centuries of naval tradition, Yeoh never got sentimental about ships—a secret she told no one but her husband—but she cared a great deal about the people she'd built up for this fight.

Yeoh never considered accepting defeat or conquest, but she accepted the fight. That acceptance brought her peace.

The umbrella of chaff explosions between her battle group and the enemy also blocked line of sight between *Los Angeles* and the corvette wing, but relay drones launched in a chain that followed the corvettes carried back a clear picture. The corvettes continued on in their swing around to the enemy's rear. The invading fleet opted to hold firm and re-form, clearly guessing the direction taken by the corvettes. They would know she was behind the umbrella, but not how close to its edge. In truth, Archangel's battle group drew closer and closer, putting themselves nearly within the outer limits of effective weapons range. The corvettes kept their distance from the enemy.

The invaders couldn't expect the real purpose of the feint. No one had tried anything like this before. If the enemy saw this coming, they would pull the escorts in closer, perhaps recall the three corvettes they'd sent out against *Guillotine*. Yet in their current formation, the enemy could still defend itself effectively. Yeoh's ploy might fall completely apart. Success would still involve ugly losses.

No one on the flag bridge could read her pensive emotions. Though officers and enlisteds mindfully kept to their duties, everyone waited on her. They saw only her famed, endless patience. Even now, she was still only faking it. She watched the corvettes curve under the screening cloud of chaff, moving at all possible speed, and decided it was time.

"Ensign Blair," she called out calmly, "instruct our guild volunteers to cease fire and withdraw on my mark. Tell them to get clear, with my thanks. Commander Santos, signal the battle group: attack speed and full energy weapons volley on my mark. That'll be one moment after I give Blair his order," she added for Santos's benefit. "We probably won't hit much at first, but it's always better to come out shooting."

• • •

Archangel's battle group emerged from the cloud of sparkling chaff and electromagnetic disruption in a close formation. Against beam weapons that remained lethally accurate over a hundred thousand kilometers and missiles that erupted with a hundred-kilometer blast radius, a "tight" formation still left the group spread out over a wide area. An unaided human eye on one ship could only barely make out the closest neighbor. Yet by the standards of the modern interstellar navy, *Los Angeles* and her companions—five frigates, ten destroyers, and a handful of corvettes—represented a concentrated force. They emerged from concealment grouped up in a wedge shape with the sole cruiser at the center behind the destroyer *Monaco*.

The invaders left one full expeditionary group lagging behind, cutting out two large and formidable assault carriers and their six escort ships from the main body of the fleet. *Argent*'s vicious ambush and her risky, aggressive tactics had destroyed three ships and crippled two more. Even now, she kept another of the invading destroyers busy. *Guillotine* had managed to bleed off three of the enemy's corvettes in a wild chase toward Raphael's moon.

When Yeoh gave the order to engage, she still brought her forces into a two-to-one fight. NorthStar fielded five cruisers to her one, along with three battleships for which she had no match at all.

The opening exchanges of beam weapons did no appreciable damage to either side. No one had time to acquire accurate speeds and headings of their opponents before the red streaks of light flashed across the space between opposing forces. Every ship then took advantage of the uncrowded nature of their formations to go into evasive maneuvers, making it harder to draw a bead.

NorthStar's fleet accelerated. Archangel's defenders continued on their way. Exchanges of laser fire intensified as the distances between opponents narrowed. Within barely a minute, the first ships of both sides scored early hits.

• • •

They'd told her she owed thirty-six thousand credits. She'd studied hard, doing everything she could in preparation for the Test, but Rose McCoy wasn't especially gifted. She'd wanted to go on to university. It wasn't a pipe dream; she had what it took for higher education. She knew that the day she took the Test on Gabriel and found that dream drawing further away, despite knowing she was good enough. Ten years later, working on the bridge of the frigate ANS *Gallant*, Operations Specialist Second Class Rose McCoy knew it still.

She had the talent. Maybe not stellar talent, but enough to make it happen. She just never had the money.

She took out loans and worked her ass off in two low-paying jobs to take the edge off her debt. Family helped as best they could. Rose passed on fun nights out and lived with her parents and put off longevity treatments because she wanted to wait for a better deal. Instead, she suffered a loan penalty based on recalculations of her expected lifespan. She turned to the navy as a path toward stability, at least, if not progress.

Basic was tough. Maybe not like the "new guard" program, but it was tough. Specialist's school was tougher in an academic and a mental sense, but she'd made it through with high marks. Sixteen weeks of military training had taught her more than she would have learned in a two-year program at most colleges. Adjusting to military life was also a challenge, but she'd made good on it and even thrived. Second class within eight years was an impressive rate of advancement by the "old guard" standards. The expansion of the last two years brought further advancement within reach.

Lai Wa still had her on the hook for nineteen thousand credits. It was low enough now that she'd qualify for tuition loans, but the most financially advantageous loans were only available if she enrolled in a Lai Wa–owned university. She'd have to give more of her money to the people who'd kept her in debt all of her short adult life.

And now she knew, beyond any doubt, that she'd never owed them a goddamned thing.

Her battle station assignment put her on *Gallant's* bridge, focusing mostly on astrogation. Rose had a clear view of the entire battle from her screens, some of which offered high-resolution visuals of ships and other contacts thousands of kilometers out. She saw *Gallant's* primary targets. She could see which of the enemy ships offered threats, which of them would likely ignore the frigate based on position, and she saw incoming and outgoing ordnance.

Rose did her job well. She routed alerts. She prioritized targets. She kept the ship's computers from chasing false leads or splitting their attention. And she knew that *Gallant* would not be able to dodge, deflect, or intercept all the weapons coming toward her. Chief Armstrong at fire control saw it, too, and hit the impact alarm with only a heartbeat to spare. Rose braced for impact just as she'd been trained.

Gallant fired a full barrage of chaff missiles, turned hard to starboard, and gunned her thrusters. Her hull shook with the detonation of so much ordnance so close by, but it was the beam weapons that got her. A laser turret from one of those cruisers cut straight into her chaff missile tubes, setting off a massive explosion to the fore of the thrusters. Another beam stabbed straight through the hull at the right angle to cut into sick bay. Yet the fatal blow came from a full-powered cannon that blasted *Gallant's* hull, including her bridge, wide open to space. The exploding missiles, in the end, served only to keep *Gallant* off balance.

The comms system filled Rose's ears with screams. Gravity went out along with the atmosphere and much of the power. Rose saw friends and shipmates blown out into space, and not all of them were in one piece when they tumbled into the void. The captain reflexively clung to the command table as it flew away.

She didn't need anyone of higher rank to tell her the ship was lost. From the looks of it, hardly anyone of higher rank was on the bridge anymore. Rose slapped the emergency release on her chair's straps, activated the magnetizing relays in her vac suit's joints, and hauled herself over to the alarm panel.

Even after such catastrophic damage, she found that the "abandon ship" signal worked fine. The lights came on wherever they remained intact. The alarm tones rang in her helmet. A new holo screen lit up just ahead of her helmet lenses, directing her to the nearest surviving escape pod.

Her station at the bridge sparked and burst. It meant little to her. The man seated beside her, though, meant something. Hernandez had a beautiful young son back on Michael. He had a wife. Family. Rose shoved herself toward her shipmate, who slumped over one side of his seat. She only needed to take three plodding steps to make it to him, having to alternately fight against and then rely upon the attraction of her magnetized boot heels to the deck to cover the distance.

He was still alive. The indicators on his helmet said so. Rose released him from the straps and pulled him out, taking advantage of the lack of gravity to fling his weightless body around. His greater mass and the motion of the ship still strained her muscles, but she got the job done.

Hernandez almost made it back to consciousness before she handed him off to another bridge crewman who'd already made it into the escape pod. Rose didn't see who it was. She let go of Hernandez, saw the faceless crewman tug her friend inside, and then turned back to see who else she could grab.

Hernandez had a wife and kid. Other people here had family, too. Rose just had some dreams about going to school someday. That consideration, already at the forefront of her mind when she saw the flashing alarms at the fire control station, dictated her last actions. She wouldn't get into the escape pod in time.

She had just enough time to turn back and hit the manual launch button on the outside of the pod, which shot away in time to save its occupants.

The final barrage of incoming missiles struck, killing *Gallant* and the last woman standing on board.

• • •

Every year, someone told Chief Gunner's Mate Marcus Keever of the destroyer ANS *Madrid* that he'd soon be out of a job. Starship weaponry relied heavily on computers. It always had. But someday soon, according to "experts" and a slew of corporate-funded engineers and whatever egghead at Annapolis or some other military academy that coughed up a paper this year, Marcus's rating would go largely obsolete. Ships' guns would go completely automated. A ship's captain would just key in a couple of priority protocols and let the computer handle everything.

In over forty years in his rating, Marcus had never once seen such a claim advanced by an actual starship captain, or anyone who'd had more than a cursory brush with space combat.

"Concentrate forward!" he yelled into the comm connection with the defensive guns. "Oh-one-five to oh-three-five! Spiral pattern! Fill it with lead!"

He turned from that to his own systems. His team knew what he wanted from them. Marcus left the defensive sweep to junior gunner's mates so he could find a good target. He jabbed his finger against an enemy frigate on his touch screen, directing the computer to handle the complex calculations for targeting, and then let the blast from *Madrid*'s main cannon fly.

He watched the cooling and power levels. He weighed the risks of another shot in the blink of an eye and then went ahead and took it, following up on *Madrid*'s strike with another. The first softened up the enemy frigate's armor. The second did serious damage, evident from the shift in the frigate's path and the venting gasses and trailing debris on its port side.

Other guns saw the opening. The frigate coughed up chaff missiles to obscure its position and spoof the targeting computers, but four of *Madrid*'s smaller laser turrets walked their beams into one another and scored another hit, this one leading to a bigger explosion.

There had been a time, long before Keever was born, when everything was indeed mostly computerized. In the early days of interplanetary and then interstellar flight, when wars back home were fought more and more with robots and drones, automation made sense. Only computers could get the math right quickly enough. But the so-called artificial intelligences that had been promised for so long never took hold. They were close, and for a long time the designers genuinely believed they'd succeeded, but disillusionment with AI grew partly out of the performance of the prototypes in combat.

Programs couldn't reliably prioritize targets the way a captain wanted. Their decisions could follow protocols based on threat levels or mission objectives or morality, but the computers never *understood* the thinking behind such protocols. They didn't, in fact, think for themselves. Modern warfare was not the only failing of AI research, but it was one field of endeavor that put the lie to all the marketing.

In the end, apart from any debate on the efficacy and legitimacy of AI, most cultures and societies preferred to know a human being was behind the pull of a trigger and not some machine. Remote control weaponry fell in prominence as electronic warfare made that approach too dicey.

Marcus was damn good at his job. He'd been through three engagements, two of them decades ago in a flare-up with Hashem and one that pit his old frigate against a Krokinthian raider. If he could stand up to aliens, he could stand up to corporate mercenaries, numbers be damned.

With the frigate turning off, Marcus shifted his attention to another target. *Madrid* rattled as missile fire came closer and closer before the defensive guns or chaff missiles made their life-saving interceptions. "Look at the whole board, guys," Marcus warned. "That frigate's backing off, someone's gonna notice we did that and focus on us . . . Three o'clock high! Three o'clock high!"

The missiles came in fast. His gunners caught them a little too late. The first one to detonate set off the other two, coming in too tight a group as they did, but the explosion rocked *Madrid* hard. Alarms blared. One of the defense turrets went out, its ammunition cooking off in a cascade that ripped past the safety cutouts and blew a gaping hole through the entire emplacement.

Gravity generators went out on the ship, meaning that, even with the magnetic grip of their vac suits, any further violent impact from a missile explosion threatened to slam people into bulkheads at dangerous velocities. *Madrid* lost emergency stabilizers. Calls went out warning of the oxygen tanks venting out into space.

The main gun was out. The others weren't. Marcus had been on *Madrid* for almost three years, all of them under the same captain. So long as she had a single defensive turret working, *Madrid* would stay in the fight, if only for the sake of taking some of the heat off other ships. Marcus quickly ran the diagnostics, saw that it was simply a matter of dislodged control lines—all of them, including the backups—and knew he could fix it.

"Hitomi," Marcus barked, "you still with me?"

"Here, chief!" answered the third class at the fire control station behind the chief's. He sounded a little shaken up, but otherwise okay.

Marcus routed his screens over to Hitomi, replacing the information on Hitomi's screens and effectively changing his role at the press of a few buttons. "I gotta go fix the control lines. Take over for me here."

"Chief?" Hitomi blinked. "Shouldn't I go?"

"I've got this." Marcus was already moving toward the ladder at the other end of their small compartment, a task which at this point required both hands and feet to keep himself from floating around or flying into a bulkhead if another jolt hit the ship. "Power and tracking are running fine! I want you shooting again by the time I make it back to my seat!"

Madrid shook as he made it to the ladder. He kept going, ignoring frightened and stressed-out chatter over the comm. He couldn't do anything more than this, anyway, nor could he do any less. He was a gunner's mate. It was his job to keep the gun running. The computer couldn't do that on its own.

He made it through the first airlock hatch in the ladder, sealed it behind him, and then climbed up through the second. He heard nothing and felt less. Marcus crawled out under the cannon's armored housing to find paneling shot away. The cables in the exposed housing were loose but uncut. They just needed some human help. A pair of hands, nothing more. *Madrid* shook again, and Marcus could feel the heat of a laser blast radiating across the hull and through his suit, but he focused on his task.

"Cables connected!" Marcus announced. He turned and crawled, as quickly as he could, out from under the cannon housing. "Hitomi, talk to me!"

"Diagnostic running, we're on in five seconds." Hitomi exerted obvious, deliberate control over his voice. "Running up a target now."

"Don't wait on me, I'll be fine," said Marcus. He pulled himself over the side and into the airlock, reaching back to close it behind him. A warning tone joined the background noise on the comm, announcing the imminent return of gravity. He felt the familiar vibration of the main cannon going at full blast through the walls of the small metal tube all around him and heard a triumphant note from Hitomi. Marcus grinned. *Madrid* was a survivor.

A thin laser beam barely missed the main cannon, but it cut through the outer service airlock and the man behind it. Marcus Keever fell down against the interior hatch, gasping for breath that would never come again.

• • •

"Frigate *Carnegie* in Group Ursa reports heavy damage. Destroyer *Atlas* in Group Ursa hit as well, moderate damage," reported Saraff.

"Tell *Carnegie* she can pull back out of formation at her discretion," Eldridge said. His gaze held firm on the command boards. The tactical display didn't fit the proper scale, of course. An amateur would be easily confused by the distances and the icons representing each ship. Properly reading such a board took months of training and practice. It also served to distract someone in

Eldridge's position from the condition of his own ship, unless the flag officer remained mindful of it. "Have we been targeted at all?" he asked aloud.

"Negative, sir," answered Lieutenant Djawadi, a *Hercules* officer assigned specifically to help prevent any disconnect between the flag bridge and the battleship it rested upon. "Incoming fire is pretty light. Nothing we can't handle."

"They don't have much they can hurt us with, anyway." Eldridge frowned thoughtfully. Yeoh's flotilla slowed his forces considerably, but that was to Eldridge's advantage. He had more armor, more guns, and a greater depth of force. He could pull any seriously damaged ships back for repairs and still push on with the assault on Raphael. He'd brought this level of power in the hopes of intimidating Archangel out of exactly this sort of pointless fight. Even laying aside the damage in this shooting match and the earlier successes of Yeoh's sucker punches with the liner and the yacht, his fleet was doing fine.

Two of the enemy's frigates disappeared off the command boards within a minute of each other. His aides announced the demise of another corvette. *Hercules* hammered a destroyer to pieces while he watched. The thing clung to life mostly thanks to defensive fire from Yeoh's lone cruiser, *Los Angeles*, but that ship bore some scars now, too, and soon enough he'd knock *Los Angeles* off the board entirely. It was the only one whose beam weapons would be powerful enough to seriously hurt a battleship, but so far she'd been reluctant to engage anything greater than her own weight.

Eldridge didn't forget about the large wing of corvettes. They'd curved back in the last minute or so to come at the main formation from behind, rather than swooping in on Group Alpha's lagging ships like he'd suspected. That would have at least forced a break in formation, but instead it looked like they were hoping to catch the main body in a pincer movement.

They didn't have the strength to close the pincers, though. Corvettes on one side, a dwindling force of frigates and destroyers on the other. Weight of numbers and firepower would tell.

"*Cascia's* down!" called out Commander Saraff. "Frigate *Cascia* just went down!"

"Group Ursa lost corvette *Mastiff*!" called out someone else.

Eldridge's eyes flared. He saw it happen on the boards as his officers reported it. The *Cascia's* death was sloppy; she'd turned her back on a crippled destroyer only to find out too late that the "cripple's" main gun still worked fine. *Mastiff* died in a brutal scuffle with one of Yeoh's corvettes.

"Tighten it up and plug the gaps, people," Eldridge growled. The losses were acceptable on a tactical level, but stupid just the same. Sloppy. His people should be better in a fleet engagement than this. Their enemy was clearly a cut above anything Eldridge had expected. They made do with fewer numbers, smaller ships, and a lot of skill and guts, or maybe faith.

Or maybe fanaticism.

The thought chilled Eldridge as he turned his eyes back to that rapidly approaching wing of corvettes, all of them named for saints. Martyrs. And the main body of ships ahead of him seemed focused mostly on bleeding off his escorts . . .

"Plug the gaps!" Eldridge barked urgently. "Group Ursa, pull *Atlas* back in tight and focus on defensive fire screens. Same goes for Group Andromeda, tighten them up!" His eyes flashed over to his own strike group. *Cascia* was down, the cruiser *Halley* and destroyer *Telesto* had taken some hits, and he'd already sent *Foxhound* off to chase after that stupid yacht.

"Sir?" Saraff asked.

"I think those ships are on a kamikaze run," he said breathlessly. "There's no other way they can hurt us."

• • •

"Oh, *now* they start tightening up. Great," Kelly grunted. She keyed the all-hands PA. "Thirty seconds to fire zone. Stand by."

"Are we gonna make it?" asked Stan.

Kelly didn't stop to offer reassurance. "Chief, you see that gap there?"

"Read my mind, skipper." The senior ops specialist running the helm nodded. With *Joan of Arc* in full battle stations, the bridge canopy was once again replaced by its retractable armor plating. High-resolution images duplicating the view appeared on the inside of the plating, enhanced by numerous tactical figures and highlighting. *Joan of Arc* followed closely behind *St. Mark*, *St. Patrick*, and *St. Luke*, but that still put her ahead of the pack.

She had a positive identifier on her target and a small, rapidly closing hole in the enemy's formation. Chief Romita kicked up the speed, as did several others in the corvette wing when they caught Kelly's signal. "Gonna have to slow down fast," Kelly warned.

"Never gonna get as slow as our practice speed was in a mess like this," Romita countered.

"Fair enough. All gunners," she called out on the comm, "prioritize this destroyer here. Let's see if we can't make a bigger hole for everyone following behind. We only get one pass at him, so make it count. After that it's full defense."

The canopy "screen" on *Joan*'s bridge showed the battle up ahead in full color with only mildly enhanced resolution. Kelly and her crew could see flashes of lasers, explosions, and some of the hotter debris floating on ahead.

Missiles and lasers streaked out from the NorthStar battle group from the moment *Joan* and the other corvettes came within long range. The ships had little need for evasive action in the first few seconds, benefitting from their small size and incredible speed, but as distances shrank and targets became more recognizable, the danger grew fierce. *Joan* dipped low from her earlier course, tilted to starboard and then port, dipped again, and then pulled up, pointing her nose straight at her target.

In a very literal sense, the crew of NSS *Pallene* never knew what hit them. She had a full spread of defenses up: antimissile guns firing away with shells that detonated either on contact or after a specific flight distance, signal-jamming electromagnetic waves, and a full-strength electrostatic reinforcement current running through her hull. She still suffered a damaging hit from *Joan of Arc*'s main gun, and that was the beginning of her troubles. All three of *Joan*'s light turrets opened up, firing in sequence to keep *Pallene* boxed in where she couldn't maneuver without suffering a hit, and then the missiles came. *Joan* fired all four tubes mounted in her wings, set in a staggered pattern, so that the burst from one detonation might clear the way of defensive fire for the rest. The first two missiles did that job; the other detonated close enough to *Pallene* to rock the destroyer hard, while the last ripped open her port side.

Joan's turrets continued to fire until she passed over the destroyer with less than a kilometer's clearance. Even with a full spread of corvette weaponry focused upon her, *Pallene* held on. *Joan of Arc* did not kill her alone. The fifteen other corvettes following in her wake were more than enough for that. Kelly and her crew were already on to much bigger problems.

"Bales," Kelly called to the bo'sun's mate over the comm, "it's go time."

• • •

Eldridge's eyes flared with alarm as *Pallene* disappeared off the board. To the other side of his flank, *Telesto* and the frigate *Sorenson* managed to kill a pair of corvettes between them, but all Eldridge cared about was the new hole in his line of defenders. *Hercules*'s companion cruiser, *Halley*, was moving back toward the flagship, and he still had two corvettes and his support ship nearby. Every one of the ships at his command kept up a constant barrage. Expeditionary Group Bravo, still largely unscathed, moved closer to help, but they wouldn't establish interlocking fields of fire in time. Even if they did, Eldridge feared it might not matter. He saw the corvettes rapidly draw closer.

It was a classic problem of dealing with religious fanatics. Most defensive strategies expected the attacker to have some eye toward his own survival. If the attacker didn't care if he lived or died, most of the rule book went out the window.

Lights flashed and alarms blared as the command bridge warned the crew to brace for impact.

• • •

No one wanted to relinquish so much control to their ships' computers for such a critical maneuver, but everyone recognized that it was too much for a human being to handle. The task demanded too fine a hand, too quick an eye, and too delicate a sense of relative speeds. For seven brief, crucial seconds, Lieutenant Kelly and Chief Romita on *Joan of Arc* had to flip the switch and let the computer take over completely, just like their counterparts on the other corvettes that had made it through the storm of defensive fire around the battleships.

Joan of Arc flew straight for *Hercules* and then leveled off at the last instant. She matched the enemy's speed almost down to a matter of meters per second and then glided along her hull as if the corvette intended to land on the massive ship. She shook from the impacts of explosive shells, but the corvette doggedly remained—even when a defense gun shell exploded right in front of the ship, sending shrapnel through both the armored bridge canopy and all three people behind it.

Every officer on *Hercules*'s flag and command bridges expected
a very different act of madness than what they saw. They figured
the screens would go black, that *Hercules* would shudder under a
horrible impact or perhaps a full nuclear explosion, and that the
damage would be terrible. Then they noticed that the corvette's
cargo bay ramp was down.

Commodore Eldridge watched in shock as dozens of men and
women in vac suits leapt out from *Joan of Arc*'s cargo bay onto his
battleship.

TWELVE

The Battle of Raphael NSS Hercules

"Our proposal does not envision a program that fully trains every recruit for every shipboard station, nor make them proficient with every piece of equipment, nor prepare them for every possible emergency situation. Such a goal is obviously unattainable. Instead, we must instill within each recruit a solid understanding of the fundamentals of starship operation, repair, and combat that will serve them in a wide variety of situations. No graduate will be a master crewman, engineer, or rifleman, but every graduate will know that in an emergency, he or she can figure things out well enough to see the emergency through."

—Gunnery Sergeant Michelle Janeka and
Chief Boatswain's Mate William Everett,
Training Proposal, Fort Stalwart, Raphael, April 2274

All seventy boarders relied on computer-controlled gear just like the crew of the ship that had delivered them. Each wore a space-walking harness over their body armor and vac suits, modified to put out greater thrust for a shorter burst than safety standards normally allowed. Every one of them knew, intellectually, that they weren't falling a hundred meters onto a hostile ship. No one "fell" in space. The ship's own artificial gravity systems would create some pull for objects outside the hull, but nothing approaching that of a planet's surface. Yet with the nitrogen jets in their harnesses firing at full blast and the dizzying view from the point of departure to their destination, it surely felt like falling.

Tanner came out in the middle of the group. *Joan's* pass along the battleship's hull didn't allow for a staggered drop. The computers handled everything, making sure the whole team jumped as one. Even with such a synchronized exit, though, the team quickly scattered across the gigantic ship's length and width. Many of his comrades never made it to the hull at all.

He focused on his own jump. No one on the team could do any more than that. Tanner kept his eyes on the hull, spread his arms out, and bent at the knees, hoping the magnets in his gloves, elbows, knees, and boots would be enough to attach him to the hull.

Screams and frightened curses filled the comm net, but the void allowed for no other sounds or any sensation like wind or a chill. A rapid, heavy breathing accompanied the sounds on the comm, but Tanner knew it was his own. Maybe some of the high-pitched swearing, too.

He hit the deck of *Hercules* like he'd been thrown out of a speeding car, and that was a blessing. His vac suit and the harness worked as designed. Tanner tumbled and sprawled against a spaceship that moved thousands of kilometers a second, but he'd been moving at almost exactly that speed and direction when he'd jumped, too. The landing didn't kill him, but it left him winded and bruised. If his rifle, damage-control kit, and other gear wasn't strapped so tightly to his body, the extra mass would have beaten him up worse.

He'd been lucky to hit at a fairly flat point on the ship's surface. Like most big ships, *Hercules* had plenty of large and small fixtures on its hull that one could grab. Aside from the turrets and missile pods, the battleship's hull was littered with umbilical connectors, chemical intake fixtures, signal lamps, and numerous handholds and clamps to aid spacewalkers on her hull—which her designers understandably presumed would only ever be the ship's own crew. All of the protrusions offered things to hold on to, but they also offered numerous danger points for someone flying in at a dangerous speed.

Tanner looked up across the deck with his heart pounding. Thankfully, he wasn't the only one to make it. At a glance, he thought maybe most of the team was scattered across the battleship's hull with him, keeping low and holding on to regain their senses. Two other corvettes, *St. Nicholas* and *Albert the Great*, had made their passes barely a heartbeat following *Joan's*, dropping more boarders in their wake on the battleship's other sides. Yet every team took plenty of losses during the drop.

Marines and navy crewmen alike shouted with terror and anger as they flew straight past *Hercules* without ever connecting. Private Kipsang, who'd been behind Tanner in *Joan's* cargo bay, almost made it but the magnets in his suit never got a firm grip for some reason. Tanner saw him slide right past, reaching out with both hands but only scraping the metal with his fingertips before floating away. Another marine, Sergeant Lawson, flew headfirst into a protruding chemical intake fixture and broke his neck, leaving him drifting off silently. Signalman Third Class Jun, another Oscar Company alumni who'd also been in weapons and tactics school with Tanner, flew right into the firing line of one of *Hercules's* defense turrets. A shell exploded upon impact with his body a couple of meters from the gun's barrels, sending hot shrapnel flying across the deck that wounded and killed more people.

Suddenly frantic with the instant loss of a friend of two years, Tanner snapped his gaze to his right. Baldwin had been at his side when they'd jumped out of the cargo bay. She wasn't so close to him anymore, but he spotted her petite, helmeted form about a dozen meters away with both arms wrapped around a protruding umbilical connector.

Hercules went into a spin to avoid the next wave of corvettes. Tanner felt it before he noticed the way the stars and the trails of debris and outgoing fire seemed to curve overhead. Attached to the hull as he was both by the battleship's gravity systems and his suit's magnetic pads, Tanner knew he wasn't in much danger of being flung off, but it made for a wild ride just the same. In a flash of movement, Tanner saw *St. Martin* fly in and try to match the spin for her drop, but a lethal hit from one of *Hercules*'s quad laser turrets cut the already battered corvette in half. Tanner thought he saw a couple of bodies fly out the back before the explosion hit, but he had no way of knowing if they were survivors or more dead men and women.

Tanner forced himself off his belly, adjusted his gear, and moved over to Baldwin, careful to assure that one foot was solidly attached to the deck before lifting the other and not at all shy about using his hands as well. The comm net that kept the boarders united—in theory—carried too many screams and shouts for Tanner to bother with it.

He grabbed hold of Baldwin's wrist, careful not to dislodge her. Then he slapped the side of his helmet to activate the person-to-person channel. "Jesse, it's Tanner. You okay?"

"I'm just catching my breath, and I am never doing that again!" Baldwin screamed angrily.

"How do you think I feel?" He looked out across the hull. More of their teammates seemed to be regaining their footing. He spotted Rivera, now a corpsman but once a fellow stressed-out recruit, heaving an injured marine up onto his back. On one hand, the presence of Oscar Company graduates in *Joan's* cargo bay for the drop felt reassuring. On the other, Tanner wondered how many old friends were already gone now like Jun.

He had several specific friends on his mind.

Baldwin followed him across the hull toward Rivera and his injured marine. "I lost that stupid comm unit bag when I hit, too. I don't know what happened to it."

"Better the bag than you."

Command tones interrupted their banter. "Regroup! All hands, form fire teams and get inside! Move your asses! Go!"

The angry, demanding voice was all but music to Tanner's ears. *Of course, Janeka made it. Never a doubt there.* "Rivera!" Tanner said once he'd made physical contact. "Come with us. I've got a breaching kit in my bag."

Rivera nodded. "Where are we gonna go?"

Tanner looked around. The starship battle still raged—he could see flashes of light and explosions in the distance in any direction. *Hercules* still put out a full screen of fire. For now, the corvettes seemed to be holding off. Many other corvettes targeted the other two battleships, far out of sight from here. Tanner had no idea how they fared. Nor did he know how many of the drops on *Hercules* had succeeded, or if most had ended like *St. Martin's.*

He pointed to the defense turret that had inadvertently killed Jun. It jutted from the battleship's hull perhaps fifty meters from his position, temporarily silenced. "There," he said. "That gun. Probably a repair access hatch somewhere."

"Why isn't it firing?" Baldwin asked, but Tanner didn't answer. He got moving.

Chatter and shouting continued over the comm net, joined now by jarring, intermittent tones as the battleship's communications techs got their jamming systems running. Before long, nobody on the outside of the ship would be able to get any signals at all.

A small ring of metal surrounded the turret, angled inward to offer better protection. Tanner and the others practically crawled to the spot, needing more than the magnetic grip of their boots to stay glued to the hull as the huge ship fishtailed and spun in an effort to avoid further boarders. Were it not for the battleship's artificial gravity field bleeding out beyond the hull and mitigating most of that momentum, everyone would have been flung off into the void. Even now, it was difficult to maintain direction and balance.

Relying on hand signals, Tanner gestured for Baldwin to move around to the left of the turret's protective ring while he crawled around the right, looking for a hatch or any other point of entry. Such access was a fact of life for ships with numerous external fixtures and moving parts like turrets . . . though Tanner expected the design of warships would never be the same after today. Especially if they succeeded.

Their search soon bore fruit as Tanner came to a sealed hatch, though it offered no exterior entry controls or an emergency handle. That was to be expected, and it was the reason why he and so many others on his team carried damage-control bags. He moved with greater confidence than he had the first time he'd tried to do this—on a destroyer's side, unrehearsed and unaided by the reassuring presence of friends. By the time he had the magnetized contact cable spooled out around the edges of the hatch, Baldwin, Rivera, and the wounded marine had caught up with him. With the breaching kit ready to go, Tanner looked from one comrade to another, got the "ready" nod, and hit the energizing button.

The hatch snapped open, releasing the air within the vestibule behind it. Tanner didn't hesitate; he swung himself over the side and climbed down the vestibule with Baldwin right behind him. Fully ensconced by the ship's artificial gravity once they were in the tube, both found it easier to use the ladder than to rely on the magnetic grips and treads of their suits. Jamming interference likewise diminished.

Baldwin reached out to touch Tanner's shoulder. "Manual control," she noted, nodding toward a spot behind him against the bulkhead.

"Good eye. You wanna take it?" He saw her nod again. He looked up and saw that the hatch above them remained open. "I don't think that thing's gonna close on its own. Keep yourself glued to the bulkhead."

"I was gonna tell you the same," she said before she pulled away. Tanner saw Rivera lean over the edge and waved him off. He drew the pistol at his side, cranked up the power on his magnetic grips once again, and waited.

Baldwin sent the hatch swinging open into the compartment below, releasing a violent rush of air. The wind died off within a couple of seconds, prompting Tanner to kill the power to his grips and drop down to the deck below. He took the landing as he'd been taught, with his knees bent and rolling to one side. He came up to a kneeling position, weapon up and sweeping the room.

Two men and one woman occupied the compartment, situated near control consoles. Tanner found them all still securing their helmets or their oxygen tanks. He'd been ready to start shooting from the moment he'd dropped into the small compartment, but a single heartbeat of observation was all it took to back him off from hair-trigger reactions. The gunnery crew had no small arms. Two of them didn't notice him right away, focused as they were on their personal life-support systems. The other held his hands up, which prompted his companions to do the same. Three shocked faces looked at him through fully transparent helmet visors.

At first, Tanner thought he'd be able to take them peacefully. He kept his pistol trained on the crew, holding on for the extra couple of seconds to let Baldwin catch up. Then he realized the woman's mouth was still moving. He fired a warning shot with his pistol, striking the overhead with a red flash of light and making all three flinch and duck downward. With his other hand, he drew a grenade from his belt and tossed it behind the gunnery console.

Intensely bright-white light erupted in their midst, along with a concussive force that knocked all three of the crewmen around. The lack of air prevented much in the way of the jarring sound that normally accompanied a stun grenade, but the weapon did its job. Tanner moved in around the console, pistol still up, ready to secure his prisoners.

"Could've warned me," grumbled Baldwin over the comm. "I almost caught that flash."

Tanner glanced up from his work binding the hands of one prisoner. Baldwin trained her rifle on his position to cover him. He could hear her perfectly well now that he was out of the jamming field. "Sorry, I couldn't wait. They were still talking," he said. "I couldn't tell if they're on a local net or if they were calling for help. It's not like I could tell them to shut up."

"I understand," she replied. "Just don't forget you're not alone here."

Tanner bound all three prisoners in the sort of riot tape police resorted to when making mass arrests. As he finished with the last, Baldwin turned away to help Rivera lower the injured marine into the compartment. By that time, more boarders had found their way to the open turret and began following through.

"Hustle up!" Baldwin warned them. "We've got wounded and prisoners, and we can't finish with either of them until we've got air in here again!"

"Belay that!" grunted one of the newcomers. "There's no time! We need this access point. We're not taking prisoners."

Tanner looked up from the gunnery console to argue that, but Baldwin beat him to it. "Who the fuck said that?" she demanded.

The newcomer stood almost a foot taller than the young woman. He wore the blue vac suit and officer's insignia of a marine captain. The tag on his combat jacket named him "MacAllan."

"You're looking at a higher rank, girl."

"And you're looking at a master-at-arms, so should I bother citing Rules of Engagement, or do I skip straight to stomping your nuts and then wrapping you up with the other prisoners right now, *sir*?"

Though his helmet made it impossible to see, Tanner was fairly sure MacAllan's jaw dropped. It was much the same reaction Tanner had, though he recovered more quickly. "Private," Tanner said, pointing to another marine, "is anyone else coming through? If not, close the hatch."

"You two are not in charge here!"

"Due respect, sir, take a breath," Tanner told him as he stepped around the console again. "I can see this is your first combat. You're right, you're in charge, but we need to do this. We'll get the hatch open again once we're finished. We just got here and we've already silenced a defense gun. We're doing good, sir."

The marine private behind the captain hesitated. Tanner didn't blame him, but thankfully MacAllan grunted, "Private, seal it up. Someone hit the vent controls. We have a corpsman here? Okay, good. Baldwin. Malone. Finish up with your prisoners."

The brief standoff ended as soon as it began. Baldwin took a couple of backward steps, her eyes staying on MacAllan until she turned to join Tanner. With the hatch sealed, air rushed back in. Before long, the whole group could hear the alarm claxons and announcements warning of boarders.

"Now I know why you're here," said Tanner over the person-to-person channel.

"He only backed down because he saw your name tag," Baldwin grumbled.

"I don't think so. I think he's hiding behind that now to salvage his pride. Regardless . . . thanks."

"For what?"

"For leading by example." He winked.

Baldwin let out a huff and shook her head, but she didn't argue the point. She just kept working.

As soon as their own helmet indicators read a viable air pressure, Tanner and Baldwin set to removing their prisoners' helmets to manually deactivate their communications systems from the inside. With that settled, they put the helmets back in place on each prisoner.

Tanner glanced over to Rivera and the injured marine, but Rivera seemed to have it under control. His patient sat still against the far bulkhead while Rivera cut open the leg of his vac suit, gave him a couple of injections, and then wrapped a gel pack with an automated corrective bandage around his calf. "Captain, we'll be good to go in a minute," Rivera announced. "I can wrap this in an airtight seal, and he'll be okay if we open up the hatch again."

"Can we leave him here and move on?" MacAllan asked. "Will he get along on his own?"

"I didn't give him anything that would mess with his head. How do you feel about it, private?"

The injured marine nodded, his helmet still securely on. "I've got my rifle. Prop me up on the other bulkhead and I'll cover the door once you're gone."

"Then hustle up, corpsman," MacAllan grunted, his eyes on a holo screen generated at his left wrist. He seemed somewhat calmer than he'd been when he'd first dropped in, though everyone's voice carried an edgy note. "Is everyone else ready? Just like in training. Stack up on the exit. Malone, you and I are in the lead."

Tanner unslung the pulse rifle from his back. "Aye, aye, sir," he said, glancing at Baldwin as he moved over to join the others. Baldwin followed.

He heard MacAllan take a breath. "Remember, a lot of the crew here will be unarmed, but don't take any risks. Nonlethal weapons only, if and when you're sure your target is unarmed and if you've got the chance to switch. Taking prisoners is secondary to the mission and to your own safety. Just like the Rules of Engagement say," he added, though it didn't sound at all conciliatory. MacAllan took another look around at his team: just three navy ratings and three marines besides himself.

"We make for the command bridge. Don't be shocked if the deck plans on your holocoms turn out wrong. That's all public consumption stuff, so the real layout of this ship will probably be different. Best guess, people. Ready?" He waited until he received six confirmations, and then nodded to the marine private with his hand on the manual hatch controls. "Go!"

Tanner and the captain tossed stun grenades through the hatch as it opened to allow for some cover in either direction. Then they stepped around the sides, Tanner going left while the captain and most of the party went right. Tanner found a passageway empty, ending in another sealed hatch twenty meters away. The other pair of hatches along the way were likewise shut tight. Alarm lights continued to flash. "Boarders on decks one, six, and eleven!" announced the PA. "All hands, secure your compartments! Repeat, secure your compartments and repel boarders! Security and marine detachments, go to channel delta!"

Nothing offered resistance. MacAllan waved the group forward, with Tanner taking up the rear. Gray bulkheads offered few signs to keep anyone oriented, and the few placards Tanner could make out from here weren't helpful. Just the same, he kept his eye on each hatch as they passed, preferring the possible shelter of any random yeoman office or gear locker to the exposure in the middle of the passageway.

"Boarding team," MacAllan spoke on the broader comm channel, "this is Captain MacAllan on deck one. Am advancing to the fore with my team . . ."

Tanner didn't listen. The group stuck too close together, moving along the passageway as if they were perpetually stacked up on a door and ready to breach. Janeka and Everett had taught Oscar Company to spread out, leapfrogging from one point of cover to the next. Marines learned it in weapons and tactics school, too. Everyone here knew better, or should. Tanner glanced back and found Rivera in close with everyone else and realized it was a case of first-time combat nerves.

"Spread out, guys," Tanner urged. "Back up if you have to, we can't bunch up like this."

MacAllan turned back to look at Tanner. With his faceplate down, all Tanner could see of the captain's face were his eyes, but they looked unhappy. "Did someone put you in charge—"

"Cover!" someone yelled out. "Hatch up ahead—"

Tanner moved without hearing the rest. He rushed right past MacAllan, grabbing at the handle of the gear locker to his left. Marines and ratings knelt against the bulkheads to either side. One or two hit the deck and readied their rifles. Tanner let the pulse rifle in his right hand drop back, its shoulder strap catching at his elbow, so he could snatch Baldwin by the collar of her combat jacket and heave.

The opposition directly ahead led with stun grenades. While MacAllan's team was prepared for the flash and thunder and got straight to shooting, the enemy did the same with ferocity. Tucked partly inside the locker, Tanner and Baldwin saw MacAllan picked up off his feet by a hail of bullets before he fell back on the deck.

Baldwin recovered quickly, kneeling and shooting around the hatch while Tanner leaned over her to do the same, firing his rifle one-handed and therefore with no serious accuracy. Yet any return fire at all, even piss-poor shooting, was better than none in such a situation. In four seconds, the team had been all but cut in half by what looked like a squad of NorthStar ship's security on the other side of a reinforced hatch that offered excellent cover.

Wounded men screamed. MacAllan's comm channel went dead. Rivera fired back from the other side of the open passageway, hanging on only by virtue of the inadvertent protection offered by the dead marine slumped in front of him.

A security officer with a riot gun went down after taking a blast from Baldwin's rifle, but he was replaced almost immediately by another man in an identical dark vac suit. Someone else threw another stun grenade through the hatch while the ship's defenders kept the pressure up. Tanner looked away, his eyes searching the passageway behind them for some sort of escape route, but all he saw were the flashes of the enemy's weapons fire shooting past.

• • •

The calm professionalism of Captain Wagner's command bridge all but evaporated with the arrival of the first boarding team. His officers entered the fight eager to test their mettle against a relatively modern and professional navy, certain that the battle would offer a learning experience but little real danger. Safely ensconced within the armor and overwhelming strength of NorthStar's flagship, none of Wagner's people expected to come to serious harm. Their biggest worry was for the safety and survival of their companion ships—a serious concern, of course, but that still offered the sort of detachment one couldn't feel while one's own life and limb were in danger.

Wagner couldn't blame them. *Hercules* was indeed a powerful ship. Between the battleship's armor, her defenses, and her escorts, a fatal shot against her from an opposing force like this would have to overcome odds akin to being struck by lightning in the wild. The command bridge felt like a bunker, with its low ceiling, strong and sturdy consoles, and armed security watchstanders outside. Yet the sudden appearance of a genuine threat to personal safety, no matter how small in scope, tore down the illusion of invincibility. Like teenagers confronted with their own mortality for the first time, Wagner's veteran officers worked with an urgency born of fear.

From what he could see in the background on his comm screen, Eldridge had the same problem on the flag bridge.

"We have a hundred and fifty boarders at most, commodore," Wagner reported. "I've already routed ship's security to the worst trouble spots. We'll take care of them. My concern is the rest of those corvettes out there—I'm betting they're all loaded with troops."

"My thoughts exactly, captain," concurred Eldridge, waving away a worried aide. "I'm instructing the rest of the battle group to tighten up now. *Ursa* and *Andromeda* have the same problems—in fact, it looks like *Andromeda* got caught worse than we did. Now we know why they were focused on bleeding off the escort ships."

Wagner glanced at the tactical screens. "Sir, I'm not sure that tightening up our group alone is going to do it. They pried off half our escorts to create the first gap, and someone needs to take on Archangel's cruiser. *Halley's* close enough for the job, but that takes away our biggest escort. We're only down one defense gun, but if we lose others before we get full control of the ship again . . ."

"Agreed," Eldridge conceded with an aggravated nod, "move us back to join Expeditionary Group Alpha. I'll put *Halley* on that cruiser. We'll get ourselves sorted out and then finish the job at our own pace. In the meantime, don't lose any more of our own guns, captain! Do whatever it takes. Get those bastards off this ship!"

• • •

"Everyone up!" Harris demanded. He stomped through the back of the assault shuttle clad in recon armor like the rest of his team. "Drop everything but personal weapons and armor! Heavy weapons and ammo on the deck. Food and supply bullshit, too. Drop it and form up outside the shuttle, on the double!"

His rangers—still technically trainees, though all of them now combat veterans—followed his orders without question. Only Soldan hesitated and gave him a curious look, which didn't bother Harris at all. Soldan had long ago earned his place in the rangers and then some. Indeed, Harris looked directly to Soldan and shook his head, holding up one hand to make sure Soldan knew he wasn't included. Harris wanted Soldan, at least, to hang on to his plasma repeater.

Harris remained behind in the shuttle only long enough to shed his own excess baggage. Pouches and gearboxes clattered to the floor. He then stalked down the shuttle's entry ramp to find his young team lined up in two rows ready for orders. All around them, larger shuttles carrying NorthStar troopers emptied out as well, though without the precision of the small ranger team. A lot of the other men and women were still dumping and sorting out gear. Officers and NCOs shouted out orders, fighting to be heard over one another and the launch bay's PA system.

Not everyone would agree on appropriate weapons for this. Some would take along grenades and heavier stuff. Others would think that too destructive. Harris saw only the necessity for speed.

"Change of plans," Harris growled. "We've been boarded. Fuckers dropped a bunch of troops on our hull and now they're moving inside. We gotta clear 'em out before the invasion can proceed. Let's not complicate this. We're a small team and we're geared up better than most of the rest here, so we're gonna haul ass up to deck one and gun down anything that isn't wearing a NorthStar vac suit. The rest of these guys will spread out through the ship as soon as they're sorted, but we're ready to go now. That lift over there looks open, so let's move!"

Thankfully, nobody hesitated to ask questions. All of his people turned and hustled for the lift.

He was pretty sure he saw Eickenberry grinning.

Gunfire in the passageway refused to let up, though now the ship's defenders clearly had the upper hand. Half of Tanner's comrades died in the first twenty seconds. Baldwin fired her pulse rifle in sustained bursts, cutting down yet more of the opposition, but the rest used the cover offered by their end of the passageway to the best advantage. She had little more to target than rifles and the occasional hand that appeared only long enough to toss a grenade. No one was dumb enough to expose anything more.

Tanner had about the same problem. He couldn't lean over Baldwin without putting a large portion of his body in the firing line. His eyes darted around, looking for anything he could do to turn the tide. Then he saw Rivera take a slug through his shoulder. The hit threw him face-first to the deck. A blast from a pulse laser struck him across the back where he lay, searing open his combat jacket in a flash of light.

It all occurred in the space of a breath.

Desperate to get to Rivera, Tanner yanked a frag grenade off his combat jacket. "Fire in the hole," he shouted and then hurled it around the corner, deliberately banking the grenade off the far bulkhead since he couldn't risk stepping out for a straight throw. The grenade went off and Tanner leapt out from cover, rolling across the deck to get to Rivera. He brought his pulse rifle up as soon as he came to a halt, planning to at least make them keep their heads down, but he saw no further laser flashes through the smoke of his grenade.

He heard plenty of gunfire. None of it came through the smoke. Then he saw one of the NorthStar troops rush through the smoke with one hand over the bloody gash in his other arm. Both Tanner and Baldwin cut him down out of reflex but held their fire as the smoke quickly cleared.

The security troopers on the other side of the hatch kept fighting, but now they fought for their lives against someone on their end of the passageway. A body slumped over the lower lip of the hatch. Blood marred the bulkhead beyond him. Two men remained, both of them now with their backs turned to Tanner and shooting wildly at someone behind them and seemingly close up.

One of them crumpled after taking a burst of automatic gunfire to the chest. The other flew back through the hatch, lifted off his feet by a snap kick right under his chin. Their attacker, a woman in the blue vac suit, helmet, and combat jacket of an Archangel marine, stepped over the lip of the hatch and the dead body that decorated it to empty the final few rounds from her magazine into her last fallen opponent.

"Holy shit," Baldwin breathed.

Tanner was already busy trying to treat Rivera. He jerked open the corpsman's bag, looking for the anticauterizing gel and the auto-suture. "Hold on, buddy, just keep breathing," Tanner urged as he set to clearing out the mess of burned flesh along Rivera's upper back. His voice shook. Rivera might have spinal damage; he'd probably lost bone, too. Tanner didn't have time to do anything for Rivera's pain. He couldn't open up the helmet, either, not with Rivera needing direct oxygen so much that the helmet was probably his best bet already.

"You guys okay?" asked their rescuer. She reloaded as she came forward, looking left to right in the passageway to take in the damage. "I heard the gunfire and came running as fast as I could."

"I think we're all that's left," Baldwin answered, kneeling beside one of the fallen marines. "Check on the other guy there!"

Rivera neither moved nor responded to Tanner's labor. Tanner slid his faceplate back, breathing heavily and working as fast as he could, but it seemed there was more blood and burnt flesh than live tissue along the wound site. Tanner placed the auto-suture along Rivera's backbone and let it go, but the indicator lights flashed out negative vitals before the tool's tiny arms started their work.

"Tissue loss severe," said the tool's onboard computer. "Patient has suffered catastrophic trauma."

"Tanner?" asked the newcomer. Alicia pushed back her faceplate and moved over to him. "Tanner, how we doing over there?"

"Patient has expired," said the auto-suture. "Defibrillation not recommended. Logging time of death."

"It's Rivera," he said, his voice cracking.

"Oh God," Alicia gasped. She knelt beside him, looking for a way to help, but Tanner shook his head.

"I can't do anything," Tanner said. "I can't—there wasn't"—his eyes shut tightly—

"wasn't time."

"You did all you could," said Alicia. "He knew that."

Swallowing hard, Tanner nodded and said, "Jun didn't make it, either. He died in the jump."

"Was this it for you guys?" Alicia asked.

"We've got a wounded guy back at the gun turret guarding the access point," explained Baldwin. She had a holo screen up. "Hey, I think they've got a relay going from outside. Check out the main channel."

Tanner and Alicia followed her advice. The jamming signal outside the ship couldn't defeat a simple line-of-sight relay going from outside the hull to a friendly receiver within the ship, and from there the boarders could at least communicate with those still making their way inside.

". . . moving back out of the fight, I think," said a familiar voice. An indicator on their holo screens listed the speaker as Signalman Third Class Sinclair. They could see through his helmet's optics, too, giving them a view of the chaos outside the ship as flashes of defensive fire continued and more Archangel troops climbed and crawled toward open access points. Sinclair seemed to be perched under an active laser turret. Another corvette swooped overhead, dropping another team. Some boarders made it. Some didn't.

"*St. Nicholas* has dropped!" Sinclair said, more or less interrupting his own report. "*St. Nicholas* has dropped! Moving off now, taking fire—we're moving away from the main battle, but the screening fire is picking up. I think they're tightening up with the rest of the fleet. None of the other corvettes could get through before *St. Nicholas* just now."

A sharp tremor ran through the deck beneath them, one that Sinclair plainly felt as well. "Something blew on the ship, can't tell what. *St. Valentine* is making her run—taking fire—shit, there's too much fire—gah!" Sinclair cried out along with the sound of cracking metal and then a sharp whistling sound. "My mask is open! Can't breathe," he cried out, and then the screen went black as Sinclair's hands came up to try to plug the hole over his face.

The connection died.

Tanner's mind raced. He got to his feet, eyes scanning the bodies in the passageway. "We're never gonna take this ship with what we've got," he muttered, stepping away from his dead friend. He had to set aside his worries about Sinclair, too—another boot camp friend, his former squad leader, and a fellow refugee from nasty academic debt. Tanner couldn't do anything for Sinclair, just as he couldn't do anything for Rivera.

He'd almost been caught unable to do anything for himself, too.

"Where'd you come in, anyway?" Baldwin asked.

"Atmosphere intake port, up that way," Alicia explained, jerking her thumb back down the passageway. "Fire team got scattered. I was all alone. Either of you see Brent?"

Tanner shook his head. "Haven't, sorry."

Alicia let out a tense breath. "Okay, we've gotta link up with some more of our people, head for the command bridge, and turn this ship around before—"

"We can't take the bridge."

The statement stopped Alicia in her tracks. Baldwin, too, stood up straight, blinking at him. "Wait, this . . . this is *you* saying we can't make it?" Baldwin asked. "You took on a pirate ship all by yourself!"

"These aren't pirates. These are trained troops and they're regrouping fast."

"Tanner, most of the crew isn't even armed! You saw it yourself with that gunnery team."

"Yeah, but more than enough of them *are.* You see what they did to us here. This was just the closest batch of ship's security grunts. There's gotta be at least two thousand marines on board, and they'll all be armed. They're probably getting organized and they'll damn sure send plenty of defenders straight for both of the bridges first."

"So, what, you're gonna chicken out?" Baldwin asked.

Tanner bent over MacAllan's corpse to snatch up the dead captain's remaining grenades. "Chickening out doesn't get anyone home alive."

Alicia watched him load up on extra weapons. She'd seen this look on his face once—right before he knocked her flat on her ass. It never happened again, but she never forgot it, or what came afterward. "So what are you thinking?"

"It's Operation Beowulf," said Tanner. "We tear the monster's arm off and beat him with it."

• • •

"Main thruster two has hostiles inside! I repeat, boarders in main thruster two! Send help, they're everywhere in here!" yelled Ensign Samantha Young. She ducked under a pipe distribution trunk, trying to dodge the blasts of electric stunners that seemed to be flying everywhere. The sight of the enemy using nonlethal weapons on her fellow engineering crewmen gave her no sense of relief. For all she knew, they wanted people alive for whatever Spanish Inquisition craziness their clergy had in mind. To make matters worse, someone had taken out the overhead power conduit as soon as the shooting had started, killing more than half the lights.

Samantha heard mostly her own breath now as she darted from one bit of machinery to the other. The whole compartment vented out as soon as the boarders breached the repair hatch. Someone should have considered this when they'd designed the battleship, she thought. Didn't anyone think that maybe, just *maybe* they'd want to make sure those hatches all had locks on them in case someone tried a crazy move like boarding a battleship in the middle of combat? How stupid were these designers?

Were they stupid enough to sign up for the NorthStar fleet right out of university? Stupid enough to take the loan payoff incentives? Great career builder, they said, excellent way to build experience . . . and now this.

Nobody else responded on the thruster two channel. Someone from ship's security yammered away at her, telling her to hold the compartment. *With what?* Samantha thought. *A crowbar?* She hadn't touched a gun since Officer Indoctrination School, and that was only a short safety course.

Samantha ducked behind the fuel consumption monitor station. Another electric pop lit up the otherwise darkened compartment. Chief Grishin made some sort of whining, gurgling noise over the comm channel, letting her know who'd been hit. She looked left and right, spotting the exit hatch a few meters away. She didn't think about matters like air pressure or where she'd go from there; she just wanted to get out and away.

She made it two steps before she found a helmeted Archangel marine in front of her. Though the other woman moved like lightning, Samantha read the "Janeka" name tag on her combat jacket before that fist came driving up into her solar plexus, reducing her to a gasping wreck on the floor.

"Someone give me an update at that hatch!" Janeka demanded over her team's comm channel. "Is anyone else coming? We've gotta move!"

"We've got two more coming in," announced one of her marines. "Got a survivalman carrying in one of our guys, must have gotten hurt."

"Then get over there and help him in, private. We need to close that hatch if we're gonna advance. The rest of you, help Fuller shut this thruster down. You've been through the program, you know how to do what an engineer tells you! Move, people! We've still got to take main engineering!"

• • •

Admiral Yeoh rolled onto her side and then got to her hands and knees, shaking her helmeted head in order to clear it. The last missile burst had hit *Los Angeles* close enough to put everyone on her flag bridge on the deck if they weren't already strapped into a chair. Looking around as she rose, she realized that even a few of the people in secure seats had been thrown for a loop.

"Thruster one is down, power to thruster two cutting out!" someone announced. "We've lost one of the starboard laser batteries! Atmosphere venting out of deck six."

Yeoh was on her feet at the command table before the damage report was finished. *Hercules* moved farther off with her frigates in tow, but the cruiser *Halley* and destroyer *Telesto* remained engaged with *Los Angeles*. Somehow, the battered ship resumed her screen of defensive fire, augmented with a rush of chaff missiles to give her a second to catch her breath.

That was all Captain Bernard's business. He could take care of *Los Angeles*. Yeoh had to keep track of the bigger picture. Perhaps only a third of the corvettes had made their drops. With that success spread across three different battleships, none of them had enough troops on board to seize control of their objectives. And now the battleships retreated into their escort formations—except *Hercules*, which had opted to run all the way back to one of the expeditionary groups.

Two of Yeoh's five frigates were gone. A third sustained heavy damage. Only *Devout* and *Resolute* remained in the fight. They harried *Andromeda*'s strike group alongside a couple of Yeoh's surviving destroyers, while most of the rest of her larger ships tried to keep the third battleship and its escorts occupied enough that more of the corvettes could make it in for their drop-off runs.

Los Angeles stood alone. The destroyer *Caracas* had done all she could to back her up, but now *Caracas* was so much debris a few thousand kilometers off to port.

Impact alarms flashed again across the flag bridge. This time the missile was intercepted further out. *Los Angeles* shook again, but not as frighteningly as it had a moment ago. Yeoh glanced at the link to Captain Bernard's status screens. Wounded as she was, *Los Angeles* could still dish out more punishment. She needed a clean shot, and if they could take the enemy cruiser off the board, the other battleship groups would have to reallocate their escorts to keep *Los Angeles* covered.

"Captain Bernard," Yeoh called out. "Can we make a good attack run at that cruiser?"

Heartbeats passed before she received an answer. "It's Commander Sutton, ma'am. The captain's dead. I'm in command now. I don't think . . . shit, that destroyer's moving in to flank us. It's all we can do to stay evasive, and that game's running out!"

Yeoh called up the cruiser's weapons status at the push of the button, thankful that Captain Bernard had been forthcoming with such access from the outset. The main cannons remained online and ready to go—they just didn't have a clear shot. Several of the secondary turrets were off-line or, in a few cases, gone completely. The defensive guns were still good—Sutton must have done an excellent job with them from the instant he took command, or *Los Angeles* would already be gone. Yet even there, she saw gaps.

"Commander, roll us to keep our belly facing that destroyer," she warned. "It's the only way we'll defend ourselves and get a good shot in with the main guns."

He didn't argue or question. The XO—now the CO—followed her advice right away, perhaps out of reflex or because he didn't have a better idea. Nothing *Los Angeles* could do would keep her from all harm at this point, but he saw the value in lunging at the larger opponent rather than remaining on pure defense until *Los Angeles* died of a thousand small cuts.

Halley didn't see the move coming. Yeoh could tell that from the larger enemy's sudden upward pitch. She wanted to get out of the way and present a minimal aspect, but she wouldn't make it in time.

Then alarms screamed and *Los Angeles* shook again. Lasers stabbed at her from beneath, gutting the armor along her belly and detonating one of her chaff missile launchers. *Halley* had blinked in the face of serious danger, but her companion destroyer saw the opportunity as soon as it was presented. She, too, pulled up to bring her main guns to bear directly on *Los Angeles*.

And then the enemy destroyer exploded.

"Take the opening, commander!" Yeoh urged.

Again, Sutton responded instantly to Yeoh's orders. She felt the slight rumble of the cruiser's remaining thrusters going into overdrive and the hum in the deck plates as *Los Angeles* lashed out with both of her main cannons. Wide red beams struck *Halley* at the juncture between the main thrusters stacked on her port side, right where the hull was already under significant heat and stress. The blast resulted in a violent explosion, putting *Halley* into an uncontrolled lateral spin.

Yeoh leaned against the command table to catch her breath, leaving Commander Sutton to call out orders to his gunners to follow up with everything they could. She turned her eyes to the tactical screen again, wondering who'd taken out that destroyer.

Now a hundred thousand kilometers out, with enough damage that she left a visible trail of gases and debris, the passenger liner *Argent* limped back into the fight.

• • •

"Didn't see that coming, did you, fuckers?" Casey growled. He held his sprained left wrist close to his chest, leaning on the broken remains of his captain's chair, since there wasn't enough of it left for sitting. He operated almost entirely off screens projected by his personal holocom and the info he could see on the hardware at each bridge station. The corpse of yet another bridge casualty remained strewn across the astrogation table, his impact having rendered the whole apparatus useless until a technician could see to it.

Casey's damage-control teams had more pressing matters to address. *Argent* hadn't sent her foes packing without gaining scars of her own. The bridge had more holes in it, which the DC team busily sealed up as best they could. The power plant could no longer rise above 75 percent of its usual output unless Casey wanted to risk a cascading failure. Most importantly to him, *Argent* couldn't possibly get into FTL now . . . which, as far as he was concerned, dictated his course for the rest of the battle.

"Tell *Los Angeles* we're beat up and our missile tubes are empty," Casey said to his comms tech. "We'll do what we can with what we've got left. Helm! That strike group over there at three-four-zero by oh-four-oh. Pick a frigate and get us within long range. Might not hurt 'em, but let's at least make 'em dance."

• • •

The blast door opened only at the insistent override signals of Tanner's breaching kit. Tanner quickly yanked the contact cable back from the edges of the door as it parted at the center. Alicia swept around the corner with her assault rifle to check for any targets. She found none. "Clear," she said. "That's two lucky breaks. Anyone think we'll get a third?"

"You count that last firefight as a lucky break?" Tanner asked. The cable quickly snapped back into the boxy kit hanging at his hip from a shoulder strap.

Alicia shrugged. "There were only six of 'em."

"We can't seal this door behind us now, can we?" Baldwin wondered. She kept her eyes and her weapon trained on the passageway to their rear.

Tanner secured the kit and picked up his rifle again. "No clue how long it'll take the relays to reset. If we're lucky, it'll happen fast, but these kits have all the safety regulators removed. For all I know, it fried the whole door."

"Nothing for it now," said Alicia. "I think that's where we're going, up to the left. Go, I'll cover from here."

Tanner moved through the open portal to the passageway beyond. But for the blast door and its closed twin that lay thirty meters beyond it, the area looked much the same as the rest of the ship. Every hatch and door remained sealed. No one wandered about. Overhead lights flashed as if anyone might forget the ship was still at battle stations.

Their goal lay halfway along the corridor. Tanner and Baldwin rushed to the tall hatch, putting their backs to the bulkhead on either side. Tanner then reached for the manual wheel on the hatch and tested it with a gentle push. As soon as he felt the handle give, he let go. "We're good," he declared. Alicia then left her position to join them, stepping up along the bulkhead beside Baldwin.

"Might be best if you two lead." Alicia got between them to take hold of the wheel with one hand, her rifle still gripped in the other. "I'll cover from here and then secure the hatch."

Neither of her companions argued. They set their weapons against the bulkhead and filled their hands with stun grenades. "You ready?" Tanner asked.

"I haven't been ready for anything since I woke up this morning," Baldwin admitted. "They've gotta have this compartment guarded by now. You sure we can do this?"

"We made it this far." Tanner shrugged. Baldwin nodded. "On three?" he asked Alicia. "One. Two . . ."

Alicia threw the handle and pulled the hatch open. To Alicia's right, Baldwin reached around the corner of the open hatch to hurl in her grenades. Tanner stepped around Alicia to do the same. His first glimpse of the compartment inside showed him something akin to a similar space on *Los Angeles*: the hatch opened onto a thin walkway and railing surrounding a circular, mostly open compartment stretching down at least one deck, with a wide, cylindrical shaft filling up much of the compartment's center all the way up to the overhead. He saw no more. Alicia slammed the hatch shut as soon as the grenades were inside.

"One," she counted again. Tanner and Baldwin each pulled another stun grenade set to fly with a flick of the thumb. "Two," Alicia said. By the time she'd said, "Three," her companions had their weapons in hand. They heard the bursts of their first barrage of stun grenades, muffled by the hatch. "One more," she said tensely, and then, "Go!"

The team repeated their move, but this time Tanner and Baldwin moved inside after throwing their grenades. They both moved to the right as they entered, Tanner watching forward while Baldwin swept her gaze and her weapon in an arc to cover the rear. They found that the compartment extended downward through three decks, with another railed walkway immediately between them and the floor below. Only a handful of crewmen in NorthStar vac suits were on the top walkway or the one below it; most of the people in the compartment sat or leaned against workstations on the lowest deck, staggered by the stun grenades that continued to detonate.

Yet not everyone below the walkways succumbed to the blinding and deafening explosions. Several men in security uniforms held up well enough under the blasts to fire back, sending lasers and bullets up toward Tanner and the others. At a glance, Tanner figured that this security team had only just arrived and hadn't taken up positions yet, given that they were all on the bottom deck. The chaos of the assault threw off the security team's aim for a few critical seconds, allowing all three attackers to enter the compartment, but the pressure quickly rose on both sides as everyone exchanged fire.

Tanner rushed at the nearest crewman, jabbing him hard in the chest with the butt of his rifle and then shoving him into the bulkhead before moving past. Beyond that point stood a ladder running the full height of the compartment. Tanner hustled for it, hearing repeated bursts from Alicia's assault rifle behind him. He looked below to see several people dive for cover, though most were too stunned to do much more than fumble around. Baldwin took a couple shots as well, putting down one of the security troopers.

None of the shots directed at Tanner struck home before he made it to the ladder. He slung his rifle and threw himself over the side, gripping the rails lightly so he could slide down. At the bottom of the ladder, he felt the sudden impact of a harsh kick at his hip. Tanner gave ground, turned, and found himself faced with a noticeably larger man in a regular, unarmored crewman's jumpsuit who came in with a second kick. Someone else rushed him from the other side, wielding one tool or another—Tanner had no time to look.

His first opponent was competent but not especially skilled. Tanner caught the man's next kick with one arm and held the leg firm against his hip while he brought his opposite elbow down on it. That didn't save Tanner from the wrench that struck his right shoulder, but a careful shot from Alicia at the top walkway ensured it wouldn't happen again. His first opponent, the kicker, fell down screaming and clutching at his leg.

Tanner moved right and dove to the deck, realizing that anyone waiting for a clear shot against him now had it. Indeed, pulse lasers struck the bulkhead behind him as a security trooper tried to put him down. He scrambled to get behind the nearest control console. Tanner could hear Alicia's and Baldwin's guns up above, but he couldn't tell yet where their attention lay. He unslung his rifle, got to his feet in a crouching position, and tried to regain his bearings. He saw holo screens, cabinets bearing burns from pulse laser fire, and just enough reflective fixtures to have some small clue of who was shooting at him and from where.

Then he realized a frightened, unarmed NorthStar crewman lay on the deck right next to him with his hands covering his head. "Oh God, man, don't kill me!" the crewman shouted. "I don't even want to be here! I only signed up for the college money!"

"Yeah?" Tanner huffed. "Me, too." With that, he pushed himself around the console again and quickly drew down on the pair of security troopers across the small workspace. He put a pulse straight through one man's helmet, killing him instantly. The other trooper stood his ground and returned fire, clipping Tanner across the shoulder, but the combat jacket deflected most of the shot. Riding high on adrenaline and focused on his aim, Tanner didn't realize he'd been hit until a breath or two later. By then he'd cut down his second enemy. Then he looked at his shoulder and realized that for all the heat and resultant pain, he couldn't be all that wounded. The jacket had done its job.

He also realized that the shooting seemed to have stopped. The unarmed crewman beside him looked on in terror. Tanner pointed to a corner. "You go sit down right there and wait for someone to tie you up," he growled. "And turn off your helmet comm unit!"

"Okay! Okay! No argument!"

Tanner turned his attention to the rest of the compartment. He saw holo screens, monitoring stations, and control consoles. In all, it appeared that perhaps a dozen people manned this compartment. By and large, most were probably there to handle any sort of equipment failure or power problem. The actual direction and output of the whole compartment ran through one specific station.

With no one shooting at him, Tanner pulled the electric stunner from his belt to deal with the few frightened crewmen in his path to the master fire control station. Most of them, still affected by the stun grenades, never saw him coming and collapsed after a single shot. One NorthStar lieutenant heaved himself up in a feat of willpower, but Tanner's foot came up into the man's gut before he could reach the controls. Tanner didn't kick gently.

"Baldwin?" he asked.

"Right behind you," came her voice. He glanced back to see her only a few meters behind. "How the hell do we figure this thing out?"

"Military tech," he grunted as he looked over the controls. "Can't make things complicated if you want people to use it in stressful conditions."

The console offered power output control, a status board showing numerous other systems, and the tactical situation laid out across several flat screens. A helmeted face on another screen shouted out a warning, but luckily the on/off switch was plainly labeled right underneath it. Tanner killed the connection between the console and the bridge. All that mattered now was the tactical situation and fire control.

Hercules fled the main line of Archangel's fleet—or, at least, what was left of it. Tanner didn't count up ships, but he knew there were all too few contacts to the battleship's rear. As Sinclair warned, the battleship would soon be surrounded by one of the other enemy formations. The computer-generated display showed icons for each of the NorthStar ships, all of them flashing to indicate a full spread of defensive fire meant to protect the battleship.

He heard Baldwin's stunner go off as she put down anyone who still seemed conscious. Up above, Alicia ran across the walkway to secure the hatch on the opposite side from their point of entry. Tanner forced himself to take a slow, deep breath, and then another, his eyes moving across the controls the whole time.

He found the power regulator. Safety override. Targeting. His gaze returned to the tactical screens.

Hercules flew into the middle of a formation of other ships. A light cruiser would soon lay off to port. A destroyer loomed to the battleship's starboard. Both of them were at least sixty thousand klicks out. The closer ships, those that the escorts came to protect in the first place, were much closer to center.

Directly above *Hercules*, close enough that she could likely be seen with the naked eye, lay the assault carrier *Saratoga*. She looked undamaged and offered a steady output of both offensive and defensive fire.

She held thousands of landing troops and knew nothing of the danger beneath her.

Closest target, he thought. *Clearest shot.* He knew that such carriers were meant to drive in through planetary assaults, and therefore were likely well armored, but his goal wasn't outright destruction. He just needed to scare the hell out of the enemy forces.

As he expected, the targeting system was surprisingly simple. The override buttons were all clearly marked and covered so no one would ever accidentally push them. Tanner canceled *Saratoga*'s "friendly" status, aimed the battleship's cannons, and fired.

• • •

The man on Brent's back wasn't particularly heavy, given the lack of gravity outside *Hercules*'s hull, but he sure made everything awkward. He clung to Brent with his arms around the marine's shoulders and his legs wrapped around his sides. Though his arms and legs all worked fine, he couldn't get around out here on his own—not with his broken helmet wrapped in electrostatic tape.

Brent wondered why no one ever thought this particular task should be included in zero-g ops training.

"Second squad!" Brent shouted. "Regroup on my position! Topside aft laser turret! Topside! Williams, dammit, I see you! Form up on me!"

Up beyond him on the battleship's hull, another marine looked around in slight bewilderment. "I can't tell which one is you," complained a voice on the comm.

Brent almost sighed. "I'm the only fucker with someone else strapped to his back! Yeah, *now* you're looking at me. C'mon, let's go."

Lasers, shells, and missiles from the battleship's guns continued to provide unwelcome lighting and a sense of chaos. Brent had recognized the problem as soon as he'd made the jump—many of the boarders got confused or frightened as soon as they landed. Much as he'd wanted to get into the fight, he'd seen the need for guidance outside the hull and had taken up the task.

Then he'd found Sinclair against the turret, panicked and almost out of air. Brent had sealed up the signalman's helmet with the first thing to come to mind and then calmed him down, but that put a clock on how much more time he could spend on herding cats. Sinclair's remaining air cartridge would run out soon.

Brent didn't know how long ago he'd hit the deck. He already felt like he'd been there all day.

"You still good to fight, Sinclair?" he asked. Given the extra burden, Brent had to bend over and keep his hands as well as his feet on the deck. Crawling along on all fours made for slow going, but it beat getting flung out into the void.

"Yeah, I'm good, corporal," Sinclair said. His tone conveyed everything Brent needed to hear: the panic had passed. Sinclair was now more embarrassed than afraid. He'd be fine. "Get me inside so I can ditch my faceplate and I'll be okay."

"Good to hear. There's a maintenance hatch right ahead of us. Be there in a second."

Other marines from Brent's squad made it to the hatch before he did. They had it open by the time he reached them. "Okay, Sinclair, I'm gonna put you down and we'll guide you to the ladder, okay? Just—woah!"

The brilliant burst of orange light far above them stood out among the rest. No one heard anything, of course, but the light alone got everyone's attention.

"What?" Sinclair asked. "What's going on?"

Brent swallowed hard. He'd been afraid that assault carrier directly above them would start dropping shuttles full of armored troops on them any minute. Now it was so much burning gas and metal. He turned from the display and found his guys similarly distracted.

"Hey! Focus, guys. No time to gawk, we gotta get into this. Move."

• • •

Status boards and holo screens across the flag bridge flashed *Saratoga's* icon brightly with an unwelcome notification tone. The icon then went gray, remaining in place to mark the wreckage. On other screens, where computer-enhanced sensor graphics presented real-time images, the destruction of the assault carrier was much more dramatic.

Many personnel on the flag bridge had their attention focused on other matters. Everyone else seemed to stop in their tracks as if unable to process the development. The cannon blast must have gone straight through main engineering, or perhaps caught some part of a central magazine compartment. No one could know, or would ever know, until and unless a salvage crew could piece together the disaster. But they all knew the blast came from *Hercules*.

Commodore Eldridge looked on in shock. The next development, however, snapped his attention back to the battle at hand: the other ships of Expeditionary Group Alpha all changed course and kicked in their engines to get away from *Hercules*.

"Report," Eldridge croaked, and then cleared his throat. "Report! No, wait. Saraff! Tell those ships to get back into formation right now! Wagner," he said, hitting the connection to the command bridge, "Wagner, spin this ship over to keep that gun pointed away from the other carriers! And get it back under control, dammit! Kill the power if you have to!"

"We're working on it, sir," Wagner replied. "Diverting troops now. But we've got hostiles in thruster one and heading to main engineering, and it looks like thruster two is—"

"Deal with it, captain!" shouted Eldridge. He killed the connection and looked to Saraff. "I don't see those ships coming back!"

Saraff looked back to him with an obvious feeling of dread. "Sir, *Tuttle* and *Thermopylae* both want confirmation that we're not already under enemy control."

Eldridge growled, stomping over to Saraff's station. "They can't take this whole ship with the handful of boarders they've dropped off."

"Incoming corvettes!" yelled out another officer.

Eldridge's gaze snapped back to the tactical screens. Four more corvettes quickly approached. This time, *Hercules* had less acceleration and fewer friends.

• • •

"Cannon two! Haul ass, go! Go!" Harris barked at his team. He spun around as he gave the order, all but bowling a couple of his people over as he rushed through.

"What about main engineering?" asked Finch.

"Forget it! Let the regular grunts handle that. Hostiles took over cannon two and we're closest, so let's move."

"Any word how many?" Narendra wondered, following as instructed.

"No, shut up, I'm listening to updates!" Harris fumed.

With their armor on, the squad could only fit two abreast in the passageway. It made for more of a racket than he cared for, but he had to accept that a stealthy approach was out the window, anyway. The de facto dispatcher on the command bridge kept babbling on about *Saratoga* being blown out of the sky and not wanting anything else to take such a hit. After a few seconds, Harris gave up and tuned the woman out. She didn't seem to know how many hostiles were in the compartment, anyway.

He stopped at one of the emergency ladder wells. "Okay, cannon two goes down from here to deck three, so we're gonna hit it on all three levels. Soldan, Clark, you're on top here. Just keep on going down the passageway. Finch, Eickenberry, you stay up here on deck one as well, but sweep around and go in from the port side. Secure the top deck and then shoot your way down, like an air assault. Bishop, you and Narendra go down the ladder well over there and enter on deck two, starboard side. Hold the level, don't try to advance unless Soldan or I tell you, got me? Patrick, you're with me. We go in on deck three."

The team split up quickly per his instructions. Half of them remained on the top deck, while the rest took the ladder well down. Given the benefit of their recon armor, they more or less dropped from level to level rather than using the steps.

"I want aimed fire in this one," Harris said as he and Patrick rushed to their destination. Soldan and the others topside gave the silent green signal to indicate readiness. Bishop and Narendra followed. "We've got friendlies in there and we want to get that cannon up and running again, so don't hose the place down. Rely on your armor. No stray shots—if you don't have a clear shot, do not pull the trigger. Slug it out if you have to. Eickenberry, I'm talkin' to you, got me?"

"Sir, yes, sir!" came the response.

Harris scowled, but let it go. It's not like he didn't want to hear exactly that. He looked to Patrick, nodded, and then hit the go signal.

• • •

Tanner pushed back his faceplate, suddenly feeling constricted by the helmet's seals around his neck and its snug fit on his skull. He looked with wide eyes at the displays. *Saratoga* remained on the screen, but its icon turned to a faded gray. The system did that to make sure people could keep track of ships lost in combat.

Where's Saratoga? someone might ask. *Didn't they come out here with us? I don't see them on the boards anymore.*

A screen made a quick damage assessment: "Target eliminated. Engine room critical likely. No signals in debris field." Another screen replayed a high-resolution image of the ship as it exploded. The console also reported the cannon's current charge—low, needing a moment to reset and change out burned components on an automated reset function—but with a standard countdown showing when the cannon would be ready again. Behind him, the round shaft running from floor to ceiling that contained the cannon's main power supply went back into recharge mode.

Business as usual.

"Tanner?" asked Baldwin. She wrapped up the wrists of another unconscious tech off to one side of the console, looking up at him with concern. He heard it in her voice, at least. He couldn't see her actual expression, what with the faceplate.

He glanced up at the walkways, where Alicia now disappeared behind the power supply shaft on her way to wire up deck two's starboard side hatch with a mine just like the others. That was her idea of "securing" a door. She didn't even blink at this. It was her element.

"I'm fine," he replied. Something felt wrong about that—it was the truth, and *that* was what bothered him—but he'd have to deal with it later. "Alicia, how we doing?"

"One more to go on this level," she said, hustling around the walkway. The few crewmen on her level all lay still, thoroughly incapacitated by all the electric shocks, concussive grenade blasts, and punches and kicks of the small team's initial entry. "If you can—"

Explosions from up above cut off her words. They erupted at both hatches on deck one and the port hatch of deck two, causing Alicia to reflexively throw herself down on deck two's walkway. At one side of the compartment, a pair of men in charred, battered suits of recon armor tumbled over the walkway rails. Another fell through the flame and smoke at the other hatch, collapsing in a heap.

The starboard side hatch on deck two flew open as well, but this one didn't explode. Alicia hadn't gotten there in time to rig one of her mines yet. Two more rangers in recon armor came through with their weapons up, looking for targets.

The captured NorthStar gunnery crew, still mostly groggy at best, did what they could to huddle against any bulkhead or console they found across all three levels of the compartment. Virtually all of them were now bound and more or less helpless. A few screamed.

With his back to the control console, Tanner shot a glance to the hatch on his right. It didn't open. The one on the other side of the compartment flew back, however, and two more rangers appeared. Tanner and Baldwin both dove for cover, but neither of the attackers fired a shot right away.

Alicia was not so lucky. The two rangers on her level spotted her and opened fire, stepping around the open hatch onto the walkway with little regard for cover. With her rifle slung over her shoulder, Alicia reacted with the weapon already in hand. She hit the mine's activator and hurled it forward, then threw herself into a backward somersault on the deck to get clear.

The blast pushed her away painfully, but it was much worse for the aspiring NorthStar ranger who stood closest to the mine. It landed face down at Narendra's feet, detonating as soon as it hit the deck. Her armor and her body absorbed most of the blast for Bishop, moving in behind her, but even he was knocked over.

Despite the flame and debris falling from the starboard side of the compartment, Baldwin found more safety there than she did on the opposite side with the other two rangers coming in. The two armored bodies from deck one now lay nearby on deck three, smoldering and sparking but otherwise not moving. Baldwin rushed for the corpses, figuring their broken armor would still offer sturdier cover than the computer consoles.

Tanner found himself stuck behind little more than a tool cabinet. Rapid-fire lasers flashed through the metal casing at its top, forcing him to cringe, but he dared to lean around the side and shoot back with his pulse rifle. He saw only one attacker coming around the huge power supply shaft toward him and realized the other would likely move in the opposite direction. Tanner fired away and managed to clip the armored figure's leg, but his pulse rifle seemed to have no effect. "Aw, fuck me," Tanner muttered, then scrambled away from his tool cabinet as the recon trooper's stream of fire shifted downward and annihilated the whole fixture.

Baldwin grabbed one shoulder of the corpse in front of her and heaved it up to get the body lying on its side to offer a little more cover. She caught a name tag that said "Soldan" with a brief glance, but paid it little mind. Like Tanner, she realized the enemy would likely split to go around both sides of the power-supply shaft. She snatched one more grenade off her belt—this one considerably more lethal than her now exhausted supply of stun grenades—and hurled it around the shaft. If nothing else, it would give the enemy pause while she figured out what she could do.

Though her legs and her back felt like they might be on fire, Alicia forced herself to her side and got her rifle off her shoulder. She fired a couple of bursts at the fumbling form of the armored ranger just a few meters away from her, now separated by a hole in the walkway and some mangled railing, but she couldn't tell if it did much good. Between the smoke and the stress, she wasn't sure if she'd hit him until her third burst, when she saw sparks against the armor.

Laser fire came down at her from above and behind, striking the walkway beside her and forcing her to roll closer to the bulkhead for protection. She looked back over her shoulder and found another of the rangers, this one a bit blackened by her mine but otherwise fine. His angle of fire wasn't good, but he could keep her pinned just by staying where he was . . . and she knew he didn't really have to do that.

"Baldwin!" Alicia shouted. "Tanner! Get out of here! Just go!"

The shooting from above stopped. *"Tanner?"* blurted the recon trooper.

Hiding behind the main control console, Tanner looked up at the sound of his name. The blackened ranger leapt over the rails from deck one to come down onto his level. "Tanner motherfucking Malone, is that you?" he shouted, sounding almost giddy.

"Do I know you?" Tanner called back.

"Hold up!" shouted the ranger Tanner had clipped, whom he now took for the leader. "Dammit, Eickenberry, I said—"

"Aw Christ," Tanner grunted before his old antagonist charged straight for the console, crashing straight through it. Though Tanner managed to avoid being pinned by anything, the impact of so much metal and weight all across his body sent him tumbling across the deck.

"Wow, I fucking dreamt about running into you again!"

"Eickenberry," demanded the other man behind him, "finish it or get out of the fucking way!"

"Relax, Harris, I've got this!"

Tanner pulled the pistol from his side holster. "Einstein," he croaked, "this is a really bad time—"

"Don't call me that!" Einstein roared, grabbing Tanner by the back of his coat and heaving him up over his head. "You think you're fucking funny with that name? Huh?" He slammed Tanner into a nearby console, knocking the gun from his hand. "I bet fuckin' Janeka's on this ship, too, huh? Is she? I'm gonna find her and kill her ass when I'm done with you. This is what they were trainin' us for all along, isn't it? This is what I wasn't good enough for?"

Tanner coughed. "Well, you *did* kinda suck at everything."

"Aaargh!" Einstein roared, slamming Tanner against the console again.

On the walkway above, Alicia had no idea Tanner was in such trouble. Her armored opponent recovered and moved in, firing in a deadly arc with his pulse rifle before leaping over the hole in the walkway. Alicia withdrew as best she could, knowing her guns were almost useless against that armor. Other boarders carried heavier weapons for such a problem, but none were here now. She'd have to handle this the hard way.

The ranger kept advancing. Alicia grabbed her last stun grenade, dropped it at her feet, and then launched herself toward the ranger's feet. Though she knew anything as formidable as powered recon armor would have audio and visual protection, the stun grenade would hopefully, at least, provide a moment's distraction— and it did. Rather than shoot her or catch her, the ranger flinched and stepped back from the blast.

The concussion shook Alicia up, too, but she pushed past it. In a flash, she was on her feet again and behind her opponent. Spinning in a full circle, Alicia delivered a forceful kick to the ranger's lower back. It knocked him up against the walkway railing, throwing him off balance.

Corporal Bishop got his bearings in time for his opponent to tackle him, which seemed crazy against someone in powered armor. She had nothing but a combat jacket and a helmet. Bishop reached back, grabbing at her combat jacket to pull her off.

Then the heated knife in her hand pierced the flexible material at the back of his neck, along with his flesh and his spine.

Tanner couldn't get to his knife. He couldn't do much of anything other than try to brace himself as Einstein slammed him into things—which, at this point, he couldn't identify. Maybe a bulkhead. Maybe a computer console. Maybe a car for all he could tell. Then Einstein held him up in the air again and threw him into another computer console, which Tanner crashed straight through and onto the deck beyond.

He couldn't tell where he was in the compartment, or who else might still be fighting, but he heard Einstein cheering for himself. That much was easy enough to make out.

"You see, asshole? Who's getting the last laugh now, huh?" Einstein prodded.

Tanner didn't answer. Hurting from head to toe, he patted himself down for weapons. His guns were gone. He was out of grenades. About the only things he had now were his knife, a useless electric stunner, ammo for weapons he couldn't reach, and his breaching kit.

He threw the charging switch on the breaching kit and began unspooling the cable from the box, letting it hit the deck in a pile at his side.

"They pay me three times what you make in that fuckin' militia," Einstein continued, "and I'm just getting started! You see the gear they give me?" he asked, stalking around the computer console to get at Tanner again. "You get anything like this in the fucking Archangel Navy?"

Black contact cable whipped out from around the console. Tanner caught Einstein across the hip with the cable, lashing out with enough force that the cable wrapped itself partway around his waist. As soon as he saw contact, Tanner hit the power button on the breaching kit, sending a powerful burst of electric pulses and override signals through the armor.

Seals popped all across Einstein's armor. Others locked up. A second later, the armor's antitheft system recognized the false signals sent by the kit and reacted as designed. From ankle to shoulder, every joint within the armor fused violently. Circuitry all along the chest piece and the legs overheated and melted.

Einstein howled in agony before he fell to the deck in a smoking ruin.

"No," Tanner huffed, "but I read the user manual once."

"Aw Christ, it *is* you," said a voice. Tanner looked up to find the one Einstein called Harris standing not far away, his rifle trained on Tanner. "I thought I recognized your face. Tough show, kid, but Eickenberry had it right. You just joined up with the wrong tea—"

Dazzling bolts of green light struck Harris from the side, plunging right into and through his body in a rapid burst. He didn't scream so much as gurgle as he collapsed under the barrage of plasma blasts, which stopped as suddenly as he began.

"Not everything is about Tanner!" shouted Baldwin from across the compartment. Tanner looked over to find her slumped against the two charred and battered rangers that had fallen from deck one, holding a large weapon in her hand with a power cable that ran to one of the corpses beside her.

"Plasma repeaters!" she huffed, holding up the heavy weapon. "Do you believe this shit? They give these guys fucking plasma repeaters!"

Tanner staggered out from behind the computer console. "Alicia?" he called out. He heard nothing, nor did he see hostiles or any threatening movement from the still bound and terrified members of the gun crew. He gingerly bent over Harris's corpse to pick up the man's rifle before continuing on past Baldwin, who remained at her spot where she could keep hold of her newfound fire superiority.

"Alicia, you there?" he asked, looking up toward the smoking ruin of the catwalk. He saw two sets of recon armor lying in the wreckage, but not his friend. *"Alicia?"*

"I'm down here," came her voice. Tanner turned his attention lower and rushed around the power supply shaft to find Alicia lying underneath the body of one last ranger. This one, too, remained motionless, with a knife embedded to its hilt up underneath his jaw. Alicia tried to push herself free of the heavy body. "Had to jump down on this one," she grumbled.

"You okay?" Tanner asked, moving over to lift some of the weight off her.

She let out an exasperated grunt. "Not really. You look pretty beat up, too."

Shots rang out from up above, just beyond the blasted entry hatches. Alicia and Tanner could hear lasers, assault rifle fire, and shouts. Tanner grabbed Alicia's wrist and heaved her the rest of the way out from under the armored corpse, wincing in pain all the while. "Ow, ribs, ow, ow." He winced, though he persevered until she was free.

Shouts and gunshots grew closer. Baldwin rolled over to lie on the other side of Soldan's corpse so she could point the plasma repeater up toward the open hatch where the noise continued. Tanner and Alicia hadn't yet made it to cover when a pair of men in NorthStar vac suits, holding laser rifles, dove through the charred hatch, turned to fire back—and were promptly cut down from outside the compartment.

"Donner," called a voice from one charred hatch.

"Blitzen!" answered Alicia and Baldwin in unison, though Tanner reflexively croaked out, "Party."

A tall Archangel marine stepped around the corner on deck two, his pulse rifle up but ready. He quickly looked over the scene and then slid back the faceplate of his helmet. "Hey, you guys okay down there?" asked Ravenell.

"Oh Jesus, am I glad to see you!" Alicia sighed. Baldwin slumped against the armored corpse. Tanner, too, let out a relieved breath, leaning against a maintenance console. "What's going on?"

"We've got about half a squad together on deck two here. They've already got people guarding the command bridge, though, and they've got it sealed up tight. We think there's an ES generator protecting the whole compartment, plus a lot of guys guarding the passageway. I dunno how we're gonna get it open. Lieutenant Thompson sent me out to find more help. Shit, are you sure you're all okay?"

Alicia looked to the others. Tanner didn't answer; he turned away from the conversation and started looking around for something, though she didn't know what. Baldwin gave a shrug. "We're banged up, but we're fine," replied Alicia. "It's just the three of us." She glanced around the compartment and at her companions. "I don't think we can hold this space."

"Maybe we oughta power down the whole cannon?" suggested Baldwin. "That way if they retake the compartment, they'll have to rev the system up again. Might at least stall 'em."

"Or blow out the controls." Alicia frowned. "Rav, I'm out of explosives. You got any?"

Ravenell shook his head. "No, I lost most of mine in the jump. Used the rest. That's what I'm sayin', I don't know how we're gonna get inside the bridge even if we can get past . . . Tanner?" he asked. "You okay?"

Tanner slumped down next to a cabinet, jerking it open and rummaging through its contents. Then he opened up the next.

Baldwin rose. "I think Tanner needs a first aid kit."

"Tool kit," he grunted.

Baldwin blinked. "What?"

Tanner opened the next cabinet drawer, reached in, and pulled out a black binder full of ordinary paper pages. He looked back to the corpse at Baldwin's feet. "Is that . . . That plasma repeater is attached to him, right?" Tanner huffed. "We're gonna need a tool kit."

THIRTEEN

Blood, Sweat, and Tears

"Sometimes I think about all those normal goals like going to college, getting my dream job, and finding someone special, and I realize I'm starting to look at them like they're tactical objectives. Like I have to fight my way through some bad guys to get to them. Then I wonder how long I'll feel like this, or if I'll start thinking that way about getting the groceries or doing my laundry. And then I think maybe just living in some small house with a bunch of cats and not giving a shit about the rest of the world actually sounds like a good plan."
—MA3 Tanner Malone, Unsent Letter, December 2276

Captain Paulson saw it all unravel with the destruction of *Saratoga*. She'd been fully engrossed in the pair of struggles fought by her own battleship, *Andromeda*—the one between spaceships across thousands of kilometers and the chaos raging within her own hull—when *Saratoga* blew apart. The moment shocked her. It stunned a fair number of her officers and, from what she saw on the tactical screens, it apparently had the same effect on several other ships.

Like many officers of her rank and age, Harriet Paulson was a student of military history. It was the kind of thing discussed at war colleges and officers' retreats. Seeing the brief flare of destruction on her screens and the slight pause in the shooting, a small corner of her mind recalled the Battle of the Nile, hundreds of years ago. She thought of the destruction of the French flagship, *Orient*, and how the spectacular explosion so shocked both the British and French that the fighting ended for a good ten minutes. Nelson, the books said, dropped several boats into the water to help recover survivors.

For that pause, lasting no longer than a couple of breaths, Paulson wondered how this might play out. Then Lai Wa's destroyer squadron tightened up around their expeditionary group—three full assault carriers at its center—and they all visibly altered course to back farther away from the battle.

Paulson snapped out of her reverie. "Son of a bitch," she fumed and jabbed a button at the personal comm panel on her chair. "Captain Leung, I have you withdrawing from the fight. Please advise!"

Leung's face appeared on her screen. "Captain Paulson," she said, "we cannot risk closing with you or the other battleships while you are compromised. We are establishing a safe distance until you regain full control."

"No, you can't do that," Paulson argued, "you'll leave us open for more of those corvettes! If we tighten up now, we can ward them off and get a handle on the boarding situations and resolve this."

"Captain, we both see what happened to *Saratoga*," Leung replied firmly. "I cannot risk a similar fate for one of my assault carriers."

"You've got a full destroyer squadron on top of your carrier group! At least send them in. We're too thinned out already here!"

"My first duty is to protect my own people, captain."

"Dammit, Leung, you're a part of this task force! You can't leave us hanging like this!"

"Your company insisted on taking the lead, captain," said Leung, her tone infuriatingly emotionless. "If you cannot control your ships, I must exercise my own command judgment. Confirm that you have full control and I will move in once more."

Paulson balled her hands up into fists. She'd never wanted to punch another woman so much in her life. "They don't have control of *Andromeda*," she said through gritted teeth, "they're just running around causing—"

"Hostiles in main engineering!" shouted out one of Paulson's bridge officers.

"Two more corvettes coming in!" warned another. "We can't catch them!"

Though Leung's expression barely changed, Paulson could see that the other captain overheard both announcements all too well. Lai Wa's field commander turned to one side and barked out a command in Chinese. With that, the connection went dead.

• • •

"Attention Group Two, Charlie Wing. Priority extraction required at *Los Angeles*. Say again, priority extraction at *Los Angeles*. Any combat-capable unit, please respond."

Though the cruiser remained on the tactical screens, *Los Angeles* fell back from the fighting. The wreckage of NorthStar's cruiser *Lovejoy* lay between *Los Angeles* and what was left of the battleship *Ursa's* remaining escorts. *Los Angeles* couldn't keep up with *Hercules* when the battleship fled for the protection of her own lines, and *Halley* stayed out of action. With that fight decided, *Archangel's* flagship had turned to get into the fight with the next closest battleship group.

That courage bought *Los Angeles* another nasty beating. Burning gases continued to spew from one of her main thrusters, now reduced to a pile of jagged metal. One of her primary cannons was gone. Computer images at this distance couldn't make out more detail than that, so God only knew how much of her atmosphere she'd lost—or how much of her crew.

A bloodstained vac suit glove reached out to tap the comms panel. Frost continued to spread over the blood on all four fingers. With no air to keep things warm, most of the rest of the blood in the compartment had already frozen up. Emergency sealing foam sat in a hardened bulge on the wrist below the glove, a rash but necessary measure taken to stay in the raging battle amid an airless compartment.

Thankfully, whoever dreamt up all the code words for this flight kept things simple from the start. Charlie Wing contained all of the corvettes assigned to drop troops onto the enemy battleships. Anyone still carrying troops was in Group One. Once a corvette made its drop, it fell into Group Two, which kept busy after those runs by engaging in anything smaller than a cruiser . . . though a few such corvettes had their hands full with just holding together.

Joan of Arc fit both descriptions.

No one else responded to the call from *Los Angeles*. That couldn't surprise anyone. Though both sides had taken serious losses, the fight continued on. Any corvette still capable of combat was still engaged. *Joan of Arc* could only answer by virtue of having just dispatched one of the enemy's corvettes mere seconds ago. That match could easily have gone the other way.

Lieutenant Kelly responded by voice, though she had to stop and swallow after her first syllable. "*Los* . . . *Los Angeles*, *Joan of Arc*. We can take the job."

"*Joan of Arc*, please advise of your combat status, over."

"Minor hull damage, some life support loss. We're down to beam weapons only. No more missiles in our tubes." She coughed once, which made her wince in pain. Her wrist wasn't the only part of her body covered in sealing foam. Shrapnel had gotten into her right hip and her thigh. "Three crew casualties. Two dead, one wounded. We're still flying."

She waited through the expected pause. "Copy, *Joan of Arc*. Proceed to *Los Angeles*."

With the helm still under her manual control, Kelly turned *Joan of Arc* down and hard to port. She lit up the corvette's thrusters, heading quickly for *Los Angeles*. "XO," she said on the ship's comm, "we're breaking off to pick up some passengers. Let's make sure we do this quick."

"Aye, aye, skipper," replied Booker's voice. "We're on it." He paused. "You okay up there?"

"I'll be fine," said Kelly. "No time to deal with it right now. By the time anyone got to me, I'd need them back at their post, anyway. Let's all stay focused."

"Aye, aye," Booker repeated. She heard him call out instructions to the rest of the crew.

Kelly's eyes shut tightly as she took in a deep, shaking breath. She didn't have time to think about anything but the enemy corvette trying to kill hers while it was still there. Now it was gone, and she had at least a minute or so before she'd link up with *Los Angeles*. When her eyes opened again, she tried to keep them fixed on the control console and the tactical screens in front of her, despite the holes and the cracks in *Joan*'s armored bridge canopy.

Better to stare at the screens than to look at the frozen bodies of Stan and Chief Romita lying on the deck.

• • •

Second Squad, First Platoon—*Hercules's* own—hardly knew what hit them.

They arrived at main engineering in good order, holding together and moving quickly while the other two squads from First Platoon were held up by engineers fleeing their posts and by the confused instructions from the battalion HQ section trying to run things from the battleship's hangar bay. Under orders from their platoon leader, Second Squad hurried up two levels to come into main engineering from deck seven, entering through the narrow maze of cooling conduits that led into the broader workshop space at the maze's end.

They found a pair of Archangel marines hurriedly wiring the compartment with explosives and shot them both down in a brief exchange of gunfire. Slowing down to confirm that none of the bombs were actually set to blow, the squad pushed in.

From out of nowhere, pulse rifle fire cut down both Corporal Swanson and Private Meeks.

"Cover!" ordered Staff Sergeant Newitz. "There! Shooter's over there! Get fire on—" He didn't get out the rest of his order. The pulse laser blast that cut straight through his helmet saw to that.

Their opponent slipped behind a support beam, fired again with a blast that all but took off Jensen's leg before he could make it to cover, and then ducked back into the shadows. Jensen lay on the deck howling in pain and shock.

"Someone check on the sarge!" yelled Gulati.

"He's dead! Shit, there's a hole right through his helmet!"

Private Masters fired off a few rounds of suppressing fire so he could look out from behind his tool cabinet and check on Swanson and Meeks. Gulati tried to cover him, but then Masters suddenly tumbled to the ground, clutching at something in his throat while blood poured out all over him from the wound.

Gulati pulled Masters back around the corner by his legs. Blood spurted everywhere. "Oh God, it's a *knife*!" Gulati yelled. "Who the fuck uses throwing knives?"

Their squad leader lay dead. A whole fire team was down. Jensen lay on the deck screaming where no one could get to him. Masters kept on bleeding to death right in front of everyone.

"Get off my ship," she demanded from the shadows. At least, the voice sounded like a woman's. The gender wasn't nearly as easy to determine as the mood.

Hiding behind a cable distribution panel, Lance Corporal Subong tried to catch his breath and think. He was already of a mind to fill the workshop compartment with grenades, but every third order on the comm system was to limit damage and protect ships' equipment. That concern ran so deeply that the heavy weapons platoons were all still down in the hangar bay waiting for orders while the rest of the ship's battalion spread out to secure every vital space they could.

"I said," repeated the woman's low, angry voice, "get off my ship."

Subong looked over to his other comrades, wanting to give an order, but he saw Donati's eyes flare. "Kiss my ass, you fucking—" Donati began, whirling around the side of another gear locker to light up the compartment with his assault rifle, but he never finished his retort. He fired wildly toward his enemy, who took an extra second to aim and put him down with three holes in his chest.

Subong decided he'd had enough. "Okay, fuck it," he hissed, yanking a grenade off his belt—only to see one much like it clatter to the floor at his feet. "Grenade!" Subong yelled, diving away before the thing detonated and sent shrapnel, flame, and debris flying everywhere.

"Get off my ship!" the woman demanded again, her voice now impossibly loud in the wake of the exploding grenade. Subong felt himself lifted up off his feet by hands at his shoulders.

"C'mon," shouted the wailing voice of one of his comrades, "we gotta get out of here!"

"What?" Subong exclaimed. He'd lost his laser rifle, and so he pulled his pistol. "No, get a grip, dammit! Turn around!"

He followed his own advice. Subong wrenched free of the two marines carrying him, got his feet on the deck, and turned. Private Gould was there in his line of vision, just a couple meters back from Subong and the others. For some reason, though, Gould didn't follow. He stood there in a weird posture, his hips thrust forward while his shoulders leaned too far back and his head tilted forward with a big, wet, red spot in his chest and a little gleaming bit of metal sticking through at the center.

Then Subong saw the extra legs behind Gould's body, and the hand that grabbed his comrade's assault rifle before it fell to the floor, and the flash of the rifle's muzzle. Bullets came flying down the corridor, many of them ricocheting wildly, while the woman demanded yet again, *"Get the fuck off my ship!"*

He ran. His friends ran with him. They ran for the nearest avenue of escape, not questioning the merits of taking one corner or another. The bullets and the shouts chased them until they came to the first path out of the corridor they could find, and it didn't matter at all to them that it led to one of the ship's lifeboats. The remaining men of Second Squad piled inside. Someone slammed the hatch closed behind them. Someone else—no one would ever rightly remember whom—hit the button to launch the lifeboat without a second thought. The lifeboat blasted away from *Hercules*, leaving a sealed hatch in its wake.

Janeka let the body fall away. She doubled back into the workshop, where one of the NorthStar marines still lay on the deck half-screaming and half-whimpering. The noise was terrible, but her own people took priority. She knelt at their sides, checking for life signs. Only one still clung to life, despite the hole in his gut.

"Thibert," she said. "Thibert, you with me?"

"Gunny? I'm hit."

She already had her first aid kit out. "I know. You're gonna make it." She cut open his combat jacket with her heated knife and placed a self-compressing bandage over his wound. Several hypo shots fell from her kit onto the deck. She picked one up and injected it in Thibert's leg, ensuring that he'd stay out of shock and easing his pain.

"I'm sorry, gunny."

"Don't be sorry. You did good. You survived and you held 'em until I could get here. I'm proud of you both."

"Where's Zacapa?" he asked.

Janeka shook her head. "Don't worry about Zacapa. You stay awake, you hear me? Stay awake. I have one other thing to do." She picked up another shot and strode over to the moaning enemy marine.

Janeka grabbed the man by the chin of his helmet and leaned in, her eyes staring at his through her faceplate and his visor. "You will not die," she told him firmly. "Your wound is cauterized. I've got a hypo shot right here." She jabbed him with the hypo gun as she spoke and then dragged him over to one side of the bulkhead, lingering only long enough to pull the pistol and knife from his belt and toss them to the other side of the compartment. Then she drew the electric stunner from her belt and gave the fallen man a solid jolt, knocking him unconscious.

"Donner!" called out a voice from an interior entrance.

"Blitzen." Janeka stood and turned toward the trio of Archangel boarders before her. "Two wounded, one of 'em ours," she said, quickly crossing the workshop to leave via the same route her reinforcements took to join her. "I can't stay. Finish setting up the charges and get both our guys out of here before you seal up the compartment. Pull him out, too," she added, gesturing to the wounded NorthStar trooper against the far bulkhead. "You hear me?"

"Will do, gunny."

She didn't wait to say more. Janeka needed to be in a dozen different places, all of them vital and all of them under fire. Deciding on the closest and most critical spot on the list, Janeka doubled back farther into main engineering, wishing she could have moved faster.

She'd trained both Thibert and Zacapa in Whiskey Company. Thibert had broken Fort Stalwart's record on the four-mile run. Zacapa had a gift for drawing. Both had done fine on their previous assignments, and both survived the jump and the fight to get this far. They'd fought to hold the workshop. They'd done everything right. Janeka would tell Thibert that, and Zacapa's family, if she survived this.

A person could do everything right in a battle and still wind up dead. Anyone. Even the ones the rest all looked up to.

Coming to the last junction before main engineering, Janeka slowed and spotted the sentry just past the open hatch. Little of the navy crewman showed—just the edge of her helmet and her rifle—but that was what Janeka wanted to see. "Donner," she called out, and waited for the countersign before she emerged from the corridor and hustled into the compartment.

Inside main engineering, Janeka found smoke, blaring alarms, and the dull but ever-present vibration of the battleship's huge fuel cell–driven engines. Navy engineers crawled halfway under machinery and up onto exposed catwalks to hurriedly cut power to the rest of the ship, with officers and enlisted ratings taking on dirty or dangerous jobs with no regard for risk or rank. At many points, they skipped straight to disconnecting conduits manually rather than try to deal with unfamiliar computer controls.

Hercules had to be forced out of the fight but not shut down cold. At this stage of the battle, the boarding team didn't want the battleship's ES reinforcement to fall, let alone main life support or other vital systems. But above all else, *Hercules* had to be taken out of the fight and not allowed to return.

Though the engineering work took full priority, Janeka, the other marines, and a good number of other navy personnel were focused on holding main engineering and its adjacent compartments. Firefights raged in a number of directions and at several levels. Archangel's forces took full advantage of the choke points and natural cover offered by their surroundings. The battlefield offered one benefit: given the danger of a misfire hitting a fuel cell container or penetrating one of the main engines, the enemy couldn't use heavy weapons or serious explosives.

Unfortunately, Archangel's people had similar restrictions. The chance of one stray shot causing a total catastrophe remained even with the limited selection of weapons on both sides.

Wounded men and women lay on the deck near one of the larger fuel cell lockers, a spot chosen by Corpsman Matuskey—the only one of his rating to make it this far—because it was out of the way and unlikely to receive heavy fire. Janeka strode past the impromptu triage station to a set of desks and computer consoles up beyond the pair of main engines, which rose up two full decks and reached at least another deck below her current spot. At the desks, she found a small handful of fellow boarders surrounded by holo screens and captured and bound NorthStar crewmen. They worked with their faceplates up, allowing her to see their stress and grim concentration.

One man in a blue marine vac suit did most of the talking. Janeka didn't interrupt as she arrived. "If Wilkins doesn't think she can hold that passageway, tell her to blow it as best she can and pull back. We can't spare enough people to back her up. Not now. Get on it, sergeant." He turned from that matter to the next without taking a breath. "La Rocca, I've got a job for you. Backtrack from here to our access point. Take some of that paint from that locker there. I want you to mark out the path for our guys, okay? Put some big red arrows on the deck if you have to. I don't care what you do. But let's mark out a clear route for the next boarding team that gets dropped off on the hull so they get straight here. We need reinforcements. Go."

The men took off. Their leader glanced over to Janeka with dark eyes and a darker frown. "Gunny, got any good news for me?"

"Workshop in deck five is secure. Much as we can get it," she said with a shake of her head. "Two casualties, one wounded prisoner. Came back fast as I could, captain." She glanced around their surroundings. "How many have we got?" she asked, gesturing to the prisoners.

"Seventeen." Captain Alvarado shrugged. "Yeah, I know, I'd rather put them somewhere else, too, but right now there is nowhere else. Unless I want to put them with the wounded. Doesn't seem like a good idea."

Janeka shook her head in agreement. "No, sir, it doesn't. No word from Captain MacAllan?"

"None. Looks like I'm running the show in here on my own unless we get another drop of reinforcements."

She glanced up to ensure that the captain's last remaining aide had his attention elsewhere. "You're doing fine, sir," she said. "No second guessing. Make decisions and stick with them until you're sure they aren't working and then fix them." She paused long enough to see him nod. "Orders, sir?"

His eyes turned down toward an open binder full of deck layouts found on a shelf in another compartment. It proved far more accurate than anything provided by Naval Intelligence. He indicated different spots on the layouts as he spoke. "We've got hostiles attempting to breach here, here, and here. Can't seal the blast doors at any of these spots. This central passageway is the widest, and it also offers a straight shot into this whole section of the ship without a line of fire on either of the main engines or any of the fuel cell lockers. I expect they'll bring up heavy lasers or plasma repeaters as soon as they figure that out, and then we'll have a real problem holding." He looked back up at her. "I've got six people up there now and a buck sergeant holding them together. They could probably use your help. Lieutenant Quincy says his guys should only need another ten or fifteen minutes with the engines," he added, making a face as if to add that he understood full well what an eternity that could mean in combat. "He can't cut anyone loose until then, so for now this is what we've got. I'll send you whoever else I can if you give a shout. Might wind up just being me."

"Yes, sir," Janeka grunted, then took off running. Behind her, she heard a pop and an electric sizzle along with an agonized shriek from one of the engineers, but she couldn't stop to help. The calls for a corpsman weren't meant for her.

Janeka's path took her aft of the ship's main engine space and past another set of consoles, most of them shot full of holes. This end of the large compartment offered somewhat more open space than the rest, which along with the broader entryway suggested it was where large equipment and supplies came through. She found the defenders evenly split on either side of the entrance with gunfire coming in from farther down the corridor beyond them. The tall doors remained wide open in a silent confirmation that they were too damaged to close once more. Spotting sergeant's stripes on one man's sleeve, Janeka rolled to his side of the entrance while bullets and laser fire shot past.

"Sergeant!" she said. "Came to help you out. Anything to tell me beyond the obvious?"

The sergeant ducked back around the corner while his other two comrades kept firing. "Not really," he replied, "other than the fact that we're all out of grenades. We've taken down a few of them, but the longer this goes on, the more of 'em show up. They're putting out light fire now compared to a few seconds ago."

Janeka scowled. "That can't be a good sign. All right, we can't hold them here all day and we can't fall back, so we're gonna have to advance and push them back from around their corner instead. There's a load lifter back that way. I'll take over here. You take one of your guys to get the lifter unfastened and running, and we'll roll it down the passageway loaded up with—"

A stuttering, high-pitched whistle and the screams of men outside of her arm's reach cut off the rest of her words. Red laser blasts half a foot in diameter cut through two men on the other side of the entrance, leaving metal sagging from the corner of the bulkhead in their wake. The other three marines all jerked back around their corner rather than risk exposure.

"Damn," Janeka spat. She rolled to the deck, coming around the corner in a prone position and firing before she saw the fat, squat infantry laser cannon mounted on its rolling tripod at the other end of the passageway. "Captain!" she called on her helmet comm. "We've got heavy weapons down here!"

She fired carefully, heedless of the wide flashes of lethal red light that came back in return from the cannon and the gunfire offered by the men moving up around it in support. Janeka took the foot off the man behind the cannon, sending him screaming to the deck, but her following shots couldn't disable the tripod. The metal was too strong.

A new cannoneer took the first one's place. The weapon fired again. Her fellow marines fought on, but yet another of them died in a sudden flash of light.

"Perimeter breach aft of the engines!" she shouted into the comm. "Aft section! Get people up here right now!"

• • •

No one needed to follow any signs or consult a map to find the command bridge. The loud, intense, and sustained exchange of gunfire provided a perfect beacon.

Alicia and Ravenell took the lead, pausing at a disabled blast door to look down the passageway. Stray laser blasts and ricocheting bullets provided ample warning against going farther, but they got a partial look at the situation up ahead. Archangel marines and navy crewmen pressed themselves up against the corners of two sides of a four-way intersection, while a good number of NorthStar troops kept up a steady field of fire from behind a waist-high portable riot barrier farther down the passageway. Behind them lay a sealed hatch marred with burns and chipped paint—but not a single hole or dent.

The two young marines ducked back around the corner to relay the situation to their companions. "That about the same way it looked when you left?" asked Alicia.

"More or less," said Ravenell. "More of our guys, about the same number of theirs. They only just beat us here, but it was enough time to set up that riot barrier. We didn't have anything heavy enough to break it down."

His eyes went to the plasma repeater in Baldwin's hands. The heavy power generator it required lay on the deck beside her. Its bearer leaned against the bulkhead, trying to catch his breath while he flipped through pages of a hard-copy manual in a metal binder.

"The officers' wardroom is right up there, on this side of the passageway," Tanner huffed once he'd found the right page. "Looks like our guys might already have it secure. There's another entrance on this side. We just passed the intersection we need. Gotta double back." He snapped the binder shut and shoved it under his belt behind his back, then hefted up the generator. "Jesus, I hate this thing already."

"Maybe we should trade off?" Ravenell asked.

"No, just . . . go," Tanner grunted.

Once more, Ravenell took the lead. Alicia guarded the rear, putting the two shuffling navy ratings between them as they doubled back to the next passageway intersection and then moved closer to their destination. "I feel like we're gonna get jumped from behind at any second," Alicia muttered.

"Sounds like the bigger fight's down in engineering," noted Baldwin. "Tried listening on the comm net, but it's too chaotic. Maybe that's where all the bad guys are going? Or maybe we're doing better than we thought?"

"Hell of a time to turn into an optimist," huffed Tanner.

Up ahead, Ravenell pounded on a wardroom hatch. "Donner!" he yelled, then paused. Tanner didn't hear the countersign, but he presumed Ravenell did since he threw open the hatch. The tall marine waved the rest into the wardroom, standing watch at the entrance.

Inside, Tanner found a comfortable compartment much like the officers' wardroom on *Los Angeles*, only larger and more ornate. The plush dining room now served as an impromptu first aid station. A man and a woman in Archangel vac suits lay on the dining tables, their outfits spattered with blood and burn marks. Another Archangel crewman stood over them, hurriedly dressing the burn wound on the woman's shoulder. He didn't look up from his work as the newcomers entered the compartment.

Tanner set the power generator down on the floor with a breath of relief, then pulled his stolen binder out to open it up on one of the other tables. Alicia pushed past, edging out of the opposite side of the compartment where gunfire continued to rage. Baldwin leaned up against the same table, opening up a screen on her holocom to check in on the comm net.

"*St. Constantine* made her drop a couple minutes ago," she reported. "So did one or two others, looks like. I think that fight in engineering actually got bigger since I checked . . . couple other groups holding choke points here and there." She glanced over his shoulder. "You sure this is gonna work?"

"It's what they trained us for in basic," Tanner murmured. "They just didn't spell it out for us."

A couple of marines entered from the direction of the firefight, one of them wearing a lieutenant's insignia. "—four different guys with heavy weapons in my platoon, and none of them made it this far," he said. "Even our plasma cutter took a hit while we fought our way up here."

The lieutenant stopped at the table beside Tanner and Baldwin. He gave the pair a quick glance. "Lieutenant Thompson. It's good to see you," he said to them both, then looked to the plasma repeater. "Damn." He slid his faceplate up before kneeling beside the weapon for a closer look.

"It's beat-up, sir," said Baldwin, "but it's functional. The damage looks worse than it is."

"I believe you, but that's not the problem. I don't think the power output on this will be enough to cut through that hatch," Thompson explained. "It'll probably clear out the defenders, but the hatch behind them and the bulkhead around it has ES reinforcement. The field probably seals up the whole bridge compartment. This is a Mark II. We'd need something stronger to break through. We'll put it to good use, though."

"Sir," Tanner spoke up, "we didn't bring you a gun." He gestured for the lieutenant to come over and then pointed to a spot on his open page. The diagrams were clear enough for a trained eye. "We brought a can opener."

Thompson frowned. "Wait, are you saying—" He cut himself off as Tanner's plan quickly became clear. "You know how risky that is?"

"About as risky as jumping between two spaceships in the middle of a battle. It won't break down the door, but I still think it'll get us through." He looked the lieutenant in the eye. "Pull your guys out, sir. I'll do it."

The young lieutenant twitched. "Pretty sure those third class stripes didn't come with a commission, kid," he said.

Tanner pushed back his faceplate in exasperation. "Sir—" he began.

The lieutenant blinked, then held up his hand. "Forget it. Okay. We'll do it your way." Then it was Tanner's turn to blink. He glanced at Baldwin. Despite her faceplate, he clearly saw her roll her eyes and look away, shaking her head with annoyance. Thompson swallowed hard. "But I can't ask you to put yourself in this position. I'll do it."

"Sir, someone needs to lead the rest of this team," Tanner argued. "You know it won't be long before more bad guys come at us from another direction. You're needed here. I'm volunteering for the job." He gave a shrug. "It was my idea, sir. I can't let someone else bite this bullet. Anyway, I'll be behind the hatch there, I'll probably be fine."

Thompson considered it for only a second longer before popping the clips on his web gear. He hit the comm button on his helmet. "Listen up! We're gonna pull back a little way out from here," the lieutenant announced, removing his combat jacket. "Crewman, get these two up and moving. I'll help. I want everyone at least one compartment away from the approach to the bridge, you got me? And don't get comfortable," he said, looking at Tanner. He held out his combat jacket. "We'll be coming right back."

Tanner accepted the second jacket. He stepped over to the gun as the others in the compartment began to clear out—everyone except Baldwin, Ravenell, and Alicia. The latter leaned out of the open hatch to shoot down the passageway toward the bridge. Ravenell took up the power generator and plasma repeater to drag them over to the hatch.

"You've gotta clear out," said Tanner.

"You've gotta get your head checked," Baldwin scoffed. "I'm not going anywhere."

"I'm serious. This is a one-person job. Anyone else in here just adds an extra body that might get hurt. No sense putting two of us in the line of fire."

His partner shrugged. "So I'll stand behind you."

Tanner looked to Alicia and Ravenell and found the pair over-turning one of the heavy, polished oak dining tables to move it closer to the hatch. The hatch lay propped partially open by a con-venient spacing bar at its top. The two marines then took up their weapons and ducked behind the bulkhead. "Aw Christ! You, too? Really?" Tanner asked.

"Really," they answered simultaneously.

"Guys, I'm serious!"

"It's like you said, Tanner, we were trained for this from the beginning," said Alicia. "We're not going anywhere, either. Now get it done or show me in that book where to point the gun and I'll do it."

"Malone, we're clear," announced Lieutenant Thompson over the comm. "Wong! Ravenell! Let's go!"

Tanner let out an irritated breath while he donned the lieu-tenant's combat jacket over his own—backward, so that the major-ity of its protective material hung in front of him rather than across his back. "I need 'em here with me, sir," he answered.

"What? What for?"

"I dunno, moral support?" Tanner muttered. He slammed his faceplate down again before he stood near the open hatch. With no one shooting back at them, the security troops at the end of the passageway had let up in their own fire. "Hey! Assholes!" Tanner shouted. "Last chance to talk this shit out!"

"Sure," one of them called back. "Throw down your guns and surrender and we can talk!"

"Okay. I tried." Tanner took the plasma repeater from Baldwin—who wisely ducked away from the hatch, as did Alicia and Ravenell to Tanner's other side—and stepped up to the opening.

He pointed the plasma repeater out and somewhat downward, angling slightly toward the security troops but not at all aiming for them. His target area bore no special markings, nor any equipment fixtures or sensors. It looked like just another stretch of deck plating up against the bulkhead corner.

The schematics in the maintenance manual behind Tanner marked it as the point where the bridge's oxygen supply ran parallel to the passageway.

Tanner turned up the power output on his plasma repeater and fired. The first few blasts struck the corner to little effect, dissipating harmlessly, but within the space of a breath the metal began to buckle and melt. The repeater wouldn't have the same effect on the door to the bridge, nor the bulkhead around it—not with an ES generator strengthening the metal on a molecular level. The deck outside the bridge was another matter.

Several of the security troopers started firing back once more. They didn't have much of an angle on Tanner. He remained within the wardroom, protected by the partially closed hatch, the overturned dining table, and even a second combat coat.

He was grateful for all of it when the plasma blasts finally cut through the deck, the insulation, and the piping. The explosion sent shrapnel and flame everywhere, shattering the table and knocking Tanner backward into the wardroom.

The blast and his landing left him disoriented. Slammed against the deck behind him, Tanner heard a strange whistling sound that seemed to rise above the roar of flames outside the room. He inhaled but found no air to breathe. Then he felt a pair of hands grab him and roll him roughly onto his belly. Someone popped one of the oxygen cartridges out of the back of his helmet—and the next. He felt one cartridge strike his arm as it popped free, but couldn't look up to see it. He felt someone's knee in between his shoulders as deft fingers inserted new cartridges, then closed the cartridge housing panel.

"Tanner? You alive?" Alicia asked for the third time. She got off his back, taking hold of his arm to pull him farther away from the hatch.

"Yeah," he mumbled. "It's fuckin' hot in here."

"No shit," she grunted.

He glanced up toward the hatch. There he saw Ravenell dart briefly out from one bulkhead across the opening into the burning passageway, then duck behind the protection of the opposite bulkhead. "I think that took care of the security team, at least," he reported.

"What the hell?" said Baldwin, crawling along the deck to join Tanner and Alicia. "How long does it take for a computer to choke off the flow of . . . ?" She stopped midsentence. Baldwin looked up to find the flames outside the hatch all but extinguished. "Huh."

Tanner heaved himself up from the deck with a grunt. "Let's see if that worked," he huffed, staggering out of the wardroom and into the smashed corridor.

"Tanner, you're bleeding," warned Ravenell.

"Yeah, probably." Outside, Tanner had to stick to the right of the passageway to avoid the giant hole on the left. Smoke soon began to clear. Tanner picked through the shattered remains of the portable riot barrier and its defenders to get to the hatch, which stood intact much as they'd all expected. He patted around for the door controls and found them still in place, though he had to wipe off bits of blood and soot.

The door naturally reported a lockout. Tanner brushed off the controls and found one of the manual communications links. He held his glove against it, sending a comms request through the electronics of his vac suit through the door panel. "C'mon, pick up. Pick up," he murmured. "Don't hide in there, you know you've gotta talk, c'mon . . ."

A sudden beep indicated an answer. "This is Lieutenant Commander—"

"Let me talk to your captain," Tanner interrupted.

"You'll talk to me. This is Lieutenant Commander Kurth. State your intentions."

Tanner sighed. "Okay, but the captain's listening, right? Commander—captain—I'm here to accept your surrender. Put down whatever guns you've got in there, open up the door, and stand down. Nobody else gets hurt."

"Nice try, buddy. You can tell that to the rest of our marines."

"*Captain,*" Tanner said, "you and I both know goddamn well that if your marines were gonna come to your rescue, they'd be here by now. They're either fighting for engineering or they're pinned down elsewhere. I've got a squad of marines and a plasma repeater out here. We can defend this passageway as long as we need. If you surrender now, the worst that happens is everyone gets handcuffs and a pat down. You've been beaten. Call the rest of this fight off. It won't do any further good."

Tanner fell silent. He heard nothing in response, but he realized the channel remained open.

"I just cut off the oxygen line going into the bridge, captain. You know it and I know it. And I'm willing to bet that right now your bridge is full of smoke and everyone's got their helmets sealed. Everyone is breathing canned air.

"I've seen your gear. I read the labels before I came up here. I've seen the emergency panels on the bulkheads. You've all got about a half hour worth of air per person. Maybe less if you've got marines in there and they didn't get a chance to grab their own cartridges before coming up."

Again, Tanner heard nothing in response. His holocom indicated the channel was still open. Tanner looked over his shoulder, where he saw Alicia, Baldwin, and Ravenell waiting. Ravenell held the plasma repeater and nodded. Beyond him, through the clearing smoke of the passageway, Tanner saw Lieutenant Thompson and a couple of his men emerge from around the corner.

Tanner turned back to the door controls. "Captain, we've cut off all your air. We don't want to kill everyone on that bridge, but we will damn well do it if we have to. Take a good look around yourself, I'm sure you care about your crew.

"Don't throw all their lives away on a paycheck none of you are ever gonna live to see."

Then a new voice spoke over the comm. "This is Captain Wagner. To whom am I speaking?"

Tanner hesitated. *Fuck it*, he decided. He popped the seals on his helmet, pulled it off, and turned back to the door panel and the camera he knew must be a part of the system.

"My name is Tanner Malone," he growled. "You know *exactly* who I am and what I'll do if I have to. Open the door."

• • •

Backup didn't arrive in time.

Janeka held the hatch as long as she could, but she knew all too well when her position was untenable. Of the six men she'd found at the entryway, only two remained alive. Both lay wounded out of the line of fire.

The enemy advanced. She kept firing until her rifle took a hit, sending sparks and shards of metal flying against the faceplate of her helmet. The infantry laser cannon fired again, striking all too close for comfort against the corner of the bulkhead to her side. Cursing, Janeka rolled out of the way.

She crouched to her feet, hit the magnetic relays in her suit, jumped up as high as she could against the bulkhead, and started climbing. "Aft entryway breached!" she reported once more. "Get someone down here now!"

"Reinforcements on the way!" called back a voice on the comm. "Just hold on!"

Janeka growled as she kept climbing, relying on the magnetic grip of her suit to keep her glued to the bulkhead. The gunny swung herself up over the corner of the entryway and waited, allowing the first handful of NorthStar marines to enter. They swept both left and right, keeping far enough apart that they wouldn't all be hit by the same grenade or arc of fire.

Then the laser cannon on its rolling tripod emerged. Janeka killed the power to her relays and dropped down onto the cannoneer's shoulders with her knees. The man collapsed with a yelp beneath her. The closest man to him let out a shriek as Janeka slashed through his hip with her heated dagger. Another trooper, standing on the cannoneer's other side, didn't know what was going on until Janeka grabbed the barrel of his gun and jerked it out of his hand.

Others rushed in. The first to get to her caught the butt of Janeka's new rifle under his chin. A second tried to tackle her, but only made himself into a human shield as she hooked one arm under his shoulder and spun him around between herself and his comrades. A third man fired in a panicked arc, catching her once in the side with a bullet that didn't quite penetrate her combat jacket while inadvertently killing his comrade on the spot. Janeka kept moving. She stepped around the side of the cannon, turned her rifle on the last jittery foe, and returned the favor. Her wound was painful but manageable. His was instantly lethal.

The rest scattered, committed more to their own survival than to any attack. They hardly knew what to make of the sudden ambush from above. Janeka kicked the cannoneer in the gut again before grabbing his weapon and spinning it around. The mere sight of the cannon turning on its former owners sent them all running back the way they'd come.

She pressed her advantage, firing a laser blast that burned an ugly black scar into the opposite bulkhead and nearly caught another NorthStar trooper, who wisely kept running. Only then did Janeka look over her shoulder for the handful of enemy troops who'd made it past the door.

Bullets ricocheted against the metal framework of a tall equipment rack and its contents within the compartment, keeping the enemies to Janeka's left pinned down. She looked to the right and found two more dead NorthStar troopers. Sergeant Baker sat up against the bulkhead, bleeding from a wound in his gut but firing.

Janeka pulled the laser cannon back from the entryway and around the corner, spinning it as she moved to bear down on the equipment rack. She didn't bother with the targeting system. With such a weapon at close range, all she had to do was point and shoot.

The blast all but cut the equipment rack in half. Its upper portion buckled and fell over onto its side, resulting in a pair of startled screams as it came down onto the two NorthStar troopers using the rack for cover.

The victory offered Janeka only a brief pause. Her side hurt terribly, as did one of her knees. She leaned on the cannon for support. Knowing the NorthStar troopers down the corridor would soon regroup, she pushed the big weapon back around Baker, breathing out a simple, "Good job, sergeant," as she moved.

Only then did she hear the voice over the PA.

"I repeat, stand down," said the deep, male voice. "This is Captain Wagner. All hands, check your personal holocoms for confirmation. You are ordered to stand down and disarm. The ship is hereby surrendered to Archangel forces. I repeat, we surrender. Lay down all weapons immediately."

A pensive silence followed. Janeka pushed the cannon the rest of the way around the corner, only to see a handful of NorthStar troopers emerge from the far end of the passageway with their hands up. Then a few more came around the corner. Then more.

"Put your hands on your heads and kneel," she ordered. Though some of the men and women up ahead hesitated, all of them obeyed. The gunnery sergeant let out another breath, leaned a bit onto the cannon again, and looked to her side.

"Sergeant Baker, you okay?" she asked. "Sergeant Baker?"

The young man remained propped up against the bulkhead, his weapon laid across his lap with his hand still around the grip.

He didn't answer.

• • •

"Everyone up from your stations, *now*," Lieutenant Thompson demanded as he and the others strode onto the bridge. Tanner came in beside him. As he'd expected, a considerable haze of smoke filled the air. "Hands up. No talking, no sudden movements." Behind them, Alicia, Baldwin, and Ravenell entered and spread out from the open entrance to cover multiple angles, though they found themselves inadequate for such a job all on their own. The command bridge of a battleship was simply too large.

Officers and enlisted ratings across the huge compartment did as Thompson demanded. Virtually every one of them turned to face their captors as they entered. The far end of the compartment held several large screens displaying tactical information. At several other spots across the bridge, Tanner could see holo screens still active, but he correctly guessed that a majority of the bridge crew had closed down their stations as soon as the captain had given the order to surrender.

Everyone remained silent—everyone, that is, except for a single, angry voice emanating from one of the speakers on the captain's chair. "Do not obey that order!" the man shouted. "You keep hold of that bridge and fight! Commander Middleton, relieve the captain and take command!"

Thompson and Tanner walked straight over to the captain, who stood at his chair. "That the flag bridge talking?" Thompson asked.

"Yes." The captain kept his hands in the air but gestured with his fingers. "I could turn it off, if you'd . . . ?"

"Do it," Thompson said. "Can the ship be run from the flag bridge?"

"Only under certain conditions," the captain answered readily, though his voice bore no great enthusiasm. He bent over to touch a couple of buttons on the armrest of his chair, making sure his captor could see each move as it happened. The voice coming from the speaker abruptly cut out. "None of the automated conditions for shifting command have been fulfilled, and I haven't transferred manually, obviously. This bridge still runs the ship."

"Can anyone on that bridge access the PA?" asked Thompson.

"Ah . . . lieutenant?" asked the captain. "Do I have the rank correct? No. No, I cut access to that before I gave the order. I didn't want the commodore to countermand me," he explained. "I'm Captain Wagner."

"Lieutenant Thompson, Archangel marines." He put one hand on Tanner's shoulder. "I've got this. Get on the helm and give me a course heading and status."

The order made Tanner stop and blink. Behind them and to the left, Baldwin instructed the rest of the captives to shift to the far left bulkhead. He looked right and saw Alicia and Ravenell with their weapons still ready in case anyone tried to resist. The rest of Thompson's team moved inside the bridge. "Aye, aye, sir," Tanner replied before he stepped past Wagner and the captain's chair.

Given the size and complexity of the bridge, Tanner had to look around for the helm. He worried for a second that he might have gone completely blank. The shift from shooting and taking captives to the tasks of running a starship, even at only the most basic level, did not occur instantaneously. Tanner looked over his shoulder to see if perhaps someone else on the bridge might be more qualified, but he saw no one. Everyone else already had their hands full with handling prisoners, except for the crewman from the wardroom, who came in with wounded marines limping along at both of his shoulders.

Tanner kept searching. Along the way, he glanced up at the big tactical screens along the far bulkhead and realized they held all he needed to sort out the most critical information.

"Lieutenant?" he called out, looking over his shoulder to Thompson and Wagner and waiting to be acknowledged. He pointed to the big screens. "We're forty-three thousand klicks inside the picket line with Raphael at one-seven-eight by two-zero-six relative to us, speed sixteen hundred kps but falling. Looks like the bad guys are scattering away from us."

Thompson's gaze moved toward the big tactical screens. So did Tanner's, naturally looking for the other two battleships. Both *Ursa* and *Andromeda* now fled the core engagements, running for the protection of allied vessels that clearly wanted to keep their distance. The graphics and labels on the tactical screens identified NorthStar's ships, a large formation of Lai Wa vessels that held tight while backing farther out of the battle, and Archangel's remaining destroyers, frigates, and corvettes. Few bore any identifying marks. Tanner could identify Archangel ships by class but not name.

Los Angeles, at least, was easily identified. Tanner's heart sank at the sight of her with no other ships nearby. Numerous icons indicated heavy damage, a very low speed, and a total lack of offensive weapons fire. NorthStar's fleet seemed to have forgotten about her. Tanner didn't know whether to consider that a blessing or an awful omen.

"Slow us down or at least turn us around, Malone," instructed Thompson. "Whatever takes us away from the bad guys and out of the fight."

"Aye, aye, sir," Tanner said again. As usual, he found most of the panels were clearly labeled and laid out in a fairly straightforward manner, but none were the station he needed. He looked for helm controls, or an override. "Shit," he muttered before checking yet another station. That one didn't work, either. Finally, he snapped, "Jesus fucking Christ, where's the goddamn helm?"

No one spoke. Tanner looked toward the captured skipper, who gestured to another of the consoles near the center of the bridge. Wagner then turned to Lieutenant Thompson and murmured, "Does he take Communion with that mouth?"

Thankfully, Tanner found the controls unlocked and fully functional. He quickly looked things over, felt the familiar nervous sensation that always overcame him when he had to steer a ship, and then reminded himself that he had plenty of space to deal with. All he had to do was turn *Hercules* in any direction other than a straight shot for Raphael. Tanner input new commands, effectively pushing *Hercules* "down" in a ninety degree turn, and cut her speed dramatically.

All the while, Tanner heard Thompson's men talk with other units over the comm network. Wagner's surrender order had made for a great many changes across the ship. With main engineering firmly in Archangel hands and now with control of the bridge, the focus quickly became one of consolidation and control. Names rang out with orders to report to the bridge, or to several airlocks where more personnel might come aboard.

The details hardly mattered. All Tanner needed was for someone with a little more experience and training to come help him run the ship. Thus far, he'd only discovered the most basic helm controls.

He glanced up from his station once more to check on the rest of the bridge, still wired from combat and ready for a sudden revolt or any other reversal of fortunes. Baldwin and one of the marines worked to pat down and bind each of the bridge officers, with several already sitting on the deck with their hands now wrapped up behind their backs. Alicia and Ravenell stood nearby, keeping the captives covered. Thompson continued speaking with Wagner.

Then the hatch opened. Tanner snatched up his rifle but recognized the Archangel uniforms coming through before he'd actually trained it on a target. He recognized the face of the navy rating, his broken faceplate practically hanging from his helmet, and a couple of the marines. "Sinclair?" he called, and then waved.

"Signalman," said Thompson as Sinclair waved, "take a station. Corporal," he said to the marine, "take charge of the prisoner detail."

Tanner kept looking over his shoulder as Sinclair moved over toward him. He grinned a bit as his boot camp squad leader took up a nearby station. "You have no idea how glad I am to see you," he said. Out of the corner of his eye—and out of Thompson's line of sight, he noticed—the marine corporal briefly slipped an arm around Alicia for about as much of a hug as they could risk. "Both of you," Tanner added.

"Yeah," Sinclair huffed. "Me, too. Bit off way more than we could chew back there."

"What do you mean?"

"Holding off a shitload of bad guys tryin' to come this way through a ladder well. Just the handful of us," Sinclair huffed. He gestured toward Collins. "That guy is fucking nuts."

Looking back, Tanner saw Collins, Alicia, and the other marines huddle to sort themselves out. Another familiar face turned his way.

Tanner gave DeLeon a conciliatory nod. DeLeon rolled his eyes and went back to his discussion.

"Anyway," Sinclair went on, "you have the helm?"

"I do, but somebody better at it than me should take over before I crash us into another ship."

"Just keep slowing us down, Malone," said Thompson, who now stood over the pair while Wagner joined his captured officers. "You're doing fine. As long as we're out of the fight, we've made a big difference. What's your name, signalman?"

"Sinclair, sir."

"Try to get us in touch with *Los Angeles*. Maybe *Rio* if you don't pick up an answer. Make sure they know we've taken down the flag here."

"Aye, aye, sir."

Tanner watched the numbers spin down on *Hercules*'s speed. He noted three Archangel corvettes already swinging in to drop off troops. In keeping with the hopes behind Beowulf, none of the enemy ships dared open fire on *Hercules*. For all the desperation of combat and the cold economic sensibilities of Archangel's foes, even corporate navy crews would not deliberately fire on their own.

Unwillingly, without conscious thought, Tanner glanced over to the tactical screens and saw the gray icon marking the remains of *Saratoga*. He didn't give himself enough time to reflect upon its presence. Instead, he looked to other matters. The fate of NorthStar's other two battleships, both of them plagued with Archangel's boarding teams, was far more pressing.

"*Los Angeles*, this is Beowulf One," said Sinclair. "*Los Angeles*, do you read? This is Beowulf One. We have control of *Hercules*. I say again, we have control of *Hercules*. Please advi—" He abruptly fell silent, giving Thompson a thumbs-up without looking away from his console.

Tanner felt another slight rush of triumph. Every development brought their entire impossible mission closer to success. His eyes lifted once more to the big tactical screens at the fore of the bridge. Computer-enhanced close-ups showed both *Ursa* and *Andromeda* trying in vain to outrun more of Archangel's corvettes, which swooped down upon them like predatory birds onto far larger but now wounded animals. The battleships tried to fight off their tenacious pursuers with fire from their lasers and defensive guns, but neither had much success. Tanner watched with bated breath.

His heart all but stopped when *Ursa* exploded.

. . .

"Linkup complete. All three struts securely locked on the hull."

"Thank you, bo'sun," came Kelly's voice over the comm. "Passengers are now free to . . . disembark from the spacecraft," she added with a cough.

"Understood," replied the bo'sun. "Depressurizing cargo bay now. Landing ramp down in ten seconds."

"Hold that order, please," spoke up a voice in the cargo bay.

The collection of men and women in gray and navy vac suits, helmets, and combat jackets struck a far different image than *Joan of Arc's* last load of passengers. These passengers bore pulse rifles and gun belts with pistols, but their combat loads fell considerably short of those carried by the boarding teams. They also lacked proper rank insignia—and with good reason.

One passenger walked over to *Joan's* XO. "Lieutenant Booker," she said, "it occurs to me that I may be the only one on my staff who has completed firearms certification within the last year. I should probably bring a bit more of an escort than I have here with me."

"Agreed, ma'am," said Booker, "but I don't know who we can spare and still get back into the fight."

Admiral Yeoh shook her head. She touched another key on her holocom. "Captain Kelly," she said.

"Ma'am?"

"Captain, your ship is damaged, you're out of missiles and you have suffered casualties. I'm pulling you out of the fight. You've done more than enough. *Joan of Arc* remains docked and locked on *Hercules*. Is that understood?"

The response came after a brief but noticeable pause. "Aye, aye, admiral," Kelly answered. "*Joan of Arc* is standing down."

"Sanjay, Ordoñez," Booker spoke up on the comm net, "you're with the admiral. Weapons and combat jacket in the cargo bay. Hustle."

Yeoh cut the crew channel again. "Lieutenant Booker, I'm ordering you to pull Captain Kelly off that bridge and get her medical attention. I don't care if you have to break the door down with an axe. Make sure she gets first aid and then move her to sick bay here on *Hercules* as soon as you can. If you have anyone else injured on this ship, you do the same for them."

Booker merely nodded. "Aye, aye, ma'am."

"Thank you."

She saw Sanjay arrive armed and ready to go. Seconds later, a hatch opened and *Joan*'s gunner's mate hurried out, carrying a rifle over her shoulder and still strapping on a belt holding two pistols as she moved. Yeoh pursed her lips at the sight but said nothing of it.

"Do not fire unless you see a weapon or clear hostile intent," she told her escorts and the handful of officers that accompanied her from *Los Angeles*. "Do not call out ranks or names. Until we get to the bridge, every one of us is perfectly happy to answer to 'hey, you.' Let's go."

Yeoh nodded to the bo'sun, who soon had the cargo bay depressurized and the loading ramp down on the battleship's hull. The party moved out carefully, with the magnetic clamping action of their boots slowing their stride. *Hercules* no longer made any sudden, violent moves. Yeoh and the others could see the flashes of lasers and exploding missiles far off in the distance. None of it came near the battleship.

They entered through an emergency maintenance hatch near an external sensor array, where a lone marine waited to let them in. The group could only go inside two at a time, closing the hatch behind themselves before opening their way into the interior vestibule and then waiting for the rest in the data analysis compartment on the other side. Shattered equipment, laser-scored bulkheads, bodies, and bloodstains lay all around. The compartment hadn't been taken without a fight—and an ugly one at that.

Guided by another marine from the boarding party, Yeoh and her group moved through eerily quiet passageways and open blast doors on their way to the bridge. Other than their first compartment, they found few signs of violence until they drew closer to their destination. There they saw the signs of Lieutenant Thompson's fight for the wardroom and the twisted, ugly wreckage of the corridor outside the bridge. A pair of marines guarded this last junction, calling for sign and countersign and even then still giving Yeoh's group a good looking over before allowing them to pass.

By the time she arrived, a half dozen more navy ratings and a couple of marines sat or stood at vital stations. None of the captives remained. Yeoh noted with some relief that in contrast to the mangled destruction outside, the bridge appeared free of damage. It only needed more of a crew.

"Engineering reports main power to thrusters will be reconnected in five minutes," someone called out. "Guess they just started cutting cables and tubes when they first got in there."

"Gunnery party has secured cannon two," reported someone else. "Reporting lots of captives."

"Yeah, that was us," answered a third voice, one Yeoh recognized. "Sorry about the mess."

Her eyes turned up to the tactical screens on the opposite bulkhead as she walked toward the captain's chair at the center of the bridge, where a lone marine lieutenant stood watch. In keeping with her instructions, the main body of Archangel's ships now adopted a largely defensive posture, apart from the trio of corvettes that still doggedly chased after *Andromeda*. The enemy seemed likewise content to stay back at long range, still engaged but clearly waiting to see the fate of NorthStar's last battleship before making another move.

She removed her helmet and stepped up next to the marine. "Lieutenant Thompson," she said, reading his name tag.

To his credit, he didn't pop to attention or salute, but the young officer clearly stiffened a bit when he turned and recognized the face in front of him. "Ma'am."

"You appear to be the ranking officer on the bridge?"

"Yes, ma'am. Not anymore, obviously," he conceded, nodding toward the handful of officers who'd arrived with Yeoh and now spread out across the bridge, "but it's been me up until now. Glad to see some regular navy officers here to take over. I had a couple of marine grunts running the astrogation table until a few minutes ago."

"We've emphasized cross-training for the last few years with good reason, lieutenant. I'm glad to see it paid off. That said, I'm here to relieve you. I can see the ship's position and heading well enough, along with the tactical situation. What's the status of the ship? What have we secured?"

Thompson gestured to a monitor station near the captain's chair, where a young woman with a yeoman's insignia sat working with several screens. The station offered a series of deck plans, which the yeoman marked out in red or green. "Engineering is secure, though that's a big space. We've got our people all over three out of the four thrusters. Two of the NorthStar marine landers took off out of here a couple minutes ago, but I think we've managed to stave off any more escapes from the launch bay at this point. The flag bridge is locked down, but we don't have control of it yet, same as a good number of other spots. And we just got a good grip on cannon two, like they—"

"Woah!" someone called out. "*Andromeda*'s changing course!"

Yeoh looked up to the tactical screens like almost everyone else. As reported, the big battleship pulled into a hard turn to starboard that never straightened out, effectively putting *Andromeda* into a broad circular path. The admiral placed a hand on Thompson's shoulder and then walked past. Her eyes stayed on the tactical screens as she moved toward the front of the bridge. Soon she stood just behind a pair of young navy ratings—one of them manning the helm, while the other tried to manage the ship's communications.

"Comms," she said coolly, "watch for anything from *Andromeda*. Highest priority."

"Yes, ma'am," replied the young signalman, "but I'm getting a lot of—ma'am, most of this stuff was locked out when we came in, but I'm starting to clear it up and I think you should—"

"There!" someone else yelled. Everyone watched as *Andromeda* pulled out of her loop and veered off away from both Archangel's formations and the loose lines drawn up by NorthStar's ships. Her speed fell dramatically. Several of her guns went dark, and then more, and then more.

"Signal from *Andromeda*," said the man to Yeoh's left. "Beowulf—" he cut himself off and instead input a few commands on his console.

"*Los Angeles*," said a voice over the bridge speakers, "this is Beowulf Three. We have taken the *Andromeda* bridge and engineering. The crew has surrendered. I say again, *Los Angeles*, this is Beowulf Three. We have *Andromeda*!"

Wild cheers erupted throughout the command bridge. Yeoh merely sighed with relief, but she couldn't blame anyone for their emotions. In truth, she felt much the same way. She'd simply carried this stress too long to expend any energy on shouting. Nor did she think the danger had passed, even when the situation on the tactical screens went through further dramatic change.

"Enemy ships are withdrawing!" called out one of her officers. "The Lai Wa formation just did a full turn and accelerated! Course heading—"

"Both expeditionary groups are pulling out, too!" yelled someone else. "They're taking off!"

"Operations," Yeoh called calmly, and then raised her voice to call out again over the din, "operations! Confirm course headings, please. Comms, please send the following signal on our channels: Flag Six to Beowulf One. Repeat until you have acknowledgments from all friendly ships. Understood?"

"Yes, ma'am," said the signalman, still working diligently at his seat. He quickly typed in and sent the message, calling up a receipt screen but then moving to other tasks. Unlike the rest of the bridge crew, his face remained grave.

Yeoh let him work. Her gaze drifted to her right, where a helmetless young man in a burned and battered combat jacket seemed to reach out and touch the helm controls as little as possible. "Tanner," Yeoh said quietly. "Imagine my surprise."

"It's good to see you, ma'am."

"You as well," she nodded, then paused. "You made a terrible mess out there."

"Due respect, ma'am, you have no proof that was me."

"And yet you look and smell like a hospital fire." She looked back to her officers. "Commander Beacham," said Yeoh, "I need someone qualified to take the helm for Master-at-Arms Malone here. Right away." She paused only long enough to see Beacham nod and step up to take the position herself rather than look for someone else for the job. Yeoh's staff knew when to delegate and when not to keep the admiral waiting.

Yeoh looked Tanner in the eye as he stood. "We've a lot of prisoners to collect. You'll be of greater use there than here on the bridge. We should start with Commodore Eldridge, or whomever else NorthStar put in charge of all this. I believe he is still on the flag bridge. I need you to arrest him, and then you and any other masters-at-arms on board will take charge of prisoner details. "

"Aye, aye, ma'am."

Yeoh watched him leave. She looked to her escorts from *Joan of Arc*. "He probably shouldn't go alone," she suggested. Crewman Sanjay and his ship's gunner's mate followed right after him.

"Admiral?"

"Yes? Signalman Sinclair, is it?" she asked, reading his name tag.

"Yes, ma'am. I'm getting calls from a lot of ships, but now that the enemy is moving out, I'm starting to pick up clearer traffic on the civilian channels. I think you'd better hear this."

• • •

No one appeared in Tanner's way as he strode down the corridors and the ladder wells to the flag bridge, a good hundred meters back and two decks down from the command bridge. *Hercules* remained more or less at battle stations per the instructions of her captain before he was removed from the bridge, though now that mostly amounted to people sitting tight at their stations without doing much of anything but worrying.

The presence of friends and comrades from *Joan of Arc* made him feel a little better. "Everyone okay on the ship?" Tanner asked.

"We lost Stan and Chief Romita," answered Ordoñez, her faceplate still locked down. "Skipper's hurt but she'll be okay. Leg wound, nothing serious."

"Tanner," Sanjay spoke up, "your helmet's back on the bridge."

"Huh. Whatever."

"Tanner, are you okay?"

"Actually, I'm beat up and I've lost friends and I blew up a whole assault carrier full of people earlier, so . . . no," Tanner admitted. "No, I'm not."

His voice cracked a little as he spoke, but he otherwise held his composure. He was among friends. At some point, he'd decided, he could admit these things to friends. And though wide-eyed and surprised by his strange, bluntly honest admission, neither Sanjay nor Ordoñez said anything to push him on it.

He did not intend to admit those feelings to a full platoon of NorthStar marines, but when he turned the corner and found them all lying in wait in the passageways and open compartments closest to the flag bridge, with portable riot barriers and infantry squad weapons deployed and ready, he realized—among other things—that they'd doubtlessly heard every word of it.

No one fired or raised a weapon at Tanner. They simply stayed at their posts and waited.

Tanner's jittery tone disappeared. "Weapons down," he said firmly.

Nothing happened.

"Who's in charge out here?"

Though the answer did not come immediately, a lone figure stood up from behind one of the riot barriers. "That would be me," he said. "I'm Lieutenant Stowe."

"Lieutenant, the captain of this ship ordered a general surrender. It's time to put the guns down."

Stowe glanced at a couple of people—probably his non-coms, Tanner thought—and then frowned. He reached up to tap at the side of his helmet, likely silencing a comms channel. "I'm afraid there's been some confusion on that point."

"Lieutenant," Tanner pressed, his voice still a little shaky but oddly polite, "the commodore's life isn't more important than yours. We don't want to kill you all, and you don't want to die. Put the weapons down. Please."

After another pause, Lieutenant Stowe said, "Third Platoon, you heard Captain Wagner. Weapons on the deck. Let's go." By way of example, he lifted his own pulse rifle over the riot barrier and dropped it on the other side, then pulled the pistol from his holster and let it, too, fall out of reach.

Beeps and mechanical latching noises followed as thirty some odd men and women crammed into open hatches and lockers set their weapons into safe modes and then put them down. Heads ducked under the riot barrier to disengage its locks and supports. Sanjay, Ordoñez, and Tanner watched as a couple dozen grim faces stared back at them.

"We're just gonna leave these guys all sitting out here?" Ordoñez asked.

"I've only got one pair of cuffs," Tanner explained quietly. "Lost my tape somewhere."

A moment later, the path lay clear. The three navy crewmen walked through the gathered marines as Lieutenant Stowe opened the hatch.

Inside, Tanner and the others saw a broad, circular compartment, much like the command bridge but with fewer control consoles and more holographic displays and large screens on the bulkheads. At a glance, Tanner figured roughly twenty people inhabited the flag bridge, all of them in vac suits, some still sealed in helmets and some not.

One officer bore considerably more in the way of flashes and pips on his vac suit than anyone else.

Tanner walked in, looking left and right for weapons or hostile intent. As it happened, everyone stayed clear of the ranking officer at the center of the bridge. Sanjay and Ordoñez walked close behind Tanner, maintaining a similarly watchful stance but also keeping a wary eye on the hatch and the gaggle of reluctantly cooperative marines behind them.

"Commodore Eldridge?" he asked as he walked up.

Only then did the man turn his eyes on Tanner. He looked the battered and filthy intruder to his bridge up and down. "What are you, a third class?" Eldridge asked distantly, then snorted. "They couldn't send an officer down for me."

"Does that make any difference?"

"Professionalism and military courtesy, son," Eldridge replied. "I imagine Archangel doesn't put much stock in that. I'm not blaming you."

Tanner's eyes narrowed. "They didn't send a *commissioned* officer because you're not a prisoner of *war*, commodore. I'm here as a deputized officer of Archangel law. Turn around and put your hands on your head. You're under arrest."

"On what charge?" Eldridge blurted indignantly.

In truth, Yeoh hadn't given Tanner a charge, nor had he seriously considered it. Still, the answer came to him right away: "Piracy. Turn around and put your hands on your head."

"Piracy? How—argh!"

Tanner cut off the rest of Eldridge's statement by grabbing his wrist and twisting it, stepping around the commodore to get control of him from behind. He had to drop his rifle to get hold of Eldridge with his other hand, but Sanjay and Ordoñez had his back. Tanner jerked Eldridge over to one side to get him against the back of his captain's chair, making sure he had the hold locked in before he reached for his cuffs.

In truth, Eldridge put up only enough resistance to make a show of it for the sake of pride. Tanner knew that perfectly well, having practiced this move to varying difficulty so many times in training. Still, even this much difficulty proved perfectly infuriating, though it only took a few seconds. The first cuff went on easily enough. The second came with only a minor struggle—but it was enough to occupy his full attention. He breathed a bit of a sigh once he had the commodore fully bound.

"Oh my God," murmured Ordoñez. "Guys?"

"What?" Tanner glanced around. Nobody on the bridge or outside it seemed to have moved. No one spoke. The only thing he heard was chatter off a nearby speaker, sounding for all the world like a news broadcast.

"—governor has offered a full surrender to the NorthStar forces," reported the civilian news anchor. "We still can't get ahold of Bethlehem Station or *any* of the other orbital facilities at this time. As far as we can tell, none of the defending navy ships in the area are still in the fight at this time . . ."

Tanner froze. Bethlehem Station orbited Michael. He looked around for the source of the voice and saw a display but found it mirrored on one of the larger screens on a nearby bulkhead. He recognized everything immediately—the continents of his home planet, the network markings in the corner, and the cityscape of the planet's capital on the split screen.

The red dots across the continents could only mean one thing, as could the fires and smoke behind the capital.

Tanner's breath caught in his throat. His eyes darted around the flag bridge, looking for more information or something to counter the images on the broadcast. Yet when he found a screen showing long-range sensor information, centering on Michael, his horror only grew.

Bethlehem Station appeared as a faded white icon on the screen, blinking softly to indicate distress signals. Grayed-out icons turned up nearby to represent a handful of smaller Archangel ships left behind to defend the planet. Looming all around Michael, Tanner and everyone else on the bridge could make out the names, classes, and positions of more than a dozen NorthStar vessels. The computer was perfectly forthcoming with details. A full NorthStar expeditionary group orbited Michael well within bombardment range, with both assault carriers and several starliners all releasing landing craft and support ships.

The news anchor continued. "We have reports of a missile strike in the middle of Hawthorne with massive civilian casualties, probably aimed at one of the defense grid cannons . . ."

Tanner's mind raced. Michael lay several light-minutes away from Raphael at this time of year, now almost on the other side of the star of Archangel. Everything depicted in these transmissions and sensor readings had occurred at least ten minutes ago, perhaps a little more. Tanner's eyes shifted to the main tactical screens, looking at the enemy ships fleeing the battle around Raphael, and he quickly confirmed the obvious, dreadful suspicion. Lai Wa's ships seemed intent on leaving the system entirely, but NorthStar's remaining forces all headed straight for Tanner's home planet.

Another screen depicted the scene around *Hercules*. Archangel's shattered fleet held in place, with some ships moving into recovery operations and others barely limping along.

Ordoñez looked to her companion. "Aren't you from . . . ?"

Tanner's eyes turned to his prisoner, who no longer looked smug or defiant. Instead, he now looked understandably nervous—and doubly so as Tanner picked up his rifle.

"You're under arrest," Tanner repeated quietly. "Let's go."

EPILOGUE

Digging Trenches

"To All Vessels: Do not pursue. Repeat, do not pursue fleeing enemy ships. All capable vessels will immediately shift to rescue and recovery operations. Remain on scene. Further instructions to follow."
—Message from Beowulf One, December 2276

She saw it all happen from the window of her prison cell. She had to stand on her bunk and its plain, cheap mattress to get to that window, but the sounds from outside and the alarms beyond her cell door left no doubt that something important was going on.

Her view was not exactly breathtaking, though it did at least look down from a hill. Like so much of the planet Michael, her surroundings rode the line between desert scrub and savannah. Fort Bradley Military Prison sat on the edges of the Fort Bradley Complex, which was home to a hodgepodge of navy facilities, training grounds, and a few other sites run by Michael's planetary government. The Civil Defense Force, geared mostly toward disaster response and other domestic emergencies, had the most people on the base. Yet from what little she'd gathered, Fort Bradley was also home to command and control for a large portion of Michael's planetary defense grid.

She saw that grid go into action shortly after the alarms started. Missiles launched from silos buried in the ground. Lasers and plasma cannons fired skyward, though at what, she couldn't say. The attack—it had to be an attack, obviously—began in the middle of the day at Fort Bradley, and thus she couldn't see much of what transpired beyond the atmosphere.

Even with all those restrictions on her view, she could tell when the defensive fire intensified. She saw the lasers that rained down from the sky to destroy several of the interceptor cannons and launch sites. And she knew what would happen next.

Pointless though it might be, she jumped down, tore the mattress off her bunk, and huddled into a corner of her cell with the mattress on top of her. She stuck her fingers in her ears, kept her mouth open, and waited for the world to end.

The wait lasted only seventeen seconds.

• • •

In the aftermath of the explosion, she couldn't really track time. She waited until she regained her senses, feeling fortunate to survive and dreading what she might find as she dug her way out of the rubble of her cell. Her luck held: she found her cell door completely smashed, with the hallways beyond it clear and emergency lighting active, though the place was a complete shambles. Walls crumbled, others looked like they might do the same, and the few windows in her wing of the prison opened out to skies so full of ash and smoke that she couldn't be sure if it was still daytime.

She didn't stop to check on any of her fellow prisoners. She found a guard killed by falling masonry, searched his body, claimed everything useful—stun gun, holocom, his restraints—and moved on, confident now that she was at least minimally armed. She had a good deal more climbing and crawling to do. More than once, she came to a dead end. Yet she continued on.

Her real break came not when she climbed through a crevasse in the prison's exterior wall but in the discovery she made afterward.

The rover pulled up just beyond her point of exit, with all three of its Civil Defense occupants stepping out to survey the wreckage. They didn't notice her as she dropped down to the ground behind their vehicle. In truth, she couldn't hold that against them. Between the shadows, the dust, and the stress of the moment, she had a lot to work with.

"Command, this is Isaacson," said one of the CDF troopers. He had his holocom going, offering up a comms screen but nothing in the way of video. "We're on-site now. Just outside the exterior walls. We don't see or hear any activity, but the whole place is a mess. No telling who's alive and who isn't."

She crept up behind them carefully. The other two, both carrying pulse rifles, slowly wandered apart from Isaacson, though not too far.

"Isaacson, command," came the response. "Understood. Make a sweep of the perimeter but do not try to enter. If you see anyone wearing less than a full guard uniform, take custody. You are permitted to use lethal force. Please acknowledge."

"Acknowledged, command. We'll be careful. If we see anyone, we'll round 'em up. Isaacson out."

She made her move then, rushing up behind the largest of the three troopers and letting him have it at point-blank range with the stun gun. She got behind him before he fell, partially keeping him upright in front of her as human shield while taking hold of his pulse rifle.

Isaacson caught on too late. He turned around in time for her to open up on him with the pulse rifle, cutting him down in seconds. The last of the CDF troopers spun around with his weapon ready, but all he saw was a blonde woman in a prison jumpsuit before her pulse rifle flashed again.

She'd have preferred to talk him into surrendering. Isaacson died with his holocom active, which meant she could raid it for info, tools, and whatever electronic cash he had on him at will. The other one would require some cracking, which she may not be able to do. With luck, however, her stunned prisoner would be sensible enough to unlock his before she had to get nasty about it.

Fort Bradley lay in ruins. Michael had clearly fallen to an invasion. She didn't know where she could go for shelter and a place to hide, but she'd figure that out before too long. All that mattered to Lauren Williams now was that she had weapons, cash, a vehicle, and her freedom.

She could work the rest out later.

. . .

"Dear Mr. Whittier,

"We must first express our sincerest condolences for the loss of your daughter, Yeoman Peggy Whittier.

"We also regret to inform you that due to the circumstances of her loss, NorthStar Investments is not yet able to process your claim for benefits on her life insurance policy. Despite claims in the media regarding the destruction of NSS Saratoga (including those made by other NorthStar officials and departments), NorthStar Investments has not yet ascertained whether the ship's destruction was due to enemy action, friendly fire, shipboard accident, or some other cause. Until NorthStar Investments concludes its investigation, we cannot disburse benefits for Yeoman Whittier or any other personnel lost aboard NSS Saratoga."

—Letter to Beneficiary, December 2276

"Hostilities began when Archangel fired the first shots—"

"You knew damn well your fleets were banned from our space!"

"—which were fired without warning by not one, but *two* warships disguised as civilian vessels, both in violation of multiple points of Union arms treaties!"

"*You came at us with an invasion fleet!*" Andrea roared back. For all the acrimony at the negotiation table, her sheer volume startled more than a few of those present. Jon Weir of NorthStar shrank back just enough for a vigilant observer to notice. Maria Pedroso, too, fell silent.

Andrea was out of her chair, leaning on the table. "You brought over a hundred warships against Raphael and another twenty against Michael, along with the raid that bombarded Augustine Harbor. You invaded and occupied a settled planet in a sovereign Union state, and you—"

"We aren't occupying all of Michael," said Maria, finding her voice once more. "We've placed the capital and a handful of military sites under our protection."

"After a bombardment that killed tens of thousands of people."

"We could say the same for the people on *Ursa*, *Saratoga*, and all the other ships we lost," Maria sneered. "In a fight that *you* started, after you took deliberate actions to destabilize the entire Union economy."

Theresa reached out to put her hand on Andrea's wrist. Maria didn't notice the move, locked in a stare-down with Archangel's other representative. "Your ships were expressly not welcome in Archangel space," Andrea said, "and they're still not."

"You're welcome to try to eject them at any time," fumed a sullen Jon Weir.

"If we might bring this back to a more practical direction," spoke up the man at the head of the table. Union Assembly President Dhawan waited until Andrea sat back down before speaking further. While he kept a deliberately calm and civil tone, he didn't patronize anyone with it. "The situation remains. Michael is under blockade, with military ships in orbit and its capital and other sites under NorthStar control. The economic matters at the core of this dispute remain unresolved. And I will remind you all again that all parties in this matter appear to be in violation of Union armaments treaties."

"Lai Wa Corporation rejects that assertion," said Lung-Wei.

"As does NorthStar," Pedroso agreed.

Lung-Wei pressed his point. "All Lai Wa starships in this incident are registered with Union fleet regulators. No Lai Wa starship on scene engaged in aggressive action against any party."

"I'm sure we all noticed that," Weir muttered.

"Showing up in Archangel space at all is an aggressive action," seethed Andrea.

Pedroso ignored the exchange. "Do you honestly think your people benefit from this in any way?" she asked Theresa. "Call the situation on Michael what you like. The fact is that a protracted conflict is plainly not in your best interests."

"Nor is it in yours," Theresa replied. "I can't imagine why NorthStar put its monthly public financial statements on hold."

Pedroso bit back her first retort. "We would much rather come to a peaceful settlement. NorthStar's position is simple. We are not interested in holding Michael for any reason other than to ensure the government of Archangel remains at the negotiation table and that they cease further aggressive action against us. All we need is a settlement on outstanding financial issues—which, again, currently threaten the entire Union economy—and the return of our ships and our captured personnel. We will then lift our military operations on Michael and elsewhere in Archangel space."

"I can't help but notice your order of priorities," quipped Andrea.

"You're not getting the ships back," said Theresa. "We're more than happy to return the ships' crews and officers as soon as you vacate Archangel space. The Interstellar Red Cross has full access to every single one of them."

"Including Commodore Eldridge?"

"The Red Cross has access to the commodore, yes. He'll be standing trial soon enough for a fairly large number of crimes."

"That's preposterous!" spat Weir.

"So is the pretext for your invasion."

"There's nothing preposterous about the economic survival of the Union."

"NorthStar and your other corporate buddies aren't the Union, Mr. Weir," scowled Andrea.

"The market numbers from the last six months indicate otherwise, *Secretary* Bennett."

"You are all correct," spoke up President Dhawan. "This situation is not good for any of the parties involved. Yet neither side appears willing to budge and both remain armed and hostile . . . again, beyond the limits of Union treaties."

"Mr. President," said Theresa, "Archangel will hand the battleships over to the Union fleet as soon as NorthStar and her allies leave Archangel space and as soon as Archangel regains her full legal military strength—but *only* if the Union fleet retains permanent custody."

"Unacceptable," Pedroso replied with a shake of her head.

"Then you can keep hemorrhaging money and influence, Ms. Pedroso," said Andrea. "I imagine you expected a quick victory would overawe the entire Union and then you could do whatever you want, but the longer you draw this out, the more it hurts you."

"We're aware of your difficulties as well, Secretary Bennett."

"Well"—Dhawan sighed—"it appears this will get nowhere, and yet this matter is too dire for the Union to remain uninvolved."

"Then you'll intervene?" asked Pedroso with raised eyebrows.

Dhawan paused, looking around the table. "I intend to approach the Union Assembly to recommend a full and thorough investigation of this matter before recommending any course of action."

"It's already taken two weeks to have this meeting!" blurted Weir. "You want to bring this to an Assembly vote after an *investigation?*"

"I am well aware of the delays caused by spaceflight, Mr. Weir. I am also well aware that everyone at this table knows the Articles of Union perfectly well. The Articles pointedly do not forbid war between member states."

"They're not member states," argued Andrea, "they're corporations!"

"A distinction on which the Articles are silent, Secretary Bennett, for which I am deeply regretful. I am similarly regretful that no court or process existed to remedy the initial economic disputes at the heart of this terrible situation. Yet those conditions remain. I am powerless to intervene on either side absent an explicit violation of the Articles or a full vote by the Assembly authorizing me to take action."

Weir's jaw fell. "How can you say that? This will be a drain on the whole economy!"

"No, Mr. Weir. As Secretary Bennett has said, the corporations represented here today are not the entire Union economy. However, you all have rather deep reserves of resources. I'm sure you'll get by." Dhawan shook his head. "If your corporation had come to me before embarking upon this course of action, I could have taken some steps to prevent all of this, but it is too late now."

With that, he stood. Most everyone else stood as well, some out of conscious observance of etiquette and others out of reflex. A few, including Jon Weir, remained too stunned to rise.

Again, Theresa put her hand on Andrea's wrist and then motioned for her to step outside. Both women abandoned the negotiating table without another word or glance at their counterparts.

"I can't believe it," said Andrea.

"I can." Theresa frowned. "This is Dhawan's chance to bleed NorthStar and the others. Oh, the Assembly will debate and the corporations will bribe as many people as they can, but the wolves just lost their wool coats. Everyone wants to see them brought down to size, but until now no one has wanted to step up to do the job. This leaves us stuck doing all the heavy lifting and paying the cost. Dhawan sees the opportunity here. He's not going to let it go."

"An amendment could take months even after it's brought up for debate," fumed Andrea. "What the hell's going to be left of us when this is all over?"

"I don't know what'll be left of Archangel," admitted Theresa. "I'm starting to wonder what will be left of the Union."

• • •

"Orders for ships, armaments, and other necessary supplies have skyrocketed at domestic manufacturers all across the system of Archangel. Following the occupation of Michael, President Aguirre and the Senate acted swiftly to put the economy on a wartime footing. While the government has emphasized a policy of keeping defense spending inside the system, some voices have noted that the contracts and orders placed by the government have happened too quickly and with little oversight. Those voices have been roundly shouted down by a government eager to maintain political unity."

—Bob Norris, Raphael Public Media, December 2276

Life on a captured battleship proved entirely different from life on *Los Angeles.*

Archangel's prized cruiser, battered and exhausted in defense of Raphael, now underwent heavy refit and repair alongside Apostles' Station in orbit around the planet. *Resolute* and *Rio de Janeiro* lay in a similar state, with so much of their hull plating and thruster manifolds shot away that they needed intensive work before they could go into combat again.

For all the weaknesses of the Archangel Navy's fleet, however, another assault by her enemies in the near future seemed unlikely. Uriel and Gabriel both held orbital and planetary defenses strong enough to hold off any conceivable invasion fleet long enough for help to come from Raphael. Archangel's capital world had similarly strong defenses, which could shoot down anything short of a full battleship strike force . . . and the only two battleships in the system orbited Raphael in friendly hands.

Those hands felt all too few at the moment, but Archangel's enemies had little way of knowing that. In the meantime it meant for a decent amount of space within the two huge vessels. For one thing, Tanner could have a couch in the junior enlisted lounge all to himself. Behind him, several other young crewmen and third classes played pool and dined on junk food and soft drinks. Despite the obvious accommodations for alcoholic drinks offered by NorthStar's recreational facilities, and despite all the stresses and loss of recent weeks, the Archangel Navy maintained its ban on alcohol on active ships.

Given the grim situation on Michael and the inability to do anything about it, most everyone on board wanted a stiff drink. Or ten. Regulations said they'd all have to wait until they could go ashore.

Though he gave it little active thought, Tanner hoped that the navy would at least abandon its faith-based naming schemes for the captured ships. Before the smoke had fully cleared from the battle, some enterprising crewmen found a few buckets of paint and covered up the name *"Hercules"* on the most obvious signs and placards throughout the ship, replacing it with the name *"Beowulf."*

Tanner much preferred that name to the usual religious iconography. He didn't know if it would fly politically. Matters like this seemed to mean an awful lot to at least some portion of Archangel's government. But he heard more and more of his shipmates invoke *Beowulf* as the ship's name despite every official discouragement, and he couldn't help but feel a little pride.

Given all he and everyone else had done and lost, he often wondered if such pride was remotely appropriate, and what it might say about him.

He sat facing the broad window looking out into the void with his feet kicked up on a small table. Rather than a vac suit, Tanner wore his dress uniform—sans the jacket laid beside him. A pair of screens generated by his holocom floated in front of him, one containing a text-only account of the Battle of Raphael, while the other offered computer-generated animation replays of the ship-to-ship battles worked up by the Uriel Media Service.

On that second screen, the "passenger liner" *Argent* rushed headlong at the destroyer *Janus*, then at the last second went into a full turn and charged at *Helene*, streaming chaff missiles in her wake. Tanner stopped the animation, reset it, and let it play again.

He'd seen that maneuver somewhere before. Not in a movie. Not in a computer game. And certainly not in person. But he knew he'd seen it before.

"Mind if I join you?" asked a familiar voice.

Tanner glanced up to find Yeoh standing beside the couch, wearing her regulation vac suit and with her helmet slung over her shoulder like most of the other crewmen. Tanner blinked, then glanced back toward the rest of the non-rates and third classes in the rec room. Most of them managed to cover up their awe and surprise at seeing the admiral in their presence. Some couldn't help but stare.

He couldn't blame them. Yeoh's presence here was a surprising breach of custom and etiquette . . . not that anyone could call her on it.

"Ma'am," he said, gesturing to the plentiful space on the couch. He picked his feet up off the table and straightened up as she sat down. "I didn't, um . . . should someone have called out 'attention on deck' or something?"

"Why? It's a rec room. And you're one to talk about regulation right now," she said, nodding at the disheveled state of his dress uniform.

"True. Memorial service."

"I thought as much. Whose?"

"Ramos. Operations Specialist Third Class Domingo Ramos. He was on *Ursa*. Oscar Company grad."

"You knew him well?"

"Well enough." Tanner shrugged. "Chief Everett was there. He said Oscar Company lost forty-three people."

"I'm deeply sorry."

"I know." He searched for words. "We still don't know what happened on *Ursa*, do we, ma'am?"

"No. We may never know. It happens."

"Yeah." He didn't press the matter. "So what brings an admiral down to the junior enlisted rec room?"

"Ten minutes to breathe and the chance to walk through the ship. I've wondered how you're holding up."

"As well as anyone else, I guess."

"Have you heard from your family?"

"They're still on Arcadia. They're fine. Worried about me and all of this, but they're fine and they know I'm okay. I've got lots of friends and family of friends on Michael, though, and . . . well. No word there, ma'am. Gonna be a shitty Christmas for everyone, I'd imagine."

"Yes." Yeoh looked at him carefully before she went on. "You've been told about the ship's logs by now?"

"No. What about them?"

"Captain Wagner transmitted them all before he surrendered the ship. NorthStar has every moment on every sensor and every comm channel right up until you and the others walked onto the bridge . . . including video of you in cannon two and the shot that destroyed *Saratoga*. In another week, maybe two, maybe sooner, you'll doubtlessly be a part of their propaganda narrative all over the Union."

Tanner considered it and sighed. "Yeah, well . . . fuck 'em."

"I thought you might feel that way. But I also thought you should know."

"We're not gonna be ready to move on Michael anytime soon, are we?" he asked.

"Not until these battleships are fully and competently crewed and the rest of our fleet is back up to fighting strength, no. Our only blessing is that the enemy doesn't want to tangle with us now, either. They didn't like the losses they took out here and they don't want to find out just how ready we are to use these ships against them. They want their toys back in one piece. But I don't believe any of that requires expert knowledge."

"No, ma'am," Tanner replied. "No, it doesn't."

"I wanted to speak with you because I've thought a lot lately about the conversation we had back in Ascension Hall all those months ago. You wanted none of this," she said, "but you stepped up. Time and again. Like you stepped up here. I'm very glad you are here, Tanner, and that you chose the role you did. A lot of other people in your shoes would've shot Eldridge on the spot."

He wasn't sure what to say to that. "Yes, ma'am."

Yeoh reached into her pocket and drew forth a small pair of chevron pins, holding them out to him. Tanner blinked. He sat up on the couch. "M-ma'am?" he stammered. "Aren't there require-ments for time in grade and stuff?"

"This ship is a little thin on masters-at-arms. I believe you've more than earned this."

He reached out to accept the pins, staring at them.

"What is it?" she asked.

"My mother made it to second class while she served, ma'am," he said. "I didn't think I'd do the same. Not in five years."

"I think she'd be very proud."

"Thank you, ma'am." He took a long breath. "But if you're looking to fix the holes in the chain of command, Baldwin's the one you should promote. You should've seen her during the battle."

"I'm well aware of her actions and her record. Master-at-Arms Baldwin received her second class pins while you were at the memorial service."

Tanner let out a laugh. "Well, as long as we've got seniority ironed out."

"To be honest, I've had a few people—civilians, mind you—tell me you deserve a full commission after all you've done." She pursed her lips. "I have explained that it doesn't work that way. Regardless, I think we both know you'd sooner throw yourself out an airlock."

"Might throw the commission out the airlock, anyway," he agreed.

She smiled, but only briefly. "It's going to be a long war, Tanner. I'm glad you're here with us for it." She glanced over her shoulder at the others in the rec room. "I imagine I should move on and let things get back to normal in here."

"Thank you, ma'am," he said. He didn't get up as she left. His eyes drifted back to the screens from his holocom, and then he looked over his shoulder. "Admiral?"

Yeoh paused and turned back. "Yes?"

He gestured to the animation floating over his lap. "*Argent* made a real difference, didn't she?"

The admiral's serene expression never cracked, but Tanner thought her response felt a bit hesitant. "They all did," she said tactfully, and then left.

Tanner turned back toward the window. Behind him, conversation returned to normal. The pair of second-class pins remained in his hand.

He reached out to the screen on his right and replayed the animation of *Argent*'s attack run again.

He'd seen this maneuver somewhere before.

ACKNOWLEDGMENTS

As a general rule, I like to know how the real world works before I take things off the rails in a sci-fi or fantasy story. Books with space navies and laser pistols are never all that realistic, but stories are better when the writer at least has some good benchmarks. In addition to a lot of Internet searches, endless demonstration videos on YouTube, Crossfire specials on the economic meltdown of 2008, and my collection of military and survival manuals, I owe thanks to several people who shared their professional knowledge with me.

Perhaps most importantly, I got a lot of valuable input from MA1 Joe Moon of the US Navy and SPC Brett Lawrence of the US Army MP Corps. Cat Robinweiler offered a lot of guidance on nursing and emergency medicine, to the point of writing a page of notes for me on one particular matter. In all honesty, the most valuable contributions they made came in the form of things that *didn't* happen in this book. That sort of thing is often invisible to a reader, but it means a lot to me as an author. I am very grateful to them, as I am to Kelsey for her help with a little bit of Arabic translation.

Once again, Lee Moyer and his assistant, Venetia Charles, were a joy to work with for the cover art. We sat down in the hotel bar at Norwescon this year to talk about picture concepts. I rattled off a couple of ideas. Lee sketched for two minutes at the most before I saw one of those ideas on paper, only he'd turned the dial up to eleven. I feel greatly privileged to work with them both.

As usual, I also have a lot of beta readers who gave me more feedback and editing help than I could ask for: Zach, Matt D., Matt S., Jenny, Phil, Tracy, Keith, Brent, Erik, Clarke, and Sean. Naturally, Erica gave it multiple reads, caught more than a few mistakes, fixed my formatting, and reliably makes my life awesome.

Lastly, and of great importance: thank you to everyone who wrote reviews on Amazon, Smashwords, and elsewhere for *Poor Man's Fight* and my other books, and thank you to everyone who e-mailed me directly. By definition, a writer should be able to put emotions into words, but I can't express just how much those reviews and those e-mails have meant to me, and how much they have contributed to the overall success of my work. Thank you for that, and thank you for picking up this book, too.

One last note: if anyone's wondering, my copy of Sun Tzu's *The Art of War* is the translation by Samuel B. Griffith (Oxford University Press, 1963).

ABOUT THE AUTHOR

Elliott Kay grew up in Los Angeles and currently resides in Seattle, Washington. He has a bachelor's degree in history and is a former member of the US Coast Guard. Kay has survived a motorcycle crash, severe seasickness, summers in Phoenix, and winters in Seattle.